FOX BECKMAN

Brendan & the Beast

D1616439

Amanda—Finally!

Contents

Prologue   iii

   1 In Which Our Story Begins   1

   2 In Which There is a Wager   9

   3 In Which There is a Journey   19

   4 In Which There is a Meeting   28

   5 In Which There is a Storm   36

   6 In Which There is a Dinner   46

   7 In Which There is a Garden   54

   8 In Which There are Mirrors and Revelations   64

   9 In Which There are Truth and Lies   82

  10 In Which There is a Hunt   95

  11 In Which There is a Discovery   111

  12 In Which There is Understanding   123

  13 In Which There is a Kiss   139

  14 In Which There is Friendship   155

  15 In Which a Mystery is Solved   172

  16 In Which Things are Done Properly   191

  17 In Which the Past is Shared   204

  18 In Which the Future Looms   217

  19 In Which Things Shatter   235

  20 In Which There is a Homecoming   252

  21 In Which There is Truth   264

  22 In Which There is a Decision   275

  23 In Which There is Love   286

Epilogue   310

About the Author   313

Prologue

Stories do not simply happen.

A story must be grown from a nascent sapling of an idea and carefully tended in the garden of imagination. A story must be nurtured, coaxed, cozened, until the roots grow deep. If cultivated well, a story may grow for years to come, thriving blossoms stretching up toward the sun.

So let us say I am something of a gardener.

Over the centuries I have aided in the rise and fall of paupers and kings alike, bestowed gifts upon the deserving—and meted out punishments upon the wicked.

Many of my sisters favor rain and fire, or stone and sea; tangible avenues of sorcery, to nudge the nature of reality. I prefer the intangible. Stories outlast any storm or inferno, living on long after the first storyteller was lost to memory. A good story grows, perennial, reinvented in new forms.

And like gardens, all stories start with the planting of one single seed.

Once upon a time…

1

In Which Our Story Begins

Once upon a time, in a fashionably modest city in the heart of northern France, there lived a wealthy and happy merchant.

Though his beloved wife was long dead, the merchant had been left with four healthy children. The eldest twins were ladies both of proper manners and proud temperaments. The middle child, studying abroad in Paris, was the merchant's only son. The youngest daughter, sweet-natured in all things and blessed with her mother's honey-gold hair, was the merchant's favorite, though he would rather lose all his fortune before admit it. She was, quite aptly, named Beauty.

While her sisters reveled in the bounty of parties and balls and salons the city had to offer, Beauty far preferred to stay at home and read books rather than mingle with good society. A great many eminent gentlemen courted the eldest daughters, especially gentlemen who understood a woman's greatest asset was having a rich father. Beauty, however, unfailingly declined all offers of marriage, claiming it was in dreadful taste for the youngest of three sisters to be wed before her elders.

In truth, Beauty didn't like any of the men that came to call; dull and shallow every man jack of them, a preening peacock with pretty lies locked behind perfect teeth. The throngs of nobles and courtiers all talked of silly things and wore silly costumes, sharply watching each other for the smallest social missteps, ready with ruthless gossip for the less fortunate.

Beauty fiercely missed her absent brother, who was honest to a fault and could always make her laugh. He was the only other person she knew who would discuss philosophy, art, or science late into the night; who didn't drone on endlessly about fashion and scandal. While he was surely in heaven at university, surrounded by like-minded scholars, Beauty was stuck at home fending off marriage proposals from dowry-chasing bores. Brendan's rare visits home were always a welcome breath of fresh air, for intelligence, sincerity, and kindness were in short supply amongst the upper class.

It was well known throughout the city her father had a penchant for gambling, and so the gossip spread like wildfire when he lost his entire fortune in one unlucky card game.

Ruin came upon them suddenly.

The merchant told his daughters, shame-faced and teary-eyed, they must move away to a smaller house in the country. He could no longer afford their maids and footmen, much less for Brendan's expensive education. Even their old governess, an ancient retainer from their days in the nursery, had to be let go. The family pawned their jewels, their fine clothes, and all but the most modest of belongings to pay the merchant's considerable debts.

The twins did not take the news well, wailing and raving. Both sisters insisted one of their many suitors would marry them and save them from the grievous fate of poverty, but they were, rather unsurprisingly, mistaken. Every swain vanished as soon as the coffers ran dry, every family friend suddenly absent, as if misfortune and scandal were catching.

At first Beauty was as distressed as her sisters, grieving at the loss of their good fortune and fine home, but she took one look at her poor father, who seemed as if he'd aged a decade in a day, and put on a brave face to pack up what few items were left after the auction.

So the now poor and unhappy merchant and his three daughters moved into a country house in the wooded lands of the south, an unfashionably rustic province inconveniently distant from any place of interest. Their new home was small, thatched, and in need of much repair. And while the merchant sought to make a living in the countryside, Beauty set herself to learning household tasks. The older sisters grudgingly applied themselves to gardening and husbandry, complaining loudly all the while.

It was many weeks before their brother made his way to their new home. Up the dusty road he appeared, bags in hand, and they all ran out to greet him. Beauty was taken aback at her initial sight of him, for it had been two years since she had last looked upon him and Brendan looked very much like a man.

"My sisters! You look more radiant than ever," exclaimed Brendan, embracing each twin with a broad smile. His smile faded as he stood in front of the merchant. "Father…"

After a too-long pause, the merchant cleared his throat and clapped his son on the back. His voice was gruff. "The journey went well, I trust?"

"Well enough," Brendan said. He brightened as Beauty stepped in for a hug, and swung her off her feet into a spin. "Look how tall you are! Country life suits you."

Beauty smiled for the first time since leaving their manor house behind. "Paris must have suited you as well. You've grown! And your hair is so much longer." She gave a curling strand of his chestnut hair an impish tug.

He ruffled her own golden locks until she protested. "It is the only way to wear it, in Paris. Bad enough I'm not noble-born, and if my hair was shorn short as a peasant's it would speak more ill of me than any lack of breeding ever could. Though I hear some aristos are trying to make wigs catch on." This brought forth a swell of questions as the twins demanded to be updated on the latest fashions, and the reunited family retired indoors.

"I will help you unpack," Beauty offered after a time, over a plate of crumbly biscuits. She hadn't yet got the hang of baking. Brendan looked up from his tea and tried to demur, but Beauty would have none of it, plucking up one of his largest, heaviest bags so he would have no choice but to do the gentlemanly thing and take it from her. She led him up the narrow stairs into the equally narrow attic.

"It isn't much," she said in apology, setting a rucksack on the crisply tucked bedsheets.

"This is fine, Beauty," Brendan assured her. "If you had seen my old first-year dormitory, you would understand why I am quite thrilled to have any sort of room with a door on it." He let a few bags slide from his shoulder unceremoniously to the floor, and then with considerably more care set his violin case on the small dresser.

"How are you?" For the first time since he'd been home, his pleasant manner slipped, concern showing in the crease between his brows.

Beauty sank onto the bed, shedding her cheerful demeanor as well. "Tired. It has not been an easy transition." She looked down, smoothing her hands over the sheets. "But look! I have learned to make a bed."

"*You* did this?" Their shoulders brushed as Brendan sat down next to her. "Made an actual bed? With your own two hands? Our governess would die of shock."

Beauty laughed a little, leaning into him. "I am trying to do what I can, to make things as right as they can be. It has been hardest on Father."

"Fitting, as our entire misfortune is his fault."

Beauty murmured a mild protest, but the knots in the relationship between her father and brother were well beyond her capabilities to ease. Besides, it wasn't as if he were wrong.

"Well," she said lightly, "we just have to keep him away from drink and gaming tables, and everything should be fine."

"Is that all? There can't be too many of those, out here in the sticks."

After a moment of companionable silence, Beauty quietly asked, "Why did you come back?"

Brendan bent forward with a sigh, his hands twining between his knees. "What else could I have done?"

"Your letters said you had offers of patronage—"

"*Might* have had offers. Nothing serious."

"You said the orchestra was looking for a new chair. You might have—"

"*Might have.* Father is the gambler, not I," Brendan snapped, then pushed his hair out of his face with an apologetic wince. "I'm sorry. It's... I didn't get it. The audition for the chair. But that is all to the good!" He sat up, tracing a flippant gesture in the air. "I would just be there thinking about my destitute family, worrying how my favorite sister is getting along without me." He flashed her a gamin grin. "Don't tell the twins I said you were my favorite."

An old joke between them. There had been a *Before* and an *After*, for their family, a great chasm dividing the depths of their sibling alliances in twain. The twins belonged to the Before, when their mother had still been alive and their father still happy, while Beauty and Brendan only knew the After.

"Besides," Brendan continued, "who wants to be stuck in one little orchestra? I want to go new places, see incredible things."

"Like all those tales we'd tell each other in the nursery."

"Exactly so. And in each of those tales, something miraculous would always follow a terrible tragedy."

Beauty returned his smile. "So then, we are due for a miracle."

"We've already had it. You've made a bed." Brendan winked, and Beauty pushed him away, laughing.

Things improved after Brendan arrived, and their small, barren cottage fast became a true home. A custom arose of gathering together in the evenings, to listen to Beauty reading her books aloud or to Brendan playing his violin. He had taken a job in the nearby village as a store clerk, and the money helped. Soon they became able to afford things like honey for their tea, cloth to sew into new clothes, and other small luxuries which didn't feel so small after living in the tight confines of frugality.

For a handful of months, things fell into an easy routine. The seasons were changing from warm to cool when a letter arrived for Beauty's father. She returned that day with her brother, having walked him back from the village. As Brendan opened the cottage door for her, he surreptitiously pressed a candle from the store into her hand.

This was the latest of many candles he had given her to read by at night. Oil lamps were hard to come by and she often went without any light at all, reading by the window in the waning light until her eyes hurt from squinting as night descended. But the two siblings shared a passion for the written word, and Brendan understood Beauty's needs exactly.

They were greeted in the small parlor by their grinning father and the twins, who both fidgeted with barely contained excitement.

"Marvelous news!" Beauty's father held up a folded piece of parchment. A shipment of valuables their father had invested in years ago and had long since written off as a loss had finally arrived in a port off the Mediterranean. He would have to travel there to prove his claim on them, and when he did, "We will be served a new fortune, my children. It will not be near so much as we once had, but I promise you! Our fortune is remade!"

* * *

The very next morning, barely after the sun crested the trees lining the sloping hills, the siblings gathered outside to help their father hitch up their only horse.

"Father, won't you take a cart along?" Brendan asked, for what was likely the fourth time.

His father barely cast him an annoyed sideways glance. "There will be no need, as I have said. When I obtain my properties, I will simply hire a cart at the port. The cart we have is rickety and unreliable."

The merchant mounted, his traveling satchel secured to the horse's saddle. "I will bring you each back a gift from the port. Tell me one thing you wish for, my children. After this venture, I will be able to afford it."

Brendan, standing behind his sisters, cast a doubtful glance toward the ground. If this venture was anything like the last one, they were going to end up not only poor but seriously in debt.

His first sister, filled with blind optimism, had already stepped up. "Father, bring me back some silk slippers and velvet hair ribbons. I tire of looking like a milkmaid."

The second sister pushed her twin aside, batting her eyelashes. "Father, bring me back a brocaded dress! A white one, with glass beads sewn in!"

"White for purity, no doubt," Brendan muttered, for her ears alone.

She shot him a venomous look.

Oblivious of the exchange, their father peered past the taller twins at Beauty. "And you, my dear Beauty. What is it you desire?"

6

"A good reading lamp, Father."

"A lamp?" The merchant looked taken aback.

"A lamp."

"But, Beauty," her father protested, "that is not a fit present for a young lady. Surely you wish to have a new dress, or jewelry, or—"

"No, thank you," she said, and from that sweetly adamant tone everyone knew arguing with her was pointless. "Though if you pick up a new collar for the horse, we can plow a garden next spring."

"What a waste of a wish," muttered one twin, the other rolling her eyes in agreement. "Absolutely hopeless."

The merchant gave his favorite daughter an indulgent smile. "I will bring for you the finest, brightest lamp one can buy, my dear."

He readied to leave, when Beauty piped up, "Brendan, what would you like Father to bring back for you?"

The merchant stopped and held a shared, wary look with his son for a long moment.

"A rose," Brendan said.

Their father's eyes narrowed, and Beauty braced for the inevitable argument. She had meant a *vegetable* garden; a practical thing, so they could grow their own food without long walks into the nearby village. She certainly hadn't meant a flower garden, since their father had done all but expressly forbid it.

No flowers grew around their cottage. She wouldn't have dared suggest such a thing.

It seemed her brother, two years older than she remembered him and several shades more defiant, did dare. "If Beauty wants a garden," Brendan went on, "then all I ask is a single rose, to clip and plant beneath my sisters' windows."

The twins gaped at him, shocked and scornful in equal measure. "That's even worse than what Beauty wanted," complained one.

Brendan hadn't looked away from his father. "Surely one rose shouldn't be terribly difficult to obtain. Should it, Father?"

The merchant opened his mouth angrily, but a flash of guilt wiped the ire away. Without any further farewell, he tapped his heels against the horse's flanks and started along the dusty path toward the sea.

2

In Which There is a Wager

After five days of uneventful travel, the wind picked up, biting at exposed skin with chill teeth, and Etienne the merchant wrapped himself tightly in his cloak. His sturdy farm horse plodded along, heedless of the grabbing branches forming an arched hallway around them. There hadn't been another soul on the road for many hours. Dusk approached. The forest was thick, the trees twisted and gnarled, and Etienne hadn't seen any sign of an inn or village.

Surely he wasn't lost.

The branches overhead were laced together so tightly he hadn't realized it was raining until a drop unerringly found its way down the back of his collar. Thunder rumbled in the gray sky. Etienne pulled up his hood and hunched low, kicking the horse into a trot, reassuring himself that any road must lead *somewhere* useful.

He must have dozed off, lulled by the rhythmic taps of the rain falling upon his cowl or the steady gait of his horse, because he awoke suddenly when his mount stopped with a nervous snort. Etienne blinked blearily, looked up, and gasped.

No port town, no village, no simple country inn stood here at the edge of the twisted forest. Instead, a huge tiered castle loomed over the countryside like a malevolent landlord.

Warm light poured out through stained glass windows, so it was not some old ruin abandoned by time and memory. A relentless cold wind gnashed at his cloak, and lightning streaked the sky. Gathering up his courage, the merchant made his way down the bare path toward the castle.

The rocky road led to a pair of enormous wrought iron gates, set between the arches of a high stone wall in a great tangled web as if the metal had been spun by spiders. Beyond it, the path continued on toward the castle, its stones all at once straighter and more uniform in their size and shape.

Etienne stared dumbstruck at the gate and the castle beyond until his horse shifted nervously beneath him. He hesitantly dismounted and pushed at the gate. It inched open with reluctance, hinges shrieking like a dying thing all the while. He stepped past the black mass of bent metal, tugging his skittish horse along.

Two rows of twisted bushes, gnarled and dark, lined the cobble path. After what felt like far too short a time, the merchant arrived at the foot of a wide staircase rising to a set of great wooden doors. The doors looked old, practically medieval, each with a massive iron knocker in the center of each. Through the deepening darkness, Etienne could make out winged grotesques and gargoyles guarding every window eave, glowering at anyone daring to approach their perches.

The merchant wished he were back home with a warm fire and a stiff drink, not here with gargoyles glaring down at him menacingly and with God-only-knew-what waiting inside those doors. Lightning again cracked apart the night sky, and before he could lose his nerve he reached a trembling hand toward the knocker, raised it, and let it fall. The sound echoed thunderously and the horse shied away, tugging fitfully at its reins.

Almost immediately the door creaked open, seemingly of its own volition. Warmth and light and the promise of shelter spilled out like cordial over the staircase. Etienne's eyes widened. He took two hesitant steps forward. And then, quite out of the blue, a hand touched his and took the horse's reins away.

He whipped around in alarm. His horse, altogether too calmly for Etienne's tastes, was led away down a path circling the castle by nobody at all, the reins floating in midair.

He rubbed his eyes, surely the victim of some trick of the darkness, or too many long hours on the road. Two invisible hands, their touch as professionally helpful as any servant Etienne had ever known, took hold of his arm and guided him indoors. He followed the gentle tug over the threshold in stunned obedience, letting away his dripping cloak be whisked away without protest.

That night he was treated to a fine meal, new dry clothes, and a pillowy bed, all given to him by eerily invisible servants. Every room was lit by torchlight when he entered and plunged again into darkness the instant he left. While the unseen servants were at first unnerving, Etienne had often heard tales in his childhood of a magical castle lost in some fearsome wood, and found it easy enough to accept this may indeed be the enchanted castle of nursery-room legend.

In the morning, a soft touch on his shoulder awoke him. He let himself be guided out of bed and into a clean set of clothes, and then be escorted through the halls toward the enticing aroma of breakfast.

He'd not realized the true elegant splendor of the castle until now, as the bright daylight spilled in through the vaulted windows. Countless rooms branched from the hallway, and every one he glanced into had walls finely papered or painted in extravagant patterns, lush carpets spread out on rich parquet floors, and every shelf and alcove decorated with priceless baubles or leather-bound books. The dining room was especially grand, high-ceilinged with walls painted in burgundy and gold. A hugely long table of polished mahogany was set with a breakfast so delicious Etienne let out a regretful sigh when he had eaten his fill.

Despite all its grandeur, it was still a strange and unnatural place, and he was eager to depart. Etienne did not hesitate to follow when guided through the ornately appointed foyer and out through the front doors, which were much less intimidating by the light of day.

The sky was bright and cloudless, the faint chill of approaching autumn not entirely dispelled. Waiting at the foot of the stone steps, Etienne's horse had been saddled, piebald coat gleaming and mane tied up in braids. Beside the horse sat two large leather saddlebags, flaps open to display their glittering contents to the sun.

Etienne stared in shock. Then he sank to his knees, heedless of the hard cobbles, plunging his hands into the bags. Each was full of more gold than he'd ever seen in one place outside of a bank. It was easily thrice as much wealth as his business venture could ever have yielded.

They were rich again! It was not enough to buy back their old lands and manor house, but certainly enough for his twins to have their dresses and baubles, for his darling Beauty to have the finest and brightest of lamps to read by. Indeed, anything else she desired as well! He would joyfully take this freely offered gold instead of wasting another week or so of travel to reach the sea. Let his former business partners take care of the ship and its modest cargo!

With a grunt he heaved the bags up and lashed them tightly behind the saddle. He turned once more to the castle. "Thank you!" he called with a grateful wave, before taking the reins and starting down the path toward the gate, the bounce in his steps belying his age.

With these sacks of gold as seed money, he could certainly regain his old wealth. Perhaps with a few wisely placed wagers, he could even exceed it.

In the sunlight, the garden around the castle was revealed to be startlingly beautiful. As if a blindfold had been removed from his face, Etienne realized he was surrounded by the most fragrant and beautiful roses he had ever beheld. Upon closer inspection, he realized the bountiful rosebushes to be the very same gnarled briars he had passed by the previous night. How different they seemed in the daylight.

The roses themselves were the darkest of rich reds, as if they had been cunningly formed from velvet. Abruptly he remembered his son's request and frowned. It had been intentionally impertinent, calling into question Etienne's ability to keep hold of anything, even so simple a thing as a rose.

Etienne chuckled. It would be quite the thing to present his family with a sack of gold in one hand and a rose in the other. His son would likely be sorry for ever doubting him. He leaned over the saddle to twist the head of a sunset-red rose from its stem.

Snap.

A dark shadow fell over him. Instinctively he cowered, the horse rearing up with a shill neigh. Both Etienne and the saddlebags slipped from its back, spilling over the ground, leaving the fallen merchant bruised and frightened amidst the twinkling coins. The horse dashed away in panic, hooves clattering on the cobblestones.

Wincing, the merchant looked up from the coin-strewn path. The first thing he saw was feet; clawed, like those of a wolf. Fear instantly soaked his limbs, but his gaze crawled up of its own accord. Clawed feet led to muscled legs, hideously bent backward at the knees and clad in dark leather breeches, as if in some mockery of normalcy. A narrow waist broadened to wide shoulders, the loose sleeves of a linen shirt billowing around thick arms. Things Etienne only could describe as hands—he knew no other name for the terrible mating of an animal's paw and a man's five fingers—clenched into fists. Horrified and unwilling, Etienne looked into the face of a monster.

He'd never in his darkest, most horrible nightmares imagined a face as fearful as the one now before him. Like something out of a woodcut, one of those old books of demons and werewolves and all the terrible creatures whose existence mankind had longed to deny as the centuries marched ever onward. Cruel lips drawn back over sharp white fangs; the flat, hooked nose with fur crinkled in disdain and fury; craggy brows shadowing a pair of strangely human eyes.

Long spiraled horns, like the Devil's himself, sprung from the creature's temples and swept back along a thick mane of hair. Pointed, elongated ears lay back low the way an angry stallion's might. Most horrifyingly of all, the creature possessed the power of speech.

"Is this how you repay my generosity?" The monster spoke in a low, guttural growl.

Etienne froze as mice do in sight of a snake, cold sweat springing out on his forehead. Baring gleaming fangs, the creature dropped to all fours and slunk fluidly around the shivering merchant.

"I instructed my servants to supply you with everything you desired. I have given you shelter. Food. Clothing. I even kindly bestowed this small wealth upon your ungrateful head. Yet you repay me by taking the one thing that was not freely given."

Etienne shrank back as the monstrous face was thrust all too close to his own. The eyes weren't right, he wildly thought. They should be yellow or perhaps green, the pupils a mere slash, like a fearsome animal's. But they were just a simple, clear light brown. Those human eyes so mismatched to the fearsome, leonine face unsettled Etienne more than even the fangs or horns or claws, or the hotness of breath upon him as the creature continued its accusations.

"You took one of my roses, which I prize above all things."

Etienne gaped like a fish, then finally found his voice, dropping his gaze to avoid those eerie, unforgiving eyes. "I-I-I am sorry, m-my Lord, I didn't mean any harm. I am of course profoundly grateful for the g-gifts you have given me, my h-humblest of apologies, my Lord—"

"Call me by no lies!" The creature roared at the merchant, the voice alone like a great blow. "I know what I am." He drew up to his full imposing height, and with one claw picked Etienne up to his feet. "You may call me Beast, for that is plainly what I am."

"Y-y-yes," Etienne stammered, knees threatening to give out from under him. "B-beast."

"How then shall you prove your gratitude? Perhaps you should pay for the life of that rose with your own."

"My own? My own life? Oh, no! Oh, good sir, good Beast! It is merely a flower! Surely the broken stem of a rose cannot be worth the life of a man?"

"And what care I," hissed the Beast, "for the worth of a man? These roses are better company than any human. They take nothing but the sunlight, nothing but water and air, and only so they, in turn, may grow. For me." He lifted one wickedly curved claw against his chest in a gesture of possession. "They are mine. Everything here," he motioned that same claw around, "is mine. You took what I offered you, and then revealing yourself as the thieving scum you are, you took *what I did not!*" The Beast's voice rose into a thunderous roar, leaving the merchant quaking and cowering once more, not that he had particularly stopped in the first place.

"Sir Beast," Etienne pleaded, mind racing. "I would that I could pay you for this rose with my life, but it is not just my life that would be ended. I have children, four of them, and they have been without a mother for near sixteen years." He clasped his hands together and bowed his forehead against them. "I beg you, good Beast. Spare me for their sake."

The Beast snorted derisively. "That is no concern of mine. What do I care of your *family?*" He spat the word out as if he disliked the taste of it. "It is you who have wronged me."

The terrified merchant glanced despairingly toward the gold coins littering the stones he knelt on. "Then allow me to return to you this gold that was your gift, to repay you for the blossom—" A furious roar silenced him. He quickly rethought his strategy. "I…I will make you a wager!"

The Beast eyed him a moment. He threw back his head and let out great, bellowing roars. It took the merchant a few moments of fearful cringing, his eyes squeezed shut, to realize it was the Beast's laughter. He peeked at the creature's face.

"A wager? Surely you jest." The Beast glared, but his pointed ears twitched, very minutely. Etienne had once, at the height of his career, been a keen merchant, and he knew when he had a buyer on the hook.

"Not at all," he assured, growing confident as he always did when the prospect of a game arose. "After all, I am now supplied with much gold, fine clothes, and a strong, temperate horse."

The Beast glared some more, this time with a weighing appraisal, and eventually nodded. Something akin to intrigue shadowed his eyes. "Your offer amuses me. Very well. We shall see if you can win yourself back in a game of cards."

* * *

Etienne took another long gulp from his glass of wine, which was perpetually filled thanks to the invisible servants attending the card game. He chewed at his lip. His cards gave him a *Numerus* of 39 points; a decent hand but not great, and sat debating his next move for a bit longer than necessary.

He glanced over his cards at the Beast, who was examining his nails in an overly casual manner. The Beast caught Etienne's look and extended his razor claws. They made a small sharp sound as they were unsheathed, like the slide of a knife against silk.

"…I will hold," Etienne mumbled, and met the Beast's bet. Unfortunately, his decent *Numerus* 39 was narrowly beaten by the Beast's superior *Primero* 40.

They played several rounds, the merchant losing each, growing more panicked with each loss. Each defeat brought on even more desperation, and Etienne would throw around a few more promises, a new wager, and the Beast would always indulge him, letting him dig himself deeper.

By the eighth hand, the merchant had not only bet his life, his horse, his gold, his clothes, his cottage, and each item he had brought to the castle, but also the entire fortune awaiting him at the southern docks. He was now understandably desperate, but also, and rather more importantly, in the vise-like grip of gambling fever.

"Everything," he said, throwing out his most eager and unruffled grin.

The Beast smirked as though he saw right through the deception. "Everything?"

"I'm vying everything I got, and I'll declare my bid at *Fluxus* 45." That was the lowest possible *Fluxus* hand. In truth, he had a *Fluxus* 70, an excellent hand. The only hand that could beat a *Fluxus* 70 was a *Chorus*, a four-of-a-kind, and what were the odds the Beast had that? It was nearly impossible! If the creature had any sense he would fold. But just in case the Beast thought he was bluffing, and laid down a *Fluxus* higher than a 45, Etienne would triumphantly lay down his 70. He had it all figured out.

"*Fluxus* 45," the Beast repeated, thoughtfully.

Etienne watched him, anxious. When the Beast folded, then it would win him half the gold on the table. He was due for a victory, he could *feel* it, the thrill of the win so close he could nearly taste it.

"I *revie*." The Beast placed down a fine silver brooch with a design picked out in emeralds.

There was a moment of silence before the merchant choked out, "You're raising? But… I don't have anything left!"

"Well. You'll just have to think of something." The Beast's voice came silky and dangerous. "Just what is it *you* prize over all things?"

Etienne *must* win. There was no way this horrible creature could beat his hand. The odds were in his favor and his fortune was all but assured. Therefore he felt quite confident as he said, "Tell you what. I'll throw in my daughter, too."

The Beast sat perfectly still. He blinked once. "Your what?" he asked precisely, as if he had misheard. One of his pointed ears twitched.

"My daughter! Her name is Beauty, and her name is enough to describe her every aspect."

The Beast sat back in his chair, paws or hands or whatever-they-were flat on the table. "Hold, man. Your daughter?"

There was virtually no chance the Beast held a *Chorus*. Feeling utterly safe, Etienne spoke like a peddler driving a hard sale. "She is sweet, kind, quiet, and well-mannered. Beautiful to behold, and a pure spirit."

"You are willing to wager your own *daughter?*" The Beast cocked his head as if he was having difficulty understanding the word.

"As long as you promise to..." The merchant chose his words carefully. "To be hospitable. Courteous. I'm sure a gentleman such as yourself would welcome the addition of a fine lady to his household."

Something flickered in the depths of the Beast's even stare. Eventually he spoke, a strange wistful note hidden in his deep rumble. "I would not harm her."

"Of course not!" Etienne smiled broadly, though it took all of his nerve to do so in the face of such overwhelming ugliness. "I would never have made the wager if I thought you would."

The Beast glanced down, where his cards rested facedown nearby. "Still, it must be said that you are a despicable person." Beast paused, drumming his claws on the table. "I accept the bet. You win, and you walk out of here alive with all your rich winnings. You lose, and I get your daughter." Eyes narrowed to thin slits. "Or your life, if you try to weasel out. Your choice, old man."

All boldness and certainty, the merchant agreed and laid down his final hand.

3

In Which There is a Journey

With the scent of home in its nostrils, the horse trotted along in high spirits, looking forward to the warmth of the barn where it would get a good brushing and hot mash, utterly oblivious to its rider's dire mood. The reins pulled the horse to a stop, and the rider slid heavily from the saddle onto the dewy grass.

Beauty had found time enough for a respite from her daily chores. At the sound of the jingling bridle, she looked up from a book of poetry. She stood, leaned her head out of the open window, and gasped. She flung herself back inside and cried out, "Father's home!"

The cottage filled with a sudden clamor as the merchant's three daughters rushed out to him as quickly as they could. Brendan followed at a more leisurely pace, tucking away the rag he had been using to wipe soot from his hands.

"You haven't brought back a cart. Was there trouble at the docks?" He tried and failed at nonchalance, instead falling somewhere between disappointment and sheer cheek.

His father turned on him, face reddening. "You! Here's your blasted rose!" Etienne threw a crumpled ball of petals at him. It struck Brendan square on the chest and fell, a few silky red petals littering the grass.

Brendan looked from the fallen rose to his father, and quirked a brow. "I take it the venture didn't go well."

"That stupid rose," Etienne spat out, "cost more than anything you could ever dream! Anything!" He then went off in a rage, pacing and ranting about many completely nonsensical things, including, to the best of the siblings' comprehension; invisible people, evil rosebushes, a haunted castle, a giant, and some sort of impossible choir.

"Oh, dear," said Beauty, wringing her hands.

One twin watched the merchant rant in front of the cottage door. She shook her head in disgust. "He's completely soused. Haven't seen him like this in ages."

Brendan put his hand on Etienne's shoulder. "Father? You must be exhausted from your long journey. Perhaps you'd like to lie down?" He added in a mutter, "Sleep it off, more like."

"You would mock me, my own flesh and blood? Ungrateful boy! We are utterly ruined!"

It was then the other twin, as she led the horse to the stable, discovered the saddlebags lashed to its haunches. As the ties came free, coins littered the earth around her feet.

"My God! Look at all this gold! We are richer than kings!" The others buzzed around her in disbelief.

The merchant wailed, "Is it worth your poor father's life?" His children traded troubled glances.

"Whatever do you mean, Father?" asked Beauty.

"We have to move away. Far away. We must leave immediately! I must rush you away, my Beauty."

"Me?"

"Come inside, my children. I have a tale to tell you." Etienne ushered them into the cottage with widespread hands. "A harrowing tale..."

* * *

The family sat in stunned silence long after the merchant had finished speaking. Brendan was the first able to dredge up a response.

"I don't quite understand what happened. You found a castle, took this rose, and then a...*beast* sprang out." He couldn't quite manage to keep the skepticism from his tone. "And then this beast demanded you hand over your youngest daughter."

His father nodded gravely.

"How did he even know you had a daughter?"

"That...that is not the point!"

"And how did he know you had more than one?"

Etienne snapped, "It's not important how he knew! Obviously he is a magical beast! I do not know how he knew, but he did! He demanded I give him my youngest daughter or die. I have one month to say my goodbyes, or to ready my youngest daughter for her journey. But Beauty!" He clasped her slim fingers in his own weathered hands. "My dear, sweet Beauty. He shall never lay his filthy paws upon my daughter! And he won't lay them on me, either, if we get out of here fast enough."

"But Father!" the twins exclaimed.

"No buts! We can move far away, to Italy or Spain. Even England, if we need to. He'll never find us there."

"Well, if he's a magical beast," Brendan said, clearly just humoring his father, "couldn't he find us wherever we go?"

"Enough questions! We have to leave!"

"Father," protested one twin. "While you've been away having your fantastical run-in with beasts and ghosts, I've gotten engaged! I'm not moving anywhere. The banker is a good man. The only one around here with any money at all, and he knows how to treat a lady."

"Still going for white?" Brendan teased under his breath, earning a murderous glare.

"Are the rest of you all mad? Have you seen the money Father brought home? Nobody needs to marry some country banker or run away to God-forsaken England. We can buy back our manor!"

"And have none left over for the future," Beauty said, a thin crease marring her smooth forehead. "It's not worth as much as it looks. If we don't use it carefully, within a fortnight we'll be just as poor as we were yesterday."

"But we *must* leave! We cannot stay," Etienne insisted.

"Beauty's right, Father. No matter how you came upon this money, we must be frugal with it. We can set ourselves up quite comfortably here, but you can't expect us to just leave everything behind us and move away." Brendan's eyes flickered with a low-banked heat. "Again."

One twin snorted. "We're not leaving because of some far-fetched tale you dreamed up in a tavern, Father."

Despite the merchant's protests, even now his memories of the castle and its Beast seemed unreal, dimming in his memory against the warm, bright reality of his kitchen table and the worried faces of his children around it. Perhaps...perhaps they were right. Perhaps he had been struck on the head and dreamed the whole thing.

* * *

After almost four weeks, the incident on the journey to the sea seemed some strange fantasy, an exaggeration Etienne's tired mind had devised.

Taking Beauty's tactful advice, the merchant had invested their newfound fortune wisely. His daughters were now well dressed, their cottage better furnished, and all three girls had respectable dowries set up. Etienne, remembering his proficiency for finances, began looking into properties within the village. Brendan continued his job as a clerk, in the afternoons returning home to play his violin, or reading in his attic bedroom, or generally giving his Father a wide berth.

All talk of a magical beast had been abandoned. Nothing bad had happened, the family was still together, and their prosperity looked assured.

Yet one day, the bite of late autumn ever sharpening the air, Etienne awoke feeling rather unwell. His breathing grew shallow, and his skin paled to an unhealthy, grayish hue. He moved shakily from room to room, or would sit in a quiet heap beside the fireplace for long stretches of time.

When he collapsed shortly after missing lunch, the sisters tucked him into bed and called for Brendan to determine what was wrong. For his sisters' sakes, he tried to seem knowledgeable and confident, though of the many subjects he had studied at school, medicine had not been among them.

"He is…sick, all right. Definitely sick. I'll just go fetch the physician, shall I?" He left with haste as the others crowded around their father's bed, wringing their skirts with worry.

When the doctor arrived, the man agreed their father was indeed ill, though from what, he could not ascertain. Etienne began thrashing and muttering. In his delirium, he grabbed Beauty's arm and wailed, "The Beast! It is the Beast's magical powers! He steals away my life from beyond! Oh, my children, I will pay for that rose."

"This rose, Father?" Brendan pulled a clay pot from his father's windowsill. He offered it to the group, illustrating the brilliant scarlet bloom growing from the dark earth. It looked innocent enough, though peculiarly long-lived.

Beauty wondered briefly why her brother had put the rose in their father's room. Likely some unsubtle attempt to needle him.

"He's killing me through the rose! *The Beast!*" The merchant collapsed back into the pillows with a piteous moan.

The doctor cast a baffled expression at Brendan. "Has he been hallucinating long?"

Brendan set the pot back on the sill. "It may have started a month ago."

"Ah. I see." The doctor clucked his tongue and scribbled notes in a leather-bound book. "Make sure he stays in bed. Keep him warm. If he feels pain, you may give him a decoction of wintergreen. I will go back to the town apothecary for something that should help him sleep. These delusions should clear up on their own, with luck."

"Luck?" asked Brendan incredulously. "There isn't anything you can do for him now?"

The doctor shrugged, altogether too nonchalant for Brendan's taste. "I must admit, this has me quite perplexed." With that news and a lingering kiss to one twin's hand, the doctor left.

The three sisters sat beside their father for the rest of the day, bathing his brow with cool water. The doctor returned with medicine, left again, and eventually their father slept, tossing fitfully and murmuring about unseen servants and card games.

* * *

In the cloak of darkness, Beauty saddled the draft horse and pulled on her traveling cloak. She breathed in deep, holding the night air long in her lungs, and patted the equine shoulder at her side. The stars winked down at her from a clear velvet sky.

She shivered, although not with the cold. There had been a thought and a will stirring in her heart as she watched her father struggle for strength and listened to his earnest madness. She could not dismiss his pain or his sincerity, so she felt only the barest of hesitation now.

Beauty guided the horse from the small barn out into the moonlight. She jumped in surprise at the figure of her brother, fully dressed and resting casually against the side of the barn, his lean body outlined in silver. The mug in his hand steamed in the night air.

"Going somewhere?"

Beauty fidgeted with the bridle a moment, and then held her head up high and stepped forward. "I know you place much stock in science. In reason. In logical, provable things. But this…this thing afflicting our father, there is no reason in it. I can see only the touch of magic, Brendan. Everything he told us was true; the castle, the beast, the rose. I can't let Father die. not while I can prevent it. We already lost our mother. I did not know her, and you barely did. To lose our father as well, to be orphans?" She shook her head. "I will go to this beast and offer myself in exchange." She pressed a light touch to his arm, her blue-gray eyes solemn as storm clouds. "Brendan, you are the man of the house, with father aging and ill as he is. You must take care of him, and our sisters."

Brendan frowned, setting the mug aside. "Beauty, think about this. You're going to go traipsing off into the woods, at night, all alone? To a place you don't even know the location of? A place, I might add, reputedly owned by a monstrous, vicious, possibly rabid beast? Have you gone *completely* mad?"

"He wants me there. I'm sure I will be shown the way. Perhaps he can be reasoned with."

"And have you thought about *why* this beast wants you? What if he's tried

24

every other food but young girl, and wants you to sate some epicurean craving? Or worse," he added, voice dropping low.

Beauty visibly quailed, but took a deep breath and regained some measure of composure. "You are just trying to frighten me. You don't even believe there is a beast."

With an exasperated scoff, Brendan threw up his hands. "It doesn't matter if there is a beast or if Father just saw a tall man in a fur coat! You can't expect me to let my little sister wander into the forest by herself. It's too dangerous!" He folded his arms over his chest, adamant. "I will not allow it."

She lifted her chin higher, her resolve strong. "I'm going, Brendan. I have to make this right."

He took in her pose for a long moment, then looked away, nibbling his lower lip. He picked up the mug and cupped it between his palms as if needing the comfort of its warmth. "You've got that blasted look again. Nothing I can say will sway you. All right. I will not stand in your way."

Beauty breathed out, clutching at the reins. "Thank you, Brendan." They exchanged a brief gaze, their identical eyes heavy with unsaid farewells, and she started forward, leading the horse behind her.

"At least have a warm drink, before you go," Brendan insisted, pushing the mug into her hands. "You'll catch your death if the wind starts up."

She swallowed a protest at the realization it was much easier to humor her brother, and took a big gulp of the tea. "Far too sweet," she said, shaking her head. "You'll waste all our honey."

"It's poppy syrup, actually," Brendan said brightly. "Father's medicine."

Beauty blinked. Her eyelids suddenly were heavy enough for the simple motion to be a struggle. "Poppy syrup?"

"I'm not sure if I got the dosage right. The doctor was somewhat vague." Brendan set the mug down and reached for Beauty's elbow. She batted him away, though her hands felt like they dragged underwater instead of air.

"You...why would you...*why?*"

Brendan snorted. "Why, indeed. As if I would let you clean up another one of Father's messes all by yourself. I'm your big brother! It's my job to keep you safe."

Beauty tried to stamp her foot in frustration but only managed a stumble, hanging onto the horse's reins for balance as she fought off a wave of sleepiness. "But if I don't go, Father will—"

"I don't give a fig for Father," Brendan said baldly, "I care about *you*. You don't need to bear the burden of his mistakes, Beauty." He lifted his chin in an unconscious mirror of her stubborn stance. "I'll take care of this. I wasn't here for you before, but I am now."

Beauty's face scrunched up in a dismayed pout. "I am going to get you back for this *so bad*," she slurred. Her eyelashes fluttered. Brendan caught her before she crumpled to the ground.

Brendan carried his sister back into the house and laid her gently on the chair next to the last popping embers smoldering in the fireplace. He stood above her, thinking furiously. She'd only try again when she woke up, and next time she'd be much more stealthy. He couldn't very well chain her to the cottage, and there was no talking Beauty out of an idea once she had grabbed hold of it. She had the tenacity of a snapping turtle.

Brendan rubbed at the bridge of his nose. She had been right, he didn't believe in his father's fantastical ramblings. There was no rampaging magic beast. However, there were too many details to discount the story altogether. Who had braided the horse's mane, and shone all the brass of the tack? Only a stable would have done so, and not one attached to some grimy little roadside inn. And then there was the money to consider. Entire sacksful of gold did not simply fall from the sky.

He padded silently into his father's darkened bedroom. It caught him unawares how pale his father looked in the puddle of moonlight, skin translucent as a ghost. Brendan had to admit, something felt distinctly *not right* about his father's illness, something that crept up the back of his spine and made shadows dance at the edge of his vision. He wasn't prepared to call it magic, but standing there looking down as his father labored for every breath, he was willing to accept the possibility there may be hidden forces at work, something he did not understand.

There was nothing else for it. He had to leave and find some answers, to either find the castle and convince his father's beast to release Beauty from her ridiculous obligation, or wander in the forest, find nothing, and disprove the whole thing. Neither option held particular appeal.

The first was unlikely, and dangerous besides, and the second only proved his father's mind had finally crumbled under the weight of his failures. Either way, Brendan did not relish the prospect. However, if he did not go then his sister most certainly would, and Brendan would not—could not—allow that to happen.

If this 'beast' had any kind of sense at all, Brendan would need proof he was who he claimed to be. He went to the windowsill and deftly snapped the full blossom, stem and all, from the dirt before stuffing it into his doublet. He pulled on his traveling cloak and strode out the door into the moonlight, to seek a man who valued his roses more fiercely than gold.

4

In Which There is a Meeting

The sky had turned black, storm clouds building. Winter was creeping close, and far too early. The horse shied from fallen branches as if any one might leap up and bite its fetlock.

After a long and tedious day of travel, Brendan had almost given up hoping for a warm and comfy inn to appear on the roadside before nightfall. He only had his father's confused recollections to serve as guidance, but there was only one path cutting through the forest, branching out only when the ocean port was already in sight. It had no crossroads or diversions, and barely enough room for an ox-drawn wagon. At least there was no chance of getting lost.

The sudden rumble of low, threatening thunder rolled over the hills. Brendan bit back a curse, wishing he could be at home by the fire, with something wet to wash away the dust in his throat.

Perhaps that had been the wrong thing to wish for, as a freezing rain started to slice through the trees. It stung as it struck, and Brendan pulled the hood of his cloak down low over his face, feeling very sorry for himself indeed. He pushed the horse to go faster, wanting desperately to get out of the downpour. The horse seemed reluctant, but he urged it forward, and they were soon delving deeper into the dark forest. He barely noticed when the dirt path turned to uneven stone clacking underneath horseshoes. His hood could not keep out every stray sluice of rain, and soon Brendan's hair grew heavy with water. He hunched low in the saddle, chin tucked to his chest, and let the steady clop of hooves lull him into a trance.

After a time a flicker of light caught his eyes. He looked up, hoping for the lit windows of an inn, or even the comforting promise of some woodcutter's barn.

The forest had opened up to reveal a craggy mountain, gray and shadowy under the darkening sky. He blinked rain from his eyes. No, not a mountain. A castle. A hulking fortress of ash-colored stone, tiered and massive, standing grand and terrible in the now-pouring rain.

As he stared gobsmacked at the irrefutable proof of his father's story, the horse halted in front of the gates and dropped its head with a weary little sigh, legs splayed wide. Brendan scrambled out of the saddle, petting the horse contritely. "Come on, boy. There's bound to be someplace warm and dry for you in...in there."

He turned to the huge gates, swallowing his apprehension. They screeched as they opened, barely muffled by the resounding thunder. He squared his shoulders and walked, towing his tired horse through the sheeting rain.

* * *

The Beast waited, perched over the door on the gutters, indistinguishable from one of the great dark shapes of the gargoyles as the rain painted them all a uniform gray. From his vantage point, he had seen the girl ride in swathed and bundled like a nun in her robes. When she dismounted, she swung her legs to the ground with unusually robust movements, walking with a bold and unmaidenly stride.

But an unusual girl was exactly what Beast needed.

He forced his mind off the thought, daring not be too hopeful for fear of nearly inevitable disappointment. He watched as she made her way down the path between the tangled roses. He could not see much through the veil of rain, only that she was slender and tall, with dark wisps of bedraggled hair peeking from the hood.

A smug little smile tugged at Beast's lips. Not for one second did he think

29

that craven scum of a merchant would balk to sacrifice his kin. No doubt the very minute he had fallen ill he slapped his daughter in the saddle and trundled her off. Beast squirmed with eagerness before remembering he had to try not to frighten the girl.

She might be his last chance.

The Beast drew his hood far over his monstrous face and crouched low as the girl neared the door. He tensed, tail lashing, and with a great leap he pounced from the eaves to the cobblestones below. He landed braced on his paw-like hands as the heavy black cloak flared out like the giant wings of a raven.

The rain-slick horse shied, pawing at the ground and frothing at the bit. The girl jumped back, the whites of her eyes visible under her hood, but she managed to hold onto her horse's muzzle. She backed up against its quivering flanks as Beast drew himself up to his full height, looming over her.

"You are late." He tried to speak softly, the words rumbling in his chest like gravel. She must not be able to see him clearly, else she'd be running for the hills.

The girl took a mouse-like step forward. "I didn't realize I was expected at all, sir." The voice was unsteady, almost quiet enough to be drowned out by the rain, but quite clearly was much too deep to be a lady's voice.

The Beast's heavy brows flew up in surprise. He shot out an arm and grabbed the intruder by the front of his cloak. He yelped, dropping the horse's bridle. Beast yanked off his hood with a sharp curved claw. The face it revealed was pale and fine-boned, with an upturned nose and blue-gray eyes, but it was unmistakably the face of a young man. An unshaven jaw left no doubt of that.

Beast snarled, "Who the hell are you?"

* * *

Despite being more frightened than he'd ever been in his life, unchecked curiosity drove Brendan to try to pierce the mire with his eyes, to make out his attacker's face. Rain fell in his eyes, and he could not discern the faintest detail. He could quite readily believe this was a true beast, just as his father had attested. The hands gripping him were stronger than imaginable, and the voice like a grating avalanche of rocks and pure menace. Brendan swallowed a lump of fear before it could choke him.

"M-my name is Brendan… My father, he came here and, well, the rose, and my sister, so I stopped her and I thought, well…" He caught himself babbling and took a deep steadying breath. "I th-thought maybe I could talk to you so you wouldn't, er, have to kill my father. Or my sister."

Fists tightened on his shirt. A leonine growl rumbled out from under the dripping black hood.

"Or me, for that matter, sir," Brendan added in a small voice.

With a snarl, the monstrous creature whirled around with Brendan's cloak still gripped in his claws, rammed the heavy castle door open with his free fist, and easily flung Brendan to the floor inside. Brendan pushed himself up off the carpet, noting vaguely how he was drenching the fine pattern of it with slightly muddy water. He pushed sodden strands of hair out of his eyes, warily watching the cloaked figure address someone behind him.

"See to the damned horse!" came the sharp command. Brendan quickly glanced back behind his shoulder. Nobody was there. He slowly and shakily got to his feet, bracing for whatever was next to come.

No amount of bracing could have prepared him as the heavy black cloak was torn off. The Beast turned to face him, drawing up and towering threateningly over him.

Brendan sucked in a shocked breath. He took a backward step, eyes going as round as twin moons. It was exactly as his father described; the thin mouth and angular jaw, a fearsome face framed by a russet and gold mane, ridged horns sweeping back from heavy, low-drawn brows. Through his shock Brendan reflexively cataloged features, wondering why his father had never mentioned the wolfish fangs or the long tufted tail. Those seemed like important details to disclose.

"What are you staring at?" the Beast snapped, claws clenched into tight fists. Brendan wrenched his eyes away and fixed them on his own hands, embarrassed to see them shaking. He tried to gather his scattered wits, fighting off the insane impulse to laugh hysterically.

Not a man in a fur coat, after all.

The Beast rumbled deep from his chest and crossed thick arms over it. "I should snap your neck for your insolence. Am I a freak to amuse you?"

"I'm sorry," Brendan whispered hoarsely.

"That coward merchant is your father, boy?"

Brendan jerked an unsteady nod, shivering as the cold of his wet cloak seeped into his bones. He didn't trust himself to speak.

"Why have you come here?" Beast demanded. "I sent for the girl."

The thought of his little sister gave Brendan all the courage he needed to answer, though every instinct told him to run like hell. "Father was…he was sick. Very sick. Beauty, my sister, she loves him dearly despite…everything, and was going to come here to save him, but I couldn't let…let her…"

"Did you think it was a brave thing to do, to march in the home of the Beast, or was it merely stupidity?" Leonine lips curled in a sneer, framing sharp white canines.

"Well," Brendan began, unsure where to put his gaze. Politeness decreed eye contact was respectful, but what if the creature accused him of staring again? "To be perfectly honest, I didn't believe there was a… Well. A beast. So, um. Stupidity?"

One of the Beast's heavy eyebrows lifted, so Brendan continued.

"And I had to come. She was so worried about Father. I thought perhaps…I could…convince you…" His words trailed off into a mumble. It sounded so stupid now, faced with this leviathan. "I can't help but feel this all is my fault, sir."

"Call me Beast!" roared the creature, the cords of his neck standing out in sharp relief. "I care not for your flattering lies!"

"I'm sorry, I…I meant it in respect." Brendan could barely hear his own voice, so quiet it came.

The Beast scowled, waving the words aside with a talon. "How is anything your fault, boy? Did you make your thieving father steal my rose?"

"Y-yes, in a way, I think." Again he struggled to meet the Beast's eyes, momentarily taken aback at their amber-brown plainness. "I asked him for one. If I hadn't requested it, he wouldn't have taken yours."

The Beast's startlingly human eyes narrowed. "Why did you ask your father for a rose?"

Brendan paused. Honesty might be his best course of action. "I didn't exactly have what you could call *faith* in my father's abilities to…do anything right, actually, so I thought I would ask for something exceedingly simple and of little monetary value."

Beast's lip curled. "It seems there is little love lost between the two of you over it. This is the same father you came to save?"

Brendan nodded, gaining little bits of his confidence. The longer he was alive, the less likely it seemed he would be eaten later. He was still breathing, which seemed to be a good sign. "Yes. Er, rather, no."

"That wasn't a particularly difficult question, boy." The Beast enunciated carefully, as if he were speaking to a half-wit. "One-word answer. Yes or no."

"Not…exactly."

"One word," snapped the Beast. "Yes or no?"

"…Maybe," Brendan squeaked.

The Beast's hand twitched as if he were fighting the urge to smack Brendan upside the head to his senses, or senseless, whichever came about first. "Try one sentence," he growled.

"I came to protect my sister," Brendan said, a quiet edge to his words slipping out from underneath his trepidation, "to stop her from throwing herself on the mercy of some madman in the woods." A full, coherent sentence. They were getting somewhere.

Beast looked as if he were holding in his temper by its raggedy edge. "Why did you think you would be an acceptable trade?"

"Ah… Well, I didn't really—"

"Fool! I did not ask for her on a passing fancy! I needed the girl!" The Beast's expression shuttered, and he turned away.

Brendan took the opportunity to really *look* at him, scrutinizing every detail. His academic curiosity stirred. Could this truly be a hitherto unknown creature? A creature capable of reason and rages—mostly rages, it seemed—and, Brendan noticed with some relief, a creature that was not killing him. Perhaps it was only a medical condition. Like gigantism, only with hair, or…or something.

After a moment, Brendan hesitantly reached out one hand, leaned forward, and asked, "Were you…born like that?"

Cobra-quick, the Beast snatched Brendan's wrist and hauled him a good seven inches above the ground, until they were face to monstrous face. The Beast seethed with outrage, eyes burning like banked coals. *"Get out!"* he roared through tightly clenched teeth.

Brendan's shoulder complained at the rough treatment, and he struggled uselessly against the iron grip before subsiding, feet dangling above the rug like a doll's. "In this weather?" he heard himself weakly ask.

The Beast looked as taken aback at this temerity as Brendan was himself. "Yes!"

"But," to his horror, protests kept spilling from Brendan's mouth, "it's freezing and it's raining, and the horse is exhausted, and I don't even know where I am!"

The Beast moved his face very close to Brendan's, half-slitted eyes promising many painful things. "I do not care. Get out of my castle. Or I will eat you," he hissed menacingly.

Brendan considered this, canted his head to the side, and said, "I don't think you will." He pointed with his free hand at the Beast's bared fangs. "See, only your canine teeth are fangs, and the rest are flat. They aren't suitable for tearing meat, and this would indicate you're an omnivore, and therefore probably—"

"Shut *up!*" The Beast yelled, abruptly dropping him to the floor in a dripping heap. "What is the matter with you? Stop talking!"

"I don't know! Apparently I babble when I'm terrified?"

"Be silent!" The command echoed throughout the buttressed hall. The Beast heaved Brendan to his feet with a rough push toward the door. "Leave. Go."

Brendan stumbled, looking at the great wooden doors with dismay.

"Do you have any idea," the Beast fumed, "how lucky you are? That you are still alive to be given the opportunity to leave with all your limbs intact? Get out of my castle!"

"I'll freeze to death," Brendan said matter-of-factly, adopting a mule-like stance.

"That is entirely your problem," the Beast grumbled, and bodily shoved him out the double doors as they opened seemingly of their own accord.

They slammed shut behind him. At the foot of the stairs, Brendan's horse stood dejectedly in the rain, water pooled on the saddle. The storm pelted down on them as Brendan trudged over and pulled himself up into the saddle. He sat there for a minute, nerves still thrumming with shock, though exhaustion crept in as fear abated. He was not looking forward to a long night of soggy and frigid travel, returning home to his family with only a bizarre story and no guarantee of their safety.

Still, the longer he dejectedly sat, the longer that ride would be, and so Brendan urged the horse forward down the long, puddled path to the gates.

5

In Which There is a Storm

The music room smelled of warped wood and neglect. Dust dulled each lonely instrument on the cobwebbed racks, and the small windows were so clouded with age they looked like smoked glass. An enormous ornate fireplace took up the entirety of the far wall, spacious enough to roast a cow whole, carved lions stalking around the mantel.

The Beast watched the flame's tongues lick the back of the metal screen. He brooded in a torn divan, its beauty long since shredded in some bygone rage. A wine chalice found its way into his grasp, and he sipped it with a delicacy his clawed hands were no longer suited for. There was a time when the room had been filled with people, all laughing and flirting and dancing. And the music, of course, so much beautiful music.

A loud hollow banging tore through the Beast's dissolving ruminations as if they were wet tissue paper. He stood, the fur bristling on his shoulders.

And then came a voice, borne on the stagnant air like a lost bird.

"Hello?"

Beast gnashed his teeth in fury. One of the servants must have let the boy in. He prowled toward the stairs as the voice floated through the hall.

"Hellooo? Look, can I just use your fireplace?"

Beast hurled himself down the grand staircase on all fours and threw the parlor door open wide. There, large as life and bedraggled as a drowned cat, the boy stood cozying up to the fireplace as if he had some kind of right to be there.

"You!" Beast bellowed so loudly the chandelier shook. "I thought I told you to leave!" The boy turned to face him, and though he was very pale he did not look at all frightened, and this more than anything brought Beast up short.

"I did leave." The boy's voice was flat. His dripping cloak suddenly lifted from his shoulders and disappeared into the aether. He jumped, glancing about in startled confusion.

"It's just the servants." Beast glowered in full force. "Is there a particular reason why you have, in fact, done the opposite of what I told you? Was I somehow not clear enough?"

"But there's no one there," Brendan protested, eyes skidding about nervously as he inched closer to the flickering fire. Evidently not even a disappearing cloak could dissuade him from that welcoming warmth.

"They're invisible, fool," the Beast told him as if that should have been utterly obvious. "I asked you a question. I told you to leave, and yet here you are, standing in front of my fireplace. Quite audaciously, might I add."

"Well," Brendan said, "after going round the sixth circle of the night on that damned road, I got tired of trying. That, and the freezing sleet, and rain, and howling wolves..." He shook his head and folded down into a wingback chair, not budging despite the rising dust. "I am not going back out there."

Beast spluttered in disbelief. "You couldn't find your way onto the main road? It's a direct trail. No curves, twists, turns, or forks. It is a completely straight road."

"Yes, I am aware. I noticed that the first time I went down it. However, on my return trip it disagreed with my memory. I passed the same blasted tree stump three blasted times. You might want to have that checked out. Your...your faulty blasted road."

The Beast blinked, taken aback. "The road wouldn't let you out?"

"That must be it," Brendan snipped, "because the road has feelings. It *wanted* me to stay." A ferocious sneeze erupted from him, and a blanket suddenly whisked into being and found its way around his shoulders. Brendan gave the blanket a wary stare. "Invisible servants," he muttered under his breath, disbelief knotting his brow until it melted away in a kind of exhausted acceptance, and he huddled down into its dry embrace. A heartbeat later a hot cup of tea was pressed from nothingness into his cold hands. "Oh. Thank you very much."

"Stop giving him things!" Beast howled at the empty air. "He is not a guest!"

"Please, can I just stay the night? I won't be any trouble."

"You already *are* trouble!"

"You let my father have a room for the night."

"And look how well *that* turned out," Beast said acidly.

"Just until morning, I swear it."

"No!"

"I'll catch pneumonia. Honestly, it's that bad out there." Silence. "And if I do, I swear I shall drag myself right back here and die on your doorstep."

Beast gave a darkly amused snort.

"Please?"

Beast heaved a sigh, his broad shoulders sagging. "Fine, you can stay. But," he amended, sticking up one wickedly curved claw, "you will be gone at first light. And I will not see nor hear one *hint* of your presence, is that clear?"

"Yes. Right. Of course. I'll be gone first thing in the morning."

With a disgusted cluck of his tongue, Beast whirled away and stalked out of the room, the claws of his feet scraping over the hardwood floors, leaving Brendan alone with his cup of tea.

Brendan settled into the chair and let the warmth seep into his skin, pushing aside all the strangeness of the last few hours to think about later. Much later. He was weary down to his bones, basking in the radiant flickering heat that felt deliciously like branding-hot hands.

A light touch fell on his shoulder. Brendan's eyes snapped open. For a panicked instant, he thought it must be the Beast coming to change his mind about eating him. But Brendan saw no one. He blinked, pulling the blanket tight over his body, and again felt the feather-soft touch to his arm.

He took a deep breath. "Is someone there?" As welcome as their attentions had been, Brendan had a hard time accepting a reality in which things like invisible servants truly existed. He looked down at his arm when he felt the touch again, amazed to see the fabric indent as if an unseen finger was being pressed into it.

That was some pretty hard evidence to refute.

He allowed gentle hands to pull him to his feet and lead him out of the parlor, back to the Great Hall, and then on through an arched corridor. Brendan tried to speak to his unseen guide as they ascended a wide, red-carpeted staircase.

"Hello? Who are you?" No answer, only a slight push to lead him down the right passage, dimly lit by candles flaring into life at his approach.

"What is your name? Where are you taking me?" Brendan persisted, yet still there was no answer. After a long, thoughtful pause and many steps, Brendan asked, "Can't you speak?"

He fancied, for a moment, the lightly guiding hands somehow conveyed a sadness, and he wondered fiercely if the guide was male or female, young or old, what he or she might look like. On impulse, he grabbed at where the invisible body should be. The hands swiftly left his side and Brendan grasped at nothing.

He stood awkwardly, hands outstretched. Then he blushed and tucked his hands into his pockets. "Sorry," he mumbled, hoping the servant hadn't been offended by his rudeness and left him alone in this maze-like hall, but the hands came back almost immediately and continued leading him along as if nothing had happened.

Soon they brought him to a door, vines and ivy carved into the dark wood. The hands left Brendan's shoulder and the door swung open to reveal a large, well-appointed room. The walls were papered in a dark pattern, saved from being oppressive by the long stretch of windows. A cozy little fire danced in the small fireplace across from the canopied bed.

Never had any bed looked so warm and inviting in Brendan's life. Though right then, a plank of wood with a sheet would have looked good to him, as long as it was dry.

The room was clean and without even a hint of the dust that seemed thick everywhere else, but it possessed the underlying scent of a room long gone unused. The fire burned merrily in the hearth, and a small plate of simple foods had been set out on a table by the window.

Gratefully, Brendan sat and wolfed down three slices of fresh bread, and drank the entire bowl of warm salty broth. A jug of watered wine had also been kindly set out, and it was sweet and quenching. He looked out the window and could barely see the ground for the darkness and the sleeting rain. He felt suddenly very alone, in the absence of the moon or even stars twinkling down at him.

A pair of hands suddenly whisked away the empty plate in front of him. Brendan jumped, having forgotten for a moment he couldn't ever be sure of being alone in this unbelievable place. It was a testament to his weariness that he didn't feel more than a flicker of curiosity as to how such a thing might be possible. Nothing would be as wonderful as sleep.

As if reading his thoughts, a corner of the bed covers turned down invitingly. In seconds, Brendan buried himself under the warm sheets, barely stopping to kick off his boots. He mumbled, "Thank you," into the pillow before he fell into a dreamless, velvet-soft sleep.

* * *

Cold fingers softly touched Brendan's cheek. He murmured unintelligibly and buried his face deeper into the pillow. The warm, fluffy, goose-down pillow, that smelled sweetly of lavender and clove.

He jolted awake at the unfamiliarity. His bed in the cramped cottage attic wasn't nearly so comfortable, nor did it smell of expensive scents. Groggily he sat up, pushing back his tangled mess of hair before he remembered where he was. The curtains had been drawn during the night, and the fire had been tended to.

"Silent as well as invisible," he muttered, filing away the information for later. He shook the sleep from his head and swung his legs off the bed. The light pouring in through the curtained window didn't have the brightness of sunlight, so Brendan guessed it must be overcast. He jammed his feet into his tall riding boots, regretting the promise to leave so early. Brendan felt like he could use a hot bath and some breakfast, but alas, another day of long, cold travel awaited him. At least it didn't sound like it was raining.

He had no idea what he was going to tell Beauty. Or his father. Brendan stood up, rubbing the corners of his eyes. His cloak, brushed and dried, had been draped over the back of a chair next to the large oaken wardrobe. Curiosity awakened after a good rest, he peered around the room trying to find some hint of the hidden servants.

"Hello? Is anyone there?" He fastened his cloak, unsure if he could find his way back down the Great Hall.

The door creaked open. Brendan stepped out of the room and into the hallway. As he walked, he found his way lit by candles even in daylight. It was a useful guide, anyway. He followed the path of lit candelabras and down the stairs until he found himself in front of the huge main doors. He heaved a sigh, but gamely fastened his cloak and pulled open the double doors.

A white flurry of snow blew in, the wind biting its way inside to extinguish the candles and stinging Brendan's skin. He quickly slammed the doors shut, and stood pressed against the wood for a few seconds, rather stunned.

Snow? The first snowfall *never* came this early.

Nonetheless, the small mound of quickly melting snow lying piled at his feet was a testament to the contrary. Brendan strode to the side window and peered out.

He could barely see twenty yards away, the sheer white landscape fading into a smooth icy wall. Trees were bare and frosted; no trace of the cobblestone path could be seen beneath its stark and pallid shroud. He could just see the mounds of rosebushes, red blossoms peeping through the blanketing snow, still alive and thriving. The snow had already drifted two feet thick against the window. A blizzard, with a full month yet until winter.

"What," the voice came hissing like wet silk over slate, "are you still doing here?"

Brendan's spine stiffened with an icy spike of fear. Slowly he turned around and faced the Beast. "Uh, good morning—"

41

"Shut up. Why aren't you gone yet?" The Beast crossed his arms over an expansively broad chest, chin lifted with the unmistakable air of commanding regality.

"Well, ah." Brendan once again tried to keep eye contact and failed, looking nervously down at his boots. "I was about to, but then I saw all this snow—"

Blinking, Brendan wondered why he was on the floor with his back against the door, and it was only when his breastbone began to throb that he realized he'd been knocked down.

The Beast loomed over him. "That," he said with a pointed snort, "was for lying."

"That was amazing," Brendan croaked, slowly getting to his feet. "I didn't even see you move..." He reflexively rubbed his chest, shrinking away from the Beast. "At the risk of getting hit again, I wasn't lying."

"What do you take me for, a fool? I was outside not an hour ago. Are you telling me that...that..." The Beast's brows climbed up as he finally noticed the whiteness outside the window. He pushed Brendan aside and cracked open the door.

The icy wind and snow whipped inside with a forlorn whine. Beast shut the door. He blinked at the woodgrain for several seconds before turning his gaze on Brendan. "I don't care. Go."

"It'd be murder to send me out in a snowstorm," Brendan told him steadily, "and you know it."

The tension was palpable as the Beast stood motionless, his expression unreadable. He then walked up to a beautiful tapestry that, from Brendan's estimate, must have been skillfully woven several centuries ago. It was an exquisite piece of craftsmanship. The Beast regarded the tapestry, as if admiring it. Then with a suddenness that made Brendan jump back like a frightened rabbit, the Beast tore it from its hangings with a feral roar, shredding it to mere threads in seconds.

Brendan stood frozen as Beast snatched up a vase and hurled it at the wall. It shattered, bits of painted white china skittering across the floor like a broken star. Brendan's sensibilities were appalled at this blatant disregard for antiquities, but his instincts screamed he might be the next thing to be thrown against the wall. Trying to be unobtrusive, he backed away from the Beast, whose shoulders heaved like moving mountains and whose talons were clenched into tight, meaty fists.

"You." Beast whipped around and shook a claw in Brendan's face, his leonine features twisted with rage. "You...you..." It was very clear he badly wanted to blame Brendan for the inclement weather. The Beast turned his back, took a step, then spun back around once more, eyes burning fury. "When this storm is over," he said with a voice of brimstone and granite, "the very *second* it stops. You. Will. Leave."

Despite himself, Brendan was once again consumed with curiosity, his gaze flickering over the Beast's twisted horns and the furiously lashing tail, and tried vainly to think of some practical, logical explanation other than magic.

"*Is that understood, boy?*" The Beast bellowed, nearly spearing Brendan through the chest with a sharp rap of his claw.

Now, Brendan was a slender sort and too clever by half, as his father had often loudly despaired. Naturally he had faced his fair share of bullies growing up, and learned well a variety of means to deal with them. Often a simple well-placed punch had done the trick, all the more effective for issuing from an unexpected source like himself. Doubtful that would end well in this particular instance. However, the most important thing was to not allow himself to back away in cowardice, even if he might be quailing inside.

Brendan stood firm against the Beast's menacing tap. "Understood."

"Good," the Beast snarled before stalking away with a frustrated growl.

Brendan let out a relieved breath. After a while, his heartbeat found its usual rhythm, and shakily, he made his way back to his room.

* * *

"It doesn't make any sense," Brendan told the room. "I've never seen so much snow in my life! Do you think it's snowing like this everywhere, or just here, I wonder?" He imagined the invisible attendant shrugged. Brendan heaved

43

a loud sigh, examining the persistent weather from the window.

"I wish you could talk," he lamented softly as another glass of wine edged toward him. "I feel like a crazy person, talking to my invisible friend." Brendan picked the fine crystal up from the table and wet his lips. He sighed and tapped a tune onto the table for what felt like the trillionth time; there wasn't much else to do. "Two days and it feels like forever."

Brendan had four times tried to leave the room and go exploring, but every time he started to creep down the stairs, the Beast had either heard with his freakishly keen ears or been alerted by his unseen servants, bellowing from wherever he was in the castle, "If you're bored, I'm sure the dungeon would be much more interesting, boy!" and Brendan would wisely turn right around and pad back to his room.

And so he sat in the chair by the fireplace, now and then glancing out the window to see if the monotonous fall of snow had slackened, or lying on the crisp-sheeted bed humming melodies to himself, or rummaging through the poorly stocked wardrobe to find something in his size that didn't look like it belonged on a medieval serf. And wasn't a dress. Every time he opened the wardrobe doors, he could swear it had acquired another dress, until eventually the whole space was filled up with ruffles and lace and he gave up entirely.

He longed for a book to read, and even more, he pined for a violin, or a lute, or even a harp; anything with strings would do. He hadn't neglected to practice for this long in years. He hoped his skill wasn't atrophying too badly, his calluses waning. Some music would lighten his spirits considerably.

Often, Brendan thought with more than a little yearning of his days at the university and the classes he missed so much. Thinking about school brought a kind of bittersweet taste to Brendan's mouth, thinking of other times and people—one person in particular—and since he didn't especially feel like picking at metaphorical scabs, he instead tried writing down some clumsy compositions that went nowhere, and asking unanswered questions to the air as the afternoon passed by.

Many times Brendan attempted to establish some sort of communication with the invisibles, but they did not write when he set a pen out with some stationary he'd found in the drawer, nor did they tap his hand 'once for yes, twice for no.'

He was greatly surprised when a slip of folded paper was brandished from thin air and set before him. It was written in an elegant but strangely archaic script.

You might as well join me for dinner. We shall talk about your sister.

-B

A conflict of emotions struggled for supremacy, relief and elation warring with apprehension and hesitance. None of them won, and Brendan was left with the knotted lump of them heavy in his stomach as he made his way downstairs.

6

In Which There is a Dinner

Brendan took several deep breaths to soothe his nerves as he approached the cavernous dining room. The halls were all still and dark, lit only by quietly rustling flames that went out as soon as he passed them. The lush red carpet gave way to a gold-hued hardwood floor, and Brendan felt entirely too conspicuous as his boot heels creaked softly, the noise echoing on the new surface.

He peered around the corner, heart thudding in his ears, his fingers curling around the oak molding. A slight, surreptitious shove at his back startled him enough for him to jump out into the open. With a reproachful glance backward at his unseen assailant, he ventured into the dining room.

The long table was made of some rich jungle wood and ornately decorated, peacocks and tigers prowling along the sides, tapering into four delicate feet that with their prominent claws put Brendan in mind of his host. What drew his more immediate attention, however, was that the table was absolutely smothered with food.

His eyes widened at the array of glazed meat, poached fish, candied fruits, braised quails, and the tall spires of soufflés. There were goat cheese quiches with hollandaise sauce, savory meat pies with shallots and cognac, some sort of honeyed dessert with browned walnuts, and—he couldn't even put names to some of the delicacies! Even when his family had counted themselves among the city elites, Brendan had never eaten so well or so elegantly.

The Beast cleared his throat. Brendan flinched, somehow neglecting to notice his host amongst the marvelous display. At the head of the table, the Beast was attired much as he had been the first night, in a white shirt under a velvet coat. He arched one furred brow expectantly.

Self-conscious, Brendan tugged at the hem of his drab doublet before crossing the floor and sliding into his seat. He swallowed down the faint but bitter dregs of fear and met his host's gaze. The twisted horns shone bone-white under the light of the chandelier. The Beast glared as if Brendan were an especially offensive piece of refuse that had impudently decided to grow legs and join him at the table.

"Are you wearing the same thing you arrived here in?"

The tone the Beast used made Brendan wish very much his answer wasn't what it was. "Ah. That. Yes."

"You come to my table in those filthy garments?" Clickity-click went his long claws, heedless of the wood's fine polish. "I did not realize you needed explicit permission to avail yourself of the full hospitality provided. Perhaps you didn't notice the big wooden thing with clothes in it? It's called a wardrobe."

Brendan cleared his throat and decided to leave his views on Beast's 'hospitality' unsaid. He looked at his hands, folded on the table's edge. "There was a disagreement about my options."

Beast raised a single eyebrow. "With whom?"

"The servants." Brendan's cheeks warmed.

Beast waited for a sizable stretch for Brendan to add anything before he gave up with a pointed, "And?"

"Well." Brendan smoothed nervous hands out across the tablecloth. "I didn't want to wear what they wanted me to wear."

The Beast sucked in air through his teeth as if searching for patience. "And what," he said, dropping each word deliberately into place, "did they want you to wear?"

A slight cough. "Taffeta, mostly. With bows," Brendan told the table, his cheeks heating even further. Fortunately, the invisible servants began to pile food onto their plates, and Brendan gratefully began eating.

"This is amazing," he exclaimed, glad for the excuse to change the subject. "I don't think I've ever eaten anything this good."

Beast propped his elbow on the table, a glass of red wine dwarfed in a furred hand. He favored Brendan with a very sardonic look. "You are a guest in this house, despite my wishes to the contrary. It so happens I am a firm believer in hospitality, no matter how annoying the company."

Brendan chuckled, and the Beast's pointed ears flicked back, the way a cat's would when it pretended it wasn't surprised. They ate, for a few minutes, without speaking.

Every so often a new dish would be placed in front of him, and though he'd never considered himself to be a glutton, Brendan ate every delicious morsel and still craved more. The Beast seemed to eat very little, and what he did eat was mostly light, though he drank a whole bottle of wine without appearing to be affected by it.

A tiny, distantly primitive part of Brendan's mind relaxed as the Beast ate salad and fruits—things decidedly not meat. So he'd been correct about the Beast's alleged carnivorousness.

He was beginning to slow down when the Beast finally spoke. "I have questions." He set down his glass with precision.

Brendan washed down his last bite with a dry, smoky wine. "I can't stop you." He tensed a little, not looking forward to any inquiries about Beauty; his brotherly instincts were to protect her at all costs.

"Your father. He kept the rose, did he not?"

The unexpected question caught Brendan off balance. "He did. But I took it with me and... oh."

"What?"

"I...I've quite forgotten about it. It must be in the room, somewhere, I would assume."

The Beast glowered, though that soon shifted into a cool, calculating look Brendan was unsure how to parse. "Hmm. It matters not." Upon waving his hand, plates of food began to be carted away, apparently floating on their own. Brendan watched in open-mouthed amazement. "Tell me about your family."

"Ah…" It took a moment to wrench his attention away from the culinary spectacle. "Well. Our family name is d'Aumale. My father, who you've met, is Etienne d'Aumale. At one time, he used to be a rather successful merchant. As successful as one can be without being born with land or titles. He met my mother while traveling abroad and she came back with him to France. After they got married, they had the twins. Marguerite and Catherine, named for Father's favorite aunts. Then they had me, and named me after my mother's godfather. He was partly Irish, so that explains *my* name. Then my youngest sister was born, and named Beauty after Mother. It's a popular thing in England, naming children after virtues. One of the few English traits Mother hung onto. She was…" Brendan looked away and forced a shrug. "She was an unusual woman. She died a few days after Beauty was born.

"After that, Father got… Well. You've seen what he's like. Thank you," he told the air as fresh wine poured from a floating carafe. "We got along all right until Father lost our entire fortune." He flashed a tight smile. "He did recently manage to bring us a whole bag of gold, though I think the thanks are owed less to him and more to you on that score."

The only acknowledgment Beast made was a slight incline of his head. Shadowed eyes narrowed a mere fraction. "Tell me about your sister."

The command made no room for argument or sidestepping. Still, Brendan gamely tried. "Which one?"

A fist slammed down onto the table. "You know damned well which one!"

Brendan set down his wine and again examined his hands, startled by the outburst. "She is… Beauty is, of course, very pretty, from an objective viewpoint."

Beast lifted one large bushy eyebrow while the other remained flat. A skill he excelled at. "Objective?"

"Of course," Brendan hastily said, "I mean, she is my sister. One does not think of one's siblings as attractive or not." He took a deep drink of his wine.

The Beast considered him with a suspicious frown. "Your father mentioned her fine disposition, but he proved himself to be a man of questionable honesty. Was he lying then, as well?"

"No!" he protested in offense, and then rethought his answer. "I mean, yes. She can be quite a brat. Spoiled." Brendan wished he hadn't been taking so many nervous sips of wine; after two days of silent solitude they had slowed his wits and loosened his tongue. "Comes of being the youngest, I believe. She's the favorite."

"And the elder sisters?"

"Oh, they're the worst," Brendan said, glad not to lie again. "I do love them, very dearly, but a more conceited pair you are unlikely to meet."

"So," Beast asked, his claws steepled before his chin, "out of all your mother's children, are you then the good son among wicked daughters?"

Brendan flushed. "Well, no—that is—" He stalled to find something that wasn't backtracking or contradictory. "That is not to say my sisters are without their good qualities. I was merely voicing their bad ones."

"Of course." Beast laid a heavy portion of sarcasm in his words.

"No need to be so acerbic. I am well aware of my own quirks and faults." The Beast didn't make any sort of response beyond one of his amazingly expressive eyebrows slanting just a hair, so Brendan kept talking to fill the uncomfortable void. "I'm very stubborn, as you well know."

Beast looked grudgingly amused, the other brow climbing up to join its partner.

"And I know what they say about cats, but I consider my curiosity a virtue rather than a fault." Brendan brushed hair out of his eyes where it had fallen out of its tie. "It got me quite far at the university in Paris."

"Did it?" The question slipped from Beast's mouth as if the curiosity had snuck its way out without his consent.

A one-sided shrug. "I got top marks in both science and history. I never achieved any great success at mathematics and scraped by at languages. Music, however, was my favorite. I learned a bit of the woodwinds, a bit more of harpsichord, and a great deal about anything with strings."

Looking reluctantly intrigued, Beast asked, "You play?"

"Mostly violin. And cello." A shadow passed over Brendan's face, and he looked deeply into his half-full crystal goblet with the same intensity a

50

fortune-teller would stare into a black mirror.

"What is a cello?"

"What is a—" Brendan broke out of his reverie to stare at his host. "A cello. You know. The big, bassy violin-looking thing you have to set on the floor to play?" Two could play the sarcasm game.

Beast sneered. "You mean a viol."

"...I most certainly do not," Brendan said, more astonished than affronted. "How have you never— Have you missed the Renaissance entirely?"

Beast huffed a little, shifting in his seat before narrowing his eyes. "And Beauty? Does she play?"

"What? Oh. No. Well, a little bit. All the girls had harp lessons when they were younger, but none of them were very serious about it."

"I see. Is there anything else Beauty likes? I should like to prepare things for her arrival."

Brendan met the obvious challenge evenly, going so far as to lay out one of his own. "I doubt very much there is anything she wants that you can give her, my gracious host." The unspoken implication of *over my dead body* was nevertheless quite present in the twitch in Brendan's jaw and the fleeting hardening of his eyes.

There was a long tense pause, the Beast's expression giving away nothing. His empty goblet was lifted by a helpful servant and refilled. A single drop of wine splashed up and leaped like a fish over the rim of the glass. The escapee fell forever, as if time had slowed, onto the white tablecloth where it fell with an ominous blood-red splash.

In one swift, fluid motion, the Beast snatched the goblet from midair and flung it into the fire. Glass shattered, the flames licking greedily at the wine. Before the stain had even seeped through the tablecloth, Beast pointed a talon at the empty space beside him with all the stinging menace of a scorpion.

Brendan felt, rather than heard, a silent shriek of pain. It clawed up his spine and made him shudder, gooseflesh prickling over his skin.

Beast stood there, breathing heavily, his brows drawn so low they almost covered his eyes entirely.

Pulse racing, Brendan sat still with shock for a moment. That poor servant, nameless and faceless, severely punished for something as innocuous as a drop of spilled wine.

Slowly the Beast swiveled his head. "Go to your room."

Grateful to get away, Brendan slipped from his chair. He turned back, belatedly remembering his manners. "Thank you for dinner," he said in his most polite voice.

The Beast's mouth twisted to the side as if tasting something unpleasant. "If the snow stops, then you will leave. If not, we will talk more tomorrow."

Brendan nodded, unable to meet the Beast's eyes.

"And wear something clean, will you?"

His mouth opened and closed on a sharper answer than was likely wise. "Certainly." He spun on his heel and walked toward the doorway as quickly as etiquette allowed.

"Boy."

Brendan halted but didn't turn around, suppressing the flash of indignation. "Yes?"

"You are allowed admittance to my music room. A servant will show you the way, if you wish it."

Surprised at this unexpected kindness, Brendan turned around, where a "Thank you—" died on his lips.

The Beast had vanished.

* * *

Once back in his quarters, Brendan glanced around for any sign of the unseen servants and immediately felt foolish for doing so. The fire was blazing hot, so he pulled his doublet off over his head and sat on the edge of the bed in only his tunic and breeches.

"Hello?" he ventured. A soft brush of air against his skin suggested one of the servants was nearby, ready and waiting for an order. "Oh good, you're there. Look, would you happen to know where that rose might be? I thought I might have left it here in the room, but it's not here. Have I dropped it

52

somewhere?"

The bed curtains quavered slightly, indecisively.

"I'd be very grateful," he added quickly, remembering how callous Beast was to these servants, how one of their number had paid for one tiny mistake and felt obliged to in some small way make up for it.

Someone took hold of his hand and laid his or her knuckles against the heel of his palm. Slowly, and with seemingly great reluctance, the hand unfurled and the rose lay revealed. For an instant, Brendan fancied he could see the outline of invisible fingers over the petals.

When he moved to accept the rose, the invisible hand snatched it away with a possessive twitch that put Brendan in mind of how, as a child, Catherine had clutched one of her dolls to her chest after Marguerite had tried to steal it.

"Perhaps...it can be kept here in a vase? That way we can both enjoy it," Brendan offered.

The presence was abruptly gone, the bed curtains still and lifeless. Spare seconds later, with a tentative brush at his shoulder, Brendan was presented with a delicate vase, the red rose rising from the neck.

"Thank you very much!" He took the proffered flower with a delighted smile. He held it up to the light and examined it closely. Despite its unnatural long life and persistent bloom, it appeared to be in all respects a perfectly normal rose. A few shiny leaves spiraled up the stem, small dark thorns hidden underneath.

He was a little ashamed of himself, of how petty it had been to plant the rose in his father's room. Now Brendan was stuck in some strange and forbidding place with no way of knowing if his father was even still alive, or if his family was all right. He wondered how Beauty reacted after she'd awakened to find him gone, if she followed him, and hoped fervently she hadn't been caught in the treacherous snowstorm.

He set the vase on his nightstand, where it glowed in the lowering firelight like a comforting reminder of home as he fell asleep.

7

In Which There is a Garden

The next day, after he arose and broke his fast, Brendan decided he would try to find the music room.

He threw open the wardrobe doors, pleased to finally see a selection of clothing befitting his size, and even more fortunately, gender. All of the clothing looked to be cut in a fashion popular many decades ago. He chose something simple from the array of brocades and silks. After moving to the country, he'd gotten used to workaday clothes and felt uncomfortable in the kind of bourgeoisie finery he used to wear. It was strange enough not wearing his old school uniform; he certainly wasn't going to start wearing embroidered velvet and cravats, and left them hanging in the wardrobe untouched.

Washed and dressed, Brendan stepped out of his room and chose a direction. The Beast had told him a servant would show him the way, but how often did one get the opportunity to explore a magic castle?

He set off down a likely-looking hallway, winter light spilling in from the tall windows gracing each cavernous corridor. Little gargoyles leered down at him from every keystone as he passed under their masonry arches. Each new hallway bore a different runner carpet, and occasionally some sorts of expensive-looking baubles and tapestries that were sometimes torn, as if by claws. Everything looked a bit less gray and dusty than it had the night he had arrived, like the castle had been gone over with a hurried feather duster.

Walking past door after enigmatic door, it didn't take long for Brendan's resolve to crumble under the weight of his curiosity. He grasped a filigree brass handle of one heavy wooden door and pulled. Locked. He tried a few more to no avail. With a regretful sigh, he assumed the rest were locked as well, resuming his search.

He took a flight of stairs on a whim and found himself in an entirely different style of architecture. Older stonework, wider halls hung with faded tapestries of long-forgotten hunts. Brendan turned a corner and the worn heel of his boot clicked softly. No carpet. He glanced down, the short exhalation of his breath echoing back at him.

A great tile mosaic, slightly faded with age, was inlaid into the ground in a deliberate pattern. The hall had a noticeable aroma to it, pleasantly earthy, not the usual mustiness of the rest of the castle. Brendan took a few steps sideways, tilting his head to take in the details of the picture.

The image of a woman, cream-colored cloth draped around her shoulders and legs, was forever stretched languidly against a verdant flower-spangled background, her arm reaching ahead to point one slender finger at the end of the tiled hall, where twining ivy and morning glories were exquisitely carved into two great arched marble doors.

Awed, Brendan approached the doors softly, mindful of marring the quiet with his footfalls. The doors looked immeasurably heavy, easily as tall as three of him, with no handles or knobs. Searching for some hidden catch, he traced carved lines of foliage. The doors silently opened inwards, moving easily on their hinges. Brendan looked inside with wonder.

To say it was a garden would have been insufficient. Not near enough to describe the beautiful trellises and colonnades, the sunken turquoise pond surrounded by orchids and snapdragons, the leafy green ferns in tall pots along the tiled walls. Scattered columns were covered in clematis and dappled ivy while fountains sang their watery burble through the conservatory. The blue-and-green tiled wall reached shoulder-high before turning to glass. Brass mullions stretched up in curves and met in the center overhead like the ribs of some enormous being. The glass panels were slightly yellowed with age, gray clouds far above still streaming down snow, the flakes melting instantly against the warm glass and dripping down the outside.

Everywhere Brendan looked, there were roses.

Feeling as if he were wandering through a dream, Brendan walked down one of the tiled paths. Now and then he stretched out a hand to touch velvet-skinned roses as red as spilled blood; delicate ones as pink as new skin; nodding blossoms a bruise-beaten blue; and some the muted gold of faded scars. Strange, and so exquisitely lovely.

There were roses with long prickly thorns, so long that Brendan had to skirt around them to avoid being scratched. Some were yellow or pink or champagne and, of course, red. Many were more exotic; sweet-smelling pale violet blooms creeping close to the ground, or odorless roses so purple they were black, each standing far apart from their sister blossoms on the bush as if they disliked one another's company. Some roses were as white as bone, bearing a scent as cloying-sweet as death.

It was the most beautiful place Brendan had ever seen. He didn't know how long he walked there among the greening splendor, eyes wide, smelling the sweet tang of earth and pollen. He dabbled his fingers in the pond, delighted to see two fat fish swimming near. One white, one black. Brendan might have wandered in a blissful daze for hours, until he looked up at the sky and realized with a jolt that evening wasn't too far away.

No luck finding the music room, but he felt more than compensated for the temporary loss. Reluctantly Brendan left the fierce, beautiful garden, hoping he could return soon. Right now, he was expected for dinner.

* * *

Feeling only marginally less apprehensive than he did yesterday, Brendan padded softly into the dining room. He'd come a bit early, in hopes of seeing the food being carted in on invisible hands, but was disappointed to see all the plates and platters already laid out, the spectacle over.

With an air of strained patience, Beast tapped his claws on the table as if he had been kept waiting for hours. Keen eyes raked over Brendan's new clothes with a scarce little nod of satisfaction. He was glad he had stopped to change into something a little fancier, even if it felt too stiff and tight for his tastes. A deep rummage into the wardrobe had yielded a gray shirt with laced cuffs and matching breeches, a silvery blue embroidered doublet that fit close around the hips, and high boots with a beetle-black shine.

Brendan bowed to his host before taking a seat. Beast nodded curtly, which was likely the heights of courtesy from him, and waved a furry hand for their glasses to be filled. Brendan thanked the air where he thought the servant should be, and took an absent sip of his wine. He watched the Beast carefully.

Anyone who kept such a magnificent garden couldn't be such a monster, despite his fearsome appearance.

In silence, Brendan ate what was placed before him, savoring the delicious cuisine with fresh amazement. If he ate like this every day, he'd be quite round before too long. Of course, any day the snow would stop and he'd be out on his tail, but it was an amusing thought nevertheless.

"Did you visit the music room?" Beast asked of a sudden, making it quite clear by his tone that he couldn't care less one way or another.

Brendan looked up in surprise. "Oh, no. I couldn't find it."

A disapproving stare over a goblet. "Did the servants not show you where it was?"

"I, ah, went alone. I just sort of...wandered around a bit in hopes I'd find it." He laid down his fork and tried to meet his host's eyes. Every time that mane bristled, or those daunting muscles bunched under royal-blue velvet, a frisson of fear brushed up Brendan's spine. He had to look away, quite annoyed with himself.

"Ah." Beast managed to fit a lot of *you're rather foolish, aren't you?* into that one word. "Then I am sure you've found many rooms are locked. Those that are locked are old and have been unused for many years. But some rooms," Beast's voice lowered in light menace, "some rooms are locked because I do not wish for anyone to enter them. Do you understand, boy?"

Brendan had to bite his tongue to stifle a nasty retort. Schooling himself

57

in politeness, he replied, "Of course. You like your privacy." It sounded infantile and obvious as soon as he said it. "Perhaps you should tell me which rooms you would rather I stayed out of, to avoid any, um, conflict."

The Beast assessed Brendan for a long second before answering. "You have proved to be a most curious specimen. I like to think I have more wisdom than to tell you what is forbidden, and thusly, of the most interest." His rough snort was almost a laugh. "Just know the servants will keep you away if you get near."

Brendan nodded, for it was the only thing he could think of to do in answer. "That big greenhouse garden isn't off limits, is it?"

"Have you been to the conservatory?" Beast had been circling his glass with a talon to make it ring faintly, but now his claw was poised over the goblet.

Brendan paused, unsure what was the best answer to give. He chose honesty. "Yes."

"No, it is not off limits." After speaking the Beast sat silently, nursing his wine, every so often looking off into the distance with an almost wistful glower.

Compelled to say something to break the tense silence, Brendan ventured, "It's very beautiful. And yet...sort of daunting."

Beast inclined his head, as if acknowledging a fact. "Do you like gardens, then?"

"Oh, yes," Brendan quickly replied, then flushed. His father had often jibbed him that enjoying flowers for their own sake wasn't something a young man should list as a virtue. "May I ask you a question?"

Beast's eyes were daggers, though the soft rumble of his answer belied their fierceness. "You may ask, but I may not answer."

"Right." Brendan swallowed. "Who are they? The servants, I mean." He managed to meet Beast's glare for an instant before his eyes wrenched away of their own accord. "Why are they...the way they are?"

Surprise flitted across Beast's leonine features. "The servants? They are just servants. As they always have been. Most of them," he added as his brow grooved, as if ill memories were bubbling to the top of his thoughts

58

like oil over water.

"But why can't they be seen, or heard? Invisibility! Such a thing. I just don't understand how it's possible." Brendan leaned forward, relieved the Beast seemed willing to speak candidly for once.

"It's obviously possible, isn't it? Or else it wouldn't be so." Beast took a long draught of his wine before continuing. "They are bound to me by great sorcery, are obedient to my will, and tied to this castle. Most of them have always been my servants, even before they became as they are. They are unable to communicate, but what would they be likely to say, anyway?"

"But how do they eat? Where do they sleep? Don't they... Well, there are a great many practical things to consider. Just who, exactly, are they?"

Beast pulled back a little, a bewildered slant to his brow. "They're just servants. They serve. That is what they do. That is who they are."

"I...see." During his time at the university, Brendan had known a few noble-born boys, and they always spoke the same way Beast did now. Servants had likely always been nameless and faceless to him even when they *had* been visible. "You said 'most of them.' Who are the rest?"

Beast's voice came as cold as the sleet pelting against the frost-rimed windows. "The others are those who have since come to my castle to gain from my wealth, making false promises and twisted lies."

A little warning bell went off, and Brendan eased back in his chair, mentally mapping the exit.

The Beast didn't seem to even be paying attention to him, his lambent gaze somewhere far away. "Your father was not the first to take something not freely offered. A few were con men and snake-oil sellers, proclaiming false cures that could be purchased for extravagant sums. Some were men of business who came to make deals, hearing tales of my wealth and power. Some were women who came hearing those same rumors, and made false vows of love, all the while looking over my shoulder and hiding the revulsion in their eyes."

There was another pause Brendan didn't dare interrupt.

"Some came by accident, like your father, and took advantage of me in some way or another. They all sought to acquire something from me; my wealth, my title, my land. So I acquired them, instead."

Brendan thought of his father, fading away into nothing, and shuddered.

"That was long ago, when people still knew of this castle and of its master. Now no one remembers the story as anything more than a nursery tale, and the only ones who wander into my land do so by accident. Or, in your case, by lack of common sense."

The uneaten food was being carried away, and their glasses refilled.

"Ah. Well. Thank you for answering my question so thoroughly," Brendan said softly. Joining the servants' ranks seemed a very real possibility if the Beast decided Brendan was more trouble than he was worth. And Beast no doubt found him to be worth very little indeed. Still, Brendan found he had even more questions now, but he clamped down on his tongue, reluctant to push his luck.

"Are you finished?" asked the Beast, indicating Brendan's nearly empty plate.

"What? Oh, yes. It was very goo—"

"Yes, yes. I will show you the music room, if you wish it." Beast swept out of his high-backed chair.

Swift with his manners, Brendan followed suit, again taken aback by the Beast's mercurial moods. "Yes, please," he stated simply, with no more than a blink.

Beast led him to a long flight of stairs Brendan reckoned he could find again, due to the great marble griffons on either side of the balustrade. Brendan hadn't been in this wing before, admiring the many long paintings adorning the hall.

"Here," the Beast grunted with an abrupt turn to the right. He pushed open a large door—third down on the right, Brendan noted—and stood to the side, a watchful monolith looming tall. Hesitantly, Brendan walked past the Beast and into the room.

The first thing to catch his eye was the enormous fireplace, practically another room in its own right. Ornately carved, as most fireplaces in the castle seemed to be, this one with great hunting cats and peacocks. Two crystal chandeliers hung above illuminating many chairs and divans with their upholstery torn to rags. Near a small window sat a large ornate harpsichord, thick layers of dust dulling its glossy shine, but Brendan was drawn to the rows of instrument racks along the far wall as if by a lodestone.

He sucked in a delighted breath. A sprawling collection of familiar instruments, even a few he could not name, were neatly displayed along the wall. Violins and violas, vielles and viols, lutes and lyres, flutes and shawms, several different types of guitars and citterns, both a dulcimer and a zither, and a large standing harp in the corner with one Moorish oud on a plinth next to it. Brendan knelt to touch a lute, and his fingers came away coated with the dust of many years.

He clucked his tongue and began to brush away the grime with his finely embroidered sleeve. It didn't clean as well as he might have wished, but soon, coughing a little at the dust, he saw the lute was a fine piece of craftsmanship, with wood the color of deep honey. He strummed experimentally, wincing at the sharp discordance. They must all desperately need tuning, strings sagging with dejection at their long abandonment, wanting the resonance of regular use to keep their voices true.

Brendan plucked at a note, carefully twisting the tuning pegs. He closed his eyes, concentrating on finding the right sound. A sudden voice over his shoulder made him jump.

"I could have the servants dust them all."

He'd forgotten the Beast was even there. "Oh, could you, please? That would be—"

In silent wonderment he stared as invisible rags were swept along each appliance, cleaning each fret and groove. A pair of polite hands took the lute from him, stripped away its dust, and handed it back clean and gleaming.

Shortly all the instruments sat shining, some still faintly humming from an efficient unseen touch. Brendan glanced at the Beast, who was watching him expectantly. He cleared his throat, bent his head back over the lute, and in a minute had it fully tuned. To test its timbre and to get a feel for the instrument, Brendan softly played a child's song.

As if all it needed was a little love, the lute's voice now rang sweet, thrumming with vitality. Again forgetting about his host, Brendan sat down in a relatively untorn chair and played a few simple bars.

"*J'ai vu le loup, le r'nard, le lièvre. J'ai vu le loup, le r'nard cheuler. C'est moi-même qui les ai r'beuillés...*" He stopped singing with the song unfinished, hands resting lightly on the lute's warm face. It felt like it had been forever since he'd last played anything.

"Play something else."

Brendan looked up, startled. It was more command than request. Even so, Brendan was secretly pleased, taking the Beast's appeal as further evidence of humanity, hidden somewhere deep inside. Fingers moving almost of their own volition, he strummed a mournful tune.

He sang the words softly, at first, until he again forgot he had an audience, and the notes rang out true and sweet in the close, forgotten air of the music room.

When the song was finished Brendan looked askance at the Beast through the fall of his undone hair.

"That didn't sound familiar," the Beast said. "French lyrics, but the melody had a strange cadence to it." He folded his arms over his chest. "I suppose this is what they teach students nowadays?"

"No, it isn't. It was an old Irish tune."

"Irish? You went to school in Paris, did you not?"

"Yes." Brendan swallowed, not liking where these questions were headed at all. "They didn't teach Irish songs, of course, but I've always liked them. They've got so much...truth." He absent-mindedly fingered the lute through scales.

"Where, then, did you learn that song?" Beast shifted his weight from one footpaw to another. "From your namesake, your mother's godfather?"

Brendan opened his mouth and found himself speechless, astonished the Beast had remembered such a detail. He tried again. "No. A friend taught me. A schoolmate. He was from Ireland." Brendan stood and placed the lute back in its place. "This has been marvelous, but I am very tired, my gracious host. Tomorrow I will tune all the instruments properly. Forgive me for saying, but they have been very badly neglected."

The Beast scrutinized him narrowly, then shrugged. "Tomorrow after dinner, I'll come and hear you play some more." Though the command brooked no room for refusal, Brendan smiled nonetheless. "Weather allowing, of course."

"What?" Brendan didn't see what the weather had to do with music.

"If on the morrow the snowstorm ceases, you will leave, of course." The words were as sharp and brittle as icicles, and clearly a dismissal.

"Of course," muttered Brendan as he made his way back to his room, an unseen servant at his elbow. All the finery and music must have muddled his mind, forgetting it was his sister the Beast wanted here, and Brendan only an unwelcome guest.

8

In Which There are Mirrors and Revelations

Brendan wallowed in a lazy half-slumber, caught between the rosy twilight realm of sleep and the land of the waking. The cold brought him fully awake. The fire must have gone out, embers dead in the hearth.

He slid out of bed and shivered. Clad only in his smalls, he quickly wrapped himself in a dressing robe. He shuffled to the fireplace and picked up a split log from the woodpile. Abruptly it was snatched out of his hand, and more logs followed the first into the firebox as a servant rushed to do the work for him. Every motion had a frenetic energy, and Brendan didn't think he was imagining the nervous tension there. Did the servant think he would complain to Beast about lackluster service? Forgetting to warm a guest's room was a far worse offense than one little spilled drop of wine.

"It's all right," Brendan said, and meant it. "Really, it's fine. You don't have to worry." The servant's motions calmed, tension easing as the fire was stoked up into a cheerful blaze.

He splashed his face in the water basin, feeling considerably livelier afterward. Some tea arrived, steaming hot and just the right amount of bitter. He turned to the window and sipped carefully so as not to burn his tongue.

The snow had lessened considerably, but a strong wind still whipped through the shivering trees like a hunting cat among young birds. A blanket of snow covered the road, high enough to reach a horse's belly. Looking south, toward his village, Brendan wondered if his family were worried about him. Well, Beauty likely was. Knowing her, she might have tried to follow him. By all rights, she should have arrived already. If Father hadn't stopped her, then the storm certainly did. A week ago Beast had insinuated the road might be preventing Brendan from leaving. Why? And was the road also keeping Beauty or anyone else out?

How strange the thought of a sentient road didn't seem like such a fantasy. How had any of this come to be? It seemed the castle and everything in it had been here a very long time. The old instruments of the music room, the outdated fashions in the wardrobe; was it possible everything here was frozen in time? Curiosity squirmed just under Brendan's skin, made him itch with the mystery of it all.

"I wish you could talk," he told the unseen servant for what was probably the umpteenth time. He picked some clothes from the wardrobe, settling on a rust-golden tunic with dark blue breeches. "I have so many questions about this place, and I don't dare ask the Beast. Look, can you— Well, maybe help me find some answers?"

The unseen servant did nothing, a sliver of uncertainty in the air.

"Please?" he wheedled. "There has to be something that sheds a little light on this whole thing." Floorboards creaked, reluctant, but Brendan pressed on. "You won't get in trouble, I promise you that. If he finds me, I'll take the blame for it, all right? I won't disturb anything. It's just I don't understand any of this, and I swear I won't bother you again if you help me. Please?"

Suddenly the servant grabbed his hand and dashed toward the door. Startled, Brendan followed, out the door and down the stairs.

The invisible servant went quickly, keeping a brisk pace down long corridors flanked by Classical statues and suits of iron. Brendan was peripherally amused by the sight of his arm floating before him, in the grip of his invisible guide. He tried to keep track of their path, but there were countless turns and twists, and three more flights of stairs before he was led into a hall half-hidden behind a massive tapestry, until he was utterly lost.

They came to a great set of golden doors. The servant pulled him through as they parted, into a vast ballroom completely constructed of mirrors and gold filigree. A great chandelier hung from the gold-paneled ceiling and brightly lit the mirrored walls. Brendan was reflected a hundred times over in each one; his own expression of amazed delight shining back at him. Even the floor was white faience so highly polished it was as if he were looking into glass. He laughed and spun about, a thousand other likenesses grinning back.

Beast must hate this room, came a strange, unbidden thought.

Impatient to be on their way, the servant again took hold of Brendan's hand and led him through the jewel of a ballroom and past another set of doors, cunningly made to blend into the mirrored wall. They went down yet another long passageway, and through yet another door hidden by yet another tapestry. How massive was this castle, anyway?

A poorly lit staircase led to a short, dark dead-end. There were no adornments or artifacts lining the walls, merely three doors. The servant released Brendan's hand. He felt a gentle push at the small of his back, urging him toward the nearest door. Deep gouges marred the surface, and the metal handle broken, half-snapped off. It took placing his full weight against the door to coax it open, the hinges keening like a mourning widow. He peered into the dark room. It smelled of dust and mouse and lost memories.

"Now where is—oh, thank you," he said as a lit lamp was helpfully pressed into his hand. He entered, eyes adjusted slowly. The room looked as if a storm had raged through it, or a pack of wild animals, ripping the drapery and scoring deep marks in the walls. Paintings had been ripped out of their frames. Overturned chairs and couches were torn asunder, fabric guts spilling ragged onto the floor. The sheer fury of the devastation made Brendan falter back a step. Thick cobwebs coated every inch of the destruction, his boots making fresh marks in the dust.

The only thing unharmed in the room was a small table in the center. A thin book lay there as if waiting for him, with a simple red cover without mark or title upon it. He set his lamp on the table and opened the book eagerly, sneezing as dust spilled into the air. The writing was spidery and fine, and with wide eyes, he began to read.

"Once upon a time," it began, "there was a handsome prince who lived in a great and beautiful castle. Now, this prince had everything he wanted, for he had many servants and chamberlains and vassals to do his bidding. His father, who lived very far away, provided him constant wealth, as the king did for all of his sons.

"So the prince had absolutely everything a young man could desire, yet his royal heart was cold and unkind. He was a cruel man who had no love for anything or anyone. He was prone to rages and great fits of temper.

"Many a young lady came courting, and each was mocked and turned away. The prince cared nothing for companionship and very soon, despite his wealth and station, no one wished to be his friend. He mistreated his servants, neglected his duties as prince, and his people grew discontent under his careless reign.

"On the prince's twenty-second birthday, an old crone came to the castle doors and would not be turned away by the footman. The prince came to see what all the noise was about and found a hunchbacked old woman yelling at his butler, screeching like a blue jay.

'What is the meaning of this?' the prince demanded.

'Oh, good prince,' said the ugly old woman in her querulous raven voice, 'I am just a poor old woman with no place to call home. My children were too impoverished to keep me, so they turned me out in the street. It is cold and my old bones ache. Might I stay here for the night, my lord?'

"The prince laughed at her. 'You, stay here at the palace? For this you bother me on my birthday? Go back to the street from where you came, hag!'

'If you turn me out, Your Highness, I will surely perish in the cold. Have mercy on me, let me stay for just one night! I can cook and mend things, if such services you need.'

'That is what I have servants for. I need nothing from an ugly old woman.' The prince became impatient. 'Again I say no! Now be gone before I have the guards on you.'

'Do you three times turn me away, cruel prince?' The old woman looked at him with a glint in her crafty eyes.

'I would turn you away a hundred times, you feeble thing. Begone!'

"But before the prince could call his guards, the old woman stood tall and threw off her rags, and her ugliness melted away. A young woman more beautiful than the moon stood there at his doorstep, her black and shining eyes hard and unforgiving as ice. She was clad in shimmering gossamer and her silver-onyx hair danced as if alive.

"Even in his pride, the prince fell to his knees before her, for it was clear she was a powerful sorceress, and an angry one at that.

'You have three times refused hospitality to a person in need, arrogant prince.' Her voice was the tinkling of slow waterfalls, crystalline like stars. 'And thus you are three times cursed; once cursed with bondage, twice cursed with solitude, and thrice cursed with ugliness. For you and those that willingly serve you are bound forever to these castle grounds, to which I give a life of their own. You shall be ever alone with yourself, for your faithful shall dwindle and diminish till they are naught but invisible wraiths, bound to your service. Your family shall not know you, and your father the King will support you no more.

'Because your beauty is a lie, your heart shall be turned inside out,' she declared, and a great pain came over the prince, and he writhed screaming on the doorstep as he was twisted into a monstrous form.

'Now you are truly a Beast,' the sorceress told him.

'Oh, great lady,' the prince-beast begged, 'do not leave me forever this way! I am sorry I turned you away, I beg you, please! Have mercy on me!'

'You did not show mercy when you thought I was but a harmless old crone. You have shown there is nothing but ugliness in your heart. But I do not leave you without hope, o selfish and pitiless prince.

'Like a Beast you shall remain, forever, frozen in time as your heart was frozen in bitterness, until the day comes when you learn to love, and are loved in return, in spite of what you have become.' With a sound like the rustling of a thousand feathers, the sorceress disappeared and was never seen again.

"And the Beast despaired, and secluded himself in his great castle with his invisible, silent servants. His people, glad to be rid of such a terrible monarch, turned to other lords and soon forgot about the prince.

'Who would love such a thing as I?' moaned the Beast in anguish, and grew ever more insular and even quicker to rage than he was before. And so it was such for two hundred years."

Brendan flipped the page breathlessly. It was blank.

He thumbed through the remaining pages, all of which were equally empty. He remained there a moment in quiet contemplation, then closed the book, picked up the lamp, and left the battered room. He paused to run his fingers over the long scratches in the woodwork of the door. Unseen hands took the lamp, and it dipped slightly, almost an interrogative gesture.

"Yes. Yes, thank you."

* * *

The rest of the morning Brendan spent happily ensconced in the music room, tuning the instruments he was familiar with and testing out the ones he wasn't. He tried his hand at the great harp, delighted by its plangent, cascading tones, and whiled away a handful of hours experimenting with some of the stranger and more foreign instruments.

At one point, after fitfully rubbing his palms against his breeches for a prolonged stretch, Brendan reached for the neck of a viol da gamba, the closest thing to a modern cello the music room contained. His hand halted as if it had hit an invisible wall, but it was only his own hesitation that stopped him. Eventually he turned away with a barely audible sigh of relief and settled down with a nice, safe violin. It didn't have the familiar little peculiarities of his own well-used one at home, but it tucked comfortably enough under his chin and sang with a good, strong voice. He played a loud, brash arpeggio to drown out the sound of the howling wind outside.

After a while his belly complained of neglect, and regretfully Brendan set down the bow and stretched his arms. It was a bit early for dinner, but he made his way down to the dining hall anyway. Perhaps he could rustle up a snack, ask a servant for a bit of cheese. On the way to the correct wing he only got turned around in the twisting corridors once, which was a marked improvement in his navigation skills.

"Wandering about, again?"

Brendan whipped around with a startled jump. The Beast stepped from a shadowy doorway into the hall. Today he wore a deep frown complemented by a red coat with mother-of-pearl buttons, and held a thin leather-bound volume in the crook of his elbow.

"Poking around in places you shouldn't?"

For a split second, a spasm of guilt flitted through Brendan's mind. After all, he had been somewhere he surely wasn't meant to be, and discovered secrets he was not meant to know. "N-no, I was just…looking for the dining room."

Beast's eyes slid off him as if he were as uninteresting as the flocked pattern of wallpaper behind him.

The silence grew tighter. Brendan cleared his throat and pointed to the book Beast held in his great claws. "So," he tried with false brightness, "what's that?"

The glare Beast leveled at him was one usually reserved for things that got scraped off of shoes. "It is a thing we call a book."

"Yes, I can see it is a book. It being so full of pages, and all. I was merely inquiring at what said book might be about?" Brendan was, just barely, able to form the tail of his words into a question, the rising tone softening its sharp edges.

Massive shoulders heaved an exaggerated sigh. "It's called *The Barrons Wars*."

"By Drayton?" asked Brendan with considerable surprise.

Judging by the skyward climb of Beast's heavy brows, he felt much the same. "You've read it?" Beast looked at him with what was nearly suspicion, as if being literate was some sort of trick.

"Yes. I quite liked it. But…Drayton only started writing in the late 1500s."

Beast stared at him with flat, guarded eyes. "So?"

"So, I thought..." Unless Beast had someone delivering current books at his castle doorstep, there was no way he could have in his possession something written so recently.

"Ah," Beast rumbled, canting his head to the side, where the winter light caught the angles of his sharp cheekbones through a high window. One corner of his mouth curled in a thin smile, and all his standoffish aggression melted out of him. Brendan blinked at the sudden change. "I see where you might be curious. The truth of the matter is, in addition to all its other myriad wonders, this castle also has the tendency to sprout new books. The way grass grows up through cobblestones, I think."

"It...sprouts books?"

"It's a nice feature. One does like to stay current," Beast said, desert dry, though the sarcasm seemed to be aimed more at himself. As Brendan tried to wrap his brain around this newest marvel, Beast asked, "What did you like about it?"

It took a breath for Brendan to mentally catch up. "Oh! The tone, and imagery. A lot of those historical epics tended to be fairly dull, and very somber. Drayton manages to keep a bit of good humor throughout."

His host eyed him for a long second, then gave a short nod. The Beast drew himself up, a regal figure in a scarlet coat and tattered-legged breeches, tucking the book back under his arm. "Perhaps we can continue this discussion over dinner?"

Brendan bit back a grin. "I'd be delighted."

* * *

"I must disagree with you there. When he wrote *Poly Olbion* he was trying to preserve antiquity, as so many poets of the time did. Drayton wasn't disparaging druids and bards; he was lamenting their loss."

"Ah, but then you are classifying Drayton as an antiquarian." Beast clicked a claw on the table in rebuttal.

"Well, of course he was."

"Nonsense. If anything, he was a monumental historian."

71

"Oh, semantics. Now you're just playing devil's advocate." Brendan flapped a hand, his cider gone cold and dessert forgotten.

Beast leaned toward him over an empty plate. "Not at all. Drayton could not admit to a forgotten past, nor could he allow a foreign history to take place of his own."

"Well, he was British, through and through."

"Exactly my point."

"I can see that. Drayton adhered to the Galfridian tradition because it gave Britain such an illustrious past, I'll give you that. But I still say he wrote *Poly Olbion* with an antiquarian slant, at the very least."

Beast grunted. "I suppose I agree. Still, John Seldon shared Camden's outlook on Galfridian mythology…"

And so on and so forth. It wasn't until much later they came to an agreeable concord on the subject of Renaissance poets, pausing for breath and reflection. Brendan furtively watched Beast while idly prodding a fork at the remains of his crepes. Quite suddenly, it struck him that he was dining with an honest-to-true *prince*, and he had to stifle a silly, boyish grin. Everything made sense now; why Beast wanted Beauty here, to free him from the spell of the enchantress.

Thinking of Beauty kicked an errant curiosity loose from the back of his mind. Brendan cleared his throat. "I've been wondering something for a while now."

Beast's face immediately grew cold, closed off.

Brendan soldiered on. "When you caught my father stealing your rose. You told him to send his youngest daughter here, in his place. How did you know my father even had any daughters?"

The bridge of Beast's nose wrinkled with what was, Brendan was increasingly certain, an expression of surprise. "The man told me himself."

"Oh." That didn't fit with the narrative his father had spun. "But why did you…" He waved a hand, searching for tactful words and coming up dry. "Why did you demand her in such a terrible fashion?"

The Beast snorted angrily, then huffed, "Look, I won the game fair and square. It was my right to—"

Palms upraised, Brendan stopped his host's tirade before it could begin. "One moment, hold it right there! What game?"

Snarl fading, the Beast cocked his head to one side. "Your father didn't tell you?"

A black, sinking feeling grew in the pit of Brendan's stomach. "Tell me what?"

Another snort. "That figures. When I caught him wantonly destroying my roses, he begged me to spare him. He even went so far as to offer me a card game, to win his life back. This amused me greatly, so I agreed. Your father, might I add, is the worst Primero player I've ever had the misfortune of playing. He became desperate enough to wager his own daughter."

Brendan bit his lip hard enough to taste copper. He stared, unseeing, at the table.

Beast leaned forward. "Are you... all right?" Silence. "I take it he didn't tell you any of this."

"*Of course he didn't!*" The answer exploded out in one quick breath. "If I'd have known—of all the—that...that..." I swear to God, he's..." The words bubbled up haltingly like lava, and Brendan's face grew hot with anger. "His own flesh—sent to certain—I can't... how *dare* he!"

Beast looked taken aback, and perhaps a little fascinated. "I can't say I'm surprised he didn't see fit to tell you the truth."

Brendan shook his head in silent fury.

Beast shifted on his haunches in the tense, sullen silence. He opened his mouth and closed it. "Er." He tried again, extending a paw forward in a conversational way. "Well, ah... hmmph." As if to cover the aborted motion, Beast beckoned for a servant to refill their cider mugs.

"I can't believe that blasted man," Brendan snapped, unable to hold his tongue a second longer. "He's never brought our family anything but misery. Losing our entire fortune wasn't enough for him. He had to wager his own favorite daughter! I mean, to do such a thing knowing if he lost, Beauty would be turned over to a—"

He froze.

"To a Beast?"

BRENDAN & THE BEAST

"That's not what I—well, yes, that *is* what I meant. As if it weren't enough he put my sister up for a bet like she were livestock, he wagered her to someone he was terrified of! And Father thought you were going to eat him, or subject him to some cruel torture, yet still he put Beauty in that same danger! The truth of your, er, appetite is irrelevant, what matters is he *thought* you were a monster. He didn't even know what I know, that you're—"

Again Brendan froze, nearly biting through his tongue.

Beast lowered his head and asked, mildly, "I'm what?"

Unconsciously Brendan's eyes swept over horns and mane, over wide, daunting shoulders. "You're... Well, that you are not as my father thought you to be."

Voice laden with sarcasm, Beast rose from his chair. "I am gratified you think so highly. It has grown rather late. I'm going to retire to my quarters."

"Oh." Brendan also stood, placing his napkin on the table. He was still considerably angry over his father, but he could tuck that away to brood over later. Right now Beast was leaving, and Brendan was bemused to find himself disappointed. "I thought you might care to join me in the music room tonight, as you indicated yesterday eve."

He didn't relish the prospect of being alone in a borrowed room with only an invisible phantom for company. What it would be like living among only mute ghosts through the long march of years? A horrible prospect, and one his host had lived for years beyond measure.

Beast looked surprised, and Brendan thought perhaps pleasantly so. "I had assumed you were in no fit state for recreation tonight."

Brendan ducked his head. "Oh, I am always in a fit state to play for an audience."

"Hm. Good. Since I did spend some considerable time shifting about the magics that sprout new books to encompass the music room, after all."

"You... What?"

"Come and see."

* * *

"See yonder dove, it mourns its love,

And flies from pine to pine.

Today you will weep at my fair love's grave,

Tomorrow you'll mourn at mine."

At the end of the song, Brendan looked up from the harp. The room was merrily bright by lit chandeliers, suffusing through with a warm cozy glow. It was quite a change from how Brendan had first seen it, all aged dust and darkness.

Before playing, Brendan had inspected the newer instruments the room had 'sprouted' with gleeful astonishment. The wall display now boasted an increase in woodwinds, a musette he was very keen to experiment with, and—because fate had decided he hadn't had a sufficiently trying day—a finely crafted cello.

His host had surreptitiously taken a seat while Brendan had been occupied with the harp. "They certainly are a maudlin people, aren't they?" the Beast remarked, something very nearly a smile upon his face.

"That wasn't even the *really* sad version," Brendan laughed. "It's hard to find an Irish song that doesn't have mention of clay-cold lovers in the grave or the like."

Beast actually laughed too, a white flash of teeth gone as quickly as it had appeared. "I have heard it said all good music is about either love or death."

"I don't disagree. And certainly the Irish wouldn't."

"You play the harp well enough. What else can you play?" The Beast waved a hand at the assorted waiting instruments like a madame displaying doxies at a brothel.

The beginnings of a boast edged into Brendan's tone. "I can play just about anything that has strings, and a few things that don't."

"Play something on the cello, then. The instrument that, as it happens, looks exactly like a viol." The Beast reclined on his side upon the divan, propping up his bristly chin with a paw.

Brendan faltered, not bothering to list all the salient differences in the evolution of the bowed strings. "The cello?"

"Why, yes! I thought you could play anything with strings. Isn't that so?"

75

Crossing the room, Brendan set aside the lap harp and ran a slow hand over the cello. He took it back to his chair, positioned it on the ground before him, and began to rosin the bow.

Beast sighed. "Stop dallying and play something, will you?" Now he was aware of it, Brendan recognized the imperious command only one born to royalty can make.

"I will play it," he said with a touch of rebuke, took up the bow, and stroked one long, tenuous note on the straining strings. Everything went still around him. Even the embers flickering in the enormous fireplace ceased to pop, as if the room itself was holding its breath.

Brendan played a slow and tender song where singing had no part, and would only mar the pure aching notes. He stretched out the resonance, drawing out each longing note, the cello's breath catching mid-note and sighing sweetly. Beast sat in perfect stillness.

When it was finished, Brendan leaned the cello on the side of his chair and folded his hands in his lap.

"Hmm," was all Beast said, "not bad."

"Thank you," Brendan said quietly, suddenly quite tired.

"Perhaps you can play again tomorrow?" Beast's tone made it clear he personally couldn't care less one way or the other, and he was simply humoring an unwelcome guest.

Brendan allowed a smile. "Perhaps. I'd like to try my hand at the harpsichord. It'll need a lot of tuning, I'd imagine."

"Very well." The Beast rose to his feet with the easy unfolding grace of a cat. Again Brendan was taken aback by the great size of his host, though he was growing accustomed to the bent-backward knees and golden pelt. It was the fangs and claws he still had problems with. "Good night, boy."

Well, he wasn't used to being called 'boy' either, that still irked him. "Good night, Beast."

* * *

Brendan sat at the foot of his bed, staring into the dancing fire. His eyes burned, and he rubbed them with the heel of his hand, swallowing a heavy leaden lump in his throat. He turned away and rolled down the bedcovers, but before he could slide into the soft oblivion of sleep, a cold, timid hand touched his shoulder. He nearly jumped out of his skin.

"Ahh! Blessed Virgin, don't do that!" Brendan clutched his chest, heart racing like a frightened mouse. There were two long depressions in the bed, the only evidence someone was kneeling on the mattress next to him.

A light touch brushed Brendan's cheek. Brendan flinched and pulled away, his hand unconsciously following the touch to the dampness on his face.

"I wasn't crying," Brendan snapped defensively. His father's voice came into his head unbidden; *You cry too much, You need to toughen up, What is wrong with you?*

"It's just… Cellos always bring up bad memories. Well, not all of them are bad, I suppose." Brendan chewed his lip. "That song always makes me think of the person who taught it to me. A friend I had at school."

The invisible servant sat silent, somehow expressing every indication of eager attentiveness. Strangely, Brendan felt compelled to keep talking, to pour out everything to this silent listener—someone wouldn't judge him or demand any explanations; wouldn't name him unnatural or wrong. His memories sat heavy in his chest, longing to be released to someone. Anyone.

"Not a friend," he began softly. "More than a friend." Brendan rose to the window, looking out at the dark snowscape and bruised, starlit sky.

"His name was Kieran. I'd been three months at the University, and I was pretty shy when I was sixteen, so I didn't have many friends. I got top marks in most of my classes, so the professors were very kind to me, but some of the older boys were decidedly not. Until I fought back and gave one of them a black eye. They left me alone after that, for the most part, but I didn't ever make many friends.

"Then Kieran came, mid-semester. He was the second son of some wealthy lord in Ireland, sent off for a proper Parisian education. When the Headmaster introduced him at assembly, he was everything you'd ever think a real Irishman would look like; green eyes, red hair, freckles, and everything. I had been so nervous when the Headmaster had introduced me, but not Kieran. He stood up there calm as you please, even told a joke. He radiated this kind of charm. Everyone was taken with him; the teachers, the students, everybody. He was small for his age, like I was, but the older students never teased him or tried to push him around. I *hated* him," Brendan laughed, ruefully. "He was good at everything, getting marks as good as mine and… I guess I was jealous.

"Then once, during free study, I saw him sitting with his back to a tree, flipping pages back and forth in a workbook. I was curious, so I walked a little close. He was struggling with a music assignment we'd been given, a few bars we had to compose ourselves.

"I was pretty snotty about it, but he was…" Brendan fell silent and drifted in memory for a moment.

"You can't put a sharp note in after the half-rest," he had said imperiously, trying to prove he knew more.

But Kieran didn't take offense at all, just wrinkled his freckled nose. "Is that so? And what would you put there, then?"

"Well, if you're going to do a crescendo like that, it should start with C," Brendan answered, a bit less venomously. "Anything else would sound funny."

Kieran looked at his workbook with concentration and pointedly changed the note to a C. Then he smiled up brightly. "Cheers. D'Aumale, isn't it? I've seen you around." Kieran scooted over, giving Brendan room to sit next to him.

He resisted the other boy's innate charm for all of two seconds before he plunked down on the grass. "Brendan," he offered, hand extended.

"Kieran." The other boy grinned, heartily shaking his hand. He adopted a concerned furrow-browed look, and said very seriously, "Doesn't the music professor have a nose exactly like a sausage?" Brendan had laughed.

Brendan blinked, looking around at his present-day surroundings as if awakening from a slumber. He cleared his throat and resumed his tale to the silent servant.

"And well, then we were the very best of friends. We did everything together. He came from a simply enormous family. Three younger sisters, two younger brothers, one older brother, and five older sisters. Eight sisters, can you imagine? I have three, and that's bad enough. He didn't have any sort of responsibilities ahead of him, because his elder brother would inherit, so Kieran was just out to have fun with life. He...he was my first real friend. We could just talk and talk for hours.

"Then I started to... I don't know. I loved the sight of him. I liked to watch him smooth his hair back, to hear him talk in that lilt. I liked the way he moved, I liked...I liked the way he looked at me sometimes. When we were alone, just talking or working on schoolwork, or when he taught me songs from his home. I didn't understand why, I just knew I liked to be near him.

"I didn't fully understand until one day after classes were over, and we were walking back to the dormitories. I was chattering on about nothing, and he just pulled me into a side hallway, pushed me up against the wall, and right there where anyone could have seen, he kissed me. At first I didn't know what to do. It was such a shock, but then... Then we were kissing right there in the hallway. A girl kissed me a few times back home, but this was nothing like that. I just... It wasn't like anything I'd ever known.

"Everything was different after that. He'd squeeze my hand under the table when we parted for class, or sneak kisses behind trees, or—I can't believe I'm telling you all this."

Brendan turned away from the window. The invisible had moved closer to the edge of the bed, poised as if listening intently. "I've never told anybody about this before." He ran his hand over his face. "It's good to have someone listen. This went on for about two months, this...courting. I knew it wasn't exactly normal, but of course you heard about it now and again, in whispers and insults. But Kieran told me he'd kissed a boy before, and there were men back home who were together. Lived together. He liked to say someday that would be us.

"He told me...he told me a lot of things. I was in love with him. It was impossible not to be. I believed it all." Brendan stared into the fireplace, falling silent. Remembering.

Remembering when they finally graduated from the common dorms to their own private rooms, remembering how Brendan had snuck over to

Kieran's room and, greatly daring, rapped on the door. How Kieran had pulled him inside, trying to stifle their laughter so as not to carry through the walls.

Brendan remembered kissing him, fingers tangled in soft hair, kissing him until he *burned*. He'd never known anything more splendid.

He remembered when Kieran started to undress him, remembered that slow, almost reverent touch exploring his skin, how it quickened into a needful surge, teeth clashing in their urgency to cleave nearer together.

He remembered boldness warring with uncertainty, remembered the bare rasp of Kieran's teeth when he mouthed over Brendan's collarbone, remembered exactly how the bones of Kieran's hips felt under his palms, remembered the taste of his mouth, the salt of his skin, remembered how Kieran said his name in that cascading lilt; one syllable falling over the next like the rill of a stream.

Brendan shook his head to drive off the lingering memories. He was silent for long minutes, arms loosely crossed over his chest. The servant shifted very slightly in the silence, bedcurtains rustling.

The sound broke Brendan out of his reverie. He strode over to the fire and folded himself in front of it, then grabbed the iron poker and gave the glowing logs a malevolent prod.

"He left school, you know. Last year. His brother died. The older one. So he had to go back home to claim his inheritance. He sent me letters. At first they were…love letters. He promised he'd be back, or he'd arrange for me to visit him…and I believed him." Brendan swallowed hard.

"He got married. His next letter was like…it was like there was nothing more than schoolboy friendship between us. As if he were pretending the whole thing had never happened. Something that made me feel like…like my heart was overflowing with happiness, we had that, and he pretended like we'd just been good school chums. After I made my peace with myself and with God for…for being as I am, for him to send that blasted letter. I was so angry with him. I didn't send back a reply. And Kieran never wrote again."

He fell into hollow silence. Cold, tentative fingers laid gently on his

80

shoulders. Brendan smiled with chagrin. "Sorry, I'm not normally so maudlin." He cleared his throat. "This was... Thank you. For listening."

The fingers pressed, and Brendan fancied they offered comfort before they retreated, leaving him as alone as one could be in a magical castle inhabited by the invisible, and haunted by his own ghosts.

9

In Which There are Truth and Lies

Even while stalking old, familiar haunts, the corridors remained mysterious things; shifting and turning, a cobweb of shadows colored by occasional pools of candlelight or the thin, watery streams of moonlight slipping in through tattered curtains.

Torches lit as Beast approached and banked down into darkness as he passed, and even he was unsure what bore responsibility for that. Despite his many long isolated years here, Beast had yet to discover exactly what was done by the servants and, more mysteriously, what was done by the willful magic of the very castle itself.

Sometimes, late at night when the moon was dark and everything around him was enveloped in shadowy silence, he thought he could feel the stone walls breathe.

He would wander hallways that stretched far longer than they had in the days when he'd been a man, stairways leading places they ought not. Beast had learned long ago if he simply thought about where he wanted to go, doors and hallways would lead him there no matter which direction he set off in. The conservatory, the dining room, the music room, and the library could all be found at a thought. He could always find his way to the armory, though he intensely disliked it; all the plate metal acted like mirrors, and were the only reflective surfaces in the entire castle the Beast had not long since destroyed—besides of course the viciously unpleasant mirrored ballroom, which was so large it was impossible even for Beast to break it completely, and so avoided it altogether. All other mirrors he'd smashed to dust, save one, which was in a wing so forgotten Beast doubted Brendan could find it even if he tried.

Beast's steps paused as he doubled back over his thoughts. He could have sworn he'd just thought of the boy by his first name, but that was something he'd made a point not to do. If he had, it would mean several things, all of which were unpleasant, and not the least of which was Beast was losing bits of his control.

The carved ivy of the conservatory doors loomed before him, and with a slight push he slunk out of the shadowy hall into the cool darkness of night under glass. The roses never slept, never faltered. Their petals were always open and upturned, velvety cold in the moonlight. The evening silvered curling fronds of ferns, the pond a placid pool of mercury.

Beast prowled regal and silent among the flora, trying to picture the girl he had been promised. His salvation, this Beauty; but his mind niggled and Brendan intruded into his thoughts as easily as he had Beast's castle.

The boy was intelligent. Could hold up his end of a conversation. Quite talented, as well. The music he'd spun earlier had been the loveliest thing Beast could ever remember hearing; morose and grieving, yet sweet as summer and just as warm. It had conjured an image of his roses, the way sunlight lit their petals to a deep fire-glow, or how they waited lambent and silvered in the moonlight.

Long ago, when everything else in the castle had ceased living, as it were, the roses in the greenhouse remained. Beast would curl beside them and watch them. They couldn't last. The rich, vibrant petals would turn papery pale and fall to the tiled floor. The stems would lose their glossy green hue and go dark, retreat from their climbers, graying with death until all that remained of the beauty they had once held would be thorns. Beast watched, fearful, for a long, long time. But day after month after year after century, the roses remained vibrant, frozen in their living unlife. He'd found an odd solace they seemed to share the same predicament as he.

The boy, though, was an unexpected change. A bit fiery, and prone to bouts of prattle and argument. If Beauty took after him in looks, she would certainly be comely enough, perhaps sharing his fine-boned features and eyes of smoked slate blue.

Beast shook his head and caught an unwilling glimpse of himself in the reflecting pool. His leonine features, his angry brow, his long pointed ears. *Monster.*

The end of the curse was near; Beast could sense it. He ever so softly cradled a rose in his paw. It glowed like luminescent blood in the moonlight, defying darkness and death. His salvation was soon at hand. Beauty would come, doubtless as distraught about her brother's wellbeing as she'd been for her father's, and Beast would finally be free.

"Yer gonna be stuck 'ere *forever*, mate. I don' 'ave a calendar or nothin', but that's a bloody long time, I kin tell ye that."

Beast ignored the voice at his back.

A little splash of water accompanied a scaly laugh. "Wot I mean is, someone's got to fall in love wiv ye, eh? An' since yer, whaddya call, *manners* is somewhat lackin', s'gonna be bloody hard, innit?"

"I did not ask your opinion!" Beast's roar echoed in the stillness of the garden. He stalked out through the huge marble doors, which obediently shut behind him.

In the garden, the crimson velvet rose trembled in the wake of the Beast's touch. A raspy voice, different from the first one, rang out. "Well. 'E's rather in a mood, ain't 'e?"

A burble of agreement. "I'd less like to see 'er mood when she finds out about all this."

* * *

Magic is a living thing. Tameable, to those with the wisdom to do such, but this is not as certain a thing as my kind like to tell ourselves. Magic can be stubborn, a thing of unpredictable moods and strange motivations. Magic can develop its own whims and wants. Become ungovernable.

Of course, this has never happened to me. My skill is finely honed, my mastery of the craft complete. It is quite safe for me to begin my stories and set them spinning on their own, to leave my garden to mature until I return, ready to harvest. I have yet to see the odd weed spring up in any of my carefully planned gardens. And if one should?

Well. A good gardener knows the value of a little ruthless pruning.

* * *

Both hands otherwise occupied, Brendan blew an errant lock of hair from his eyes. The impudent strands stuck onto his eyelashes, effectively distracting him from his harpsichord repair. He stood up straight, arching his back, barely avoiding smacking his head on the raised soundboard. He'd been working all bent over for some odd hours, and he wasn't ready to even begin thinking of tuning.

The repair was a long, meticulous job, but Brendan enjoyed it. Lately his mind felt like it was spinning in all directions, spread out too far for him to gather, so he relished the opportunity to apply himself to some healthy, difficult work. Besides, he was starting to get cabin fever, looking out of his small room at the prison of snow outside.

Thanks to the music room's enormous fireplace, the temperature and humidity of the room had been kept relatively constant, so the harpsichord hadn't warped beyond repair, fortunately. Brendan had wiped down the yellow-ivory keys with alcohol and painstakingly cleaned the interior earlier that day, before dinner. The invisibles had been a great help in providing the appropriate oils and cloths. Luckily no mice had made a home inside, as that could have seriously damaged it further than Brendan's skill to repair. It had become customary over the last few days for Brendan to play for his host after dinner, but today he demurred to instead put the harpsichord to rights.

The soundboard was cracked, but not on a bridge line, and the pinblock was intact. Casework in otherwise fine condition. Brendan struggled a bit over some rusted wrest pins, resigning himself to those notes remaining flat no matter what he did. He sighed. Harpsichords got incrementally harder

85

to tune with every year of neglect, and this one had been neglected a very, very, long time.

He had nearly finished when an unseen servant brought him cool water with a few refreshing mint leaves. He took it with thanks, laughing at how accustomed he had become to the supernatural servants.

The only work remaining was to deal with the most rusted of harpsichord strings. Brendan glared at it. It would be delicate work to tune, as the tension could snap it. Weighing the risk was tricky; either leave it alone and have an annoyingly dissonant note, or break it trying and have no note at all. But if he managed to pull it off, the results would be well worth it.

Brendan twisted the wrest pin ever-so-gently, tapping the corresponding key. He leaned in, closing his eyes to better concentrate.

There was a tiny sharp sound like a crystal breaking, and a swift swish by his ear. He jerked back. The loose string curled and bobbed in the air, broken off at the wrest pin.

"Blast," Brendan muttered in annoyance. He would likely be able to compensate for the loss of the string with some fancy fingerwork, but a few songs just wouldn't sound right. He supposed he was lucky it hadn't sliced his face open.

His cheek did feel a little warm, he belatedly realized. He put his hand to it. Sharp pain lanced through the side of his face, his fingers coming away bloody.

"Oh!" He clapped his hand back over his cheek, vanity panicking. A cut like that could easily scar.

"What's going on?" Brendan spun around. The Beast glowered from the doorway. "A servant grabbed my arm. What's happened here?"

"I… The string…it snapped, and—" Brendan waved at the harpsichord in explanation, feeling all at once embarrassed and awkward and glad. Beast marched over and lifted Brendan's hand from the cut with gentle authority. Brendan, stunned by Beast's—was it concern? Was the Beast actually concerned for him?—complied and let the Beast examine the wound. It stung fiercely, a liquid trickle tickling his cheek.

A low grumble of displeasure. "It's bleeding quite a lot. Come. It needs tending."

Brendan followed in dumb astonishment as Beast led him out of the music room and down the hall, his blood-slick hand covering the laceration.

The Beast turned them down a hall and then they were in the dining room. Brendan stopped in his tracks. "But we were upstairs! How did we—"

"Yes, yes, the halls shift about. Come along, you'll get blood on the rug." The Beast beckoned impatiently, going through the servants' entrance into the kitchen. Brendan took a deep breath to stop both his reeling brain and protesting logic, and followed his host into the kitchen.

"It was stupid, I knew it would probably break, I shouldn't have had my face so close to it…" Brendan kept up a penitent litany as Beast fished a cloth out of a nearby drawer. A water-filled bowl had already been set out on the counter.

The Beast dunked the cloth into the bowl and wrung it out. "Come here," he ordered. Brendan hesitated for only a moment, then padded close. The Beast was the most unpredictable man—for Brendan now knew the Beast still was a man, under all that fur and rage—he had ever met. Was it only a week ago Beast was threatening his life?

"Here, take your hand away… There." Beast made a little click of his tongue. Brendan nearly laughed. The sound reminded him of his old governess. "It doesn't look too deep. I don't think you'll need a bandage. Here, be still."

Brendan froze awkwardly as Beast bent down to dab at the cut. Brendan flinched.

"Stop twitching," Beast rumbled, trapping Brendan's chin in a large, careful paw. He pressed the wet cloth to Brendan's cheek, expression closed and unreadable.

Brendan gasped as the linen touched his tender cut. "Cold." He tried a little laugh that quickly died of nerves. "Thank you." He was suddenly very aware of Beast's proximity; the paw on his face, how close together they stood.

Beast dipped the cloth into the water between daubs. "You are welcome. It wasn't very clever of you to get bitten by the harpsichord."

Brendan's eyes made the halting journey up to Beast's face. The hand on his chin was softer than it had any right to be, and very warm. The Beast's gaze was distant, betraying no emotion, but his eyes were quite a pleasant shade of honey-brown, like autumn leaves and woodfires. He smelled of the crushed velvet of his red jacket, and another scent too, like clean musk. A little bite of panic caught hold, and Brendan shifted his weight from one foot to the other.

"This is very kind of you," he said softly, voice shifting up nearly into a question.

Beast's hand froze, and Brendan mentally cursed himself for speaking before he thought. "The servants aren't very good at medicinal things. I'm nearly done. It wasn't all that deep. It's stopped bleeding. I'll put some iodine on it and that will be that." Beast left the cloth afloat in the bowl and turned to pick through one of the cupboards.

"Do I really need iodine? I mean, it doesn't even hurt anymore."

Beast snorted with one hand in the cupboard and was customarily sarcastic. "No, let's skip it. And in two days the cut will get infected and scar. Is that what you want?"

Brendan could only shake his head in contrition.

Beast found the little brown bottle and unscrewed the cap, filling the dropper with the stuff. "Now this time, no fidgeting." Brendan stoically bore the nasty sting of the iodine with no more than a wince.

"You seem to know your way around the kitchen," he mentioned as the Beast put the medicine away.

"Does this seem strange to you, that I would know my way around my own kitchen?" Brendan couldn't tell if he was angry or amused.

"Well, I'd just thought...with the servants..."

Beast crossed his arms over his broad chest and leveled a half-smile. "I know it may be hard to believe, but sometimes I like to do things for myself, boy."

"You know, I do have a name!" Brendan immediately regretted losing his temper, but would not back down and gave no outward sign of remorse, meeting Beast's eyes in challenge.

Beast's smile vanished so quickly it might never have been there. "Really?

I hadn't noticed." He swept past Brendan and paused at the exit. "It's late. Go to bed." He pushed through the door, leaving Brendan standing there awkwardly, cursing his too-quick tongue.

* * *

The roses were even more beautiful by night. It was well past midnight, the falling snow and the distant stars seeming as one through the glass ceiling. Brendan wandered the moonlit paths of the garden, attempting to align his unsteady thoughts.

He was in an enchanted castle with invisible people, halls and roads that lead wherever they wanted to, and a two-hundred-year-old transformed prince. Brendan circled a cluster of irises alongside the night-silvered pond. He'd always longed for adventure, in the way most well-read youth did, wanting to see new places and experience wonders the likes of which he'd only imagined.

The first unimaginable wonder he'd ever come across had barely been further than a day's journey away from home.

Not that there was much home waiting for him, anymore. Brendan folded down onto the stone tile next to the pond with a heavy sigh. Reeds and lilies thatched over the water's mirror-like surface in a latticework of shadows. No classes, no friends, no career to aspire to nor passion to follow, no one special to hold close. All Brendan had now was his family, with all the highs and lows that entailed.

He worried about Beauty, dealing with all their family hardships alone without him. Brendan dabbled his fingertips in the water, watching ripples spread as he envisioned his sister in this very spot, had he not upset the apple cart and stepped into her place. Beauty had a good heart; she could learn to see past the Beast's appearance, in time. Maybe she'd break the spell, become a princess, and never want for anything again.

Brendan threaded damp fingers through his hair. "How come even the thought makes me feel sick to my stomach?"

"Love'll do that to ya, bruv."

BRENDAN & THE BEAST

Brendan nearly fell into the water. He twisted around, eyes darting, but he was alone. "Who's there? Where are you?"

"Down 'ere."

Brendan looked down. Beneath the quicksilver skin of the pond, two long shapes twined and stuck their heads up above the water. He blinked. "You're…fish."

The white one grinned toothlessly, whiskers curling. "Koi, to be precise. Not the blushin' flirty kind, unnerstand. Koi with a K."

The black one, more difficult to see in the darkness, winked a bright eye at Brendan. "We ain't the coy kinda koi. Nice night for it, innit?"

"Uh…" Brendan swallowed. "You'd think I'd be used to things like this happening around here. Um, hello."

"'Allo, luv," chirped the white fish, "nice to meet ya."

"Pleasure." Brendan cleared his throat, hands folded in his lap. "Are you enchanted people, too?"

The black fish jumped into the air with a derisive flick of the tail, landing in a noisy splash. "O'course not! We were never '*umans*," it answered upon resurfacing, disdain in its scratchy voice. "The nerve o' even askin'."

"Sorry," Brendan said reflexively. *I'm apologizing to a fish. My life has become so strange.* "So, er, have you always been here, then?"

"Sorta." The white fish swam a lazy figure-eight. "We two were imported, right? Long time ago. Didn't use to talk then, o'course. Then the castle went all wonky, and all the two-leggers went ka-poof or ka-roar, an' we got right keen, we did."

"Aye! Dead smart, we are. Go ahead, arsk us a question. Anythin' at all."

"But be warned, squire. When it comes to the important questions, the personal ones, one o' us answers truth, and the other speaks only lies." The white fish swam around the black one, a sliver of moon snaking around shadow.

Incredulously, Brendan scoffed, "What good is that for?"

"Wot?"

"One of you speaks truth and one of you speaks lies?"

"Aye."

"Why on earth would you do that?"

"Oh, well, if *you* think it's silly, I'll go and brin' it up wiv the laws of magic, shall I?" And to think Brendan had once thought a fish couldn't sound sarcastic. "Just arsk us a bloody question already."

"All right." Brendan thought for a moment until he came up with a question no fish could possibly answer. "What's seven thousand, three hundred and ninety-two divided by sixteen?"

"Four 'undred and sixty-two," piped both fish at once.

"That...sounds right." This was, by far, the oddest thing that had ever happened to him, up to and including meeting the Beast.

"It is." When they twined together, it was difficult to tell which fish was speaking.

"Six twenty times twelve?"

"Seventy-four forty, that's easy."

"Squared?"

"Eighty-six and a quarter." Both fish grinned. A grinning fish turned out to be a disturbing thing to see. Brendan tried another tactic. Mathematics had never been his forte anyway.

"What year did Charles the First become Holy Roman Emperor?"

"Eight hundred."

"Hmm." Brendan thought for a moment. How versed could fish be on musical trivia? "Who wrote the opera *Dafne*?"

"Jacopo Peri."

"Ah-ha, I have it. How many demisemiquavers in one semibreve?"

"Oh, ho. Thirty-two, fancy lad."

He was being bested by a fish. It was downright embarrassing. "All right. What did my sister Marguerite want for her fifteenth birthday?" He lifted his chin in triumph.

"She asked yer father for a sapphire brooch, but wot she really wanted was Catherine's opal earrings. She nicked them from 'er nightstand. And when you caught 'er at it, she made ye promise you'd never tell, or she'd tell yer father you snuck out at night ta ride 'is best geldin'." Fishy eyes twinkled up like pearly gems.

Brendan's mouth hung open in shock. "How…how did you know that?"

"We know a fair bit o' stuff!" The black fish sounded smug. Brendan didn't think he liked that one very much. "Ye might even say we know *everythin'*."

"Right, there's a word for that… Nippy-something. Nippotant. Nipple-tent…"

"Omnipotent?" Brendan guessed.

"Oi, that's the chuffin' one!" the white fish said. "We're omnipotent fish. Omnipo-fish." Both koi gave a warbling chuckle, pleased with their wit.

These talking fish knew everything except the word for knowing everything? "I think the word you're looking for is omniscient, not omnipotent."

"Cor, ain't this one a wee little know-it-all." Brendan didn't think he liked the white fish very much, either.

"When you spoke before, what did you mean by 'love will do that to you'?" It made a sort of sense; he did love his sister very much and wanted to keep her safe.

"Oh ho, 'e wants to know about love, does 'e? That's a mighty *personal* sort o' question, squire."

"And you answer only either truth or lies, is that right?" Brendan kept his eyes locked on the fish as they swam about, intent on outwitting them. "Fine then, which one of you speaks lies?"

Both fish nodded at each other. "That one."

"Ah ha! But if you speak the truth," he pointed at the white fish, "then the black one lied saying the other did."

"Unless I was the one lyin', aye?" Brendan deflated. "S'a good guess, luv. Go on then, try again."

"Okay." Brendan nibbled a fingernail. He once read about a riddle like this before in a book and tried to recall the hero's ploy. "Okay. You, black. If I were to ask the white fish if you were the liar, what would they say?"

The fish clicked its tongue in good humor. "Gettin' clever, are we? Well, they'd say I was lyin'."

"Ah-ha! But then if they said yes…then you'd be telling…the truth! Yes, I've got it. So then they'd be the liar! But if you are lying, and the other said no, you told the truth…then you would have just lied. Um. But then the white fish would be a liar too… Wait a minute… Is that right?"

It was far too late at night for logic puzzles. Brendan rubbed at the bridge of his nose in irritation.

The white fish laughed with a burbling rasp. "Uncross yer eyes, luv, you'll go blind. S'no use tryin' to suss out which one o' us is truth and which one is lies. We ain't *never* goin' to let ye know."

"Well, then what good are you?"

"Tut, tut. Manners, squire. Such a temper. A perfect match, ye would be." The koi started making sinuous circles around each other under the reeds, making it nearly impossible to tell who was talking.

"A perfect match with what? Could you please come out where I can see you?"

They didn't oblige him. "Wiv you an' Mary Queen o' bloody Scots! Who do you think?" There was an aquatic snigger under a leaning flush of lilies.

"I don't know what you mean." Brendan tried to peer into the inky shadows.

"O'course ye don't. S'too early yet," came one cryptic fishy mutter. The other koi quickly added, "Or rather, it's too late in the day, s'wot we mean. Ye should be goin' off to bed, right? Gettin' a wee bit tired, I'd wager."

"But you didn't answer my question! And I am not tired." A traitorous yawn split his face. "So, I'm a little tired. Can't we talk some more?" Likable or no, these fish were certainly intriguing, even if they were confusing enough to give him a headache.

"Plenty o' time for that, two-legger. Off wiv ye, now!" Both fish leaped out of the water and dove down deep to the bottom of the pond, splashing Brendan in the process, and wouldn't resurface or speak again.

"Talking fish," Brendan grumbled, pushing himself to his feet. "What next? Dancing silverware and enchanted footstools?" He picked his way down the garden paths, out the great marble doors, and across the lovely tiled mosaic woman stretched across the floor. "I suppose you speak in riddles and rhyme, hmm?" Her silent smile remained unchanged as Brendan passed by.

Back in his room, the fire had been tended to, and a glass of warm cider set on the nightstand next to the slim vase holding the rose. As he slipped down underneath the heavy coverlet, he looked over at the rose, still in the full bloom of health, its petals port wine-red in the firelight.

"You realize this is all your fault," he told it, pausing a moment just to make sure it didn't talk back, before falling into slumber.

10

In Which There is a Hunt

For the first time since he had arrived at the castle, Brendan awoke to a blue sky.

The fire crackled softly. He stretched and slipped out from under still-warm sheets, feeling oddly distant, as if some far-off dread was trying to form in the pit of his stomach. He pulled on clean breeches and a thick woven sweater waiting neatly folded on a chair. It looked like something a grandmother might have knitted, and it fit loosely around his slim frame in a comfortable drape.

He wiped away the soft blur of condensation from an icy windowpane and inspected his pale reflection, wishing for a proper mirror. He sighed, mouth hitching to one side. Well, at least the blasted scratch didn't look as if it would scar.

He stepped out of his room. As he approached what was usually the end of the hallway and the beginning of the path toward the dining room, there was an open door he could not recall having seen before. Either it had been closed, or it had not been there at all, and Brendan took its appearance as invitation and walked through.

Beyond the small foyer, arched glass doors were swung open onto a stone balcony. Brendan's breath clouded in the winter air.

Beast stood with his hands clasped behind his back, his wide shoulders sloping gently downward, mane wafting in the cold breeze. Brendan tucked his hands under his arms and stepped out, the wind catching his hair and sending a few chestnut locks into his eyes. The stone leeched warmth from the soles of his socked feet, and he wished he had thought to put on his boots.

He sniffled a little to announce his presence. "It's cold out. Or does that not bother you at all?"

Beast didn't turn but merely looked back over his shoulder. The corner of his lip twitched with something like humor. Brendan realized he must look ridiculous, swathed in wool and shoeless. "Not particularly." Beast returned his gaze over the wintry garden and the skeletal woods beyond.

Brendan took a breath. "It's stopped snowing." They regarded the morning stillness, side by side, in silence that was not quite companionable. "So, with the snow all…not falling and such…"

"You are quite free to leave," Beast said, his voice just slightly overlapping Brendan's. He was a study in neutrality, neither indicating suggestion nor reticence. Another silence stretched.

"Although… The snow must be extremely deep." Brendan glanced at Beast out of the corner of his eye, rubbing frigid toes on the back of his calf.

Beast did not look at him.

"After a storm like that. Would be suicide to leave, even if the horse could manage the snow. Which I doubt. And I'm not thrilled at the prospect of trying."

Beast shot Brendan a sidelong glance, then snapped his eyes forward as his expressive ears flicked back. "Your incompetence would hinder you endlessly."

"So… I guess I'm staying a while longer."

"It would appear so." Beast turned on his heel and strode back inside. After a moment, his husky voice returned from the hallway. "Do you not plan on eating, then?"

Brendan swallowed a smile before he turned and followed.

* * *

Breakfast had been a quick and civil affair, with fluffy eggs poached to perfection, warm croissants, light white wine, and slices of cinnamon-baked apples. Brendan's appetite had surged with an abrupt sense of optimism, and found himself shoveling in twice as much as he usually did.

The Beast inquired about Brendan's scratch—*it's perfectly fine, thank you very much, doesn't hurt at all*—which led to polite discussion congruent with the lightness of the meal. Beast seemed half-interested at best at news of the Parisian courts and the current king, so Brendan changed the subject to one he was much more conversant in; music.

They discussed obscure composers that had worked for the Medicis, mainly Italian organist Antonio Squarcialupi and Flemish polyphonic singer Heinrich Isaac, musicians Brendan had to admit he knew very little about. Beast seemed surprisingly knowledgeable, and interested to hear about the new talents in France, such as Corelli, Lully, and Couperin, all of which Brendan enjoyed immensely.

After Brendan had excused himself with a promise to later demonstrate the style of Pachelbel, he went back to his room. He felt a little silly saying to the air, "If it's not too much trouble, I could really use a bath, please," but the servants rushed to oblige. The fire had been stoked to a pleasant blaze, and he waited in the uncomfortable chair at the dressing table, wishing for a book to read. The earlier conversation had sparked his interest, and he wondered where he could find some history books—though in this castle, they were probably labeled under 'Current Events.' There just had to be a library somewhere in the labyrinthian palace.

A large copper tub was carried into the room and set right in front of the fireplace. Buckets of hot water poured in with quick efficiency, marvelous to see. Brendan didn't think he'd ever get used to the sight of such a thing. Then the empty buckets were carted out, a washcloth and bar of bark-brown soap set on the tub's rim.

Brendan hesitated only a moment before deciding it was silly to be modest in front of the invisibles. He pulled the sweater off over his head, breeches and smallclothes soon following suit. The fire was pleasantly warm on his skin as he padded to the round copper bath and stuck one foot in. Prickles ran up his leg. The tub was luxuriously large and deep, and slipping in he found, to his delight, he could submerge his whole body quite comfortably. The tub they had back at home was a trifle too small and usually resulted in cold knees and a sore back.

Brendan closed his eyes with a contented purr as heat soaked into his bones. He slid down until his chin just met the steaming water and allowed his thoughts to drift.

Perhaps he should see his horse that morning. Maybe have a talk with those ridiculous fish. He hadn't realized how oppressive the snowstorm had been until it let up, and was left now feeling restless. He washed, the square of soap smelling sharply and pleasantly of cedarwood, an exotic decadence Brendan took a moment to revel in. Taking a deep breath, he ducked under the water, scrubbing his fingers through his hair.

Then he stood, water slicking down his body and hair clinging to his face. A towel presented itself from nothingness, which Brendan gratefully took as he stepped out onto the hot marble hearth. The towel was thick and Brendan dried himself quickly in front of the fire, beginning to feel a little awkward being naked with God-only-knew how many invisible servants in the room.

Mostly dry and in new smallclothes, he wished aloud for a mirror. But the only mirrors Brendan had seen in the whole castle were in the glass ballroom, and it would certainly not be worth making a trek all the way there just for a shave.

Right away the servants brought in a brush, lather, and a straight razor. Though he'd always been envious of boys at school who could grow proper beards, Brendan supposed it was lucky his didn't grow in fast enough to warrant daily taming. He shaved, the lack of a mirror causing only minor difficulty. He ran a brush through his hair but afterward left it to its own devices, as it would dry in natural waves that Brendan would admit he was quite fond of.

When he'd come back from Paris, Catherine had teased he'd become too vain, but she was one to talk. It took her the better part of an hour to get ready in the mornings.

He dressed warmly in thick breeches and the same sweater he'd worn at breakfast, and found thick gray woolen socks in a drawer. Tall winter boots appeared at the foot of the bed when he turned back. He thanked the servants and made his way downstairs, heavy boots clomping with each step.

Just as he came down off the last step, he realized he didn't even know where the stables were.

"Is there a door leading to the stables?" he asked the air, hoping a servant had followed him down.

"Yes, there is." To his credit, Brendan didn't jump this time. Beast strode out into the hallway, an open book in his large furred hands. He lifted an eyebrow, which he seemed to do whenever he was condescending. Which was often.

Brendan inclined his head a polite degree. "Good afternoon. I'm on my way to see my horse. To make sure he's all settled in," he added, in case Beast thought he meant to leave.

Beast glanced down at the volume he held, brow furrowed and lips pursed. He looked very bookish, and Brendan had an amusing image of Beast with tiny reading glasses perched atop his wide nose, and smothered a smile. Beast slammed the book shut with one hand, dust swirling, and held it out to his side. A gracious servant promptly tucked it under some invisible tunic.

Brendan realized he had probably watched that book disappear the very same way a man lost in the desert would stare at a cool jug of water pouring out on the sand.

"Well. There's no doubt you'll manage to get lost if you go with a servant. This way." Beast flicked the cuffs of his wine-red coat and spun on his heels. Brendan's boots thudded hastily behind him.

* * *

Beast slowed down, shortening his stride so the boy could walk alongside him; easier for Beast to sneak looks out of the corner of his eye. Hair dark

99

with damp, face freshly scrubbed. To Beast's keen sense of smell, he had the aroma of water and wool, with the faint spice of cedarwood soap.

Brendan stuck his hands in his pockets as he kept pace with the Beast, looking eagerly outside every time they passed a window. Beast felt much the same way. He wanted to dig his claws into the dirt and snow and grit, longed for the crunch of dead leaves under his steps, the scent of trees and earth in his nose. It had been a long time since he'd last been hunting.

"So," Brendan interrupted Beast's thoughts, "do the servants take care of the horses? I thought they couldn't leave the castle."

A very irksome question. "There is only your horse. The house servants and stable hands can leave the castle, just not the castle grounds. They can go no further than the outer gardens." Nor could he. Beast didn't appreciate the reminder. Though the servants, the roses, and he himself had not aged, the same had not been so with his animals. The mews and kennels stood empty, inhabited now only by sparrows and spiders.

The boy, thankfully, fell silent. The hallway opened to a crossroads of sorts, and Beast turned at an age-blackened suit of armor to a much wider passageway, high ceiling vaulted like that of a cathedral.

"This certainly is a long way," he heard Brendan mutter. "Castle must be bigger on the inside than it is on the outside."

Beast ignored him, flicking an ear in mild irritation as they passed walls decked with crossed axes and swords. When Brendan slowed down to look at them, Beast growled annoyance, and the boy shook himself from his inspection and rejoined the pace. A pair of enormous doors loomed, wrought iron strips over each door forged into rampant lions.

"That's the library," Beast remarked casually as they passed by, watching for the boy's reaction. His wide gaze was now one of near-worship, face aglow. They walked for a stretch, silent but for Brendan's boots and the click-click of Beast's claws on the hardwood floor.

"Do you think..." ventured the young man, eyes darting up at Beast and back down again, "might I be allowed there, sometime?"

Beast shrugged as if he didn't care much one way or the other. "As long as you don't damage anything."

"Of course I won't."

"And not today," Beast added, more for the sake of making rules than for any true reason, curious if the boy would obey.

"All right. Thank you," Brendan said fervently.

Beast said nothing for a long time, and when he did, his voice had gone softer than he had intended. "You are welcome."

Once outside, an iron fence lined the way to the stables, snow crunching underfoot. Roses, defiantly blooming through their ice-rimed leaves, twined around the fence.

"The roses are beautiful," Brendan said, his breath written in steam on the air. Beast wondered, for a hint of a moment, if the boy would be warm enough in cloak alone, without gloves or scarf, before reminding himself it wasn't his problem.

"Yes. They are." Beast was a little alarmed that an audible undercurrent of honest fondness stuck in his answer. That was becoming a distressingly increasing occurrence as of late; falling into unguarded lapses, voice and manner as difficult to control as his unruly thoughts.

* * *

The stable was one of the largest Brendan had ever seen, and the emptiest. Each of his footsteps echoed. Beast stalked in ahead, looking more ill-tempered than usual. "There are dried apples in the tack room, if you like," he grumbled. He leaned against a stall, crossing thick arms over his chest with an impatient shifting of his weight.

"Oh! Thank you." Brendan ducked into the room, found the shriveled apples in a glass jar, and as an afterthought grabbed a currycomb as well.

The stable's single occupant stuck his long head over the stall door and whinnied softly in welcome as Brendan approached.

"Hello, my friend. I have something for you." He unlatched the door and patted a broad piebald flank, crisp straw underfoot. The horse whuffled eagerly at the treat in his palm. The big gelding looked well cared for, but must be lonely all by himself in these huge stables. Brendan scratched his mane. "Did you miss me, Jean-Luc?"

Beast snorted. Jean-Luc flattened black-tipped ears but didn't stop lipping at Brendan's hands. Brendan felt himself turn a fierce shade of red. He'd forgotten Beast stood so close.

Leaning his elbows on the stall door, Beast's fangs flashed in a brief grin. "*What* is that horse's name?"

"Jean-Luc," Brendan mumbled into his hand. "Marguerite picked it." Beast still smirked. Brendan brushed with long, even strokes, the gelding's coat quivering with pleasure. "I would have named him something else."

"Like what?"

"Hmm, I'm not sure. Something more fitting to him, like—"

"Like Dog Food?"

"Hey!" Brendan shot Beast a dangerous look. "He's good draft stock. Got some Percheron in him, somewhere."

"Mongrel, then?"

"Nothing wrong with that! What makes you the resident expert on equines, anyway?" Each stroke of the currycomb grew shorter, matching his temper.

"I used to breed horses. These stables and the surrounding paddocks used to be filled with the best horses in the realm."

The grooming came to a close, to Jean-Luc's disappointment. Brendan leaned an arm across those somewhat-Percheron hindquarters. "You used to breed horses?"

"Oh, yes. I had the best. Friesians. Arabians. Even Andalusians purchased most extravagantly from Spain." Beast's eyes fell to the empty stable next to them. "All of *them* had good names," he added with a smile. Quite shockingly, this one didn't look mocking.

"Really?" Brendan didn't have extensive hands-on experience with horses, being city-born, but for the sake of status his family had owned a few when they had been at their wealthiest. "Good runners, then."

"And hunters. I had one Friesian in particular. Charlemagne." Beast didn't look at Brendan but up at the rafters, where sparrows and finches fluttered from beam to beam. "The best stallion in the stables. Night-black, sired by a Germanic warhorse who was rather infamous at the time. Never could a fox outrun him. Even the coursing hounds were hard put to keep up with him."

Brendan stared, amazed the usually so taciturn Beast was telling him, the unwelcome pest, about his pre-bestial past so candidly. In his mind, Brendan could clearly see the fleet hunting dogs, and the coal-dark shape of Charlemagne throwing himself headlong through the forest after a red wisp of fox.

Beast swept thick golden hair from his face and shifted his weight, upper body rippling with muscle under crimson velvet. Brendan blinked and looked quickly away.

"Charlemagne. That *is* a good name. Did you hunt a lot, then? What game?"

"Many things. The surrounding woods used to be rich with game." Beast looked straight at Brendan, for the first time since they'd entered the stables. "Do you hunt at all?"

Brendan found it difficult to return eye contact. Beast's eyes burned into him, and his breath snared in his throat. "When I was younger. Mostly pheasants and rabbits and things like that."

"Any fox hunting?"

"Fox hunting is for gentry nobler than my family, I fear. A pastime for nobility with nothing better to do with their time, no offense meant."

"There is none taken. Fox hunting was more about the hunter's skill than about actually catching the animal anyway." Beast smiled, a truly amused and scorn-free smile reaching all the way to warm brown eyes. Brendan ducked his head, hiding what surely must be a gobsmacked stare.

"So I hear. What other sorts of animals are in your forest?"

"Deer, boar, hawks and merlins, all sorts of fauna. There used to be many wolves, but now I see them rarely. Lions, too."

"Lions?" Brendan asked, incredulous.

"That's right. Kings and lords used to import them from far-off lands and let them loose only to hunt them. This was all very, very long ago, of course. Before my time. They're long since extinct. I doubt the winters agreed with them."

"Huh." Brendan thought about that for a moment, giving the horse one last pat before unhitching the stall door and joining the Beast in the open. He tossed his hair back from his face, smiled brightly, and was just about to suggest they go indoors for a hot lunch when a shadow fell across Beast's face.

Beast's breath puffed in the cold air like a bull's, his piercing human eyes set in that inhuman face focused and unforgiving. "I will make one thing clear. The only reason you are here is because of your sister. That is why the road let you in; because you are to serve as my bridge to Beauty. Do you understand? You are here to witness my fine hospitality, to be convinced I prove no danger to her. That's why the snow won't let you leave. That, boy, is your one purpose in being here. We are not, God forbid, *friends*. Do not for a moment think you are a welcome guest outside of your capacity as intermediary. Is this clear?"

Stung and bewildered, Brendan stared at Beast, mouth agape. He hadn't even *said* anything. His tongue was ready with the shape of something cruel; perhaps, 'My sister will never want anything to do with you. You're a monster. She would never stay with something like you.'

But I could. The silk-whisper thought bloomed in the back of Brendan's mind, so shocking him that he couldn't find his voice.

"Don't forget it." Beast swept past him into the open courtyard. "Go back inside. All this talk of game has made me hungry. I'm going hunting." Then he turned his back and stalked away, snow crunching under his heavy, clawed feet.

* * *

Silence. Wait. Start to move, quiet as a falling leaf, over the snow. Paws spread wide to keep from sinking, brown cloak as camouflage. Movement—freeze.

Beast watched a hare make its wary way through the brush. Too small for good hunting. The hare caught scent of him, froze in terror, then dashed off out of sight, kicking up a white flurry. Beast prowled on all fours under the heavy pine boughs, ignoring the raucous scolding of crows and squirrels. He found what he was looking for: deer tracks. Wide, deep ones. Probably a buck, weighed down by his antlers. Nostrils flaring, Beast began to track.

It's not as if he was unaware I wanted his sister here. No, just concentrate on the hunt.

There. More tracks. Follow them, so silently the snow doesn't even creak under his weight. Flex sharp, strong claws. Muscles tensed like coiled springs. Liquid strength and power.

He looked as if I had struck him a physical blow.

And what of it? I don't care if his precious little feelings got hurt one whit. There! Ahead of the grove. A young buck. Eight-pointer; not bad, really. Probably newly kicked out of his herd by the lead buck and hadn't found his own doe yet. Creep oh-so-quietly around the tree… Watching. Waiting. Anticipation rippling through anxious muscles.

If he were being honest (and honesty was one of the things the Beast had always prided himself on, for good or ill) he would have to grudgingly admit the castle had been a touch more interesting lately. A little. And maybe, yes, just the teeniest, tiniest bit less empty with the boy's company. The absolute smallest bit, of course.

Damn it, keep your mind on the task at hand.

When he'd helped the boy with his harpsichord injury, like a fussing aunt, the realization that it was the first time he had touched another person in over a hundred years had hit Beast like a hammer blow. It had been so long since there had been anyone to talk to.

Stop this maudlin nonsense. I find my solitude soothing. Much better than people always wanting something from me.

The buck moved, nibbling the tips of a hawthorn bush, slender foreleg delicately poised. Stalk closer, freeze still as the deer looked his way. Stay completely still as a stone.

He's so damnably sincere about everything. And he looks at me, really looks, not just staring over my shoulder. As if he weren't afraid of me in the least. Always smiling for one reason or another. The way he smiled at me in the stables was…

Damn it! Stop.

Now, while the buck's head is down. Now! Now!

Beast sprang. The young buck jumped to run, but wasn't nearly quick enough for the swift fangs and claws of the experienced hunter.

His anger and tension much sated, feeling entirely primal and savage, Beast began the long trek back to the castle, alone but for the dead deer slung over his shoulder and his own traitorous thoughts.

* * *

Brendan rest his hands on the oaken doors of the library. He should just go in, despite Beast's orders. Why shouldn't he? After the cruel things the Beast had said, it would be a very satisfying act of defiance to disobey him.

But that is all it would be: an act. Brendan turned away from the temptation of the doors and made his way down the echoing hall. There would be no point, and things were tense enough between them without him spitefully adding to the friction. He was still a guest under Beast's roof. He sighed. He could see the library tomorrow. At least it was something to look forward to.

He should have said something, should have stood up for himself. It rankled, being called 'boy,' the way Beast talked down to him, or eyed him with obvious disfavor. He hadn't wanted to hit someone so badly since his first week at school.

As he made his way back, Brendan absentmindedly tugged at any doors he passed. All were locked. He ambled along without any real direction when he noticed an extraordinary door he could have sworn hadn't been there the first time Beast had led him down this passageway. It was certainly the type of door one noticed, with a brass handle exquisitely carved to look like a wide, unblinking eye, and tiny squares of glass set into the wood so it glittered like a beacon fire.

Somehow Brendan knew it wouldn't be locked.

The door opened easily into a round room that clearly hadn't seen entry in years beyond counting, ancient cobwebs breaking and quivering as he

106

passed. The room was unusually cold, the air stale. Six full-length mirrors leaned up all around the curved wall to reflect a central point, perhaps at one time in the distant past serving as a grand lady's dressing room. Now each mirror was shattered to pieces, their edges blackened with age. A half-moon window spilled light down into the center of the room, where a shard of light shone brightly in Brendan's eyes.

The room had no other furniture save for a small plinth in the very center of the pool of light, a single handheld mirror set upon it, the kind people kept on their nightstands. Curiously Brendan approached, his splintered reflection repeated a thousand times around the room in broken glass shards, and picked up the mirror. He turned it over in his hands.

In stark contrast to the room, the mirror was warm to the touch. Aside from its unusual warmth, it was a very ordinary silver mirror, new and untarnished. Not a single cobweb touched it.

He smiled wryly. He had just mentioned that very morning he wished for a mirror. Perhaps this was the castle's way of granting it. Brendan held it up and glanced at his reflection. The mirror felt good in his hands. Strangely good. Warmth and comfort suffused through him, skin tingling. It felt like a warm glow in the nursery fireplace when he'd been a child; it felt like his mother's softness. It felt like sunlight through the classroom window; it felt like learning something new. It felt like reading indoors on a rainy day. It felt like playing the perfect song on a violin. The mirror felt like...home.

It clattered to the table as Brendan dropped it in alarm. Clearly this was no ordinary mirror. But any hesitation was quickly outmatched by curiosity. Cautiously, he picked it up again. This time, it still felt good to hold, but not with the same engulfing euphoria.

Brendan inspected it for a long time, but the mirror kept its secrets. Could it be considered stealing to bring this back to his room? It wasn't like anybody was using it, sitting untouched in some spidery old room. Besides, how often did one get the opportunity to study a magic mirror? Feeling thoroughly seduced, he put the mirror in a pocket and pulled his sweater down over the handle.

He spared one last look around the cold, broken room before leaving.

He pushed the glittering door shut and started to walk away toward the stairway that would take him to his room. When he glanced back over his shoulder, a chill ran up his spine.

The door had disappeared.

* * *

Brendan jabbed at the fragrant venison with a silver filigree fork. He wasn't especially hungry, appetite worn as thin and threadbare as his mood. The Beast had some nerve to sit there across the long table looking so blasted pleased with himself. His earlier outburst at the stables still stood stark in the forefront of Brendan's mind.

"You know," Beast drawled with an archly raised brow, acknowledging Brendan's existence for the first time all dinner, "I do believe it's customary to thank someone if they, say, went through considerable effort to provide you a fresh-caught meal."

Now, what Brendan meant to say was "Quite right, do forgive my manners," or perhaps, "Could you pass the salt?" but what instead came sharp and fast from between his lips, was: *"Allez a l'enfer."*

Beast nearly dropped his fork right into the gravy. "I'm sorry, what?"

Brendan stared back at him, anger momentarily derailed by the realization of what he had just uttered to his host with such scathing acidity. "Uh… Pass the…salt. Er. Please."

The Beast continued to stare. "Did you just tell me to go to hell?"

"Er. No?"

"Then perhaps you'd care to speak louder, boy."

Brendan shot immediately out of his chair, his hands slamming down on the table making fine dinnerware clatter. "My name," he uttered through gritted teeth, "is Brendan Mattheus-Etienne d'Aumale."

"If I had wished to know your full name," the Beast growled back, "I would have asked for it, boy."

Brendan's eye twitched. "Have you always been this much of an arrogant, self-centered *prig*?"

"Some backbone from you at last. Interesting." Beast sneered. "You assault my manners when I have been a gracious host; given you meals, a room, my prodigious hospitality?"

"You're a prodigious ass," Brendan said, unable to help himself.

Beast looked taken aback for a single heartbeat before doubling down on his rage, bellowing down the length of the great table, "You should be thanking your lucky stars that I refrained from tossing you out into a blizzard!"

"I am not entirely certain that was a courtesy," Brendan said curtly, spinning away from the table toward the door, his fists clenched at his sides.

Beast closed the distance with animal swiftness, looming between him and the door. His eyes were narrowed under the shadow of his brow. "You are sorely testing the limits of my patience! Never have I seen such ingratitude, and from a creature as unworthy as you—"

Blindly flung but true, Brendan punched the Beast square on his broad, leonine nose.

So fast it must have been on pure instinct, Beast snatched Brendan's wrist and held it painfully tight. His face went utterly blank, eyes round. Brendan braced himself, standing his ground, but the Beast did nothing apart from hold his wrist immobile and gawk at him.

No telling if it was long minutes or just a few fleeting seconds that ticked away while they glared and breathed and...stood...at each other. Brendan couldn't tell if the flush he was feeling was simply anger, or if Beast himself just gave off that much heat.

He is not...ugly. Not ugly at all. Merely...strange. And interesting. Looking past horns and fangs and fur, he noted the chisel of cheekbone and cut of jaw; the hard set of his mouth; heavy eyelids lined with thick, dusky gold fur that was somehow much more striking than mere eyelashes. Everything about the Beast was striking, more so than anything Brendan had ever seen before.

He lifted his chin and kept his gaze staunchly locked on Beast's, refusing to back down. After another moment of waiting, and then another, waiting for Beast to retaliate, to hit him back, to do *something*, Brendan dredged up his voice. "Well? Are you quite finished?"

Beast glared for another long, painful moment. He took an abrupt breath and pushed Brendan away, his expression shuttering. "Yes. We are." And with the finality of coffins being nailed, the Beast turned and stalked from the hall.

11

In Which There is a Discovery

The warm greenhouse air was oppressively warm as Brendan stretched out beside the reed-rimmed reflecting pool. All around, moonlight caught each flower in an eerie, luminous glow.

He'd changed out of dinner clothes into a comfortable green doublet over a loose wheat-hued tunic, tucking the new-found mirror into his belt. Beside the night-black pond, Brendan turned the mirror over in his hands, hoping the calm of the garden and the prospect of a mystery to puzzle over would banish the eddying muddle between his ears.

"Looking right knackered, luv. Come wiv more questions?" The white koi circled the pool once, looking past fishy whiskers with an amused intelligence that had no place on a fish. The midnight fish shortly surfaced and swam a loop around its pale twin, saying nothing.

"Oh. Good evening. Do you have a moment to talk?"

"Not like we 'ave appointments to keep. Had a bit of a fallin' out wiv the Master? Thumped him a good one!"

Brendan looked away. "I didn't come to talk about that. I wanted to ask you about this." He held the mirror out for inspection.

"Oh ho! Got the mirror, 'ave ye?"

"I know there's something...special about it. I just can't figure out what." He considered his next words, mindful of the aquatic prophets' tenuous grasp on honesty. "How is it used?"

"Nothin' easier. All ye gotta do is hold it in yer hand, ask it to show you somethin', look at wot it shows ye, and Bob's yer uncle!"

Brendan's brow creased with confusion. "What does my uncle have to do with—"

"Anyroad," the white fish interrupted, "it's a right handy jobber. Don't always show wot ye expect to see, though."

"Huh." Brendan scrutinized the mirror another moment before slipping it back under his belt, putting his curiosity aside for another time. "Thank you."

"Polite thing, ain't 'e?" murmured the white to the black. To Brendan it said, "Anytime. Anythin' else we can do for ye?"

Brendan looked down at his hands, twisting in his lap. "Could you tell me why...why he...and why I..." He gave up with a frustrated sigh.

The hitherto silent black fish now spoke. "Look, it's dead simple. Ye can do one of two things." A small fishy eye fixed Brendan in place. "Ye can go back home, get yer sister packed up and send 'er off 'ere in your place. She'll stay 'ere for a couple o' months, and 'oo knows? Maybe fall in love wiv the Master."

"And then the curse will be broken."

"Maybe so, maybe no." The black fish looked smug, which was a disturbing thing to see on a fish.

"Why do you say that?"

"I'm only sayin' the curse is a double-sided affair, is all." Brendan opened his mouth, but the fish talked over him before he could speak. "So ye could do that."

Brendan fell silent for several heartbeats. "What's my other option?"

"Ye can stay 'ere for a bit, and see wot 'appens." The black fish gave him a conspiratorial nod, an impressive feat for a creature without a neck, and dove beneath the water.

"Well, no use whingin', that's wot I always say." The remaining fish swam a little figure-eight in front of Brendan. "It'll be a new day tomorrow. Go 'ave a sleep, right, you'll feel more chipper in the mornin'."

Brendan stood and scrubbed a hand over his face, exhaustion creeping in.

"You're right. Thanks again for your help. Good night."

"One more thing, luv." Brendan turned. "Bloody good punch! Just pow, right on the snoot! Ha!"

* * *

Not a word of greeting was uttered at the next morning's breakfast.

The servants had prepared a light meal of cheese and fresh bread, fruit, and a lovely walnut endive salad that went mostly uneaten. The silence was so taut it could be cut with a limp endive.

"Did you sleep well last night?" Perhaps the Beast asked out of some latent sense of hospitable obligation. His tone sounded like it was being held hostage, forcibly civil by threat of knifepoint.

Brendan shoved a few walnuts around his plate. "Fine, thank you."

They both picked at their food.

Brendan coughed. As a guest, courtesy demanded more of him. "And you?"

Beast grunted, one broad shoulder rising in a lackluster shrug.

"Er... How is your nose?"

"I think I'll survive." It was so wickedly acerbic it nearly left welts on the ears, and that was it for the morning's conversation. Brendan had left the table politely enough and walked the way he'd been shown down to the stables.

Even as the oppressive fall of snow had dissipated, it had been replaced by an empty sense of loneliness weighing down every corner of the castle. He didn't know how the Beast had survived with it all these long years. Brendan sighed, leaning his forehead against a horsey muzzle. Jean-Luc lipped at his hair, warm breath redolent of hay and oats.

He was getting better at finding his way through the castle. He certainly didn't understand the magic, how it worked, or what whims motivated it to shift about. But it wasn't lapping hallways back onto themselves anymore, or multiplying stairs under Brendan's feet. He'd likely be able to find his way to the library today, and there was nothing that cured a lonely afternoon quite as well as a good book.

Eventually he headed back indoors, thumping loose snow from his boots, and after a few hallways, his path met the sizable blockade of the Beast. The rhythm of Brendan's heart snagged, as if missing a step on the stairs, and he cleared his throat to cover a sudden unwelcome attack of nerves.

"My lord," he said, with much the same flat tone he would have told no one in particular 'A tree' or 'Thursday.'

Beast glared balefully for a second before inclining his chin the barest degree.

Brendan became starkly aware of the snow melting in his hair where the horse had snuffled it out of its ribbon, wet straggles catching on the side of his throat. More snow was likely still clinging to his boots. He was probably tracking it everywhere.

"The snow is still quite deep," he said.

"And yet I remain certain the roads will soon open and travel will again be possible. Thankfully." Beast grinned sharply, a quick, feral flash Brendan was unsure whether to answer with humor or affront. "Something to say?" the Beast prodded, but Brendan was determined to not let himself be so easily goaded.

"I was looking for the library."

Beast blinked, head tipping to one side. For just a fraction of a moment, he looked chagrined. "I will take you there," he grumbled, so low Brendan thought at first he misheard.

"What, honestly?"

Beast scowled a little, likely regretting whatever mad whim had possessed him to offer in the first place. "Yes, honestly." He strode ahead, leading the way down the hall. The path subtly shifted, oak bleeding into teak, tapestries shifting into framed art the way the autumn turned green leaves into gold.

"This is unexpected of you," Brendan said, a tiny delighted note wriggling into the words.

"It will be for the best, I suppose," Beast said tartly, though Brendan thought the lift of his ears belied his true mood. "You can read up and finally gain some degree of understanding about the matters which you try to debate."

Despite himself, Brendan smiled, far preferring this over tense, antagonistic silence. He'd missed these verbal parries and ripostes, the clash and clang of their conversation.

"This coming from a man who has been shut up in his castle for so long he doesn't even know the vernacular any longer." In the past, this sort of sally had been met with a snort of amusement and a wry comeback Brendan very much looked forward to countering.

But Beast stopped dead in his tracks, turning on a heel to fix Brendan with an unreadable expression. "What did you say?"

"I—"

"Never mind. It was clearly nothing." Beast turned and resumed his pace, and Brendan almost stumbled over his feet to keep up. So mercurial. The man was a far more complex puzzle than any Brendan had unraveled before.

Wrought iron lions grinned in sideways leers, paws poised over the handles of the library doors. Beast wordlessly pushed them open and strode in. Brendan followed, swallowing his excitement. Surely he could find something new, something he hadn't read bef—

He stepped inside and went slack-jawed with awe. The library was far more than large, it was cavernous. Boundless. It surely held every book that had ever been or would be written.

He took a few dazed steps forward, almost afraid to turn around and discover, unbelievably, even more books behind him. There were books enough for a dozen lifetimes, filling a space larger than most theaters and might even put some cathedrals to shame. High windows of stained glass spilled illumination on thousands upon thousands of books, shelves wrapping around the entirety of the room like billowing swathes of multicolored silk.

"Problem?" Beast's deep timbre held open amusement. Brendan tore his gaze from the spectacle to look at him, and was struck by the warm color of his eyes; clear honey sheened over dark wood.

"No," he managed. "No, no problems. This is… Beast, this is breathtaking."

* * *

For a very long moment, Beast could only stare at his guest, bathed in cold winter sunlight but glowing with even zeal from within. He looked equal parts hungry and reverent as he went to the nearest book-lined wall and ran a hand across a leatherbound spine. His blatant thirst for literature and appreciation for knowledge was suddenly much more than a dinnertime amusement.

Beast watched him, entirely captivated. Very few things had held his attention so raptly in long years, perhaps before even the curse. Wonderment was, by now, an alien sensation. Yet he still knew it when he felt it. On rare occasions, his roses would evoke it; beautiful, fragile, eternal. A comfort. Seeing that emotion now painting his guest's fine-boned features somehow kindled it anew within himself, and Beast looked around his library as if seeing it for the first time.

It *was* quite wonderful. Breathtaking, even. When had he stopped seeing it that way? When had it become just another room?

Keeping himself tightly composed, Beast moved with broad strides to one of the bookshelves, a long ladder rolling itself helpfully out of his way. Using a single claw, he gently edged a book out from where it was wedged between two other volumes, clad in creased red leather and clearly handbound.

"This is an epic poem you may be interested in. Very old. Given to me by an elder brother who had been traveling in the northern regions of the world, where the Norsemen live." When was the last time he had even thought of Barnabie? A vague image of a tall ginger-haired man with eyes the same dark amber as his own lingered at the back of Beast's memory. "It may be ill-suited to your tastes. It is about violent men. But it is greatly interesting."

"What is it called?"

"Beowulf." Beast proffered the book. When he took it, Brendan smiled at him; a small thing, but warm with genuine thanks. Did he even realize he was doing that? Always smiling in that infuriatingly open, candid way?

Beast forced himself to shrug off the lingering tumult from Brendan calling him a man and not a beast, in the hallway outside. The boy hadn't even seemed to notice he had let the mistake slip past his lips, and now that lambent little smile wasn't helping matters any, either.

Beast did not intend to smile back, but the corner of his lips tugged up of its own volition.

"Thank you. Truly, thank you, this is all more than I ever expected. This is..." Brendan looked away, tucking an errant lock of hair back behind his ear. "It's strange. This room feels so much more...inhabited, I suppose, than the rest of the castle. Like all these words, all these different voices, are keeping us company. It's...less lonely."

The light clung to Brendan's eyelashes in a way that made Beast grasp blindly for a response, so he merely padded to a plush chair studded with small brass bolts and sat, content to wait for Brendan to explore as he pleased. He did not usually take a seat in front of his guest, hating the way he awkwardly folded into chairs with his misshapen, bent-back legs. At least behind a dinner table, most of his deformities were hidden. But currently his guest was too distracted with book-lust to witness such a thing.

Holding the gifted book to his chest, Brendan moved toward the shelves and hesitated. "May I...bring books back to my room?"

"Of course. When you've finished something, a servant will return the book for you, so you needn't worry about that."

"I can bring them back myself."

"You may rethink that once you've started climbing to the very top, but suit yourself."

Brendan grinned a little, looking at Beast sidelong. "It will take me quite a long while to need the ladders, my lord Beast."

Beast bared his teeth in what was nearly a smile. "Normally I would agree, but your nature is so contrary, you will doubtless choose some erratic method of picking books, and this will undoubtedly lead you to the ladders much sooner than you would ever actually need to."

Brendan laid the book on a nearby table and stepped up onto the closest ladder. He began to pointedly climb it, as high as he could scale. Beast rolled his eyes.

"An extensive collection of medieval lyric poetry!" Brendan called down. "And all this Provençal literature, why, I didn't realize you were such a sentimentalist." He plucked one and tucked it under his elbow.

Beast snorted and did not offer a reply. Brendan reached for another book, wobbling perilously on one foot. Beast tensed. "Don't fall," he said, a strict command and no gentle warning.

Brendan merely scoffed, "I'm not going to," but began to climb down regardless, relieving the shelf of one more selection before he dropped deftly from the third rung onto the carpet, all books in hand. "These shall make a fine start, I think. I'll take these back to my room and change into something dry. I was…" Brendan coughed a little, cheeks reddening. "I was thinking, later, of walking the outer gardens a bit. I would enj—that is, if you would care to walk with me—"

Beast pushed out of his chair. It was unaccountably difficult to tear his eyes away from the boy's face, recalling with sudden and vivid clarity the way his pulse had raced beneath Beast's fingertips when he'd caught his wrist.

That unexpected punch had left Beast utterly rudderless. No one had ever dared do such a thing before in his whole unnaturally long life, either before or after his curse. All Beast could do at the time was stare, keen animal senses noting the cedarwood scent of him, the steady pound of Brendan's heart in his throat; the defiant sculpt of his slim shoulders; how he glared back, fearless and flushed with anger; eyes that were normally a calm silver-blue all lit up like lightning over a storming sea. Oddly, it had reminded Beast of his earlier hunt, of following tracks in the snow.

"Doubtful. I have traversed the gardens too many times for them to hold much fascination for me. Do not wait for me," he called back across his shoulder, and made his escape back to safe, familiar solitude.

* * *

Later, Brendan could not help but fancy he was a bold explorer of the northern climes himself as he strode through the snow. He summited the high steps and raised banks of the outer gardens; a winding, wending maze of symmetrical shapes separated by low shrubs blanketed with snow.

The outer gardens were fascinating in their strangeness, especially compared to the more classically laid out rose gardens of the courtyards immediately circling the palace. The gardens fed neatly into the iron-wrought fencing girding the encroaching forest, keeping the bare branches from creeping onto the castle grounds. Brendan explored the strange geometrical shapes of the statuary and intricately designed mazes of walkways through them. One path had great slate squares paved into the shape of an ouroboros, and he followed the scales of the great serpent all the way down its back to where it ate its own tail before it led him into the next section of the garden.

The Beast had not accompanied him, nor had Brendan seen his host since the library. He had sat a while with the book the Beast had given him, stroking the supple cover before opening it. Marvelous that it should be in such beautiful condition after so very long, but he chalked it up to either magic or the attendance on the book's behalf by an invisible servant.

The poem itself was intensely captivating, and indeed very violent. Beast had not mentioned the book was annotated by a French hand in polite little scrawls in the margins, explaining the odd cultural reference or location. It was fascinating. The culture of the Norsemen was so intriguingly foreign, that even if the story had been only half as well-crafted and gripping as it was, Brendan still would have been loath to put it down.

Though only halfway through, the book had left Brendan feeling a bit wild and wanting to prowl, so he did. The garden here resembled a wedding cake, with huge rectangles of white marble stacked upon each other, each slightly smaller than the one below. He stood on the penultimate step and looked across the smooth blanket of pure untouched snowfall overtop.

The light was failing now, evening crawling near. How incredible it must be to see such a place as the northern edges of the world with one's own eyes, where all year was this illusion of crushed diamonds scattered across white velvet, catching the dying sun. Brendan walked around the perimeter of the final layer of marble, facing the palace, the sun setting on its other side.

He smiled, then. Maybe over dinner, he and the Beast could discuss the poem. And after, perhaps, he could play again, try out the harpsichord. He absently touched his cheek, where a scar would have rested had it not been for Beast's timely and thorough care.

"You know," he mused to the expanse of white, "I truly think he might have some good qualities under there."

He strode across the platform with great, ridiculous Viking steps, squinting into the last light as it peeked over the towers of the castle, and then the ice broke beneath his feet and the light was gone.

Later he would feel exceedingly stupid, for having not realized it wasn't a dais he tried to walk across, but a frozen pool. But at that moment all Brendan felt was stillness, no breath in his lungs and no purchase under his booted feet; and then a cold so intense it stung like fire until he felt nothing at all.

* * *

Beast moved with a hunter's speed back toward the castle, the boy slung over his shoulder. Thankfully he was still breathing, but he'd stopped shivering, which Beast took to be a bad sign.

He kicked open the entry door and raced with blind determination through the halls of his palace, his prison, trusting the doors to arrange themselves as necessary. The frozen edges of his fur started to thaw, frost-crackled clothes soaked through from his heedless crash into the icy pool to pull the boy up from the depths. He ignored the chill. He'd survive.

Beast carried Brendan into the guest room, roaring, "Hot water!" The tub was filled almost instantaneously.

He reached for the laces of the boy's doublet and hesitated, looking down at his sharp talons with consternation. Pinching wet, half-frozen cloth between claws, Beast peeled away layers until he was able to slip the too-pale boy into the bath.

Color rushed back into Brendan's skin, cheeks and shoulders going pink as steam rose up into the air. Relief flooded through the Beast; he'd be all right.

Brendan slipped further down into the tub, chin dipping below the surface before Beast realized it would be a wasted effort if he had saved his guest from one body of water only to let him drown in another.

Beast bent awkwardly to cup the boy's head in both hands above the water, utterly at a loss. He'd never done anything like this before. He was drawing on knowledge from his own frigid winter hunts and things he vaguely remembered reading in books. Maybe he was making things somehow worse; that would be his style, to be sure.

Beast scooped some hot water in his paw and let it stream through unbound chestnut hair. He kept his eyes aimed very firmly above the waterline.

The bath began to cool, steam dissipating. Towels had already been set to the side, as well as a thick robe. The fire had been kindled, and was now merrily roaring away.

"You," Beast muttered, "are a foolish, impossible, and very unlucky guest."

Brendan's breath stirred, and his eyelashes fluttered. A single sound made its way through his chest and into a low, protesting hum.

Beast huffed a laugh. Contrary even at death's door.

He carefully drew the young man out of the bath, wrapped him in a towel, and then a few more for good measure. Trying to stand Brendan on his own two feet proved fruitless, his slim weight swaying into Beast. Beast rolled his eyes and eased the boy into the robe, letting the towels fall away.

He tried to guide Brendan toward the bed with only a supporting paw under his elbow, but the young man nearly tumbled to the floor. After catching him, Beast scowled. Well. He'd already carried him this far. What were a few more steps to the bed?

So Beast scooped him into his arms and carried him those few steps. The covers slid back, a down quilt pouring out from nowhere and spreading across the bed. Beast set Brendan down. He hesitated, frowning, suddenly feeling clumsy and lost and not at all sure whether sticking a half-drowned person in bed and leaving him there was the best way to handle things. He had no idea what he was doing, and nobody but himself to ask.

Stirring from absolute stillness, Brendan reached up and tangled his fingers in the uneven mass of Beast's still-damp mane, a plaintive sigh rising from the back of his throat. He clung close as if on instinct, pushing his face into Beast's firm shoulder and breathing in deeply. His lashes fluttered, lips curving into a dreamy smile.

The Beast held very still.

Brendan's nose traced a slow line from Beast's jaw to cheek. He pressed his lips against the corner of Beast's mouth in a brief, weak, but very unmistakable kiss, before slipping down to rest in the crook of the Beast's neck with a contented sigh.

His breaths evened out, a soft rhythmic caress across the rabbiting pulse of Beast's throat. For a long while—he had no concept of how long precisely—Beast sat contemplating the color and composition of the quilt.

Eventually, he extricated himself from under the young man's weight, piling the covers up around him as Beast sat back on his haunches, expression deeply shrouded.

He couldn't say how long he silently watched before he finally turned to leave. Beast hesitated at a side table to run the pad of his great clawed thumb gently across the crimson cover of his long-dead brother's book. It shifted with the motion, seated unevenly on the table. Beast lifted the edge of the tablecloth, and stared at what was, possibly, at least until very recently, the single most precious thing in all his world. Beast drew in an abrupt breath, the kind of noise that startled birds in a forest to flight.

The magic mirror winked balefully up at him with the firelight, and an old, smoldering, quiet rage, the likes of which the Beast had not felt for some time, began to kindle.

12

In Which There is Understanding

Beauty fussed with Brendan's buttons, muttering under her breath about saucy painters. Brendan shooed her away to her chair and stood at his appointed place behind her, while their father struggled into his best suit coat with the help of his valet. Marguerite gave big doe eyes to the painter as he set up his canvas, and Catherine adjusted that god-awful hat of hers, jabbing pins into it like a warrior preparing armor for battle.

Self-consciously, Brendan fiddled with his own velvet hat. He hated the thing, with its horrible big feathers. He never wore hats if he could get away with it. *And if that painter lets his eyes drift south on my sisters again, so help me God, I'll—*

"All right! Everyone quiet!" Etienne ushered everyone into their places with great mother-hen sweeps of his arms. "Anyone who's not getting their portrait painted or painting one, please get out of the room. Now, my children, we are going to sit down, or stand up as the case may be with your brother and I, stop fussing with our clothes and hair—I'm talking to you, Marguerite, put that comb down—and we're going to let the man paint the bloody picture. All right?"

"Father!" Beauty chastised, a hint of amused scandal in her voice. "You're getting all red. Come stand here."

It took another few rushed moments for everyone to get situated, but soon they were all in place; the three sisters sitting side by side, menfolk standing at their shoulders. The artist made small adjustments, holding a brush in one hand while picking stray lint from Etienne's sleeve with the other. He pinched a crease into Brendan's cravat, then made a move as if to adjust the scarf over Beauty's lap, but he caught the venomous look Brendan shot him and subsided.

And so the d'Aumale family sat together in silence (except when Catherine hissed a little gossip to Marguerite, but Etienne surreptitiously prodded her shoulder and they both fell into sullen silence) as the painter hunched over his canvas, eyes darting from them to his work.

Brendan peeked down at Beauty. His hand lay on her shoulder, and he squeezed gently. She turned her face up and flashed a quick smile.

Her face burst into tiny stars, spiraling away into the whiteness spreading around him. It was bright. Very bright.

* * *

Brendan opened his eyes and regretted it. His skull felt like it had been beaten with an icicle and then stuffed with wool. He flung up an arm to block out the light, eyes slit. The curtains of the other window, still shut, were suddenly thrown open.

Brendan moaned. "Please. Too bright. Have mercy."

A hand tugged at his shoulder. Blearily he looked up, which was pointless because the servant was eponymously invisible, and croaked, "What?"

A heavy stoneware mug of thin porridge pushed into his hands, warming their lingering chill. "No, thank you, I'm not hungry." He tried to hand the mug back. The invisible pushed it back at him very firmly, quite clearly brooking no nonsense.

"Fine, all right. I'm drinking it." Brendan took a small sip and found he was hungry after all; extraordinarily so. And a little shaky.

Then he remembered.

Cold swallowing him, so cold it squeezed all the breath out of his body. The shadow of broken ice above him. The vice-like grip of a strong hand on his collar. "How did I get here? Did you... Did you save me?"

The air had a slight tremble of a head shaking.

"No? Then... Oh, no. No." Brendan set down the porridge in dawning horror. *"He* did, didn't he?" He took the affirmative silence for a yes, and groaned in absolute mortification. "Good God, I'm a massive idiot. I can't believe—It's been one mistake, accident, or calamity after the other ever since I came here." He palmed his face and muttered through his fingers, "He's going to be angry. Is he angry?"

The servant laid a ghostly hand on Brendan's shoulder and gave him two brisk, encouraging pats.

That didn't bode well.

No use putting it off. Brendan sighed and slid out of bed with care, and frowned at the thick, loose robe draped around him. It was not even remotely familiar, as Brendan always slept in his smallclothes.

"Thank you," he mumbled to the air; the thanks because he was pretty sure it was an invisible servant who had done it for him, and the mumbling because he was both embarrassed and none too pleased his clothes had been changed without his knowledge or permission.

The dimming light through the windows looked to be near evening. This meant there was half a day, a full night, and another nearly full day missing from his memories.

After a few tries Brendan managed to stand up on his own, and then he did a quick body check: both legs and arms, all ten fingers and toes, and other such important extremities were still present and accounted for. No bruises, scrapes, or broken bones. He was shivering a little, though he didn't exactly feel cold. It was more like his body was reminiscing about the sensation of cold, shivering only out of habit.

His strength grew the longer he moved around the room, pulling on the wool sweater he'd taken a liking to and tying back the tangled mess of his hair. Only the tiniest bit shaky, he padded from the thick warmth of his room into the notably cooler hallway. The corridors were dark. The flames of the wall sconces were low and guttering, giving the castle an eerie, unwelcome cast. If the castle truly resonated with the moods of its master...

Brendan bit his lip and twisted the hem of his sweater. He hesitated at the top of the stairs, squared his shoulders, and made his way determinedly down.

The hallway felt strange, as though a quiet ripple crept beneath the rugs or flitted from torch to torch. As he walked, the color of the carpet shifted a different shade. Brendan frowned at the floor. "No, not to the music room, thank you. I want to go where Beast is." The color shifted back so slowly as to seem reluctant.

He'd just bossed around a hallway. Brendan's life had certainly bidden sanity a fond farewell.

He padded past the Great Hall, following the faint crackle of a fire to the open archway of the parlor. The fire's lambent glow silhouetted a high wing-backed chair, its back to the door. Brendan could faintly hear breathing over the pop of embers.

"Good evening," Brendan ventured, but his voice came rough and thick. He cleared his throat.

Beast did not reply, beyond deep, heavy rumbles of breath.

Brendan had gotten pretty familiar with being pointedly ignored.

He skirted the firelight toward the chair. "I'm sorry," he began, because it seemed like a good place to start.

The low growl stopped.

Well, that was a little better.

"Are you," Beast said, the gravel of his voice offset by its silken cadence, elocution deceptively, dangerously soft.

Not better at all, then.

Brendan stepped further into the light, examining his host's posture. Beast was flung near sideways in the chair, head and shoulders hunched, profile low and heavily shadowed. It seemed to be a pose carefully orchestrated to project an air of nonchalance and, as it revealed its manufactured nature, failed utterly.

"I should have known better." Brendan looked down at his twisting hands. He'd needed to be rescued like some absolute simpleton who had never seen a frozen pond before. Mortifying. It surely wouldn't do much to convince his host he was of much worth or quality. And just when Brendan thought he was maybe making some headway on not being called 'boy' all the time.

"Should you have." Beast dripped disdain. He wasn't sneering yet, but that likely wasn't far off.

"Look, it was a foolish mistake. I didn't even think to ask if I should be careful—"

Beast tossed his head back with a barking laugh that trailed off into a derisive snort.

Brendan stared, somewhat wide-eyed, and continued. "—as I thought I knew the gardens well enough by now and *why* are you being so *strange?*" he demanded, then wished he hadn't, as was frequently the case whenever he opened his mouth without first considering what was about to come out.

He had the awful, creeping suspicion the Beast's mood may have to do with Brendan's clothes maybe not being changed by the invisible servants, but his brain skittered madly away from the idea whenever it tried to surface.

The Beast scowled. "Strange? This is not strange. This is *anger.*"

"Oh," Brendan said with more than a little exasperation. "Well, how refreshingly new. Never seen that emotion from you before."

Beast raised up in his chair while his head lowered significantly; a bull preparing to charge. "You would dare show such impertinence? This *insolence?*"

"This isn't insolence, this is *anger*! You haven't got a monopoly on that, you know."

"What right have you to be—"

"Did you undress me yesterday?"

A ringing silence. The fire didn't dare crackle too loudly. Beast stared at him, looking much like the rug had been yanked out from underneath his feet.

"Yes," he finally said. "And I…put you in some warm water."

Brendan had no idea what to say to that and hadn't even meant to ask the question in the first place. "Oh. Warm water, like…a bath?"

"Something like a bath. Yes." The silence stretched on.

"Oh. Well. I see. Thank you, I suppose?" In the next span of silence, a horrifying thought congealed in Brendan's mind. "That… After…you

127

know... Um. That water was really very cold."

"You could have easily frozen to death." Beast looked a little lost, diverted from what was surely a carefully cultivated rage by the unexpected turn in the conversation. "If you hadn't drowned first."

Brendan's voice wavered to a bit higher register than normal. "Yes, which—because that water was awfully cold. Really, terribly cold."

Beast had seen him *naked*. Naked and *cold*. That just wasn't fair. The implications hung at the fore of his mind like one of his father's heavy cargo crates being hoisted onto a ship deck, looming and creaking over the planks.

"Yes," Beast snapped, "I am perfectly aware, due to a number of clues such as copious amounts of ice and the way you were turning *blue*, the water you fell into was, in fact, cold."

"Well, I'm just saying!" Brendan insisted, red-faced.

"I know you are," Beast yelled back, "because you keep saying it!"

"Yes, well." Brendan switched tactics. "Why? You didn't have to... Why didn't you leave it for the servants?"

Beast snarled, "What, are you upset my claws may have scratched your delicate skin? Now you expect the servants to be at your beck and call? You are a finicky, hypocritical little thing, aren't you?"

"That isn't—"

"And in addition to being an ungrateful, deceitful thief!"

Brendan blinked owlishly, baffled to a point beyond fear or wariness. "I... What? I didn't take your blasted pool, I just fell into it."

Now it was Beast's turn to look confused, heavy brows crowding in puzzlement. "What are you talking about?"

"What are *you* talking about?"

The wing-back chair toppled over as Beast flung himself from it and into the full illumination of the firelight. He thrust forward something small and silver from the shadow of his cloak. Brendan had sense enough to reel away from it, then freeze with encroaching dread.

"This!" Beast hissed. "This! You stole this! I have given you endless hospitality, I have opened rooms to you that have been closed for centuries, tended to your injury with my own two hands, given you—" His shoulders hunched. "I saved you from certain death, and yet you stole from me." A loud snort of disgust. "Always, they take the one thing not offered. But then I should have expected no less from the son of a dishonest merchant."

A sudden ember burned in Brendan's gut. "How dare *you*, my lord. I am no thief. My father is a witless fool when a wager is involved, and shortsighted, and self-serving, and—I find I could easily list off his worst qualities all day—but he was never a dishonest man in his business. And in any case, I am *nothing like him!*"

"You stole from me just as he did. Therefore, you are a thief." Beast's lip curled, expression going chilly. "I was a fool to believe you were different from all the others."

"I did not steal from you!" Brendan yelled, the powerful ring of his own voice surprising him.

"Then how did this little item come to be hidden in your room, hmm? Will you claim it walked there itself?"

"You never forbid me from unlocked rooms—"

"That door was locked!"

"No." Brendan clipped each word short, barely reigning in his temper. "It wasn't. I touched the knob and it opened."

"I locked it myself!"

"I have no ability to open locked doors without a key," Brendan said tersely, forcing his hackles down. "Therefore, you must be mistaken."

"Are you calling me a liar?" Beast asked in the soft, nearly calm sort of tone he took when he was about to start tearing up décor.

"Not lying. Mistaken."

"So the door simply opened for you, did it?"

"Apparently. A mysteriously unlocked door is far from the most outlandish thing I've witnessed here. A door appeared, it was open, so I went in. And then. Er."

"Then," Beast prompted, pacing on all fours around the toppled chair. Brendan swallowed to see him in such an animalistic mood. It seemed long ago the last time he had been genuinely frightened of the Beast. *They all sought to acquire something from me,* Beast had told him, of those who joined

129

the ghostly ranks of the servants. *So I acquired them, instead.*

"Well," Brendan said, searching the floor for his thoughts. Unfortunately, they weren't there, so he looked back up and met the Beast's ire head-on. "Well, the mirror was in the middle of the room! Just lying there, in the clear open! All shiny, and on a plinth! Was I *not* supposed to touch it?"

"No! And even if you did, touching is a far step removed from *taking*!"

"You never said I couldn't...take things," Brendan said with far less conviction than he had a moment ago.

Beast glared in furious disbelief. "That needed to be spelled out?"

"No! I mean, possibly? What harm in taking it to my room? Only borrowing. Just moving it from one room of the castle to another couldn't cause any trouble, I thought." He shifted his weight from foot to foot. "It just—I picked it up out of curiosity, I swear I was just lifting it to look at it better, and then...it felt... It was warm. And it..." He stifled a sigh, shoulders sloping downwards. "It felt like home."

Beast was still for a long moment. "You must hate it here very much to be so homesick."

Brendan blinked; the Beast's bubbling anger was underpinned by a faint shadow, a dark mood lacing through the words that sounded like...

Brendan had, through occasional chance and rare misfortune, come across the truly cruel before, and counted himself among the lucky few that he'd managed to maneuver his way through life thus far avoiding any direct confrontations with the sort. But avoidance was not ignorance, and by necessity—being on the smaller side and his proclivities what they were—he knew what warning signs to look out for. He'd seen anger as an extension of fear, a desire to control, and more troubling as a veneer over some dark delight underneath.

But what lurked underneath Beast's ire was none of these things, and indeed sounded very much like *despair*.

And with the lens of perception shifted into place, several little clues added up, and the puzzle behind Beast's ever-changing moods slid into clarity.

Beast glared imperiously into the fireplace, his words coming in a seething rasp from the bottom of his throat. "Allow me to do you the favor, then, of rescinding my hospitali—"

"Wait," Brendan demanded; clear, resonant. To his astonishment, Beast's mouth snapped shut, his expression wary.

Of course Beast was quick to think he was being taken advantage of. To hasten to push away before someone else could do it first. The way his moods and manners shifted, mercurial and unpredictable, always keeping Brendan on his toes.

Well. Two could play at that game.

"You're hard to know," Brendan said softly.

Beast flinched back, wariness blooming into alarm. "What?"

"Has no one ever wanted to get to know you before?" Brendan took a small step forward, and Beast took one back. "Has anyone truly tried?"

"What is— You think to distract me from the matter at hand." Beast scowled, drawing up tall and forbidding, arms folded over his broad chest.

"I am sorry about the mirror. I didn't think there was anything wrong with my keeping it to look at for a while. But I should have asked, and I own that mistake."

Claws clicked against parquet as Beast shifted his weight, chin rising imperiously before it dropped, anger bleeding out of his posture.

"And I'm not homesick," Brendan felt it important to add. "I thought going to university in Paris was to be the greatest adventure of my life. Anywhere away from home would suit in that regard, but this place? This castle has been more incredible and bewildering and *wonderful* than any experience I could have ever hoped for. I feel truly fortunate to be here, to see what I've seen. Everything here goes against all I've ever known or learned or believed in. Endless corridors that shift and change, people I cannot see, and multitudes of books in languages I don't even recognize. And there are these fish," he said with sudden, earnest distress, looking up at Beast's shadowed face.

"These...these chatty blasted fish in the conservatory, and they know things there's no way they could know, and I don't...I just don't know...what that's about. At all. I think I've been coping pretty well with everything

131

else, but those fish are truly beyond my ability to comprehend." Brendan swallowed before continuing. "And then there's you. There's you, and I don't understand you at all. I wish I did."

Beast did not make a single move for what felt like ages, the pop of embers in the fireplace the only indication that time itself hadn't stopped. Finally he shook himself, clearing his throat. "I suppose it is...possible...my reaction was unwarranted." Every word seemed as if it had to be dragged forcibly into being. "Perhaps...I have been too hasty in my accusation."

"Hmm." Brendan squinted as if peering for a far-off horizon. "There's an apology in there somewhere, I could almost swear it."

Beast snorted, a slight twist of humor in the line of his mouth. He righted the armchair with one hand and sank into it. Another chair slid up to the fireside, and Beast waved at it in invitation. Brendan sat. "As for the mirror," Beast declared, "I am willing to agree we have both been in error, and we may consider the matter settled."

Brendan's eyebrows inched upward. "Magnanimous of you," he said, in as neutral a tone as he could.

To his surprise, Beast hunched down a little, ears lying flat. "I'm well aware my social skills leave much to be desired."

"Well, yes. But they do say every rose has its thorn, don't they?" Brendan offered, propping his cheek on his fist.

Beast turned a horrified look upon him. "Are you...comparing me to a *rose?*"

Brendan winced. "Er. I think I did."

"Good thing your inability to craft a metaphor does not extend to your facility with musical instruments," Beast grumbled.

The unexpectedly sweet compliment resonated through Brendan, a light touch strumming over harp strings. He coughed to cover his pleasure, and asked, "So does the mirror really do anything special, or is it just warm to the touch?"

"Of course it does something special. It's a magic mirror."

"Well, the fish told me as much, but I thought they might be pulling my leg," Brendan said. His curiosity, perhaps his foremost natural state of being, perked up with interest. "Is everything here magic?"

"It's an enchanted castle. There may be a bread knife or two that remain mostly mundane, but yes. Everything here is magic. Well spotted."

Brendan didn't bother hiding the roll of his eyes at the familiar sarcasm.

"I was going to destroy it," Beast offered, unprompted. Brendan leaned forward, silently encouraging him to go on. "I wanted no mirrors of any kind in this place. But when I touched it... It somehow seemed to..." He spread his claws expressively. "It made me forget...things. My troubles." Beast looked away at the flickering fire for a moment. "It is at times a source of tangible comfort, at others a window to other places. On a few occasions, it has served as a window to the past. But why or how or when it chooses to act as these things, I do not understand or control."

"A window," Brendan murmured. "To anywhere? Or anyone?"

"Though usually a thing one has reason or wish to see."

"Yes, the fish told me something like that."

"You've mentioned. You've spoken to the fish, then?" Beast's voice warmed with amusement. "I wouldn't take anything they said to heart."

"They're infuriating," Brendan agreed. "Which one is it that tells lies, and which one tells truths? They were both being awfully cryptic."

"I have no idea. As far as I can tell, they're both terrible liars." Brendan could swear he saw a smile under all that fur. "Even after two hundred years, and many clever attempts to trick them into telling me, I've not discovered their true natures."

Brendan brought his heels up onto the seat and clasped his hands over his knees. He debated over his next choice of words, but seeing as the two of them had seemed to reach a more candid exchange, he said plainly what was on his mind.

"Two hundred years is a long time."

Beast looked at the fire for long seconds before replying. "It is." Silence began to stretch between them, but before it could become uncomfortable, Beast added, "You must be starving after your frigid fiasco last night. Shall I have something brought up for you?"

"I am hungry, but still a little weak, I think. I'm not sure if I can stomach a lot of rich food." The huge fireplace was warming the last remnants of chill from Brendan's bones, and he wasn't inclined to move.

"I'll have the servants bring up some soup, then. I've eaten already."

"That sounds good. Thank you."

His host grunted in reply and waved a large paw to direct the invisible servants. Two small tables floated in and planted themselves beside each wingback chair. A pair of glasses of dark cabernet appeared on each table, and a blue stoneware mug was handed to Brendan. He wrapped his hands around it, relishing the heavy mug's warmth and the steaming fragrance of the broth. The soup was hearty and filling, a mouthful warming Brendan's whole body right down to his toes. He was pleased to spy a small pearl onion in it, always a favorite of his.

"I thought I might play a little harpsichord tonight."

"Ah, yes. Take some revenge on it, perhaps?"

"I would be honored if my gracious host could attend." He readied himself for disappointment. He'd come to value the appreciation an audience afforded him.

Not just any audience; he liked playing for *Beast*.

Beast tilted his shaggy head, swirling his wine like an experienced sommelier. "I may be able to clear my busy schedule."

Brendan tried to bite down a delighted smile. He sipped his soup as they sat in companionable silence. After he polished off the last of his wine, the wineglass swiftly refilled.

"Thank you," he told the unseen servants.

"Why do you do that?"

"Why do I do what?"

"Why do you thank them? I've seen you. Speaking to them, asking questions you know they won't answer." The Beast waved a hand. "They don't care, you know. They don't have the capacity."

Brendan stared at Beast, the mug of soup forgotten an inch from his mouth. "Don't have the capacity?"

"Yes. It doesn't matter if you're polite to them or not." Beast's brow creased.

"Wha— Of course it matters! What do you mean, it doesn't matter?"

The furrow in Beast's brow deepened. "Just that. It doesn't matter. They're only invisibles."

Brendan's jaw dropped. "How can you say— They're still *people!*"

"No. They *used* to be people. Now they're...like shadows. You don't thank your shadow. They do what they're told; they cook and clean, but they don't *think.*"

"How can you possibly know that? How can you know they don't think and feel? Can they tell you?" Brendan set his mug down so hard soup sloshed onto the table.

"Well, of course they can't tell me. That's why—"

Brendan cut him off. "Just because they don't look like human beings, that means they aren't human beings? Is that what you're saying? How can you truly believe that? I mean, what about *you?*"

There was a dangerous silence. "What about me?"

"Oh, come on. A man like you doesn't think these poor forgotten souls are worth any courtesy? Aren't worth respect? Or is it that you think nobody is worth it?" Brendan pushed himself up and paced to the fireplace. Beast glowered, his paws tightening on the chair arms until his talons bit deep into the wood. All those times he called Brendan 'boy' surged to the forefront of his mind. "Is that it? No one but you deserves respect? Are you just like so many other arrogant, bullying men—"

"*Stop calling me a man!*"

Glass crashed to the floor with one sweep of Beast's paw. Brendan jumped a step back. The chair tumbled over as Beast flung one of the little tables into the fireplace, the greedy flames hissing as they licked at the varnish.

"*I AM A BEAST!*"

A stabbing pain struck Brendan square in the heart. Beast stood there among the wreckage, chest heaving, eyes cast down.

Brendan stepped toward him. "You're not. Well, when you act like this, sure, it's pretty beastly, but... You're not a monster."

Finally meeting his eyes, Beast glared at Brendan for long seconds. "You said you want to know me. You don't. Not really. There's nothing to know."

Brendan swallowed, taking a small step forward. "I happen to think there's a good man under there I'd like to know very much."

Beast looked stricken, breath shuddering once. Words rasped in his throat, unsaid, and he cleared it sharply before trying again. "It's... When...you call me a man, you aren't...mocking me. Are you."

Brendan was now close enough to lay his hand on Beast's velvet-clad arm, and wished he dared to. "No. I'm not."

Beast turned such a searching gaze upon him that Brendan's knees gave an alarming wobble. "No. I can see as much. I...will try to not react so vehemently in the future."

Brendan ventured a tentative smile, trying very hard to not notice the fine fall of Beast's tawny hair over his brow, to quell the itch to push it back behind a pointed ear. "And I will try to not infuriate you so. It's a tricky job, you know. I'm never quite sure what will and what won't."

Beast exhaled sharply, looking away from Brendan's offered smile. "I believe I was the one to anger you, this time. I didn't realize you felt so strongly about the servants." Who were, incidentally, clearing away the broken glass and righting the chair as Beast spoke.

Brendan considered his words carefully before he spoke, which he'd be the first to admit was a refreshing change of pace. "The way I see it, there are two kinds of people. There are those who don't recognize others as individuals. Rather, they are only tools to be used, or bodies to be seduced, or mirrors to reflect their own superiority. They're not real people. No one else is important. No one but themselves.

"Then there are those who see every single human being as their own person, with whole private worlds of complexities. These people see everyone has potential for greatness." Brendan paused a moment. "I suppose, what my point boils down to, Beast, is what kind of person do you want to be? Alone and superior in the great, dark void? I imagine that must be a very lonely and frightening world to live in."

Beast regarded him for a long moment, face still, as though he were carefully guarding against any emotion. "And what sort of person are you?"

"The sort who sees worth in people. Something doesn't cease being valuable simply because you can't put a price on it, Beast."

"You're very young to be so perceptive."

Brendan lifted his chin. "I don't think I'm much younger than you. I mean, if we ignore the two hundred years difference, of course. Am I right?"

The Beast took a step back, throat bobbing on a reflexive swallow. "Perhaps. I don't exactly keep track of each year."

A wave of weakness hit Brendan. He brought up a hand and rubbed his eyes. "I'm more tired than I thought I was." He leaned against the side of the hearth, then slid down to sit on the rug with his knees drawn up, elbows resting lightly on them.

"You still need time to recover. It might be wise to skip your harpsichord demonstration tonight."

"I agree." Though not pleased at the prospect, he definitely didn't feel hale enough to perform a concert.

From his seated position below, Beast's form was brought into sharp relief by the golden firelight, his curved horns shining. He was undoubtedly the most striking thing Brendan had ever seen, with his brooding eyes and broad frame. Like he took up more space in the world than most men. And there was no doubt he certainly was a man... Brendan's eyes drifted of their own accord.

Startled at his own thoughts, Brendan tore his gaze away and swallowed hard.

Beast gracefully folded his legs beneath him to join Brendan on the hearth rug. "Tomorrow then, if you're feeling better."

Brendan tried to shake off his disquiet, but it clung. "I meant to say earlier, thank you for allowing me to stay here, even after the storm had abated. I know it wasn't part of your plan, but... It's an incredible place."

Beast smoothed the lay of his coat before speaking. "What would you be doing back home, had your father never darkened my doorstep? What ambitions motivated you? What plans did you have for your future?"

Startled, Brendan instinctively shied away from answering, as he had many times when his sister had prodded him on the very same thing. What use was it to linger on dreams that would never come true? "Wha— Why do you ask?"

A wry smile angled his way. "You claimed you want to know me. Can I prove any less?"

Face suddenly burning hot, Brendan looked down, as if his shirt cuffs had become full of great interest. "Didn't really have any plans, I suppose. Get a job. Support my family."

Beast's eyes narrowed in an incisive look that shone light into shadowy places Brendan didn't like to examine too closely. "Curious. I've only seen you be evasive before when questioning you about your sister."

"I'm not being evasive," Brendan protested, clucking his tongue as if this was the height of absurdity. "I'm forthright to a fault. Ask any of my friends."

"I suppose you have dozens of those." Surprisingly, it didn't seem like a jest, like Beast naturally assumed Brendan had his pick of boon companions.

"I… No. Not since school. I never really had the knack for it."

"I see." Beast hesitated, clearly choosing his next words with care. "Upon reflection, I suppose it would be difficult for you. Being unbearably nosy and all."

Brendan smiled. "Ah, yes. You're exactly right."

"Friendship is overrated. People always wanting something. Needing favors. You're probably better off." Gazing off into the fire, Beast seemed lost deep in thought and memory. "I never had any."

There was a long, tense silence, wherein Beast sat still as a statue, looking like he wished he could snatch his words back and swallow them unsaid.

Brendan spoke as softly as a cat padding over snow. "You have one."

Beast was still for a long moment. He turned the barest fraction toward Brendan and smiled; a barely-there sliver of honest pleasure. "I suppose I do."

It was at that exact moment Brendan realized he'd fallen in love.

13

In Which There is a Kiss

In the old days, Beast's court had been full of 'friends.' A pack of courtiers always spinning their advantage, fawning admirers or royal sycophants who plied with falseness, and would only tell of truth if it benefited them. It had been so long since Beast had known anyone whom he wanted to call friend that he scarcely knew how to recognize the feeling now.

Between waking and sleeping, he wondered if the gentle warmth seeping into the cold, forgotten reaches of his soul could be the glowing ember of friendship.

Slipping into slumber, he readied for yet another night of animal dreams; dreams of stalking and running, dark and colorless save for the color of blood. Dreams he had dreamed for two hundred years. Dreams fit for a beast.

Instead, the Beast found himself inside the sun-dappled confines of the hedge maze at the southern edge of the castle grounds. He knew implicitly, as is the way with dreams, the center of the maze held a very fine prize for him, so he took a step to seek it out.

He was so shocked to find himself walking upright, like the man he used to be, that he almost jolted awake. Then the calm dream logic sank in, and Beast was only mildly surprised at his boot-clad feet, at his hairless hand brushing stray locks from his human face. He walked, for a drifting, unknowable time before he arrived at the maze's heart. A silver fountain presided over the tiled center, a spray of water catching the sunlight in brilliant spectrals.

Brendan sat there on a bench, a basket at his side. Beast was pleased to see him there, in this secret place, and a little bemused by his own pleasure. Why he should be so pleased to have his privacy invaded, he had no idea.

Sunlight cast its golden glow on the young man, an errant breeze toying with his unbound hair. He smiled—that infuriatingly oblivious smile that made the Beast's insides clench every time he saw it—and saying nothing, indicated the Beast should join him.

As Beast took a seat, Brendan dipped a hand into the basket and pulled out a single, perfect blackberry. Slowly, his gaze not budging from Beast's, he bit into it, the rich color vibrant on his lips. Frozen, Beast could not take his eyes off Brendan's mouth, pink tongue flicking out to catch stray droplets of sweet juice. Beast wished he would say something; anything, wanted him to break this silence between them more than he could remember wanting anything in his long life.

Brendan offered a berry to Beast with a slight smile. His eyes were the blue-gray of mountains at a distance, of a horizon one was bound to seek.

The dream swirled and changed, color bleeding away until the world was black and white and savage. Beast ran on all fours over thick drifts of snow with a vague sense of loss, chasing something he could never catch.

* * *

Many rooms and an untellable number of hallways away, Brendan was not sleeping well. After some restless shifting, he pushed off the twisted sheets and tried to will himself to sleep. The rose, still blooming and perfect on the nightstand, caught the moonlight on its dark petals.

Why had Brendan gone and done something so abominably foolish as fall in love with the Beast?

With a muffled groan, he flipped over and buried his face in the goosedown pillow. A confusing mess of emotions eddied through him, all fighting for dominance. One second, elation sang with the heady joy of it, and then dropped him into paralyzing fear of what would happen if the Beast ever, *ever* found out. A swift stab of hope; could there be even the slightest possibility of the Beast actually returning his feelings? Hope drowned in the clamor of doubt, a litany of reasons why the Beast couldn't possibly care about Brendan, especially in *that* way. At the merest hint of what pleasures *that way* entailed, the swell of drunken happiness would resurface and start the whole blasted cycle over again.

He was the worst kind of fool.

There was no point in trying to get back to sleep. Brendan stood up and stuffed his feet into some boots. He needed to sort some things out, and there were only two people in the whole castle he could talk to about it. Given a generous definition of people.

* * *

The thick garden aroma did wonders to calm him. The rich scent of greenery and loam took Brendan back to his childhood, playing in the mud while his mother tended her flowers. One of the only clear memories of his mother he had.

The only light coming through the arched glass ceiling of the conservatory was the cool crescent of moonlight, silvering everything it touched as with a paintbrush. He knelt down at the edge of the pool, his light-fingered touch raising glistening ripples over the water.

"Excuse me," he called softly, "might I have a word?"

A slick dark shape slithered up to the surface in a lazy loop. "Ye may 'ave several. I sense wiv my awesome powers of omniscience ye can't sleep, right?" The black koi winked a bright, glassy eye at him.

"What astonishing insight. Where's your...associate?"

"Sleepin'."

Did fish sleep? How did they keep from floating to the top? If, indeed, the other fish was sleeping at all. It depended on whether or not he was being lied to, and Brendan had very little way of being sure. Another reason to look into the sleeping practices of fish.

"Lookin' a wee bit distracted," the fish noted with clear amusement.

"Sorry. Just...tired. Listen." He dug his hands into the mossy earth on either side of his knees. "I think I'm starting to understand what you were talking about earlier... You know. About. Love." He glanced around for eavesdroppers, then felt silly for doing so.

"Ah," said the black fish softly.

A gleaming white head broke the surface of the pool. "Oi, some of us are tryin' to sleep."

"Button it." The black fish bumped into the other. "'E wants to talk about you-know-wot."

"Ooh, finally. Was gettin' tired o' waitin'. Look," the fish said to Brendan, "there's not much we can tell ye in plain speech. There's laws an' things."

"I know, I know, the truth and lies caveat. That's fine. It's just... I have no one else to talk to." He looked away, feeling uncertain in a way he hadn't since he'd been a confused, scared youth.

Both koi watched Brendan, then shared an inscrutable, fishy look.

"There's naught we can tell ye about your partic'lar problem at 'and, luv—"

"—but we can tell ye a smidge more about the castle. A few mysteries ye don't already know."

"Oh? Like what?"

"Like, fer example, 'ave you ever wondered where all the food in this place comes from? Not like there's anyone skippin' off to market, right?"

"Yes! I have wondered!"

"It just so 'appens there's magic cupboards in the kitchen. Anythin' ye request will appear, and then the servants can cook it up a treat. Neat, eh?"

"Really? That's fascinating." Brendan's curiosity was already racing on ahead of him. "Anything at all? Could I request, I don't know, roasted crocodile, or something really exotic like that?"

"Sure can, squire. Even things not in season." For some reason, the white koi flashed a quick unreadable look at the other fish before it continued. "Y'know, like beets, or...blackberries."

"Really? Blackberries are my favorite. They only grow down by Lyon, and we could only get them fresh up north for a week or two in summer."

The black fish grinned. "Well, 'ere ye can! You just need to arsk."

Every time Brendan thought he had this place figured out, he discovered something new and wonderful. Not that any of this new information helped him wrestle with his tangle of emotions, but it was nice to be distracted from them.

"Thank you both."

"Oh, no, thank *you*," the white fish said in a syrupy tone.

"Well, we gotta get our beauty sleep, squire," added the black. "Off with ye."

"Of course. Good night. And thanks again."

With two identical splashes, the koi plunged under the water and did not resurface.

* * *

The next morning Brendan rifled through the wardrobe, nervously comparing each potential outfit against another, before realizing this all was getting downright silly.

He'd eaten meals with Beast before. This was but one more breakfast. He decided on a plain cobalt doublet to wear over a plain white shirt, and plain gray breeches tucked into plain black boots. There. Plain as anything. Not trying to look fetching or anything ridiculous.

He washed and shaved in the washbasin and pulled his hair back into a low tail. It was getting a bit too long to wear loose. He'd have to ask if the servants could trim it up.

His host was already seated when Brendan arrived in the dining room, the Beast leaning on his elbows and swirling a glass of *vin d'orange*. Brendan entered with a self-conscious tug at his doublet. Beast looked up from the fireplace with a small twist of the lips that just may have been a smile.

"Ah, there you are. Did you sleep well?"

Brendan was so distracted by that smallest of smiles he had to wrench his attention away to concentrate on getting in his chair. "Um, yes,"—a little white lie—"and yourself?"

Beast looked away quickly and sipped his drink. "Yes, fine. I take it you are recovered from your...episode?" Despite his gravelly tone, the glimmer in his russet eyes bespoke good humor.

"I feel much improved, thank you." Brendan tried to scrape up something else to say that wasn't too terribly stupid. Fortunately, the servants chose that moment to bring in breakfast. Brendan took a few bites of eggs in the building silence before breaking it with the first words that popped into his head. "Do your servants have any barbering skills?"

"Why, do you need a leeching?" Another miniature smile, fang tips barely showing.

Brendan returned the smile. "Your knowledge of the tonsorial arts is a little out of date. I just need a haircut." He pulled the end of his ponytail in front of his shoulder to demonstrate. "It's a bit longer than is acceptable."

Beast grunted. "Acceptable for whom?"

"Well... I don't know really. Standards of men's fashion."

Beast took a few bites of toast before saying, "You should leave it long. Grow it out."

Prickly from lack of sleep, Brendan was quick to bristle at the implication. Beast never took him seriously. "What's that supposed to mean? That I'm better off looking like a girl?"

Beast glared at him sharply. "What? No! I just meant it was common in my day for men to wear their hair quite long. That's all."

"Oh." Brendan rubbed his eyes. "Sorry, sorry, just a little tired still, I suppose."

Beast's ire evaporated. "You *were* quite ill. Gave us quite a scare."

"'Us'? Is that like the royal 'we'?" Brendan asked with a wry smile, chin propped on his hand.

Beast looked alarmed. "Why would you say that?"

"Oh, please." Brendan rolled his eyes. "I've figured out you're royalty. A prince, if I'm not mistaken. I'm not an idiot, you know." No sense in mentioning a certain book had helped along his hypothesis immensely.

"People who aren't idiots don't saunter out onto thin ice and nearly drown themselves."

"I was hardly sauntering." Cheeks hot, Brendan stabbed an errant slice of plum. He grasped for a change of subject. "You know what would be delightful? Some blackberries with breakfast."

Beast's head slowly rose, his eyes wide.

Brendan smiled reassuringly, not sure what caused Beast's poleaxed expression. "I mean, you know, not for today, obviously. How about tomorrow? You can get them here, yes? We could share some. Maybe with some sweet cream."

Beast shoved his chair back and stood up without his usual grace, nearly clumsy. "I must go!"

Brendan's heart sank as he stood up, too. "Did I say something wrong?"

Beast didn't quite meet his eyes. "No! You just...finish your breakfast. I forgot...I had something to attend to. I'll just...go do that."

Beast spun on his heel and was almost out the door before Brendan called after him, "Wait!"

Beast turned back, arms crossed over his thick chest, his aggravation an intangible but effective shield. "What?"

Brendan twisted his hands together. "I... I'll be in the music room practicing in an hour or so. Would you...care to join me?"

The tips of Beast's ears flicked forward. "Yes, all right." He stood there another second more before making his getaway.

* * *

Beast would have been mortified to confess to anyone (if he possessed any acquaintances other than the one presently plaguing him) the matter he had so desperately needed to attend to was a bout of forceful, frustrated pacing across the thick rug of one of the castle's many parlors. Head spinning from more than the repetitive motion, he flung himself into a heavy wooden chair and stared bemusedly at the now-shredded floral pattern of the rug.

Damn.

Doubtless, the invisible servants had heard Brendan's request, and doubtless, it would be fulfilled. Without question, the master of the house had absolute will and Beast could prevent it if he chose, but...he could not bring himself to do it.

Truth to tell, Beast had not eaten so well in more years than calendars could contain since Brendan's arrival. He'd had no need; he hunted himself, and if he did not, he bid the servants bring him meat, sometimes thick breads or cheeses, simple things that rended well under fangs and claws.

Blackberries. How long had it been since Beast had tasted blackberries? He could not say.

Beast hadn't even really remembered the details of his dream until that moment, only recalled strange and dim sensations. But the mere mention had filled his senses with the too-vivid memories of a dream he'd been glad to forget.

Of course his infuriating, unexpected guest would have known just the right thing to say to make Beast question himself. Of course there would be some convenient little aberration to throw Beast's plans awry and damn him to untellable eons more of solitude, trapped in a body so familiar he could only recall his original form in dreams.

His castle was a prison. A living one, one that changed at will to keep Beast caged. Now it had given him dreams of temptations, things he never before would have called such, and dangled the possibility of seeing them realized. What could it be but a test, the way the snow had been? The question was: had he failed it? Should he have been stalwart from the beginning and sent the boy back to his home? Sent for the girl?

Or perhaps...perhaps, before a heart so cold and feral and dusty as his own could learn to love, it needed to open to something simpler.

Beast's first true friend. No wonder he was getting ahead of himself with the wrong person in mind. It wasn't the boy's fault, surely; the magic was as much to blame as either of them. But still, it didn't sit right, the thought of having her brought here now when Brendan was still recovering, still acclimating. Perhaps bringing the girl would be too much, an axe blow to the tender new sapling of their friendship.

No. No, but he was wrong, he *had* to be wrong. What better time than now? With friendship newly forged, good spirits between them, finally reaching an amicable accord.

Brendan's words from last night rang in his head; *'So what it all boils down to, Beast, is what kind of person do you want to be? Alone and superior in the great, dark void? I imagine that must be a very lonely and frightening world to live in.'* With only that handful of speech, he'd introduced another way of living, offered a sliver of hope into an otherwise bleak existence.

It was a realization as surprising as it was terrifying, that Beast no longer wished to be alone.

* * *

Later, Brendan favored the Beast with a demonstration on the refurbished harpsichord while his host reclined against a silk divan.

The song was difficult, especially with the improvisations Brendan had to make to work around the broken string. However, the rest of the notes Brendan had labored so hard to tune sounded quite divine, if he did say so himself. He closed his eyes to savor the melody, head bowed over the keys, chestnut curls escaping their tail to brush his cheek. The cut there had healed without a mark, as Beast had predicted.

Fingers flying over the keys, Brendan refined the details of his Plan. He had carefully chosen the perfect song to play on the lute after the harpsichord. A mournful Irish folk song that sang sweetly about love, but also warned life was too short to waste one second of it. In addition, it had been a song Brendan learned in the months *after* Kieran had left him, which was of vital importance.

With a flourish, Brendan played the finale of the cantata, the last note reverberating through the room.

Beast looked up with a muted murmur. Brendan performed a joking half-seated bow; he'd hoped for more of a reaction. He had been playing at his able best, after all.

"Very fine. Do you feel hale enough to play something more?" Beast asked as Brendan traded the bench for a chaise lounge.

BRENDAN & THE BEAST

"Oh, I think I can struggle my way through another song." Brendan smiled as he checked the tuning of the lute. Beast's answering smile was done more with his eyes than with lips, but Brendan's pulse quickened nonetheless. He ducked his head over the strings to hide the flush in his cheeks.

The servants brought cups of hot chocolate, a decadence Brendan had only enjoyed once at the fanciest of parties at his university. It tasted like liquid gold as it ran down his throat, but he focused on the large bulk of Beast as he drank, wondering how those lips would compare in sweetness. It must have been ages since the man was last kissed. Surely he had been, before?

Beast lifted his cup with a pointed "Thank you," while rolling an eye back at Brendan.

He beamed. Beast's gaze snapped away to fix on the small cup dwarfed in his hands.

Brendan cleared his throat. It was a good Plan. It would work. He strummed a few clear notes, plucked up his courage, and began to sing.

"Cold blows the wind over my true love,
And gently drops the rain.
I've never had but one true love,
And in green-wood he lies slain..."

Now, in his Plan, after Brendan had finished the song, Beast would look surprised. Maybe he'd lift an eyebrow in that compelling way he had and say something like, "Are you sure you got the lyrics right? The beloved ghost and the bereaved were both men." Then Brendan would look at him archly and maybe with just the smallest fraction of a seductive smile, say "Oh, I got the lyrics right."

Here things got a little sketchy on the details, but Brendan's Plan came back into sharp focus when Beast would say something like, "The song is right! Why are we wasting time? I am completely interested in ravishing you this very second," and then the Plan got very, very focused indeed.

But instead the Beast just sat there peering at his chocolate, with the same expression of mild approval he wore after every song Brendan played. What was he supposed to do now? The Plan pivoted on the Beast's reaction! The

148

Plan was being ruined! What about the Plan?!

"What did you think?" he blurted, hand still spread over lute strings.

The Beast looked up and tilted his head to the side, a trifle vaguely. "A good tune." He fell silent, looking pensive.

Brendan wanted to scream. "You weren't really listening, were you?"

"No." Beast swirled his chocolate, now gone cold. "I was...thinking."

Exasperated, Brendan waited in vain for anything more. "About?"

Beast looked as if he would speak, stopped, and drank more of his chocolate. Brendan watched in confusion as Beast repeated the actions all over again—open mouth, close mouth, sip chocolate—as if he were trying to put off breaking bad news. He was about to crack the silence himself when Beast abruptly rose to his feet and gave Brendan a companionable clap on the shoulder.

"Nothing, nothing. We can discuss it later." Beast paused, hand still lingering on Brendan's shoulder, the touch radiating heat.

Brendan sat perfectly still with breath caught in his throat, not wanting to make a single move to startle the Beast, as if the touch were a wild bird he held in his hand. It was the first time the Beast had voluntarily touched him when he wasn't furious or when Brendan wasn't in danger of dying.

Beast tore his hand away and bowed a tiny fraction, a regal, archaic gesture. "Thank you for playing. I did quite enjoy it. You must play me more of that style. We really had nothing like it in my time."

Brendan bowed back as well as he could sitting down with a lute on his lap. "Of course."

"I will see you at dinner." Another very small, very formal bow, and the Beast left.

* * *

Brendan spent the rest of his afternoon enjoying a brisk ride with Jean-Luc, taking a light lunch in his rooms, and perusing Plato in the library. All these pursuits, neither equestrian, gastronomical, nor scholarly would distract him from thinking about the Beast. His hands. His smile. His voice— God,

149

that voice!

Brendan had, in weeks past, been able to rationalize his fascination with the Beast as purely scientific. But he couldn't keep lying to himself—his interests were anything but academic. He sighed, setting the book down next to the library armchair, the slanting rays of the sunset cutting coppery paths across the room.

He didn't exactly know how it had happened, but it would be foolish for him to deny it had. Even as ridiculous and impossible as he knew his hopes were, his thoughts lingered. Wonder if those fangs would get in the way when kissed…

Brendan shook his head, trying to clear it in vain. Really, what was the best he could hope for? Would Beast even understand his advances? Would he understand them and be insulted to the point of rage? Even worse, would he feel sorry for Brendan, think he was sick, look at him with disgust—or worse of all, pity?

But haven't there been hopeful signs? Lingering glances, touches…

Beast was likely just terribly lonely. Would Brendan be taking advantage of his long years of solitude? And would he be in some way helping to keep Beast locked in his castle, as wondrous a place as Brendan may find it, keeping him from finding a way to break the terrible curse laid upon him?

And, of course, more practically, there was the dilemma of anatomy. Exactly how much of the Beast was…a beast? Was it wrong to find Beast attractive, with his horns and fur and clawed hands? Probably not, as he was attracted to the man, not the mane. He liked how Beast looked in spite of those features, not because of them.

It was all a moot point anyway, Brendan sharply castigated himself. It was laughable to think the Beast was brewing a secret desire for Brendan, too, when he barely tolerated him. But what if…

Brendan scrubbed a hand over his face, groaning. He had not been lying when he told Beast he was well aware of his own flaws. Rating somewhere below his stubbornness but not as high as his impulsive tongue, he was a champion at over-thinking an issue for so long the offending problem had long gotten bored and wandered off of its own volition. He was doing it now, tying himself into knots over things that would never come to be.

What did he have to lose, in trying? The Beast wouldn't harm him—Brendan somehow knew this with a certainty rooted deep down into his very bones—so what really did he have to fear? The loss of his pride and vanity? He could do without those. A broken heart? He'd lived through that once. He could live through it again.

But he'd never know what he might have had if he didn't try.

* * *

It was nearly a new moon, and the conservatory was in fine form. The cool scent of jasmine enfolded Brendan in its aromatic embrace as he wended his way down the path, admiring the lambent glow of white roses in the sliver of waning moonlight.

Dinner had been savory pheasant in tarragon sauce, with garden vegetables tossed with lemon juice and olive oil. Conversation had been as light as the meal. Beast had inquired after how Brendan had occupied his day, which led to a long discussion over dry white wine on the merits of the *Republic* as it compared to the *Symposium*. The whole time Brendan had been acutely aware of himself, second-guessing the way he held his wineglass or the way he spoke as if Beast would suddenly see his intentions written on his forehead.

As he ambled around a vine-covered marble column, he froze. A handful of steps away, Beast sat on one of the low benches hidden within the flora. His large hand cradled one delicate rose blossom, his dark eyes cast in darker shadow. Brendan debated whether to join or creep away, but Beast turned toward him, a single ear flicking back.

"I heard you coming." Beast's eyes had a slight green glow of a cat's. Brendan suddenly remembered the term from one of his lessons: *chatoyance*. "Are you enjoying the garden?"

Brendan swallowed his apprehension and stepped closer. "Very much. Do you...often come here at night?"

"Yes. The jasmine," Beast said by way of explanation. Brendan followed

151

his gaze to one of the twisty trees, spangled all over with flowers like little white stars. "They bloom only at night."

"They're very lovely."

"Don't stand there like an idiot. Come and sit."

Brendan hesitated.

"Don't worry, I'm not angry. I am gratified someone else enjoys my garden as much as I do."

Brendan perched on the far end of the bench. He could act normal while seated next to the object of his affections among starlight and the soft perfume of night flowers, in what was surely the most romantic setting known to man. No problem.

"I don't often get to show it off," Beast added with a twinkle of good humor, and it took a moment for Brendan to mentally catch the thread of their continuing conversation.

"Well, gardens aren't something I get to talk about often, either." Brendan's fingertips bit into the edge of the marble bench. Beast looked at him in inquiry. "Oh, it's…it's nothing. Just…" He sighed. "My father didn't like me to bring them up."

"Why not?"

"Because of my mother, I think. When I was very little, she would take me out to her flower garden and I'd help her plant and weed. She loved flowers. Tended to the manor garden herself, wouldn't hire anyone to do it. After she died, Father dug it all up. Put in cobbles." Brendan pushed at a loose thread on his breeches. "I think it hurt him to be reminded of her. So, whenever I'd mention greenery of any sort, he'd take the opportunity to belittle me as much as possible. He said flowers were only suitable to give to girls you wished to court. Because only girls like flowers."

One of Beast's thick brows quirked in disbelief. "I had known the man was a fool, but I hadn't realized the enormity of his ignorance. Are the splendors of God's green earth restricted to only one gender?" The sweep of his hand encompassed all the life around them, from the glistening pond to the fragrant jasmine. "I've always believed an appreciation for growing things showed strength of character."

152

Brendan smiled, warmth kindling in his belly. After a moment of companionable silence, Beast asked in a low rumble, "You were very young, then. Do you still miss her?"

"My mother?" He took a long breath before best deciding how to answer. "I always miss her. Not a second goes by where I don't feel this little ache, here, behind my heart." He put a hand to his chest, tapping the crest of his breastbone. "Most times I don't remember it's there. But then I see or smell something that reminds me of her, and it throbs, like...like a cut on your fingertip."

Beast peered at Brendan, a little aghast. "How can you live like that?"

Brendan's mouth opened on a sharp retort.

"No, don't... Let me explain." Beast held up a palm, looking for all the world like a man who had drawn idly at a string only to find it attached to a great tangled ball he was now obliged to sort out. "Isn't it better to let it go? To be free of that pain, rather than loving so fiercely you still feel the loss of it after so long? How can it be worth it?"

"That's the stupidest question I've ever heard. Of course it's worth it. Every second."

"I don't understand. I certainly don't miss my parents. Of course, I don't think I'd ever spent more than ten minutes alone with either of them in my whole life. I was raised by nursemaids and tutors."

Brendan watched Beast's rueful expression, his mood softening. He'd been lonely long before he'd been a beast, then. "The price of power, hmm?"

"Something like that." Beast tipped his face up to the slim curve of the moon with an unreadable look in his chatoyant eyes.

Brendan took a deep breath and made a decision. Beast's question had sealed it for him; was the risk worth it?

His answer was a most emphatic *yes.*

Brendan scooted closer. "I've enjoyed our conversation, but I think I shall retire. Good night, Beast." Heart in his throat, Brendan leaned in and gave Beast a small peck on the lips, throwing all his careful caution to the wind.

Brendan's breath caught. It had been only the lightest touch, a scarce press of dry lips, but it felt as if lightning had struck straight through him, or like he'd been submerged again in that frozen pond with the shock of impact thrumming through his bones.

He pulled away, heart threatening to punch through his ribcage, and looked up into the Beast's luminous eyes. Over them, golden brows crashed together, and Beast opened his mouth on what might be query or protest or...

He kissed Beast again, harder this time, desperate to shut him up and quick, his fingertips at the corner of Beast's sharp jaw. Beast went utterly still. Then he fisted a hand in Brendan's collar and kissed him back.

He kissed back. Brendan might die on the spot from that one simple truth, that Beast was actually and truly *kissing him back*. The sudden searing rush, lips moving firm against his, the fabric of his doublet tightening under Beast's grasp, the scent of jasmine and musk thick in his nose. It felt like all the air in the greenhouse had been stolen away, the only breath left what they shared between them. Brendan gasped and pressed closer.

Beast jerked away. Quietly, with no expression, he husked, "Good night," and left Brendan alone in the garden.

14

In Which There is Friendship

That night Brendan had very interesting dreams indeed, dreams that left him flushed and wanting upon waking. At home, in the privacy of his cramped attic bedroom, he would have thought nothing of finding a little ease at his own convenience. But here he could never be sure if he was truly alone. Nothing to take the wind out of his sails, as it were, like the thought of an invisible voyeur.

With a sigh, Brendan rolled out of bed and performed his morning ablutions before dressing. The thought of breakfast made him more nervous than he had been since the very first one, back when he still hadn't been sure if the Beast would eat him or not. After the events of the previous night, Brendan had no idea what to expect. Maybe he should skip breakfast today.

He really hadn't planned on that kiss. He'd had a vague, nascent idea of courting Beast slowly, building up a strong friendship that would naturally lead to something more; but it just *happened*. He hadn't been thinking, raw from Beast's probing questions and the way Beast sat there looking so…looking so *kissable*.

Brendan sighed. What's done was done. He'd committed to seeing this through to whatever end, and bore himself up straight and tall. Perhaps it was unwise, but he couldn't bring himself to regret what he had done. It'd been a pretty sensational kiss.

An invisible servant brought him a comb. Brendan brushed out his night tangles and searched the vanity for the ribbon he had placed there last night.

"Excuse me, but do you happen to know where I can find something to tie up my hair?"

A soft breeze brushed by him. All the drawers of the vanity opened, and a big show was made of wind ruffling through each one. After only a few seconds, the drawers shut themselves and the breeze whisked by Brendan's arm as if in apology. It was very strange, as there had been new hair ribbons readily supplied for him so far. What reason would the servants have in hiding such an innocuous thing?

He shrugged. No matter. He'd just have to wear his hair loose. He had far bigger—and furrier—concerns on his mind.

* * *

When Brendan walked into the dining hall, it was with his head held high and shoulders square and unashamed. Relief and disappointment warred within him when Beast's usual chair proved empty. A quick search revealed he wasn't anywhere else in the room, or out on the balcony, either. Brendan opened the glass doors of the balcony, surveying the white-blanketed grounds. Numerous tiny bird tracks traced their journey on the wide stone rail through a new layer of fresh snow, but no sign of Beast.

The aroma of eggs and ham finally caught Brendan's attention. He sat and noticed a small scrap of paper atop his plate. The writing was cramped and old-fashioned.

It snowed but little last night, and the morning is clear and cold. Excellent hunting weather. Expect me back no later than noontide. Enjoy breakfast.
-B

A bowl of blackberries waited beside his plate, as well as a small pitcher of cream. Delighted, Brendan set the note aside and did as he was told.

Afterward, he threw on his cloak and headed toward the stables. A servant provided him with a woolen scarf long enough to wrap around his throat thrice. Sufficiently muffled, Brendan enjoyed the sound of the glittering, powdery snow crunching under his boots. He and Beauty used to call it 'diamond snow' when it laid itself thick and sparkling on the veranda of their nursery, when they were very young and their father very wealthy. They would fling handfuls of it at each other before their governess had ushered them back inside, clucking about pneumonia.

One winter Beauty had been severely scolded for dumping a bucketful of snow in the twins' beds. Brendan smiled under his scarf, remembering Catherine's indignant shriek. It had echoed throughout the entire manor and even gotten Father out of his office; a nearly unheard-of occurrence in those days.

The stable was warm and smelled reassuringly of fresh hay and horse. Brendan slid the door shut behind him and unlooped the scarf from his face. Jean-Luc nickered with excitement as Brendan lifted the latch of his stall to let himself in. The big horse bumped his nose against Brendan's chest, and they both enjoyed a few minutes of companionable ear-scratching. A blanket had been secured around Jean-Luc, and the horse had been given a pail of still-steaming hot mash.

"Glad to see they're treating you well, old boy." He patted the broad neck as the horse went back to lipping up mash. Jean-Luc had been one of the best things Brendan's father had bargained for, after losing the family fortune and moving out to the provinces. Not very fast and not much to look at; but ever dependable, never balking at any task the d'Aumales had set before him, whether it be yoke, plow, or saddle.

Fingers tangled in coarse mane, Brendan leaned his forehead against the warm column of Jean-Luc's neck, breathing in the familiar horsey smell. "I wonder if you miss them all, too. Never thought *I* would, that's for sure."

Brendan decided against going for a ride, leaving Jean-Luc to his cozy stall and warm blanket, tucking his chin into the scarf to escape the icy bite of the wind as he walked back to the castle. There was maybe an hour before noon, and he wanted to be sure to catch Beast when he came back from his hunt.

Once changed out of winter clothes, Brendan tucked Beowulf under his arm and asked the hallway to take him to the main parlor, which it did with amazing alacrity. Still marveling over that particular miracle, he settled

157

down in a relatively untorn chair. The mutilated furniture and torn wall hangings stood in stark contrast to the refined white wood paneling and finely carved mantle that hinted at the parlor's better days.

The first time Brendan had been in this room, he had been exhausted, dripping with freezing rain, and still in shock over his first glimpse of the Beast. Now he placed his hand over five great tears on the armrest, and his hand outstretched to its limit couldn't quite span their width. After a few moments of contemplation, he opened his book and got busy reading.

Beowulf had just suffered a dragon bite when Brendan heard approaching footsteps. The Beast stomped heavily into the room, clutching his left arm close to his body. With barely a glance at Brendan, he stalked over to the fireplace and threw himself into an armchair. His jacket sleeve had been torn away, exposing a wide gash.

"Your arm!" Brendan dropped the book and stood up. "What happened?"

"Elk," Beast grunted. He hunched over his injured forearm and licked it.

Brendan clucked his tongue in an unconscious imitation of his old governess. "What are you doing? Stop that. It's going to get infected." He drew close, assessed the damage, and asked the servants to bring hot water and bandages.

"I'm fine," grumbled the Beast, turning away. Brendan knelt and took Beast's arm, tearing off the tattered remains of the sleeve in an eyeblink. "It is nothing!" Beast snatched back his arm and wouldn't meet Brendan's eyes.

"Stop being so stubborn. You helped me when I got attacked by a rogue harpsichord *and* fished me out of a freezing pond. Let me help you. We're friends, aren't we?" Brendan tucked his unbound hair out of the way behind his ears, smiling up at Beast. "Don't you trust me?"

Beast stared for a few long moments. Wordlessly, he stuck out his arm.

Brendan smiled and began cleaning the gash. He bandaged it, touching only where necessary, barely refraining from running his fingers through the short silky fur on Beast's arm.

In short order, Brendan sat back on his heels with a satisfied nod. "There. Not too shabby a job, if I do say so myself." Brushing off his breeches, he stood and returned to his chair, giving Beast some space. Never smart to crowd a wounded animal, and Beast seemed precariously close to that line at present. Brendan glanced at the hand-shaped claw marks on the armrest and kept his tone light. "A keepsake from the one that got away?"

Beast's frozen expression thawed, and his huge shoulders dropped, tension draining out of them. Brendan was learning to read him correctly, it seemed.

"It does happen occasionally," Beast murmured, running a talon over the neat white bandages. A servant brought in a new coat, this one a fine brocaded blue with silver edging. He shrugged off the one-armed jacket and put on the new one, adjusting the fall of his shirt collar underneath. "This buck was quite a giant. His rack of antlers nearly cleared the treetops." He shot Brendan a sideways smirk.

Brendan grinned. He recognized a good old hunting tall tale when he heard one, and waved encouragement for Beast to continue.

"I began to give chase, but this buck wouldn't move. He bellowed loud enough to shake a few stars from the sky and charged me. I dodged, but he was damned fast. Sliced me like a fine cheese with one of his fifty points."

"He didn't run?" Brendan leaned forward, rapt. "He came at you?"

Beast nodded, watching the fire. "The males can be very dangerous when they're in rut."

Brendan looked away, red creeping up his cheeks.

"I should have known better," Beast admitted. "I was...perhaps a bit foolhardy to even consider him suitable prey. I'm glad he'll be out there still, siring good strong fawns to make fine sport in a year or two. Why were you in here, anyway? The parlor lacks the amusements of the music room or the library." He glanced around at the shabby surroundings as if noticing them for the first time.

Brendan cleared his throat and looked at his hands, clasped in his lap. "I was here waiting for you, actually."

Beast tensed up again. "Oh?"

"I wanted to ask you,"—Brendan's courage quailed, and he changed his mind at the last moment—"if you'd like to try riding Jean-Luc." An offer he'd truly been considering, just not what he'd planned to say at this moment.

159

Every single one of Brendan's carefully laid, logically mapped plans had fallen flat, whereas allowing his impulses to take the reins had gone, thus far, surprisingly well.

Beast couldn't have looked more shocked if Brendan had suggested he grow a new tail. "What?"

"I know he's not as fine as the horses you're used to, but, you know, I thought… He's a good mount, and I thought you'd like to. Um. Ride. Again. It's fine if you don't want to, I just thought—"

"You thought I'd like to ride again." The sentence rolled on Beast's tongue as if he were tasting a new wine and found the vintage good. "Yes. I would." An actual smile flashed over his leonine face so fast it might have been imagined.

Brendan stood up with a courtly bow, only a little teasing. "Shall we then, good sir?"

Beast rose from his chair, shaking his head. "You're mad, you know that?" He turned to leave, not bothering to check if Brendan was following, which of course, he was.

* * *

Jean-Luc stamped nervously as the Beast approached.

"There, there, my friend." Brendan gave the draft horse a reassuring pat. The texture of his voice deepened, the way it did when he sang, rich and soothing. Realizing his own ears were pricked far forward to catch every note, Beast shook himself and stepped forward with a palmful of sweet dried apples.

When the horse was calmed, Beast mounted up. Brendan murmured praise and handed the reins up to Beast before stepping away. Under him, the horse shifted, hoofing the frozen ground with an eager whuffle of breath.

He was in a saddle again. It had been a long, long time.

"You're smiling." Brendan tipped his head to one side, nearly grinning himself.

Beast sat up a little straighter in the saddle. He tried an imperious glare

160

he suspected didn't come off as such. "Well, what of it?"

Brendan wordlessly shook his head, watching from a relaxed lean against the fence lining the riding path.

Mollified, Beast gathered up the reins and kicked the horse into a walk. Despite the long decades, it took only seconds for his body to remember how to move, how to react, how to feel what the horse was feeling, shifting his weight along with every step.

His elation must have shown on his face, because Brendan chuckled through the ridiculous scarf obscuring most of his chin. The chilly breeze tugged his hair into an auburn halo. "Oh, go ahead. Take him for a run."

"Are you sure?" Muscles bunched under him, the horse as eager to be moving as he was.

"Yes, I'm sure. Go, already! Jean-Luc is champing at the bit!" A wide grin flashed at him over the woolen scarf, and Beast returned it without consciously deciding to do so. He was in no way prepared to think about what had happened between them last night; or indeed, even admit to himself anything out of the ordinary had happened at all. But something fluttered in his stomach at the sight of that bright smile, at the ease with which he'd given one back.

"*Yah!*"

Jean-Luc burst into a canter, mane streaming, his hooves cutting up platter-sized chunks of frozen turf as they raced down the wide path. Beast laughed aloud at the ecstasy of flight.

He glanced back. Brendan watched him gallop, expression rapt.

It had been a long, long time since Beast had been in a saddle. But it'd been even longer since someone had given him a gift.

* * *

Beast remembered the next few days as a series of moments.

The Library

The afternoon rays slanted bright across the library, dust motes dancing in the air.

"Here, listen to this." Brendan read out an amusing passage from his book, a fictional account of a wandering Visigoth pilgrim. Beast found, somewhat to his surprise, he enjoyed listening, as that trained musician's voice made Brendan a fine orator.

Beast set his own book down open in his lap. "Do go on."

His guest flashed him a small smile and continued to read.

The next day, Beast searched out a passage he'd always liked to read aloud to Brendan, who listened with such captivated focus that Beast sought out another, and another.

Days that had once felt painfully eternal no longer seemed long enough.

The Music Room

"What in God's name are you doing?" Beast asked, making it clear he would have been no less shocked to find Jean-Luc in Brendan's place, standing in the middle of the music room instructing Beast's servants to replace furniture.

Brendan stood with hips canted to one side, a finger against his pointed chin as he watched a plush divan float into place. "Oh, hello. I'm switching out the old, torn-up stuff in here for undamaged things. I think the servants have hidden storerooms full of fresh furniture. A little to the left, I think," he added to the floating divan.

Beast puffed up in indignation, his tail lashing once. "Why?"

"I did mention the furnishings were old and torn-up, didn't I? I started asking them if they could repair the tapestries—"

"They're servants, not wizards."

Brendan ignored the interruption. "—and then if there were suitable replacements they could bring. Doesn't it look better in here?"

Beast started to glance around dismissively, but blinked. It *did* look better. Brighter, shinier, less tattered. Funny how he never noticed how claustrophobic the room had become. "I...suppose I have no objections."

"Good," Brendan said with a disarming grin. "Because I've already done the parlor in the east wing."

The Game Room

A midmorning ride had become their custom on clear days, and while walking back, Brendan pointed at an open door along the hall. "What's in here?"

"That? That's the game room."

"You never told me you had a game room!" Brendan lightly shoved Beast's shoulder in reproach.

Beast stood stunned as the young man brushed past to enter the room. So casually he had done that; given him a playful push, as if such a thing weren't extraordinary at all. His palm brushed the swell of his upper arm, over the ghost of Brendan's touch.

"Come on, let's play something."

Beast could not think of a good reason why they shouldn't. Beast won Fox and Geese by the barest degree, followed by Brendan declaring victory at Nine Men's Morris, though it was by another slim margin.

His guest was much better at gaming than his father had been, though it would perhaps please Beast more if he were just *slightly* less adept at them; Beast disliked losing.

He suggested Rithmomachia, which he was certain he would win.

"Rithmomachia?"

"Yes, haven't you heard of it?" In his day, Rithmomachia was required learning in all schools.

"Of course I've *heard* of it. My grandfather was very keen, I recall. But I've never played it. No one plays Rithmomachia anymore!"

"What? No one plays The Philosopher's Game? The finest exercise in mathematics and strategy? Widely regarded as the greatest game of all time?"

Brendan leaned his chin onto his palm. He had fine, long-fingered hands Beast tried not to stare at as they drummed a brief tattoo against his lips. "I believe they stopped teaching it after the invention of the zero, and fractions and integers, things of that ilk." He cast an encouraging smile through his fingers. "They teach chess now, though."

Though discomfited, Beast set up the chess board. Unbelievable this poor

163

substitute could have replaced the Philosopher's Game. Chess certainly couldn't allow one to find harmony within the Pythagorean theory, could it?

After half an hour it was abundantly clear Beast was well on his way to losing this inferior game, and feeling old and out-of-touch, he smacked the board off the table with a snarl. Pieces showered the ground, the board coming to rest upside down at Brendan's feet.

The other man merely looked at him, unimpressed, and it inspired an unexpected flicker of shame. "I, uh." Beast thought quickly. "I saw a bug."

The corner of Brendan's mouth twitched. "You saw a bug."

Beast sat sternly with all the dignity he could muster, then sighed. "You are a good player," he said, though the admission cost him. Brendan's face pinked, lips pressing tight as if trying to conceal a brilliant smile. Beast wished he wouldn't.

"So are you." Brendan bent to pick up the board, and servants helpfully set the pieces back into their squares. "When you take the time to think things through. You rush headlong into the thick of things, with no regard for strategy or subtlety."

"Yes, well. I wouldn't count subtlety as one of my more evident traits."

"No, I suppose not." They laughed together for a moment. Brendan took a deep breath, squaring his shoulders as if stoically resigned to his fate. "All right, teach me Rithmomachia, then."

And Beast felt a glowing warmth he told himself was friendship.

Beast's Bedroom

His dreams were back to shadows and sounds, the familiar dreamscape of sensation with no true shape. The hot, pulsing rush of the hunt, as familiar as the long years he had endured.

But then the nature of the dream shifted, almost imperceptibly at first, but then became quite clearly a different kind of hunt altogether. An ache blossomed with vivid flashes of color and barely-formed glimpses of something very like sweat-slicked skin. This was not the savage glimpse of dream violence that would only be soothed by a real hunt, but a very different ache, indeed.

Though Beast couldn't see, not properly, the way he saw with his waking eyes, he could still *feel*. He could feel—

Jerking awake, the Beast threw out a blindly flung claw. A bed curtain tore from its moorings with a shredding of seams. His breath cut a rasping, heavy swath through the silence of the night as he sat stark upright, sweat cold under his fur. The dream had left behind a familiar whisper of jasmine and cedarwood that soon faded from Beast's mind, leaving nothing but a dull, lonely ache.

The Parlor

The days had grown short and dark, winter now in full swing. When the snow grew thick and the evening wind too cold even for his thick pelt, Beast listened to Brendan play. Elegant hands moving over keys or strings, deft and graceful, creating music out of nothingness.

His favorites were the times Brendan played violin; he could play anything with strings, as he'd boasted before, and not without cause. But his ease with a violin was something else. In Beast's time, a virtuoso of his skill would have been invited to play at the finest courts and paid well for it. Had the outside world changed so much that the bearer of such talent could only aspire as high as 'getting a job' to 'support his family'?

Beast looked down at his own hands. The curved claws could retract a little, not as much as a cat's might, but were every bit as wickedly sharp. He extended them to their utmost. How long it had taken to relearn holding a wineglass, turning a page, even how to dress with these deadly claws. What were these hands good for? Certainly not for creating anything.

He watched Brendan with envy until it struck him: he'd never done *anything* useful with his hands, even before he'd been cursed and changed. Beast had never done anything useful, period. He'd go out hunting with hounds and hawks, never needing to draw a bow himself. He'd listen to minstrels play in this very room, never bothering to pick up a lute himself. He'd read books others had written when the weather was too bad to hunt, and only when absolutely unavoidable, he had ruled.

In fact, now the Beast thought about it, the only impact he'd ever had was temporarily lessening the amount of wildlife in his forests and dog-earing pages.

* * *

Late afternoon grew into evening; colorful slats of sunlight filtering through the stained glass library windows dimmed and faded, but Brendan did not notice.

Only a flicker at the corner of his eye drew his attention from *A History of Finnish Sagas and Norse Eddas*, as a servant lit the lamps and sconces around the room. A fine, brass oil lamp at Brendan's elbow threw plenty of light onto the pages. The warm glow made the library feel cozy and close, enormous though it truly was.

He stared for a moment at the flickering flame as it danced on its wick. Beauty had wanted one of these. What was she doing right now?

Was she reading by the light of a cheap tallow candle? Did she look up from her book and think of him, of her lost brother? Had she waited for a letter, for any kind of sign? It must be about…two months, Brendan realized with a start, since he had left in the night. Did she think he must be dead? Was she wracked with guilt that her brother had gone in her place?

"She's going to kill me," he muttered to himself.

"Hmm? Who's killing whom?" Beast's head rose from his thick tome. Brendan jumped a little and flushed with embarrassment.

He'd been cautious not to mention Beauty, unwilling to tread on treacherous footing, but Beast was his friend, wasn't he? Who better to confide in? With some trepidation, Brendan said, "Beauty. When she was going to sneak off. I…gave her tea laced with poppy syrup."

"You *drugged* her?"

"Just a little! Just to…knock her out," Brendan said miserably. "So she wouldn't follow me. She must have been furious when she woke up. I feel awful about it, to be honest." He didn't look up as the silence stretched out between them, gnawing at his lower lip. He knew it; he'd ruined everything by bringing her up.

Beast heaved a sigh and closed his book. "You did it to protect her." His tone was unusually placid, and as Brendan looked up, he couldn't read the Beast's veiled expression.

"Kind of you to say."

"Would you— Never mind," Beast grumbled.

"No, would I what? Please continue."

Beast took a deep breath and spoke all in a rush as if plunging into cold water to get the shock over and done with. "Would you like to see her in the magic mirror?" Brendan had become accustomed to Beast's tiny little tells; he was hiding a great deal of nervousness.

Brendan considered carefully. On the one hand, suppose seeing Beauty would rekindle Beast's interest and thereby put an end to Brendan's extended stay? What if Beast found her to be very beautiful indeed? On the other hand...

"Yes, please. I would very much like to make sure she's all right."

Beast stood up and straightened the cuffs of his shirt. Brendan had noticed, not without appreciation, that Beast had lately left off wearing an over-jacket unless he was venturing outdoors.

"The mirror is being kept in a room of my suite. You can have a look, and then retire with your mind at ease." Beast didn't exactly smile, but it was close enough to make Brendan's heart skip in his chest. His heart did all kinds of foolish things around Beast. "Follow me."

The walk was short, the hallways changing to suit their master's fancy, neatly bypassing three flights of stairs to lead them to a set of gray doors. Two grimacing gargoyles peered down from alcoves above, lintels inscribed with sinuous dragons and other fantastic beasts. Several gouges marred the paint.

Beast pushed open the doors and stood aside to let Brendan in first. Beast cleared his throat, running a clawed hand through his shaggy hair. "You can wait here in the foyer. I'll...go get the mirror." He turned to another door, then added as if in afterthought, "Make yourself comfortable."

When he left, Brendan felt free to gawk. Beast's own suite!

167

The foyer was large and opulently decorated, mostly in grays and silvers, though as torn and neglected as everything else in the castle. Pairs of tall candelabras guarded each of the three closed doors leading out of the foyer and further into the suite. There wasn't much else to look at, so Brendan sank down into a sofa only to immediately come back up, coughing at the cloud arising with him.

As he patted the dust off his clothes, the Beast stepped back out into the foyer. "Ah. Sorry about that. Here." He proffered the mirror at arm's length. Brendan took it, enchanted warmth prickling up his wrist.

"I… Thank you, Beast."

Beast shrugged with an air of carelessness. Brendan inspected the mirror, uncertain.

"I can leave, if you'd prefer," murmured Beast with unusual perspicacity.

"No, I just… How do I make it work? I tell it what I want, and it does it?"

"Pretty much. Go on, then. It won't bite you."

Brendan held the mirror up and, feeling a little foolish, spoke to his reflection. "I would like to see my sister. Wait, I've got three. Um, Beauty, please." He ignored Beast's amused snort.

The handle warmed in his palm as his reflection swirled away into silvery blankness. He gasped, automatically flipping the mirror over to check for trickery. "Amazing. How does it work?"

"Magic," came the dry retort. An image coalesced on the surface of the glass: Beauty, as clear as if he was there seeing her in person. He spent a few seconds in dumbstruck wonderment before truly processing what his eyes saw.

She looked well, writing some sort of correspondence on her small desk. She was dressed simply, but in good, new fabric. A fine oil lamp lit her work, Brendan noted with satisfaction. The money their father had brought home was being put to practical use, if Beauty had anything to say about it.

Beauty smiled over her letter, quill scratching across the paper as she wrote. "I can even hear the quill! That's remarkable!"

Over his shoulder, Beast's soft laugh sent the hair over his ear stirring, and his heart into an uneven trip. "You see your sister looking quite well, and you remark upon the capabilities of the mirror. One would think you would dissect it if you could."

She really did look well, even smiling from time to time as she wrote. Who could she be writing to? A swain, perhaps?

The image faded away to silvery swirls. Brendan set the mirror down on the mantel, then turned to face Beast. "So. Now you've seen her."

Beast stood very still and said nothing.

Brendan's mouth thinned. "Well, what do you think?" He kept his voice light, empty of the apprehension icing his veins.

Beast did not meet Brendan's gaze for a long moment. When he did, those honey-dark eyes trapped the breath in Brendan's lungs. "She looks like you," he said simply.

Brendan was acutely aware of how near they stood, of how little it would take to close that distance. "Thank you. For letting me see her. It does set my mind somewhat at ease."

"Only somewhat?" Beast asked, a tease hinting low in his voice.

Brendan surged up and kissed Beast with enough strength to rock them both back a step. He snaked his arms around Beast's neck and clung there, knees suddenly shaking and heart thundering in his throat. Under his lips, Beast's mouth was soft but unmoving. Brendan pulled back, fearing he had made a dreadful mistake. This was a much more forceful approach than he had taken in the garden, kissing Beast lightly while the scent of night jasmine drifted about them.

Beast's eyes were wide, almost wild. Then with an intensity Brendan had never seen in him before, Beast cupped Brendan's head in both huge hands, pulled him back up, and pressed their mouths together in a fierce clash of lips.

Blood roared hot in Brendan's ears as he clung to Beast's thick mane, tipping up his chin to slide into a slower kiss, one that left him as dizzy as if he'd drunk a whole bottle of wine by himself.

One of Beast's hands dropped down to the small of his back, and Brendan moaned against parted lips. The sound jolted Beast, pulling his head away, breath fast and heavy. "I—" One syllable flush with uncertainty.

"Shh," Brendan whispered, and advanced on Beast so quickly the other man retreated a step, backing into the door. With Beast effectively trapped, Brendan reclaimed the kiss, any resistance crumbling against him. Desire plucked at his heartstrings, drowning out all rational thought. He hadn't yet introduced the aspect of tongues into the kiss, and before he could rectify that, Beast thoroughly distracted him by threading a hand into his hair. It felt incredible, and eyes fluttering shut, Brendan fell out of the kiss and into the caress, pushing his head into Beast's hand.

He snapped his eyes open. He met Beast's dazed stare, licked his lips as he pressed his hips insistently against Beast's, and said something stupid.

"Is this the door to the bedroom?"

It took Brendan a senseless second to realize he had misstepped, and by that time Beast had already disentangled himself from the embrace. His claws scrabbled at the door, blindly searching for the handle behind him.

"Yes, and, uh, it is quite late, and I... Just, good night!"

The door slammed in Brendan's face. He blinked, paused, raised his hand to knock, paused again, and turned around. "*Merde*," he muttered, mortification crawling over him. It had been going so well! Why had he gone and done such a foolish thing?

The *why* was pretty self-evident, as Brendan adjusted his clothing. Not thinking with his brain.

He took a deep, steadying breath and walked out of the suite—after first waiting a minute or two in the hopes maybe Beast would change his mind. However, the door remained closed, and no sound at all permeated the heavy stillness in the foyer. Brendan ducked his head and left.

Again in his own bedroom, he stood with his back to the door and spoke to the empty room. "I am a complete idiot."

He flung himself onto the bed so hard the canopy shook. He tried to think about cold water, dead things, anything but those strong hands, the firm press of that large body, those amazingly intense eyes...

Not. Helping.

After regaining a modicum of composure, Brendan rolled over and lay spreadeagled on the coverlet, not bothering to toe off his boots. How was he supposed to face Beast tomorrow morning?

Perhaps the Beast would pretend like nothing had happened, as he had after the garden. But... *I don't want him to pretend nothing happened. I want... I want more.*

He could talk with the omnipofish, as he'd mentally dubbed them, but the only thing more embarrassing than what had just happened was to be reduced to asking relationship advice from fish.

Despite everything, a smile spread across his face. He knew enough to tell when a man wanted him, and Beast had definitely wanted. Brendan's smile grew until he had to bite his lip to contain it.

15

In Which a Mystery is Solved

Sleep had been elusive, Brendan only snatching a few hours by the time dawn crept its stealthy way through the gaps of the bedcurtains. He lay among the tangled sheets, tired but wide awake, the morning sun growing stronger and brighter until he finally gave up and arose with a heavy sigh.

Immediately, the servants set to work with gusto. The air hummed with activity as sheets were stripped, pillows plumped, and a hot bath filled. Most days, the servants were so furtively unobtrusive about their chores that Brendan had difficulty even noticing them, but today he could only spare a little distracted curiosity over the change as he bathed and shaved. Something had the servants all atwitter, but Brendan was too busy with his own problems to try to puzzle it out. He slipped a collared jerkin over his shirt, feeling like an utter cad for his thoughtless words last night. He wasn't sure how he could even look Beast in the eye after that shamefully forward display.

A pair of invisible hands seized his collar. Brendan jumped in surprise. They turned down the askew collar, smoothing it out with brisk efficiency. He blinked as they plucked a stray thread from his shoulder, then spun him about to face the door.

"Um. Thank you?" He felt thoroughly mother-henned. His shoulder was given an encouraging pat. He took a deep, steadying breath before opening the door and walking down to breakfast.

His heart skipped a beat to find Beast standing before the great fireplace, his broad back to the door. Brendan wiped palms gone clammy with nerves on his breeches before addressing Beast's hunched shoulders.

"Good morning." Beast didn't speak or turn around. As half-expected; the Silent Treatment, surely soon to be followed by the Pretending It Never Happened. Brendan cleared his throat and spoke again, louder, allowing the Beast to pretend he hadn't heard him the first time.

"Good morning, Beast."

That regal profile turned just a fraction, outlined in the morning light. Even from that concealing angle, Beast's face was lined with distress, more so than just an ill-advised kiss would warrant. Brendan drew near and ever-so-daringly laid a hand on Beast's arm.

"Are you all right?"

Beast spoke so softly that Brendan had to strain to hear it. "Do not touch me."

His hand slid from the velvet-clad arm like a lead weight.

"You are bewitched," Beast continued, in a tone that rang ever so faintly mournful.

"Bewitched?" After a second of blank surprise, Brendan laughed, the sound of it too loud in the echoing hall. "What do you—"

"It is *she* I am meant for, not for you."

Brendan stared open-mouthed, stung but at the same time perplexed by the hesitant gentleness of Beast's voice; near a whisper, as quiet as a hare in the snow.

Large paws clenched at Beast's sides. He took in a long breath, leonine tail lashing once before stilling. "You asked once how I got this way. Long ago, I angered a sorceress. She said I was full of vanity. Pride. That I was...ugly inside. She did this," Beast gestured at himself, still speaking with such strange, quiet dispassion, "to teach me a lesson. She said I would remain a monster until I found love. And now, do you see?"

Beast finally turned to face him, emotion thickening his voice. "Do you see that now I am close, so close to what may break the spell and free me, the witch sends my salvation's *brother* instead! Your arrival was all her design. The roads turning you back, the snow keeping you here, all her plot to keep me a prisoner. Last night..." Beast faltered and turned back toward the fireplace. "You are under a spell of her devising. You do not feel as you think you do."

Brendan broke into a nervous grin. "Ah. Well. I think I may have something to tell you." He pulled gently at Beast's arm to make the man turn. "There's something I need you to know about me—"

The Beast abruptly shook off Brendan's touch and whirled around, his mane ruffling. "I do not need to hear it," he hissed. "I do not want to hear the lies she put into your head. It pains me enough to..." He looked away, shutters closing over his expression.

"Look," Brendan said with what he felt was exceptional calm, "if all that is true, if I'm under a spell, then answer me this: *why did you kiss me back?*"

Silence stretched between them. Beast's thick brows crowded close over his arched nose. Brendan took a deep breath. Now or never.

"Is it because you feel as I do, that there is *more* between us?" Brendan tried and failed to catch the Beast's eyes, feeling like he was toeing the edge of some great cliff, about to plummet, with his heart beating so thick he could taste copper at the back of his tongue.

"You are speaking nonsense." Beast's voice dropped until it was nearly in a register too low to be heard, barely stirring the texture of the air. "What more can there be between us but friendship?"

Brendan grabbed the Beast's clawed hands, not flinching at their sharpness. "Beast, this is ridiculous. There's no spell. I'm not bewitched."

Beast's hands twitched in his own, but he did not pull away. "You are!"

"Fine," Brendan huffed, "you're right. I am bewitched. By your passion, your intelligence, your kindness. I am bewitched by your eyes, your voice, by the strength and compassion in your heart, by the good man I know you are; the man I am so grateful you've started to let me see." Gaze steady, Brendan pulled up one of Beast's hands and pressed a slow, deliberate kiss to his large palm.

Beast breathed in sharply, throat bobbing as he swallowed.

"Still think there's nothing here but friendship?"

"Enchantment."

Beast hadn't yet pulled away, both hands still clasped between Brendan's own. "You know, I can't help but notice you don't claim *you* are bewitched, Beast. Only I."

Curved horns caught the firelight as Beast shook his head. "She would be unable to. I have some small defenses of my own. But you don't. She's made you believe in something that can never be possible. Desire born only of falsehood and sorcery."

Brendan's heart gave a great lurch, and he licked his lips nervously, looking down at their interwoven hands. "I've only ever desired men. My whole life." He swallowed thickly. "In school there was...a young man...whom I cared for very much. We were...lovers, for a time." He had to pause, sucking in a shaky breath, then lifted his chin. "He wasn't the only. Just the first. Not the point. The *point* is I am not bewitched, Beast. This is the way I am."

"Lovers?"

"Yes."

"How?"

Cheeks flaring like hot coals, Brendan cleared his throat. "The...usual way?"

A muscle jumped in Beast's jaw. "I've never heard of such a thing."

"Are you being serious? Oh my God, you *are*. You haven't— You can't have been *that* sheltered!"

"I was not *sheltered*," Beast protested, looking both bewildered and thoroughly annoyed by the unexpected turn the conversation had taken.

"As long as people have existed, there have been those who seek out the affections of their own gender. How could you never even have *heard* of... I mean, you have all those Classical books in your library! The histories of Alexander, the Grecian plays, the poems of Sappho... *The Satyricon*, for God's sake!"

"Surely that is all just satire." Some of the Beast's old growling rumble crept back into his voice.

"Satire!" Brendan couldn't help but drop Beast's hands, nearly doubling over laughing. His head felt light, nearly giddy with nerves.

"Well, I certainly don't see how it could be possible!"

"I could show you," Brendan blurted fervently, then flushed hot, hardly believing he had dared to say such a thing out loud. Beast looked as if he'd been rendered entirely speechless, lips parted and eyes wide. Brendan shook off his embarrassment and stepped closer. "Beast, believe me, what I feel for you is real, not some kind of witch's spell."

"And...what do you feel for me?"

The only answer he could give Beast was to stand up on his toes and kiss him.

After what felt like an age, Beast's arm slid around Brendan's shoulder, a deep, visceral growl thrumming through his chest. Encouraged, Brendan swiped his tongue across the seam of Beast's lips, chasing a surprised gasp.

"I've dreamed about doing this," he whispered against Beast's mouth. No reason to hold back now, to hide his truth any longer, not when his heartbeat was already thundering so loud it could surely be heard outside the castle walls.

"You have?" Beast whispered back, his breath shallow, the set of his pointed ears betraying a slight tremor.

"Mm. Repeatedly." He guided Beast's lips back to his own, unwilling to let them go unclaimed a second more. They parted just enough for Brendan to slip his tongue inside and deepen the kiss, his head swimming at the warm, welcoming ease of it.

As it turned out, the fangs didn't get in the way at all. One mystery solved.

Heat rushed through him as they crowded close, bodies aligning sweetly. A thick arm tightened around Brendan's shoulders, talons burying into his hair.

"I've dreamed of it too," Beast breathed in a slow growl that slipped all the way through Brendan's bones, warming him like a fine liquor. They kissed for an eternal moment longer, then Beast abruptly pulled away. "Wait. Sappho? Really?"

Brendan could not constrain the laughter that bubbled up.

And the day eased into several.

* * *

The Library

Brendan puzzled through a Roman text, drawing upon every scrap of his Latin lessons to do so, when he stumbled across a particular line in a poem. A very *explicit* line in a very *detailed* account of the history of Alexander the Great. One *particular* conquest of his; and not one involving a battlefield.

This gave him an Idea.

"Beast? How good are you with Latin?"

"Good enough. Better at Greek." His host didn't look up from his book.

"There's a paragraph in this I can't quite parse. It's translated into Latin *from* Greek, so maybe you'll have better luck with it than I have. Could you translate it for me?" He passed the book over. Beast's eyes skimmed the page, froze, and widened. Brendan tried not to grin.

Beast needed time to think. To process. In one fell swoop, Brendan had thrown the man's whole worldview into chaos, and he was happy to give him a little distance while Beast figured himself out. He didn't want to push too hard.

But surely a *little* pushing couldn't hurt.

"Where did you find this book?" Beast asked slowly. There was no way to tell if he was blushing.

"Over there. Why? What's it say?" Eyes wide, the picture of innocence. "I was able to translate something about thighs?"

"If you climb back up there you'll find a Latin dictionary." Beast handed the book back.

Temporarily thwarted, Brendan sighed, sat back, and continued reading.

The Music Room

"There is no way this is happening."

"Just trust me, it'll work."

"No, it won't. I'm not...shaped right."

"Oh, come on. Your fingers are perfect for it!"

"This is not going to— How are they 'perfect for it'?"

"The claws. It's like you have little plectrums on each finger. You'll see, you'll be brilliant."

"Well, that's something no one has ever told me before."

"Can't imagine why not." Brendan smiled radiantly. "Here, hold it like this. On your lap." Beast shifted uncomfortably as the harp was placed in its proper position.

"Put this hand here," Brendan's hand traveled Beast's arm to place his clawed fingers along the correct strings, lingering longer than was strictly necessary. "And this one here. There. Now you just stroke it gently." He leaned forward over Beast's shoulder, sure to breathe his words directly into a long, pointed ear. He was both amused and gratified to see the ear flick backward in response, much like an agitated cat.

The broad expanse of shoulders moved beneath his arms, and Beast strummed once and only once, discordance twanging as every string on the harp snapped.

In the silent moment that followed, the two stared dumbfounded at the wreck of an instrument in Beast's lap, broken strings waving haplessly like reeds in the wind.

"I'll go get new strings. It will only take me a moment to restring it."

"I'll go get the iodine," Beast replied wryly, and stood and left before Brendan could retort.

The Game Room

The evening had passed without much event, and the pair retired with some dark sweet port, playing games for the last few hours. Beast had, after some cajoling, agreed to subject himself to another chess match, but soon enough his misgivings proved correct.

He whipped a finger across the board to point with incredulity at the two offending pieces. "What is that? What is that you just did?"

Brendan froze, hand poised over a pawn. "What? What did I do?"

"That...that shenanigan with the king and the little piece that looks like a castle!"

"The rook?"

"Yes, the rook, I knew that! That move is clearly cheating! Neither of those pieces move in such a fashion, nor may they do so at the *same time!*"

"I castled my king. It's a perfectly legal move."

"'*Castled your king?*' Now you're just making things up!" Beast crossed his arms over his chest in affronted dignity.

"I am not! Just because you were not aware of the rule does not mean it does not exist."

"That is utter nonsense!"

Brendan's eyes narrowed a tiny fraction. "First you accuse me of theft. Now I am a cheat, as well?"

"If the shoe fits..."

Brendan abruptly stood. "It may take me days to find a chess rulebook in that enormous blasted library of yours, but by God, I will do so!" As he strode across the parquet, Beast stood and swiftly caught Brendan's arm.

He stopped and turned, a wary look in his eyes. "What?"

As if Beast had any idea; as if his body hadn't outrun his sense every time he got close to Brendan. "I don't...rightly know. Just...stay."

Frown melting into a grin, Brendan leaned up on his toes with a gentle kiss. Beast's already careful grip on Brendan's arm softened, drawing him closer. When the kiss broke, Brendan murmured against Beast's lips, "Do you forfeit the match?"

It should have been infuriating, the way Brendan offered a constant and unrelenting challenge. And it *was* infuriating, to be sure, but also... *exhilarating*. Beast gave him a crooked smile. "Never."

"Good," Brendan purred, looking up through his lashes. "Though next time you impugn my honor, I'll have no choice but to demand satisfaction."

Beast's tongue failed him as heat raced through his body. He had no idea what he could possibly offer by way of satisfaction, but found he wanted very much to find out.

"Sorry," Brendan said, regret softening the storm-blue of his eyes. "I'm trying to give you time." With a self-effacing grimace, he puffed a breath upwards, riffling the hair at his brow. "Spoke before I thought."

Beast had been given nothing *but* time. Centuries of it.

"I like the way you speak," he admitted, sifting his fingers through the rich chestnut of Brendan's hair. The way Brendan spoke to him, the way he looked at him, it was almost like he forgot he was speaking to a monster.

The way Brendan looked at him, Beast could almost forget it, too.

"I'll have to remember that." Brendan's grin was so brilliant it put every one of Beast's riches to shame, and he let himself be pulled down for a proper kiss.

Beast's Bedroom

Night approached and as the hallway lanterns lit themselves, Beast turned to his guest after a late dinner and bid him a good night. He headed to his rooms, looking back at the curious echo of footsteps behind him. Brendan followed close in his wake, hands clasped behind his back as if out for an afternoon stroll. Unsure of how to respond to such a thing, Beast remained silent and kept walking.

At his bedroom door, Beast pivoted on his heel and drew himself up. He cleared his throat. "Good night."

Nodding, Brendan leaned far forward into Beast's personal space. "It is particularly lovely." His smile walked a blade's edge between gentle and predatory. "I agree. It is a *very* good night."

Beast had no clue how to proceed and wasn't terribly keen to reveal how much trepidation he was hiding. Kisses were one thing (how had he lived so long not knowing they could be like this, each one sparking fire in his veins? Worse: how was he going to live on afterward without them?) but anything further was another matter entirely. Surely Brendan would rethink the whole thing if he saw more of Beast's terrible form. The thought tore at him, the inevitability of it.

"Yes. So. I shall bid you a good night, then. Since we've established it is, in fact, a good one."

A very slight smile curled at the corner of Brendan's lips. "This is the part where you invite me in," he said as if teaching grammar to a student. "To your room."

Beast swallowed. "Is that…is that proper?"

"Beast, we're sequestered away from the outside world in a magic castle. Is propriety our biggest concern?"

"I take your point." Beast cleared his throat again. It didn't have to be anything more than a drink, or a chat. There was no reason to tie himself into knots. "You are, of course, more than welcome to join me in my drawing room."

Brendan smiled radiantly. "Thank you." He trotted through the door before Beast could hinder the proceedings with further courtliness, and lounged with particular languor on a half-mauled settee in the corner. Beast couldn't help but find Brendan's expression to be unfairly expectant.

He scraped together some tattered remnants of his manners. "Would you like any,"— Brendan's eyebrows climbed a fraction of an inch upwards—"tea, or a nightcap?" The eyebrows fell back to their usual place.

"No, thank you. I'm fine." Brendan stood and sidled around the antechamber, peering through each open door into the rooms beyond. "Spacious." He leaned against a doorframe with both arms loosely crossed over his chest. "Fit for a prince." He flashed a quick wink.

Beast rolled his eyes. "Nothing we aristos like better than wasting usable space to show off our quality."

Brendan snorted with laughter. Beast hovered nervously around a wardrobe. What did real people do before bed? What would make him look normal? It had been a long time since he had made any sort of preparation for sleep other than to shrug out of his clothes, curl up on his bedcovers, and close his eyes. Brendan's voice rang out behind him, breaking him out of his reverie.

"I must say, that is a rather impressive bed. Is the headboard made of oak?" A pause. "It's nice. Sturdy-looking."

Suddenly struck by how farcical his life had become, Beast huffed and turned, planting his hands on either side of the doorway. "Look. You seem to be laboring under the misapprehension that I have any idea what to do in this situation. Whatever...this rather unique situation may be. I have no frame of reference for any of this."

Over the space of two heartbeats, Brendan's expression shifted from taken aback, to thoughtful, and finally apologetic. "Then allow me to bid you good night, my most gracious host." With a small bow, perhaps a concession to Beast's earlier courtliness, Brendan took his leave.

Beast stared after him, flabbergasted, and as the door shut, shouted, "That doesn't *give* me a frame of reference!"

The Parlor

"What had you planned on doing with all that education once it had finished?" Beast hesitantly picked up Brendan's hand and held it in the air, unsure of what to do with it now he had it.

The previous night, after Brendan had left for his bed, Beast had read up on all his Classical books, the ones he always thought were satire, or perhaps just effusive descriptions of uncommonly strong friendships. New light was thrown upon the deeds of Alexander and Hephaestion, Achilles and Patrocles, and even Emperor Hadrian. He had made it barely ten pages into the Satyricon before setting it aside. Too ridiculous. And too filthy.

After hours of what could only be classified as studying, Beast still felt just as much at sea as he had before opening a single page.

Brendan shot him a quick smile, cheeks flushing very pink, and eased their hands down to rest comfortably entangled on the couch cushion between them. He slipped his fingers around Beast's as he answered, a touch breathless.

"Well, I didn't have to do much with it, really. Our family was wealthy enough for me to take up Father's business at any time I pleased. I was sent to university to teach me some culture and gain connections, and to keep me out from underfoot until I came of age to inherit. I had thought," he ducked his head as if embarrassed at the confession, "to become a musician, but that's not in the cards." He shrugged, avoiding Beast's eyes.

"Why not?"

"Because…" A shadow passed over Brendan's face. It didn't suit him. "I wanted to travel all over, play for different orchestras: here in France, Italy, maybe even Germany. But that takes patronage, which takes the correct social cache, which my family lacks." His laugh was cut with an unfamiliar note of bitterness. "And this was *before* my father made an extremely public disgrace of himself, losing our manor to the gaming tables. Any chance I might have had was lost along with our entire fortune."

Beast frowned, squeezing Brendan's hand. "Natural talent doesn't figure into it?"

"It used to," Brendan said, wistful. He cleared his throat, shaking off the strained tone. "Now natural talent gets you only so far and no further. Unless you're rich enough to bypass politics entirely." He said that like it was an amusing joke, like of course there was no amount of wealth able to accomplish such a feat.

"Anyway," Brendan hastened to say, clearly eager to be done with the topic. "Once we had to move to the country, all our old plans fell apart. I figured I'd probably save up money from working as a clerk and someday buy the grocers, perhaps. I don't know. I haven't thought that far ahead."

Beast turned Brendan's hand over in his own giant paws. He carefully traced the delicate lines across the palm with a single talon, and brushed the small calluses adorning each fingertip. He admired Brendan's hands a great deal. "I can't imagine you selling cabbages."

"Hey, I'd be great at selling cabbages."

"Hmm, likely true. You're annoyingly persistent."

"Persuasive," Brendan corrected, smile growing sharper. The sight made Beast's stomach flip over.

"I could certainly be persuaded to buy anything you're selling." Leaning down, he caught Brendan's lips in a slow kiss. Brendan gasped, the pulse in his wrist quickening beneath Beast's thumb. Beast freed a hand to card through his unbound hair.

Any second, Brendan would take a good close look at Beast's fearsome visage, come to his senses, and run away. But right now, his startlingly bright eyes were very sure, layered with some heavy emotion Beast could not name. A slim hand reached up to the curving outline of one of his horns with soft, questing fingertips. Beast jerked away.

"All right," Brendan whispered against his lips. "I won't touch them, if you wish."

"No, I... That's not..." *Do they bother you so little?* The words were too fragile on his tongue, so Beast swallowed them unsaid.

Instead he firmed his grip in dark hair and poured himself into the kiss with renewed vigor. He'd been taken by surprise by every kiss they had shared so far, and it was fair play to instigate one of his own at last. Testing, he swiped his tongue over Brendan's, earning a pleased murmur he drank right in.

He'd kissed others, in his life before, though not often. It took some thought to remember the motions; how to breathe through a kiss, how not to bump noses, how the slick rasping slide of tongue made his own breath come faster... Marveling, Beast let his free hand fall into Brendan's lap.

Brendan gasped sharply into the kiss and pushed his hips up into the Beast's palm in an unconscious reflex. Alarmed, Beast broke away and snatched away his hand, certain he had hurt the other man.

"I'm sorry," he said wretchedly, ashamed of his great unthinking strength and fumbling claws. It would take so little for them to draw blood. "I did not mean—"

"Don't be," Brendan replied in a husky tone Beast hadn't heard him use before. It sounded very...interesting. He wanted very much to hear it again. "I would not object if it happened twice."

The pulse raced in that pale throat. It struck Beast of a sudden: he himself had been the cause, *he* had done that; made Brendan gasp, made his eyes glaze over, made him writhe under his hand. His throat went dry at the way Brendan looked up at him with simple, trusting openness, as if he would be amenable to anything Beast wanted. Anything at all.

Beast's heart skipped in his chest, though not with passion. Having such utter trust aimed at him was terrifying. What should he do? *Was* there a correct course of action?

Distance; that was the key. He leaned back, which was more difficult than he had anticipated, as warm and pliant as Brendan was, worse than forcing himself to climb out of a toasty bed on a cold morning.

"What was his name?" he asked softly. "The...lover you had at school." The word 'lover' had been surprisingly hard to speak. Too personal, too

184

intimate.

Brendan blinked, eyes clearing a little. "Kieran." By way of explanation he added, "He was Irish."

"Ah." Some pieces finally came together. "The songs."

"Yes. He taught me most of them."

"I see."

"He moved away and got married. I was quite upset at the time."

Beast watched him closely, heart catching a little. "And now?"

Brendan traced the edge of his thumb along Beast's jaw, a slow, revelatory smile spreading over his face. "I'm not anymore."

He scooted closer and tilted his head back, a gleam of challenge in his silver-blue eyes. Yet another challenge Beast found he could not back down from, so he leaned in and kissed him again as the fire crackled in the hearth.

* * *

Though winter's most severe weeks were now passed, snow still fell in large, fluffy clumps on the conservatory ceiling, where they melted and ran down the glass in winding rivulets. Inside the greenhouse, the air was as warm and moist as summer, and the loamy fragrance of growing things was a tangible pleasure.

Beast had always enjoyed a meander through his garden, and his enjoyment was enhanced by the accompaniment of a friend. Even the stroll by the fishpond hadn't been unpleasant, though the two koi had been bickering with one another over the nature of the universe in a most irritating fashion.

Soon the conversation returned to literary avenues, as it often did.

"I don't see your point," Brendan said, walking beside with two paces for every one of Beast's. "What reason for Polo to make everything up? What's the point of going all that way only to come back with—how did you put it? 'A heap of lies.'"

"Money," he said with a short bark of laughter. "People want to hear what they think they already know; foreigners are hedonistic cannibals, noble savages, and heathen bigamists. Who would want to read a travel account

185

about how people from strange and foreign lands happen to be pretty much like everyone else? 'Witness the savage inhabitants as they get up early for work! See the foreign devil have a light lunch!'"

"Well, I think his version was much more interesting."

"Which just proves my point."

Brendan laughed. It was a good laugh, deeper than his slightness might indicate, with a mellow richness honed by years of vocal training. He hid a yawn behind his hand before speaking. "I'll grant you that. This has been a very engaging evening. I thank you for your company, Beast." He set a hand on Beast's arm, and the touch sent a frisson up his spine. Though they had yet to share more than kisses and caresses, Beast's thoughts scattered every time those slender fingers made contact. "I bid you a good night, Beast." His smile robbed Beast of his ability to think, and the other man had already turned to take his leave when Beast remembered the proper response.

"Good night, Brendan."

Brendan froze in his tracks. He slowly turned back around, expression completely indecipherable. Beast had no earthly idea what had so struck him.

"What did you say?" The tremulous softness in Brendan's voice took Beast aback. Had Brendan misheard him and thought Beast had leveled some terrible insult?

"I...just said good night. What did you think I said?"

Brendan stepped forward with such boldness that the Beast took a baffled step back.

"I thought I heard you say my name."

The ardent heat behind those words astonished him. Good thing no one could see the hot flush under his fur. "Surely I've said it before."

"You haven't," Brendan said silkily, taking a panther-like step closer. "Believe me, I'd have noticed."

Before Beast could cobble together a reply, Brendan had closed the distance between them and attacked Beast's mouth with the ferocity of a wild animal. Slim, strong fingers dug into his biceps as Brendan licked his way into Beast's mouth.

Beast's body acted of its own accord, grabbing Brendan's slender waist and pulling him closer. He smelled deliriously good, a heady mix of cedarwood soap and warm skin filling Beast's nostrils. He couldn't get enough of it, licking and nipping a trail of kisses up Brendan's neck and along his jaw, relishing the rapid pulse as it flickered under his lips. The rasp of stubble dragging across Beast's tongue intoxicated him in ways he never could have imagined, that proof of maleness sharp under his tongue.

Another proof pressed into his thigh as Brendan slid his hips against him, a dizzying crush. Brendan hauled himself up by Beast's shoulders and took the tip of an ear between his teeth, applying light pressure that sent sparks shooting behind Beast's eyes.

"*Putain*," he swore with deliberate clarity, because otherwise he'd be a wordless, moaning wreck.

"Scandalous language," Brendan smudged into another hot, panting kiss, smiling as he did.

"You first kissed me after you'd almost drowned in that pond." Beast wasn't sure what possessed him to bring this up at this exact moment. Perhaps it felt like a secret he wasn't permitted to keep.

"I... What?"

"You were delirious." Beast nuzzled where Brendan's collar ended, trying to find how far down that pink flush went with his tongue alone. "You didn't seem to have a clue who I was or what you were doing."

"God, that's embarrassing. Can we forget that whole thing ever happened?"

I doubt it, Beast didn't say. He'd cherished the memory of that kiss that wasn't a kiss for far too long, back when he'd thought it was the only intimacy he'd ever be allowed to have again.

"Consider it forgotten," he lied magnanimously, licking a stripe up Brendan's throat.

Brendan moaned and pressed his hips tight, the exquisite pressure leaving Beast breathless. He couldn't even remember the last time he had experienced anything close. Decades ago, at least, if not far, far longer.

Brendan shuddered in his arms and husked, "Bench?"

"Bench." Beast dragged them over to the nearest seat without putting an inch of air between their bodies, and they tumbled onto the marble in a graceless clinch, Brendan straddling his thighs to resume the feverish kiss.

After mere seconds of this bliss, Brendan pulled back, worrying his bottom lip. He ducked his head, hair falling into his eyes. "So, um. What would you like?" It was the first brush of uncertainty Beast had ever seen from him, though he wriggled a little in Beast's lap, clearly eager to please.

Beast swallowed. He traced the shape of Brendan's shoulders, once again struck by how strange and marvelous it was to have another person touching him, after so many lifetimes of solitude. To have *this* person.

Women he had been with, so long ago, had usually been professional courtesans or the occasional young widow, always forthright and outspoken about what specific acts they were willing to perform. Once, he had asked a courtesan if she could at least pretend their congress wasn't such a businesslike affair. It was awful. The fluttered eyelashes, the forced endearments. Beast hated the artifice of it, the falseness of feeling. He'd never asked for it again.

Sex had always been one of his onerous princely duties; settle land disputes, allocate treasury funds, bed a harlot. Oh, he had done it often enough—more often than he had settled land disputes, certainly—for his passions had run high and the momentary release had been welcome. That was all it really had been, a temporary easement of tension, no different than a hot soak after a long ride or a massage after a boar hunt.

Never, in all his days, had Beast known a heady rush of arousal so keen as when this man so much as smiled at him, or when a lock of that dark hair spilled over those smoke-blue eyes, or when the scent of that warm skin filled his breath. Even now need pierced through him like a knife, and the depth of it frightened him as he had never been before.

If he let Brendan touch him with those slim, skilled hands, he could play Beast as easily as he did a lute. This time, at least, *Beast* would be the one leading the charge.

He plunged his tongue into Brendan's mouth, sliding both hands along his arched spine and then further down to cup his buttocks, so firm and round that Beast couldn't help but groan aloud into their kiss.

Brendan shivered and pressed impossibly closer, thighs tight at Beast's hips. The insistent swell of his hardness was as daunting as it was thrilling. But this wasn't so different from what had occurred in the parlor not so long ago, and he had some idea of what Brendan might enjoy.

He dipped his hand down and cupped the bulge in Brendan's trousers.

Brendan made a strangled sound in his throat, hips snapping forward as his head fell back, hair flying wildly into his eyes. *"Putain,"* he rasped.

"Scandalous language," Beast teased, feeling eight feet tall. He pulsed his grip, careful with his claws. Brendan scrabbled at Beast's shoulders, his chest heaving. He poured himself into a biting kiss, grinding into Beast's palm.

"The things I'm going to do to you when I finally get you in a bed," Brendan growled into the kiss, and *God*, that was... Beast had admitted out loud he liked the way Brendan spoke to him, so really he only had himself to blame.

He'd wanted to lead the charge, stay in control, but all of that was as good as shattered. He wanted nothing more than to hear that voice ragged with arousal, to feel that body shudder once more against his, to whisper again into the flushed shell of his ear: "Brendan."

Brendan cried out as he came apart in Beast's arms.

The garden was still. Brendan trembled, his breaths evening out by inches. His arms, still draped around Beast's broad shoulders, went as supple and relaxed as willow boughs.

"I...don't think that's ever happened when I've had my clothes on," he said with a shaky laugh. A crease appeared between his eyebrows, embarrassment stealing over contentment. "Er. I don't want you to think I'm normally that...fast."

Beast silenced him with a kiss, cupping his face with both hands. "Then I'll take it as a compliment. It's been a long time, yes?"

Brendan blushed. "Yeeess... But it's been even longer for you, hasn't it?" The understatement was uttered so close to Beast's ear it tickled every fine hair. Beast shivered.

"It...it has," he breathed. Brendan smirked and reached for the ties of

Beast's breeches. Beast wrapped a gentle hand around his wrist, halting him.

"You don't want me to..."

He wanted a hundred mad, impossible things, not the least of which was for Brendan not to regret doing something now before he'd really seen the extent of Beast's monstrous nature. Likely it was already too late for that, to avoid regret altogether, but Beast could at least minimize the damage by giving them both some time to reconsider.

God, it was selfish, but he hoped Brendan wouldn't reconsider.

"I think," Beast said in the graceful rise to his feet while straightening his cuffs, "it's high time we do this properly."

"Properly?"

"Yes. In a bed, perhaps? I understand that is the usual thing. And I confess I'm greatly curious about all these things you claim you will do to me there." Beast enjoyed seeing the flush creep across Brendan's face like a sunset. "It's quite late, so I propose we retire to our rooms for the night. Tomorrow after we break our fast, we adjourn to my chambers to...to continue tonight's conversation. Is this agreeable to you?"

Brendan's mouth opened and closed several times before he could find his words. Immensely gratifying he'd finally been caught off-guard. "Agreeable, yeah. Yes. If you're sure—"

"I am." It was the worst, most disastrous idea in the history of ideas, but Beast was utterly certain he was going to go through with it anyway.

Brendan's teeth caught his lower lip to contain a joyful smile. "Then I will see you at breakfast tomorrow, Beast."

Drawing on every ounce of his royal bearing, rusted though it was by centuries of disuse, Beast dropped into a courtly, formal bow. "And I shall bid you a good night, Brendan Mattheus-Etienne d'Aumale."

At that moment, the wide, shining smile Beast received seemed to make every long year of his imprisonment worth it.

16

In Which Things are Done Properly

The first thing Beast did upon waking was order that his rooms be thoroughly cleaned.

In truth, the *very* first thing he did was have a complete, if not wholly unexpected, nervous breakdown. He'd fallen asleep readily enough the night before, a remarkable feat considering what had transpired that evening; the things he had committed to with his own voice, the things he had done with his own hands. Then he woke up, and it all came back in a tangled rush. His claws snagged at the sheets, any certainty he had felt last night now dissolving in the confused jumble of *what the hell am I doing?!*

Beast allowed himself a handful of private moments to panic. Then he gathered himself and set the servants to work.

They dusted and polished, replaced anything torn or tattered, beat out the rugs, and made up the bed with fresh sheets. Beast tried not to think about the *why* too closely. If he stopped to think, he might collapse in a boneless heap of cowardice upon the scrubbed floor.

So instead he performed his morning ablutions, dressed, and made his way down to breakfast. He'd meant to be early, but Brendan had arrived even earlier, already seated at his usual place with a steaming mug idly in hand, watching winter birds flit about the windowsill.

The morning light was kind to him, not that it needed to be. The light could be downright hostile and Brendan would still make it look good. His upturned nose and pointed chin granted a fine-boned elegance that wasn't quite delicate enough to mistake for anything but masculine, especially with a hint of unshaven shadow tracing the slope of his jaw.

At the click of Beast's clawed steps, Brendan turned about with a warm smile. "Good morning." He had left his hair down again. It was unreasonably fetching.

"And to you." He slid into his seat, and the food was served. Beast took several bites before he even noticed what he was eating. His knee bounced under the table.

"So I'm just going to come right out and ask this." Hands flattening on the table, Brendan met Beast's eyes with a resolute set to his chin. "Are you going to pretend nothing happened last night?"

Beast set down his fork, faintly proud of himself for the steadiness of his hand. "No. I am not."

All of Brendan's breath left him in a rush. "Oh, good." He displayed that careless smile that always scattered all of Beast's carefully composed thoughts. "Then I should thank you."

"Thank me?"

"For a nice evening. A pretty spectacular one, actually." At Beast's blank confusion, he added, "It's customary."

"Ah." Beast took a long drink of whatever-was-in-the-cup to buy some time. "Is it also customary to say I enjoyed myself immensely, and look forward to similar actions in the future?" Even across the long table, Beast saw the way Brendan's clear eyes darkened with what had to be arousal.

Brendan's tongue flashed across his lips. "In that case, what do you say we forget about the rest of the food and go up to your rooms?"

If Beast's ears were less keen, he might not have picked up the faint tremor. At least he wasn't the only one feeling nervous. He set his napkin on the table and stood up. "Follow me."

Only after closing the bedroom door behind them was Beast suddenly seized by a feeling of intense dread; of inevitability. Any moment, Brendan would change his mind and leave. If Beast could just gather his courage, he should reach out, should pull Brendan into his arms and somehow convince him to stay.

They stood silent for a few slivers of eternity. It was Brendan who finally closed the distance, hands sliding over Beast's shoulders. The bravery of this small action struck him—this little gesture, one Beast had found himself unable to do, and returned the embrace because to do otherwise was unfathomable. And suddenly it all felt as effortless as breathing.

Their lips met easily, a dance they'd practiced the steps to more than a few times thus far. Beast stroked a hand through Brendan's hair, liking it very much, the way the loose waves wound around his fingers. His lips still tasted of tea and sautéed pears.

"Beast," Brendan said, pulling back far enough to afford a glimpse of his teeth catching at his lower lip. "I have a question. And, er. It's…kind of a big one. Important, I mean."

He could scarcely believe Brendan was still here in his bed-chamber, in front of him, not running away; in fact, moving nearer, pressing his slender frame close. "Hm?"

Brendan swallowed, his cheeks blazing crimson. "Right. So. This question. That I have. It's. Well."

"Just ask it, Brendan," Beast murmured with exasperation edging into fondness, wrapping a strand of that bewitching hair around his claws to give it a gentle tug. Brendan's eyes fluttered closed.

When they opened, he took a deep breath and firmly asked, "Is everything human down there?"

Beast's hand froze their explorations. "What?"

"Okay, look. I have to know beforehand. Exactly how much did the transformation change you? I mean, you have all your…" Brendan motioned in the general direction of Beast's lower half.

"Yes! I have all my…" Beast waved his hands emphatically. "What kind of question is that?"

"An obvious one? Look, Beast." Brendan laid both hands on each side of Beast's face. "It's not going to change anything. I just need some advance warning here. I think it's a reasonable request."

There was a prolonged silence. Beast felt very hot under his fur.

"Everything is...normal."

Brendan let out a tiny breath. "Well, that's...something of a relief." He smiled brilliantly and pulled Beast's head down for another kiss.

* * *

In mere seconds, the kiss grew heated, and Brendan surged into it with a soft, eager sound he was surprised issued from his own throat.

He pushed Beast back as he walked, leading him step-by-step closer to the bed. Beast's arms wrapped around him and lifted him off his feet. Before Brendan could gather his wits, his back pressed into the plush mattress, Beast's breath hot at his throat. Brendan arched up with a shocked gasp into the welcome weight atop him, head already swimming.

Beast fixed him in place with an intense hunter's glare. "You're...sure, about this?"

The question must have cost him. Brendan did not let his gaze falter. "I'm sure." Craning up to further express his sentiment with the language of lips, he slid his tongue slowly over Beast's bottom lip before pulling it between his teeth. Beast groaned, breath stuttering.

His tongue swept into Brendan's mouth, talons tangling in his hair. Beast shifted down and lightly placed a bite onto the sensitive strip of exposed skin above Brendan's collar, where neck met shoulder. Brendan shuddered, eyes sliding shut as Beast's tongue traveled the dip of his collarbone. A press of sharp teeth turned his knees to water.

His voice shook. "If...if this has all been an elaborate scheme to devour me, now would be a good time to spring the trap."

A low laugh rumbled against his skin. Lips dragged up from Brendan's jaw to his ear, and he gasped as Beast bit him again. "That would be one convoluted trap," Beast murmured. "Would have been a lot easier to eat you the night you wouldn't leave. Could have saved myself a lot of headaches."

Brendan managed a breathy laugh and pulled Beast back into a slow, searching kiss; exploring, tasting. He was lost for long moments, drifting with delight, eventually surfacing from his pleasant haze with the realization

Beast wasn't just prolonging the kiss for the pleasure of it; he was stalling.

"Something wrong?" he whispered.

Beast sighed heavily and pushed up on his elbows. "I... I don't..." Thick brows furrowed with frustration.

Brendan smoothed the pad of his thumb over each eyebrow, over tendrils of russet hair spilling across Beast's forehead. He slid a hand over one curved horn, marveling at the feel of warm, ridged ivory. This time, Beast did not flinch or pull away.

"It's all right. Talk to me."

Beast huffed, not meeting his gaze. "I know how to do *this* part. I...don't know how to proceed...for the rest."

"Ah, that old frame of reference problem." Smiling, Brendan drew his tongue along the curve of Beast's jaw. The short fur felt interesting against his tongue, unexpectedly silky, not all too dissimilar from skin. Beast drew in a quick sip of breath.

"There's no need to rush, you know," Brendan said. "We can just do this, keep kissing. We don't have to do any of...the rest." He let his head fall to the pillow to better watch Beast's face. Eyes gone dark, pupils swallowing iris. A pink tongue flicking out to wet kiss-bruised lips. A flaming tongue of lust curled in Brendan's belly.

"No," Beast breathed, "I want...the rest."

Sending up a relieved, blasphemous thanks to every saint in the heavens, Brendan yanked Beast down for another kiss. "The rest, it is then." He rolled, pushing the other man onto his back, and straddled him.

"First thing," he declared with a warm, mischievous smile, "is to remove some of these clothes." Without waiting for a response, he pulled off his shirt and flung it away. He licked his lips, nerves suddenly jangling. He could almost *feel* Beast's gaze on his skin, the hunger there nearly overwhelming. "And now yours."

He touched the hem of Beast's shirt and large hands clamped down over his, instantly, like a reflex.

"I don't—" Beast's throat moved through a thick swallow. "I think that should stay on."

195

BRENDAN & THE BEAST

Brendan tipped his head to the side. No sense in not being perfectly frank. "Beast, I'm going to lose my mind if I don't get you naked. Let me see you."

Beast did not move, face tight.

"Please."

After a breathless pause, Beast nodded, his grip loosening. Hands free, Brendan grinned and hastily shoved away fabric, finally baring a chest he'd spent a lot of time imagining.

Definitely the *one* thing he wanted to avoid was staring. It would not do to make Beast unnecessarily self-conscious. But it was hardly his fault that he couldn't resist.

Without the vestments of civilization, Beast looked impossibly even broader and larger than he did with them; muscles well-defined even under the golden fur, which was as short and smooth as it was on his face and arms, except in the center of his brawny chest where it grew in longer tufts. Brendan desperately wanted to sink his fingers into those curls, until he noticed Beast's small, tight nipples, hairless and bitable, and was caught in indecision. What to lavish his attention on first?

Apparently, he had stared in admiration too long, for Beast abruptly sat up and started to squirm out from under him. "I understand," he grunted, expression shuttered. "We'll forget this ever—"

Brendan lunged forward and pushed Beast back down, surprised when he managed it with his slighter frame. "Easy. I'm looking at you because I *like* the way you look, Beast." Beast still looked uncertain, tension pulling his muscular shoulders into a tight hunch. Gently Brendan stroked them, over collarbone to chest, hands skating down across the firmness of his stomach before traveling back up to repeat the whole caress. Beast relaxed minutely with every path his hands traced, eyes sliding shut, letting himself be soothed.

Brendan bit back a wild, exultant grin. Keeping to these light, undemanding strokes was driving him mad, but he restrained himself. As tempting as it was to rush in headlong, he had to be careful with Beast. This was, in some ways, his first time, and Brendan wanted to give him something special, something he didn't think anyone had ever bothered to. Beast's trust was a precious gift, and Brendan had no intention of proving it ill-earned.

His thumb brushed a nipple, and a short, hungry sound rumbled in Beast's throat. He pushed up and delved his tongue deeply into Brendan's mouth, closing a fist in Brendan's hair as his hips rocked up, once, hard, and Brendan thought he might pass out from sheer, delirious bliss.

"More," Beast said, voice husky with heat.

"Yes," Brendan agreed, throat dry. He dipped his fingers underneath the hem of Beast's breeches, brushing the line of his pelvis. Beast arched into the touch and gasped wordlessly. His breath quickened, which was pretty gratifying considering Brendan hadn't even done anything yet.

Beast met Brendan's gaze, a single canine furrowing into his lower lip. A new light sparked in his honey-dark eyes, a determination like nothing Brendan had ever had focused on him before.

He was shoved back up, his knees bracketing Beast's powerful thighs, and a single talon hooked under the ties of his breeches and deftly unfastened them. That undivided, lambent stare was almost more intense than the oversized hand that reached in and took firm hold of his aching length.

"Ah!" The sudden certainty was nearly as arousing as the touch itself. Beast watched him with something like amazement, and as Brendan shuddered under an experimental stroke, it spread into a slow, lupine grin.

Before he knew it, Brendan was flat on his back and Beast over him. Big hands tugged at his breeches, which clung stubbornly to his hips. "Take these off?" Beast asked in a breathless growl.

"God, yes." With Beast's help he managed to kick them away, shucking his smallclothes while he was at it. And suddenly, he was naked in front of Beast. For the second time, remembering his near-drowning with a little leftover embarrassment. Hopefully Beast found this experience a bit more impressive than the first, or at least agreeable enough to continue doing that remarkable thing he had been doing with his hand.

Beast grazed a touch along Brendan's thigh and settled on the curve of his hip. His eyes were shadowed, betraying no trace of feeling. "You look..." Beast exhaled, eyes suddenly flooded with a myriad of emotions that disappeared too quickly to read. He squeezed them shut for a full second, then took Brendan's face between his hands and kissed him firmly. He drew away and said with a barely discernible quaver, "You look...very good."

Warmth rushed all the way to Brendan's toes. He would have answered, but Beast's tongue drew a moist line down the middle of his uncovered chest, and all his wits were instantly dispersed by agile hands and insistent lips.

Brendan nearly fumbled in his eagerness to get into Beast's pants. He pressed one hand alongside Beast's straining hardness, heat suffusing all the way through the thick fabric. Beast bit his lip hard, as if to contain a fountain of words. Brendan watched in fascination as his piercing gaze lost focus, the breath stuttering past his lips.

"Yes?" Brendan asked softly, the press of his palm solid and certain. One last chance for Beast to change his mind.

"*Yes,*" dragged harsh and thick out of Beast's throat. Brendan tried to bite down a grin as he peeled the waistband down over Beast's hips and took the matter well in hand. The eager sound Beast made almost broke him. With his free hand, he tried to yank the breeches down out of the way.

Beast stilled his hand and turned onto his back. Brendan took the opportunity to lean in, burying his fingers in the thatch of chest curls, and sunk his teeth into the swell of Beast's pectoral. Beast arched into the bite with a guttural choke.

"That's." He panted. "That's very distracting."

Brendan flashed a wicked smile. "Is it? So sorry." He teased the furry whorl leading down Beast's stomach. "What could I possibly be distracting you from, dear Beast?"

Beast indicated his last remaining garment with aggravation. "From getting these off."

"Ah, my apologies. An important task, one I support fully. Please carry on." He settled back on his haunches to watch.

Beast squirmed out of his breeches easily enough until the knees; it seemed he had minor difficulty maneuvering the bunched cloth over his long, backward-bending ankles and taloned feet. The way his tendons stretched and flexed was fascinating. Brendan wished he could explore those strange planes and angles, but he had likely used up all his allotted gawking time admiring Beast's mouth-watering chest.

Speaking of mouth-watering, Beast was a little larger than normal, as Brendan had expected (not that he'd made a habit of spending several late-night hours speculating over the lurid details of Beast's body, no, certainly not) but not alarmingly so. He was, however, as hard as a bar of iron underneath silky skin when Brendan touched him. Beast tipped his head back, lips parted, his breath gone shallow.

It was like a curtain thrown wide, sunlight pouring into a shadowed room, the way Beast's ordinarily taciturn features fell open, the clear play of emotions written with every breath and twitch and sigh. Enthralled, Brendan swiped his thumb up and over the crown, wiping away a bead of moisture.

Beast shivered, sat up, and *growled*.

It reverberated all the way into Brendan's bones, his pulse leaping Beast drove him down to the mattress in a powerful surge. He was delightfully heavy, masculine scent redolent of crushed velvet and earthy musk, nails pricking into the crest of Brendan's hipbones as Beast thrust their lengths into exquisite alignment.

Wildly Brendan bucked up and pushed their mouths together, a searing, desperate clutch, matching the roll of their hips. Beast moaned against his tongue, and any resolve Brendan might have had to go slowly crumbled into ruins. He burned with need, a flood of embers smoldering beneath his skin as dipped a hand down to bring them together with a delicious, throbbing friction that set sparks off behind his eyes.

Beast tore out of the kiss with a feral growl, hands braced on either side of Brendan's shoulders. He looked down between them in open fascination, feasting his eyes as they strove together. His shaky exhale ghosted against Brendan's over-hot skin, and then he poured himself back into a hard, driving kiss; fingers clutching, legs entwined, all bruising teeth and apologetic lips.

It hit in a sweet, sudden ache; a welcome wave crashing tumultuous over him, rushing and roaring in his ears and after so many nights of dreaming about this, of wanting it so much he thought his heart would burst; dear God, it was *perfect*, and Brendan tripped and tumbled over that edge with a glad shout.

Beast tensed above him, and Brendan gasped, "Yes, yes," unable to express in sensible words his need to see Beast fall apart.

Beast pulsed hot over his hand in a shuddering swell, riding it out with his face pressed into the crook of Brendan's neck, burying a short gasp that just might have been his name.

Eventually time restarted, the world resuming its slow spin.

Brendan drew away his cramped hand with a pleased hum. Beast gave his neck a final bite before rolling onto his side, one arm still slung across Brendan's middle. Muscles in his forearm trembled as Brendan ran his fingers over them, through fur slick with sweat like a horse after a long ride.

He made use of the edge of a bedsheet, which wasn't the most elegant of solutions, but needs must. Wordlessly he offered it to Beast, who looked sheepish until Brendan snorted and pulled him into a kiss, not drawing away until he felt an answering smile against his lips.

God, but he loved that smile. Had anyone else ever really seen it? Suddenly overcome, Brendan took a rattling breath and pushed his face into Beast's chest, twining his arms around that broad frame.

"All right?" Beast asked with concern.

Brendan hid a beaming smile against Beast's breastbone, certain if he looked up, his love would radiate out and Beast would see it and he would *know* and it would ruin everything, Brendan's whole world shattering apart around him.

"Very," he said.

At the back of his mind the fear had crept that once the moment was over, Beast's curiosity sated, he would snap to his senses and become his old, hermetic self. But here he was, doing the opposite of pushing Brendan away, winding an arm tight around his waist.

Brendan wished fiercely this moment could be preserved, a jewel of memory frozen in time, unchanging forever.

The back of a knuckle caressed his cheek. He looked up and got caught in Beast's eyes. He couldn't decide if their warm color was more like dark amber or molten honey. Something easy to get stuck in, in any case; a fly-trap hue.

Brendan leaned his face into Beast's palm. "Do you want me to go?" He silently cursed himself. What was it about this man that made him always say the wrong thing?

Beast slowed his exploratory caress. "No," he said softly. "Do you want to?" His fingers flexed minutely against Brendan's cheek.

"No," he breathed.

A long pause. "Good." Twining a curl of Brendan's hair around his finger, Beast reeled him in for a slow, lingering kiss. Even spent, it brought a rise of gooseflesh. "We can have lunch here, if you like. Are you hungry?" Realizing he was, enormously so, Brendan nodded. "I'll send for provisions straight away. Are you..." Beast hesitated as if he was unsure of the proper pleasantries. "Are you content to remain here while I bathe?" He drew away and levered himself up to his feet.

Brendan raised a brow, trying to compose his voice into a nonchalant tease. "Oh. Feeling a trifle unclean?"

"What? No! It's that...sweat makes me all...spiky." Possibly he was blushing under his fur, though it was impossible to be sure. The knot of worry in Brendan's belly eased.

"Well, we can't have that, can we?" He lay back with a warm chuckle, hands crossed behind his head. Beast lingered, trailing his gaze over Brendan's nude body, and he could almost feel the tangible weight of those honeyed eyes on his skin. "I could join you, if you like," he offered, a touch breathlessly.

"I think...not this time." He gave Brendan a small, quiet smile before taking his leave.

Brendan smiled up at the silk-tasseled canopy above him, stretched all the way to his toes with a dreamy sigh, and waited.

✳ ✳ ✳

Beast twisted the brass knobs of the bath and let the basin fill. He was glad he had so long ago invested in the installation of running water, a luxury only available for the wealthiest, and even then it had been cost-prohibitive to outfit more than one or two rooms. It would have been decidedly awkward to have the servants fill a bath while he had a naked man in his bed.

A naked *man* in his *bed*.

Beast rested his hands on the rim of the sink, staring at the space on the wall where a gilt-framed mirror had once hung. He wondered if he looked any different. He certainly *felt* different. Not just the usual lassitude that came after sex, as he dimly recalled was the case, but perhaps something he found in Brendan's eyes; the naked want, or the warm, open acceptance.

Yes. That might be it.

He had been openly curious and even admiring as Beast lay bare, and hadn't flinched. Not once had his eyes darted away or his hands hesitated.

Beast had to clench his fingers on the porcelain at the thought of *those hands* to keep from melting to the floor. Steam curled around him.

Beast scrubbed quickly, toweled off, and threw on his dressing gown. On his way through the suite, he was surprised at how lived-in it looked, with new candles in the candelabras and fresh silk upholstering the divans. He'd gotten so accustomed to the shambles he'd forgotten how the castle used to look.

He poked his head out the foyer doors and announced, "Two lunches to be served up here. Nothing too fancy. Leave it on the sideboard of the foyer, *not* the bedroom itself." He pictured Brendan's disapproving frown, and added a "Thank you." He couldn't manage to keep the sarcasm out of it entirely, but it would have to do. Rolling his eyes at himself, Beast went back to the bedroom.

He was arrested at the threshold by the sight of every long, lean line of Brendan stretching across Beast's bed, arms up overhead with fingertips brushing the sturdy oaken headboard. Languidly he smiled up from the messy nest of the sheets, as unrealistically beautiful as some kind of siren tossed upon the seafoam, bringing with him fathoms and fathoms of trouble.

"I can't imagine why you bothered with the bath," the siren said, slyness creeping into his smile. "You're just going to have to take another one later." He drew in his limbs and rolled to the edge of the bed, where Beast had unconsciously drifted like a wayward ship. Brendan rose up to his knees and draped his arms over Beast's shoulders, eyes sparkling. "I can cope with a little spikiness."

Beast's knees threatened to wobble. He slid his arms around Brendan's waist, marveling at the feel of smooth skin underneath his palms.

"This was a good idea," Brendan continued, idly tangling his fingers in the towel-damp spill of Beast's hair, "coming up here right after breakfast. Now we can spend the whole day in bed, if we like."

The knot of Beast's throat bobbed as he struggled to keep his composure. "It was a good idea, wasn't it?"

Brendan's body stretched into a sinuous line as he pressed his lips to Beast's ear. "I have a few good ideas of my own, you know." His low murmur was heavy with promise, and a need so recently slaked began to surface again.

"Really," Beast breathed, aware of how his voice shook but unable to stop it. "All of your ideas thus far have been quite exceptional." The edge of a slick tongue traced the outer curve of his ear, which reflexively twitched forward. "Would you care to elucidate these ideas? I can assure you I am agog." A light laugh sent a shiver down his spine.

"I could be convinced." Brendan sank back down onto the mattress with a cheeky smile. "After lunch. It's your fault we skipped breakfast, you know."

Beast laughed.

And so they talked idly of unimportant things, laying together on the rumpled bedcovers, until Beast heard the slight click of a closing door, and retrieved their trays from the foyer. They ate stretched out on the bed, indulgently heedless to crumbs or spills, and Beast felt more alive than he had in any memory of his life before.

17

In Which the Past is Shared

Brendan's first good idea, after the empty luncheon plates were set away on the nightstand, was to thoroughly catalog and document Beast's physical peculiarities—purely in the interests of scientific inquiry, of course. He started with one of Beast's large hands, grazing the knuckles with his lips. Beast sucked in a sharp breath, then relaxed with a sound much like a purr.

The things I do for science. Brendan pushed up the sleeve of the dressing gown and drew his tongue in a broad stripe along the thinly furred skin of Beast's wrist. The muffled purr deepened. *Ah, he likes that, check.*

When he glanced up, Beast's eyes had narrowed. Brendan froze immediately, worried he had somehow misstepped. "What is it?"

"You have the strangest expression on your face."

His cheeks grew hot. "Oh?"

"It's the same look you get when you're translating Latin."

"You watch me when I'm reading Latin?"

"Well, when you *try* to read Latin." Beast smirked sharply, moving Brendan onto his back and settling atop him with no effort at all.

"Not all of us had two hundred years to study it," Brendan huffed in mock indignation. It was hard to pretend offense while Beast cleaved to him like a second skin, nose nuzzling in Brendan's hair, but he made a valiant effort nonetheless.

Beast snorted, teeth flashing in a grin. "So to what do I owe the look of such intense concentration? Are you running equations in your head? Remembering the names of all the tendons in my hand, perhaps?"

"Maybe I'm trying to learn *you*." The words came out breathier than Brendan intended.

Beast propped his weight on his elbows and looked down at him. "You're doing fine so far," he said quietly, then brushed his lips against Brendan's temple. "Better than you are at Latin, anyway."

Brendan laughed. He had a witty retort on the tip of his tongue, he really did, but completely forgot it when Beast eased down and kissed him. Brendan hummed appreciatively, running his hands over the watered silk of Beast's robe. All this talk of books and reading when they far better things to do with their time.

All this talk of *books*... A slow, skulking thought had been creeping in the shadows of Brendan's mind for some time, and now it finally sidled into the light.

Like a Beast you shall remain, forever, frozen in time as your heart was frozen in bitterness, until the day comes when you learn to love, and are loved in return, in spite of what you have become.

That strange and beautiful book he'd read so many long weeks ago, hidden in a dusty broken-mirrored room, the words written true in a way Brendan couldn't express, as if they had been penned with a steadfast conviction mortal hands could not possess.

The phrasing had stuck like a pebble picked up in a horse's hoof; deceptive in size, but digging in deeper with every step.

So here was the crux of it, then—Brendan had Beast in his arms, and knew beyond a shadow of a doubt that he was irrevocably in love with him. He hadn't even felt this way with Kieran, this utter unquestioning certainty that what he felt was *real*. Not mere infatuation, or some permutation of lust, but love. He loved, and knew it down to his marrow.

And Beast remained as he was.

Beast did not love him.

Logic hadn't been among his favorite university subjects, but he'd been good at it nonetheless. The curse would only be broken when they loved one another, and it wasn't broken: *ergo,* Beast did not or could not love him. There was no other conclusion to draw.

It wasn't an issue of something as trivial as *shape*; Brendan had fallen for Beast as he was, *in spite of what he had become* (how could an ancient book have gotten even that so very right?) and he had no wish for Beast to change. For all Brendan's bravado, all his forthright words and his unhesitant actions, a deep-rooted fear twined around his gut like a thorny bramble. After Kieran had left him, he'd barely been able to pull himself back together, and what he felt for Beast was…was a great deal *more*.

At the start he'd known Beast would most likely reject him—or even worse, *laugh* at him—but accepted the risk and gone ahead anyway. Wonder of wonders, he hadn't been tossed out on his ear, but that didn't mean his feelings were returned. Beast desired him, perhaps, but did not love him. The proof was in front of him, looking down with a crooked smile.

"Now what's that look for?"

You're going to break my heart, and I'm going to keep giving it to you anyway. Brendan managed a smile, pushing the thought back down into its shadowy refuge.

"Just thinking."

Beast propped his head on a loose fist and adopted a serious mien. "Good, you should definitely get some practice in."

Brendan laughed and shoved the other man off him. *"Bâtarde béat!"*

"More scandalous language. And the basest of lies. My parents were married," Beast drawled.

Brendan broke into chuckles again. He'd never seen Beast in such good cheer, and a warm glow suffused through his chest to think he might be the cause.

"What were they like?" He settled close, lifting himself up on one elbow. "Your parents. You've met my father, unlucky you, you know what he's like."

Beast managed an awkward half-shrug from his supine position. "They were… I don't know. The King and Queen. Distant." His gaze suddenly sharpened. "Your father… Does he know? About…you know." He made a vague motion that seemed to indicate Brendan, himself, and the bed they lay on all in one swoop. "About you?"

"Oh! No! No. Definitely not. He'd disown me in a heartbeat." He hadn't intended the bitterness, and cleared his throat to mask it while he idly traced the ornate pattern of the duvet. "Distant, hmm? I remember you once saying you were raised by nursemaids and tutors."

Beast watched the path of Brendan's fingers. "I suppose I was." Silence fell between them. "Do you want to see them?" Beast suddenly asked, pushing himself off the bed.

"Do I want to... *What?*"

Beast smirked, extending a large hand to pull Brendan to his feet. "Just get dressed and follow me."

* * *

It wasn't until it was too late to turn back, passing through the wing with Brendan's soft footfalls close behind him, that Beast considered this may not have been a good idea. He hadn't been in this part of the castle in years, and while there was no telling what sort of state it was in, that was not what gave him pause.

This room was full of his secrets.

Brendan stepped lightly to his side, the brush of his shoulder sending a little frisson of electricity up Beast's arm. He'd never get used to that, the sensation of touch. So strange, so addictive.

"Are we here? Not that I have any idea where *here* is."

"This," Beast said with the lofty air of a proclamation, "is the portrait gallery." He swung the door open before them.

Chandeliers flared to life, chasing shadows into their cobwebby corners. The network of halls was clearly old and unused, once-fine carpet now graying and curled, and the air had a staleness that faded as the light grew brighter. Frames adorned every wall in vast multitudes.

Brendan looked around with unguarded delight. Hiding his trepidation behind an arch smile, Beast swept his hand forth grandly, an invitation to explore at leisure.

Brendan stepped up to the first portrait and gave it a measuring look. Beast followed, sticking close to the shadows.

"Who's this?"

The painting was not in good shape, frame marred with rot and the canvas murky with age. Through peeling varnish a pretty young woman posed in an elaborate headdress and embroidered houppelande, her delicate hand set atop the head of a sleek ashen hound.

"It was customary for nobles to send portraits of their marriageable daughters to any eligible princes."

Brendan threw Beast a startled look. "You were supposed to marry this woman?"

"Hardly. I'm not even sure who she is. We must have received dozens of portraits like this from all over. It was considered crass to not hang up every damned thing you were given. Can't just throw them out, after all; nobility are worse than packrats. Anyway, it was sent to my elder brother, not to me."

"Is this the elder brother who traveled with the Norsemen? The one who brought you the book?"

"You remembered. Yes. Barnabie." Said aloud, the name sparked a small and unexpected bout of panic. He had brought Brendan here on the whim of a passing fancy, thinking he would enjoy seeing something new. But now Beast felt exposed, strangely more so than he had when he'd been naked a quarter-hour ago.

A sudden desire to run seized him. He quickly mastered it, admonishing himself. *Has he not already learned so much of you and not yet turned away? What does it matter if he knows of your family, too? All that is here are the faces of dead people.*

Beast's mouth tasted bitter. He walked ahead, skipping past several faded portraits of strange princesses.

Brendan kept apace. "Is there a portrait of him?"

"I believe so. This way." He led Brendan to a large, gilt-framed painting near the end of the hall. Iron-wrought sconces gave each painting emphasis and luminance, this part of the gallery in better shape. A slight breeze revealed the presence of the invisible servants as they lit more candles around them, the gloom fading.

Beast jerked his chin at the painting. "This is he. Eldest brother Barnabie."

Brendan was silent for a moment. Beast ignored the painting and watched him instead, already knowing what he would see: a tall, stern man with a beard as elaborately groomed as his finery. The man's serious eyes, though slightly too small to be thought handsome, had the same steely intensity as those of the falcon perched on his forearm.

Brendan said, "He certainly looks like the type who could hold his own among the Norseman."

Beast snorted. "He certainly was." He suddenly remembered the stubborn jut of his brother's jaw when he had an idea he just wouldn't let go of. He tore himself out of the memory, again suppressing the desire to flee. To distract himself, he waved at another painting.

"This is Cousin Colette, a comtesse, died a year after this was painted. Wasting sickness, I think." He led Brendan down the hall, naming people of interest as they went. "Marquise Claudette, second wife of my uncle Antoine. Uncle Hugo, with his terrible little dogs…"

Occasionally Brendan would stop and inspect a painting more closely, which made Beast fight the urge to fidget. "These two?" Brendan inquired. Painted in the Gothic style, two young men were seated in a grand parlor. Beast could see why it had caught Brendan's interest; both men held musical instruments.

"That gangly one on the left is my other brother, Henri. The other is one of our cousins, what was his name… I can't recall. A minor baronet, I think." He leaned in and lowered his voice as if imparting an important secret. "Henri didn't actually play, so you know. He just thought it would make him look more rakish."

"Really? A fraud, was he?"

"Unfailingly so. An absolute *scoundrel* with the ladies."

Brendan laughed heartily. He had such a good laugh, almost musical. Beast found himself saying absurd things just to hear it more often.

Finally they arrived at an enormous painting nearly spanning the entire wall, its gilt frame easily a foot thick and plentifully carved with rosettes and flourishes. An art-loving spider had made its home in the upper corner until an invisible hand brushed it away.

"King Frederic and Queen Brigitte." How odd that looking at the faces of his parents, saying their names aloud, stirred no trace of feeling; but then, they had ever been strangers to him.

Actually—and the thought struck like a sudden slap—every painting in this hall was of a complete stranger. This gallery, Beast realized, was a monument to isolation, a visual treatise on a lonely, friendless life. He had been surrounded by throngs of people and close to no one.

And for the first time in his life, he suspected it was his own fault.

Beast puzzled through this revelation while Brendan considered the royal pair. "They look very elegant." He turned to Beast with a soft smile. "You have his eyes, you know."

Beast shrugged one shoulder, affecting carelessness. "Well, there you are then, the portrait gallery. It must be nearing dinnertime, I should think."

As he turned to lead them out and away from these strange, empty faces, Brendan reached for Beast's arm. "Wait. Your very own portrait gallery, and none of you?" His smile widened. "Color me incredulous."

He…felt like an imbecile. He really should have expected this, shouldn't he? Of *course* Brendan would want to see him as he had once been. The handsome prince. This had been a terrible idea. But it was too late to take all this back, to just stay in bed and to never set foot in this dark, spidery hall ever again.

So Beast snorted. "Turn around." Behind them ran a long row of shredded wreckage. Canvases drooped utterly destroyed and rotted from their broken frames. Beast gestured to them with dark humor. "All of these along this wall are of me."

It was a good thing, really, that none were left. If Brendan could see Beast-as-he-should-be, and then looked back at the Beast-as-he-was-*now*, the inevitable disappointment on his face would be… It would be… Well, it would be something Beast did not wish to see.

Breath held, Beast watched from the corner of his eyes. Brendan took in the ruined paintings for a moment, then turned back with a wry smile. "I like how you just left the empty frames hanging there. An interesting design choice."

This startled a laugh out of him. "Well, you know me. I like my décor shabby as possible."

"I had a portrait painted, once. The family did, I should say, all of us together. It hung in our manor's vestibule before everything went to auction to pay off Father's debts."

"I'm sorry."

"Oh, don't be," Brendan laughed. "We all looked cross-eyed. Terrible likenesses."

"I didn't just mean the portrait."

Brendan's laughter melted into a half-formed, fragile smile. "Well, what can you do," he said with the cheerful resignation people spoke of flooding riverbanks or the terminally ill; tragedies that can not be mitigated but only be endured.

Then he paused, glancing from wall to wall. "You've told me all their names."

"Yes?"

"Hugo and Henri and Lady this and Uncle that, and so on..."

"Yes?" Beast didn't see where this was going.

"What is yours?"

Run run run run.

He checked himself, and stilled.

I...

It's...

Beast dug down into his memories and came up with nothing. His brows furrowed, and his answer dredged up in a low rasp. "I—I do not remember."

He stood there in cold silence, in a tangle of disbelief, embarrassment, and—most surprisingly of all—grief. He thought he had mourned for his lost self untold years ago, but to discover he didn't even recall his own name?

Now there was no one left who remembered him. No one would speak his name in memorial. Not even himself.

He stood there at the precipice of some great yawning gulf, only the sound of his own echoing heartbeat in his ears, until Brendan stepped forward, took Beast's hand in his own, and pulled him back from that edge. His hands were warm, and his smile warmer.

"No matter. I know everything I need to know about you already."

Beast's throat felt like a shredded canvas. "Don't you *care?*"

"Not really. Whoever I would have seen in those pictures wouldn't really be you."

Beast's eyes dropped to his bootless feet, to those hated claws, unable to give a name to the feeling behind his heavily thudding heart. His gaze dragged slowly up, locking onto slate-blue.

With a desperate growl, he pushed Brendan up against the wall and kissed him. Brendan gasped under his lips, surprise sliding into enthusiasm as he kissed back, and Beast lost himself again under the watchful gaze of a dozen half-remembered cousins.

* * *

Brendan melted under the onslaught, responding quickly despite the gallery's faint miasma of dust and mildew. Kissing Beast was like experiencing a force of nature. He'd never been bodily held up against a wall before, and it was proving to be a novel delight.

Teeth followed tongue against the sensitive curve of his neck, and he groaned, scrabbling for purchase in Beast's shirt. He slid his hands underneath the hem, muscles rippling under his fingertips. The tight press of their bodies had him hissing in pleasure, head thumping back against the wall.

Beast's voice was hot and gravelly at his ear. "Could I convince you to move this somewhere more comfortable?"

"Beast, at this point I think you could convince me the sky was orange." A growl underlaced Beast's low laugh, sharp teeth latching onto Brendan's earlobe. "*Ah!* With stripes, even."

212

Beast kissed him deeply enough to steal the breath from his lungs, then peeled away to say, "Your room is closer than mine."

"Does that matter? I thought the hallways went wherever you wanted them to."

Beast's eyes had gone dark as woodsmoke. "Doing that requires some… concentration. And I am in no fit state to concentrate on anything besides you at the moment."

Brendan forgot how to breathe. Then Beast took his hand and the next thing worth remembering was shoving bed-curtains out of the way and being pressed back into the mattress, their clothes littering the hardwood floor of his room.

Hungrily he swept his tongue into Beast's mouth, then drew the lower lip between his teeth with a gentle tug. Beast groaned and bucked his hips. Brendan rolled them until he straddled Beast's waist.

"Let me try something," he breathed into Beast's pointed ear, taking his strangled gasp for assent. He kissed his way down Beast's body, taking frequent detours along the way to tease and nibble, mentally cataloging what made Beast's lungs catch or his limbs twitch. Soon Beast was breathing in shallow catches, muscles quivering faintly.

Brendan wriggled lower and bit at the sharp jut of Beast's hip, mouth watering with anticipation.

"What are you—"

And then in one easy movement he took as much of Beast as he could into his mouth.

In the periphery of his vision, Beast's head rocked back, his whole body arching up like a bow about to be fired. He went utterly silent, as if his body had no intention of wasting precious attention on something as foolish as breathing.

Brendan hummed in pleasure; at the weight, the texture, at the welcome taste blooming on his tongue. After a while he disengaged briefly, voice colored with amusement. "Breathe, Beast."

Beast shakily sucked in a lungful of air, knuckles taut-clenched on the sheets. Extremely gratified, Brendan pressed a warm little laugh against wet skin before concentrating again, until the slide of his lips and tongue completely unraveled the man beneath him.

The broken gasp of his name came like a benediction, and he too fell apart.

After, Brendan rested his head on that broad chest, closed his eyes and drifted, lost in that aching ocean of a heartbeat.

Beast's breathing took a long time to slow, hands carding through the messy curls fanning across his chest. The husky rumble of Beast's voice reverberated pleasantly up through him. "No one has done *that* for me in…a *very* long time."

"Mm." It seemed an enormous task to move, even if just to reach for the duvet and pull it up around them. Instead Brendan stayed where he was and tucked his cold feet underneath Beast's legs, shamelessly stealing his heat. Beast didn't even complain, which in Brendan's opinion was enough reason to fall in love with him all over again.

"Are you all right?" Beast asked.

"Mmhm."

"I mean, are you…*all right*? That is to say, are you, ah. Content?" Somehow Beast made the last word sound almost salacious.

Brendan craned his neck back to look at him without lifting his head, and smiled languorously. "Mmhmm."

"You're sure?"

They had progressed way beyond the point of verbally dancing around indelicacies, as far as Brendan was concerned, and he couldn't resist an opportunity to tease. "Are you asking if I…broke my arrow? Cleaved my pin? Had the little death? You want to know if I summited the Pyrenees?"

"Oh, my God," Beast muttered in utter mortification, shoving at Brendan's shoulders not nearly hard enough to dislodge him. "You're awful." They wrestled in a brief pantomime of pique until Beast caught Brendan back up into his arms with a scuff of low laughter.

Settling in, still chuckling, Brendan hid his yawn against the curve of Beast's collarbone. "I'm not surprised you didn't notice. You were otherwise engaged. Sweet of you to check."

"But. I didn't even touch… Just from that?"

"Mmhm. Being on the other side has its own rewards, you know."

Beast was silent for a moment, claws gently tracing across Brendan's shoulders and raising a line of goosebumps in their wake. "I see." Brendan couldn't help a displeased grunt as Beast maneuvered him back into the pillows and pulled the covers over him. "Here, you're freezing." He smoothed the duvet with a thoughtful expression as Brendan lazily watched. Beast said softly, "Well. If that's the case, I might have to try it sometime."

Once, when Brendan was a lad of thirteen, he had been invited to an acquaintance's country estate for part of the season. They'd been on a long ride through the outlying fields, where the ripe summer wheat met up with the liminal edge of the forest. They heard a high, piercing screech, brought their horses to a halt, and watched an enormous eagle swoop down to land on a fallen branch along the trail, not two yards away. Without even glancing at one another, both boys knew not to move even a little, and they sat silently watching the eagle for what may have been minutes or hours, barely even blinking lest it frighten the majestic creature away.

Brendan felt the exact same way now. Finally he brought up his hand, tangled it in the Beast's thick mane, and pulled him down into a kiss, not trusting his voice in the slightest.

When Beast pulled away, running his tongue over his lips, he cleared his throat and asked, "Are you hungry?"

Brendan stretched. At the moment he was definitely more interested in sleep than he was in dinner. "No, I'm fine. You go ahead, though."

Beast gave him a lopsided smirk. "How have you managed for the past months to conceal how exceedingly slothful you are?"

"You're *supposed* to be lazy after sex," Brendan protested. "You're the one who has to get up and fuss about with baths and dinners. It's unnatural."

Beast snorted in amusement. He stood and cast about for his clothing, plucking pieces off the floor. Appreciatively, Brendan watched him dress, then suddenly snickered.

"What?"

"I just realized. In the portrait gallery? If the servants didn't know before, they sure as hell do now." He grinned puckishly as Beast stared at him, and

BRENDAN & THE BEAST

very possibly blushed.

* * *

Something had gone awry.

Magic, like any living thing, can balk at being leashed, though we of the sorcerous persuasion are loath to admit it. Likewise, both gardens and stories can go wild, baleful, throwing up thorns and brambles, the expected harvest gone to rot and worms.

Cloaked I went down long roads, twisting through woods until greening fields prevailed into a village bursting all over with the spring.

The cottage was tucked between beech trees that strayed out from the oaks of the dark forest bordering the town. The roof was well thatched, the last vestiges of snow melting off it in rivulets, and slips of smoke curled out of the chimney. A young mare shared a patch of sweet new grass with a few fine goats, and a low stone wall surrounded a garden of fragrant kitchen herbs.

Under the windows grew a thick tangle of rosebush, blooming early with deep red buds—I knew those roses. Looking at them rankled, deeply. Frost crept outward from the hem of my cloak, blades of new grass withering at my feet.

This was not right. The correct players were not in their proper places. My story dared to try tell itself.

Easy enough to mend.

I pulled my hood up and slipped away to blend into the dusky shadows, waiting for the approach of nightfall.

18

In Which the Future Looms

When morning slanted bright across tangled sheets, Brendan awoke alone.

He stumbled out of bed, yawning hugely, and scrubbed his face in the washbasin. His stomach gave a loud grumble, scolding him for skipping dinner the night before, so he bathed and dressed quickly, barely bothering to run a comb through his hair before tying it up out of the way. Funny how there seemed to be plenty of ribbons on the dresser today.

Hunger wasn't the only reason for his haste. A happy, fluttering eagerness lightened his steps, and he nearly floated down the stairs.

At the sight of Beast reclining in his usual chair, everything clicked into place. Brendan was sure he must be smiling like a fool, as he took his seat. "Good morning," he said, picking up a grapefruit spoon and toying with its sharp edge to give his hands something to do.

"Good morning to you, too. Did you sleep well?" Beast leaned forward, chin in hand. He wasn't exactly smiling, but the slow curve to his lips hinted he wasn't far from it.

"Very. You could have joined me, you know."

"Is that so?"

"If you wanted," Brendan hastened to say, all at once unsure if that was an intimacy he had any right to offer. Sleeping together was one thing, but *sleeping* together could be quite another. Brief post-coital naps notwithstanding, Brendan had always snuck back to his own room after a dalliance, the risk of getting caught too great to chance discovery.

What would it be like waking up while still being held in Beast's arms?

The kitchen door swung open, and covered platters carted out along the empty air and set before them. Silver cloches whisked away, and Beast gestured toward the meal with a gentlemanly flourish. Brendan let the issue drop and tucked in to eat.

"So, what shall we do today?" Beast asked after a good portion of breakfast had been devoured. "Bit cold for a ride. Library? Or I could beat you at Rithmomachia again."

Brendan swallowed a bite and groaned theatrically. "You keep bringing that up. Must I relive my ignominious defeat? Will it haunt me ceaselessly to the very grave?" He raised his fist and shook it melodramatically, the effect slightly marred by having a fork in it.

"All right, all right, no Rithmomachia. Perhaps a music recital?"

"It *has* been a while since I've gotten in some practice. Although…" He let his voice drop into a deeper, throaty register. "Yesterday we spent practically the whole day abed. Perhaps we should do something a little more…vigorous?"

Beast's heated eyes met his own. "I know just the thing."

* * *

Brendan panted heavily. He shook damp hair out of his eyes as a droplet of sweat rolled down the middle of his back. Beast wasn't even winded, which Brendan found to be utterly unfair.

"You're terrible at this," Beast laughed. "Didn't they teach fencing at that fancy university of yours?"

"They did, but after the introductory classes, I elected to take tennis instead." Once he caught his breath he squared up *en garde*. Beast's lunged, and Brendan barely sprang out of the way, the *fleuret* missing his hip with an alarming swish.

"Have you read *Flos Duellatorum*?" Beast asked airily, twisting his wrist in

218

an elegant flourish.

"Can't say as I have." He barely sidestepped another well-placed swipe. He returned one of his own, which Beast batted aside as easily as he would shoo a fly. "Italian, is it?"

"Yes, a treatise by Fiore dei Liberi on fencing technique. Very informative. You might find it illuminating."

"I'm on to you. You're trying to distract me with literary zeal." Brendan flashed a grin at Beast over a clumsy parry.

"Am not," Beast said with affront too thick to be anything but put on. "I'll have the servants bring it to your room later." Another thrust came much too close for Brendan's comfort. "Don't worry, there are lots of pictures."

Brendan only managed a scoff, trying to concentrate. The flashing épée looked utterly natural in Beast's great claws, and when he wasn't ducking wildly out of its range Brendan admired his easy steps, the cool confidence in his every motion. It was distractingly appealing.

Brendan darted in on the offensive, and after Beast parried he followed through with a fine riposte.

"Nice," Beast murmured, falling into a defensive stance. Their blades met, ringing out in the *salle*.

Brendan beamed, ridiculously pleased at the praise, and the distraction proved his downfall.

Beast's arm shot forward cobra-quick, the tip of the *fleuret* landing squarely over Brendan's heart. The impact shoved Brendan back a step.

"Okay, okay! Touché, you win!" Brendan backed off, lowering his sword. Beast drew himself up and saluted, looking a little too smug. Brendan saluted back, because those were the rules, and muttered, "You just better hope you never go up against me in a tennis match. I came in third at a tournament."

"Alas," Beast said, a mocking hand to his heart, "these grounds are bereft of tennis courts. These tales of your athletic prowess must remain sadly unconfirmed."

Brendan rubbed at his breastbone, where the prod of the épée had struck hard, even through the padded jerkin.

"Are you hurt?" Beast asked, concern softening the caustic edges of his voice.

"No," Brendan scoffed. "I'm fine."

"Are you sure?"

He rolled his eyes. "It might bruise, but I am not some delicate flower."

Beast watched as Brendan unbuckled the leather pads, hands jerking impatiently at this unfamiliar task. "Did I say something wrong?"

Brendan sighed and turned back to Beast, gathering his damp hair into a tail before tying it back up. "No, no, you didn't. It's me, I'm sorry." Saying nothing, Beast stepped closer. Brendan chewed his lip for a moment. "It's just… Sometimes I feel like you don't take me seriously."

He was entirely unprepared for Beast's hands to come up and cup his face between them. He went still, heart stuck somewhere in his throat.

"Is this serious enough?" Beast covered his mouth with his own for a deep, honey-sweet kiss.

After a long second of eternity he pulled away, and Brendan released a shaky laugh. "You tell me."

They looked into each other's eyes for a lingering moment.

Beast tore his gaze away, stepping back. A troubled look might have flashed across his leonine face, but Brendan said nothing and continued taking off his armor.

When their equipment hung on their appropriate pegs and swords mounted back up on their racks, Beast suggested they take lunch in the solarium. A bright, open room with high ceilings and ivy-covered windows, no doubt green and beautiful in summer. Snow had piled in the corners of each glass pane, limiting their view of the gardens and making the solarium feel more private, almost cozy. Unlike most other rooms in the castle Brendan was familiar with, very little was torn or in some other way ruined; most likely because every surface of the solarium was either glass or dark wood paneling, and it would be quite a task even for the Beast to shred up a hardwood floor.

"So," Brendan later began, mopping up leftover sauce with a crust of fresh bread, "you learned fencing in the Italian style, did you?"

Beast lounged on a settee with his particular brand of casual grace Brendan had always admired. "They invented all the best techniques. Surely you aren't going to accuse me of an unseemly lack of patriotism?"

Brendan laughed out loud. "Not at all. I'd be drawn and quartered if I admitted this in certain circles, but it's the same story with music."

"Such is the way of things," Beast chuckled, swirling a glass of garnet-red wine before taking a drink. "Steal from the neighbors and claim it your own all along."

"Have you ever been?"

"Been what?"

"To Italy," Brendan said with a good-natured roll of his eyes.

Beast's smirk disappeared. "No."

"I've always wanted to go." Brendan watched snowflakes melt against the solarium windows. "Visit all the famous concert halls and opera houses. I've got a list of places I want to see one day," he offered, a little shyly; it felt like divulging a deeply held secret, opening the shell of his most impossible hopes to let Beast glimpse the pearl within.

"Do you."

"Oh, yes. Italy is high on that list, maybe the second or third spot. Where do you most want to go?"

"Where do I most want to go," Beast repeated, each word clipped short.

Brendan looked over sharply. He knew that quiet, creeping quality of Beast's tone; the one that always preceded some violent outburst, a rumble of thunder before the breaking of the storm. "Beast, I—"

"No, this is an excellent line of inquiry." Beast sat up very straight, eyes flint-sharp, and set his glass down on the table with a loud clink. "Not at all sheer idiocy. Asking someone shackled to an eternal prison *'where do you most want to go.'*" His voice went high with mockery, lips curling in a sneer.

Brendan cupped his elbows in his hands, stomach twisting. "I'm sorry, that was… I wasn't—"

"You weren't what? Thinking? What a shocking change of pace for you."

Spine stiffening, Brendan gave Beast a flat stare. "Rather uncalled for," he murmured, a barely-voiced reproach.

Beast's shoulders dropped. He buried his face in his hands. "I know," he said after a tense minute, words muffled. He sat back up and met Brendan's level gaze. "I didn't mean it."

Brendan inclined his head the faintest fraction, the silent challenge of his gaze not faltering. Beast's eyes darkened slightly, and the little hairs on Brendan's arms all stood up, as if he were in an electrical storm.

"Come here," Beast rumbled in a soft, silky voice.

Brendan ignored the way his heart tripped against his ribs and lifted his chin. "No."

Beast growled low in his chest, then subsided. Brendan waited.

"Please," Beast finally said, just contrite enough for Brendan to rise and walk around the low table until he was in front of Beast, their knees nearly touching.

Beast reached up, his taloned thumb slowly drawing a circle around the point of Brendan's wrist. He swallowed and let himself be pulled down into Beast's lap. Settling into a comfortable drape, his hands curling over broad, velvet-clad shoulders, sliding his mouth over Beast's. He tasted of wine, the tart smokiness suiting him down to the ground.

Beast broke away to mumble against his neck, "Sorry." His hands nearly spanned the breadth of Brendan's waist.

"Forgiven. You didn't even break anything this time. I'd say that's progress." A low laugh ghosted against his cheek. "I am, too. I spoke thoughtlessly."

Beast said nothing for a while, face hidden at Brendan's throat. "What is at the top of your list?"

"Hmm?" Brendan shivered at the brush of lips tracing the line of his jaw. "Oh. Greece."

Beast took a long drag of air, claws pricking through Brendan's doublet. "That's mine, too. The place I'd go."

A sting struck Brendan square in his breastbone, a far more forceful strike than the épée. He bit down on automatic platitudes like *I'm sure you shall,* or something even more foolish like *Perhaps we can both go together, someday,* and instead answered with a kiss, slowly exploring when wine-tart lips parted enough to let him in, touching the smooth ridges of Beast's horns simply because he could, and gave the slight suggestion of rolling hips.

Beast rumbled deep in his chest and pressed up, licking into Brendan's mouth, and time dissolved for a while.

Only when furred hands encircled his wrists did Brendan realize his own hands had been wandering steadily southwards, even going so far as to untuck Beast's shirt from his breeches, quite without any conscious memory of doing so.

"Not here," Beast murmured.

Brendan tried to catch his breath, mystified. "Why not?"

Beast's eyes darted about like he was on the lookout for enemy spies. "The servants. They could be watching."

"Er. Can't you ask them to go away?"

"I *could*, yes, but... Well, they've been rather fractious of late."

"*Fractious?*" Brendan fought off a laugh. "Well, we certainly can't have that. Fractiousness leads to far worse things: first contrariness, then recalcitrance, then onto downright insubordination."

"It's your influence, you know," Beast shot back with a frown. "They see you disobey me, and they think they can do the same."

Wiping his smile away, Brendan sat back and adopted the quietly livid expression that never failed to convince his sisters he was furiously angry with them. He'd won a lot of quarrels with that look until Beauty learned the power of the hurt sniffle, which reigned supreme in any sibling squabble.

"Oh, I'm to be obedient, am I, Your Highness?"

"No," Beast said hastily, "that's not—it isn't—"

Brendan's mock sternness melted into a roguish grin.

Beast rolled his tawny eyes in exasperation. In one swift motion he threw Brendan back against the pillowed arm of the settee and clambered on top of him. "You are *infuriatingly* vexing. Do you realize that?"

"As long as I'm not *fractious*."

Beast buried his face in Brendan's shoulder and laughed silently, his amusement quaking pleasantly through Brendan's body. When the laughter had run its course, Beast stood up, eyes bright. He pulled Brendan to his feet, twining an arm companionably through his own.

"Would you mind terribly if I escort you?"

"Depends on where we're going," Brendan rejoined easily, as if his wits didn't abandon him every time Beast went out of his way to touch him; as if those broad hands didn't set his heart racing every time they were on him.

"The music room. You did say it had been too long since you've had some practice." Brendan had little choice but to keep up as he was led from the solarium, taking two steps for every one of Beast's. "And it has been too long since I've heard you play. I had my heart set on a proper recital."

Charmed beyond measure, Brendan grinned, a flush claiming his cheeks. "Well, if my gracious host desires a recital, then a recital he shall receive."

So that night he played, and with every measure tried to say what he couldn't speak, as if the dulcet notes themselves could carry his love through the air.

* * *

Marking the passage of days did not come easily to Beast. He'd long since been living season-to-season, rather than day-by-day, and it had taken some practice to get back into the habit of thinking in *yesterdays* and *tomorrows*.

The winter sun was fading into evening when Beast rapped on Brendan's bedroom door. It slid open at his knock to reveal the young man curled up in front of the fire, his nose in a book, the flickering firelight catching red in his hair. He briefly glanced up before going back to reading.

"Come on in. I'm almost finished."

Beast stepped inside with a fond shake of his head. The lack of a second chair meant he sat down on the bed, sprawling his awkwardly-bent legs out in front of him. Brendan looked to be on the last few pages, his eyes avidly darting back and forth. Must be a good read.

Beast leaned back on his hands, content to wait, letting his gaze idly travel the room. Piles of books on the side table awaiting return to the library; a hairbrush on the windowsill sitting atop a nest of ribbons; a lute and a gnawed quill on a desk strewn with papers. The pages had parallel lines sketched across them and a crowding of notes prefaced with a treble clef. A lot of sections had been scribbled out, and a sparse number of others circled.

A rose stood in the vase on the nightstand. In fact, judging by its dark hue and nuance of shape, it was the very same rose the merchant stole—the very one Beast used to focus an oathbreaker enchantment through as punishment. How odd he'd forgotten all about it. After a moment's consideration, he found he didn't mind. It looked good where it was, at Brendan's bedside.

A short time later, Brendan shut the book with a sigh of satisfaction. "Sorry, I was miles away, there."

"No need to explain. I quite understand."

The fire had died down. Brendan stood up with a stretch and went around the room lighting lamps and candles. "Anything in particular you came to see me for?" The flirtatious look he darted over caught Beast unawares. It took a second to remember why he'd actually come.

"Ah... Yes. I had thought an evening ride might be pleasant."

"Oh." Brendan gazed out the window, where the sunset still lingered among clouds the color of autumn leaves. "He'll be anxious for some exercise, I think."

"I thought the same, myself."

Brendan said nothing for a long moment, attention still fixed on the distant vista below. "Did you know it's nearly March?"

He hadn't. "Winters can be long, here."

Brendan's head dropped, tousled hair snaking from his shoulders to shield his face. When he turned back around, his hands trembled ever so slightly, probably imperceptible to anyone without the keen animal senses Beast possessed.

"Beast," Brendan began, eyes averted. "Do you... I need to... Is this..." A thick exhale of frustration. "Never mind." Then he threw himself at Beast.

Want tightened inside him, no less potent for its suddenness. He caught Brendan in his arms and fell back against the bed, eagerly twisting off the other man's shirt. He pulled his head down, teasing a nip at Brendan's lips before claiming them in a searing kiss.

It was easier every time; easier to give a little more of himself, and easier to take, like a locked door had been flung open inside Beast and all his long-restrained desires pouring through.

Brendan's clever hands unfastened an array of buttons, and in mere moments every stitch of their clothing lay scattered around them. Beast flipped on top in one smooth movement, licking at the bared hollow of throat, drunk on the taste of salt-sweet skin. His tongue rasped along the fine edge of Brendan's jaw, reveling in the contrast of textures; smooth skin and rough stubble.

Brendan hummed with pleasure, then opened his eyes. "Sorry, I... It just occurred to me I haven't shaved for a while."

It took a long moment for Beast to translate his thoughts into words. Had he ever experienced anything similar during any of his previous romantic encounters, if they could even be called that? No. But was Beast deriving more pleasure out of the simple scrape of this man's nascent beard than he'd ever felt with any part of a woman? Assuredly yes.

"I...kind of like it," Beast breathed, voice small and weak to his own ears, a reflexive rush of shame following the admission.

"Do you?" Brendan whispered, delight evident in his eyes as the reflected candlelight painted them into blue agates.

Beast's only answer was to kiss him, so long and so deeply that when they broke apart he gasped for air. They finally found a rhythm, hips aligned and bucking hard. Brendan writhed against him, his slender, calloused fingertips digging into Beast's biceps hard enough to bruise. And the *sounds* he was making...

From the very beginning, Beast had noticed Brendan's pleasant voice, enjoyed the rich, silvery tones of his singing, and how interestingly husky it got in the mornings. But like this, breathless and raw with need, a voice like the melt of bittersweet chocolate...

"God, your *voice*," escaped him, and he buried his face in the crook of Brendan's shoulder, eyelids squeezed tight. "Say something, anything—"

"*My* voice?" Brendan sounded surprised, even taken aback.

"*Yes*," Beast hissed, and tugged him into an intense, grasping kiss.

226

When Brendan pulled back, a wicked spark lit in his eyes. "I'm learning all *sorts* of things about you today." The throaty burr in his words was unmistakably intentional.

Beast groaned, grinding against Brendan's thigh, far closer than he wanted to be so soon.

"What would you like me to say?" Brendan purred. "How good you feel, how handsome you look? How much I— I want you?" A break, quickly covered, like he might have intended to say something else.

Beast shut his eyes tight, determinedly not thinking about it, what it might mean, whether any of it was true. He latched their lips together, heart galloping at the way Brendan kissed in sharp nips and languid licks, all advance and no retreat. That alone would have been enough to finish him, but Brendan grasped for his hand, braiding them together, and guided them both down in tandem between their rocking hips.

Beast learned the way of it, as if he were being shown the moves to a dance or a duel. Brendan keened and shivered, a shuddering spill over their joined hands. Beast followed a spare second later, and for one slim, perfect, golden moment, every trace of *yesterdays* and *tomorrows* vanished and left only glorious, reckless *tonight*.

When the world came back to him, he found the sheets had been drawn up to his chest, and Brendan stretching out languorously beside him. Staring up at the tasseled canopy, Beast slowly caught his breath, all those tomorrows creeping back.

He sat up. A muffled sound of protest beside him.

"Moving around again already?" Brendan wriggled deeper under the sheets. "We can take the horse out tomorrow. Relax, lay back for a bit."

Beast said nothing.

"Unless you want to go again, of course. I am definitely in favor of that."

"You didn't have to say that."

"Say what?"

The word scraped as it went, leaving him raw. "Handsome."

Beside him, Brendan sat up too, playful tone gone. "I didn't—"

"The curse is not just going to go away. This. What we're doing. It's not… She wanted to punish me. The sorceress. And. I don't—" Not at his most articulate. He took deep breaths to steady himself, his words hanging in the air like candle smoke after the snuff.

Shifting closer, Brendan slid a hand over his own. "So then, how do we break it?" His tone was sensible, as if this was an equation that could be solved.

Beast moved his hand away. "We can't."

"We could try to find this sorceress, or someone else who knows how to undo it—"

"Do you think I haven't tried?"

Beast got up and stalked nude to the window, glaring down at the garden, his precious roses stark black against the snow. "Even if there was a way, I…I don't know who that person even *is* anymore. I don't know how to be him again. There's none of him left." Beast dragged a palm over his face, and caught his own reflection in the dark window. He quickly looked away. "I don't even remember his name, or what he looked like. Not really. I am just… I'm only this, now. This is all that's left."

Slender arms slid around his waist, tugging Beast back into an embrace he was weak enough to encourage, leaning back against Brendan's slight but solid frame.

"Come here," Brendan said gently, guiding him a few steps toward the hearth, where the light was best. He reached into a desk drawer and drew forth the silver handheld mirror. Beast frowned as it was presented to him.

"How did—wasn't this in my rooms?"

Brendan flashed an impish smirk. "I stole it again." He offered the magic mirror once more. "Come on. Do me a favor and look into it."

Hesitant with uncertainty, Beast took the mirror, holding it at enough of an angle for it not to catch his face. Brendan pressed close to his side, and Beast waited to be enlightened. "Well? What am I supposed to be looking at?"

Brendan's smile softened, and his hand wrapped around Beast's, tipping the mirror down.

"You."

Beast was startled enough that he did look, eyes quickly skidding off the sight of his own hated face. He swallowed hard, something like hurt and anger and shock all mingling together in a leaden lump in his throat.

"*Why?*"

Brendan put his head on Beast's shoulder. "Because calling you handsome wasn't just pillow talk, Beast. *Look*. Really look."

The simple act of looking at a piece of glass should not make his heart thud so unaccountably fast, or cause bitterness to coat his tongue. But unable to deny Brendan even this, his eyes caught; and he looked.

"See?" Brendan brought up a hand to trace the sharp cut of Beast's jaw, to stroke a line over his proud nose, to thumb the umber-gold sweep of his brows. "A face a fellow could get direly attached to, don't you agree?"

An overwhelming flood of warmth drowned Beast's bewildered disbelief, a tide that left him floundering for breath. "You...are *utterly mad*."

"Maybe so," Brendan allowed. "Or maybe the better I get to know you, the better I like what I see."

Utterly. Mad.

Dropping the mirror to the nearby chair, Beast scooped Brendan up in his arms and pushed him back to the bed, letting his passion run fierce and wild, and for just a little while let himself believe it.

* * *

Brendan tumbled back, sinking into the pillows as he curved up into the slick glide of Beast's tongue dragging down the middle of his chest. His heart jumped as Beast kept going; a wet, heated caress along the dip of his navel. Breath held in anticipation, Brendan felt as if a rosined bow had been drawn across all his thrumming nerves in one legato stroke.

Beast laughed softly against the skin of his thigh, and rasped, "Breathe, Brendan."

Brendan managed a shaky little laugh before he knew nothing but the searing heat of Beast's mouth, quivering from head to toe in aching pleasure. "Oh, God, Beast." Beast gave a deep, answering hum, and Brendan tried

229

desperately to keep his hips still.

"That's perfect," he gasped, because apparently Beast liked the sound of his voice, liked the way Brendan spoke as no one had ever dared to before. He let his octave drop low, threading his fingers into golden hair. "I knew you'd be good at this. You like it?"

Eyes squeezing shut, Beast exhaled sharply through his nose and redoubled his efforts, and either he'd been paying very close attention to Brendan's technique, or perhaps Beast's instincts were just *that* good because even so soon after last time Brendan was already brought right to the edge.

"Wait, wait." Brendan pushed at Beast's horns. "It's too much, I can't—" When Beast crawled back up, Brendan pulled him close so their foreheads touched, breath mingling. He swallowed hard. "What do you want?"

"I want everything."

Brendan shivered, managing a weak laugh. "You don't know what everything is, Beast."

Beast thought this over for a moment. "No, but I still want it."

"God," Brendan whimpered, just barely aloud, against the other man's lips. He pushed Beast firmly onto his back and sat astride him, peppering frantic kisses all over his face and chest while muttering, "Yes, yes, I want that, too." He wanted it more than he could ever remember wanting anything, his heart setting a staccato beat against his ribs.

"Don't move," he ordered, and slid off the bed to rummage in a dresser drawer. When he regained his perch, Beast gave the glass vial in his hand a curious look.

"What's that?"

In an offhand, nonchalant sort of way, Brendan said, "Bath oil. I kept it from the last time the servants drew me a bath. For no reason."

Beast looked slightly baffled. "Why did you—"

"For *absolutely no reason whatsoever*," he stressed, face burning. "I mean, I wasn't…planning anything."

Beast hiked up one thick brow. "You're being especially cryptic today."

"Oh, *I'm* cryptic," Brendan groused, leaning forward to scatter more kisses to Beast's face. "Hello, kettle. You're black."

He adored the way Beast laughed under his lips.

The teasing kiss quickly became heated, and soon they were both gasping for air, bodies striving closer and closer as if their skins kept them too far apart.

Brendan wrenched himself back with considerable effort, his voice unsteady in his own ears. "I'm going to do something. Tell me to...to stop if you need to." He wasn't sure how Beast would take this, if he'd be interested, or if he would even like it, but—

"I trust you," Beast said simply, running a steadying caress up his arms. Brendan had to drop his head, biting his lip behind the shield of his disheveled hair, lest he confess his heart and ruin everything.

When he regained some semblance of composure, he poured out a palmful of oil, sat back on Beast's thighs, and took him between slick hands. Beast bucked up wildly into Brendan's grasp, nearly throwing him off.

"Easy," Brendan soothed. He shifted higher, and Beast's eyes went wide with realization.

"Can...can we do that?" he asked hoarsely.

Brendan's only answer was a swift, wolf-like smile.

He'd need to go slow, but the oil was a considerable help. Brendan eased down, relishing the delicious stretch, the slight near-pain burn, until he could not sink down any further.

By that time, Beast's eyes had rolled all the way back in his head. He gripped Brendan's hips tightly enough to leave sharp little pinpricks of his claws, just enough to indent skin. Brendan shivered, bracing his palms flat on Beast's heaving chest.

"All right?" he asked.

The sound Beast made wasn't anywhere close to language. He visibly gathered himself to answer, "Just...don't move for a second."

Brendan trembled with the effort of keeping still, aching to move, to get *more*. Finally Beast gave him a shaky nod, and he snapped forward with relief. Beast's cry matched his own; a natural harmonic of notes sliding together in synchronicity. Brendan leaned into an angle that had him keening, pleasure flaring hot and glorious inside him, goosebumps prickling up every inch of skin.

Voice fragile as wet silk, Beast whispered, "Are you all right?"

"Yeah," Brendan groaned as he rocked. "It's...it's good." A woeful understatement, but he couldn't wrangle together anything better, brain a fuzzy mess of building rapture. "This is... I can't explain."

"No one told me...*that* felt like anything special," Beast said haltingly, like he too was having trouble with coherence.

Brendan laughed low and sultry, falling forward onto his hands. "It's a *secret*," he whispered in Beast's pointed ear. "Otherwise everyone'd be doing it."

Beast wrapped strong arms around him, one hand curling tight into the tangle of his hair. It was too much, the full length of Beast's body burning underneath him, *in* him, the controlled power behind his every thrust, the firmness of his hand encircling Brendan, the way Beast gazed up at him like he'd never beheld anything finer; Brendan utterly lost himself.

He was dimly aware of sinking his teeth into the taut muscle of Beast's neck; of grabbing handfuls of his mane and pulling hard; of the desperate sounds tripping from his own tongue; of the steady rhythm of their bodies in an endless, ecstatic glissando that swelled, crested, and broke into a melodious coda more perfect than any he'd ever heard.

He had something of an encore as Beast rolled him over with a desperate growl, instinct alone guiding his ankles to lock around Beast's waist and hang on for dear life as each thrust ignited violent aftershocks that left him broken and begging. One last snap of hips and Beast fell forward onto his elbows, shuddering with a guttural gasp.

When they found their breath, Brendan tilted his head up to draw Beast into a kiss, slow as honey dripping raw off the comb. Afterward Beast regarded him silently, shadowed eyes half-lidded with satisfaction, a subtle smile playing at his lips.

Brendan cleared his throat and steeled his nerves. "Off to fetch a snack, or take a bath, or something?"

Beast shook his head, russet tendrils tumbling into his eyes and catching on his lashes. "No. I'm not going anywhere."

Joy swelled through Brendan, and he smiled so widely his cheeks protested. He lifted the covers, and Beast curled up close around him.

* * *

You're hard to know, Brendan had told him. *I'd like to. I happen to think there's a good man under there I'd like to know very much.* If there was even a glimmer of truth there and not just wishful thinking, then Beast would have already sent Brendan far away.

He watched Brendan sleep beside him, chestnut curls falling across closed lids. Gently, so as not to wake him, Beast smoothed them back across his forehead.

It was a certainty now, a truth spearing him through as clear and sharp as a shard of glass, that everything the Beast had ever done in his long, long life had been a mistake. No surprise this was yet another. All of his choices had been the wrong ones, and most especially the ones leading Brendan into Beast's bed. Into his thoughts. His heart.

A cage might be attractive if it was gilded prettily enough, but no amount of fine trappings could erase the fact it was still a cage. The long years within had stacked up heavier and heavier, leaching all light and color out of the world, until the stagnant solitude of time was all Beast knew.

Then this stubborn, vexing, nosy, *infuriating* man, brilliant and beautiful, had brought it all rushing back, as vivid and rich as Beast had forgotten life could be.

And he couldn't stay.

Brendan had his whole life unwritten ahead, his pick of far more suitable lovers, the whole world at his feet. What could Beast possibly offer him? The prettiest spot in his prison? A life cut off from his family, never visiting the places he so longed to see, wasting his talents on an audience of one?

How could Beast bear it, watching Brendan grow old and unfulfilled while he remained unchanged, all affection they once had for another withered into bitterness?

The sooner Brendan left, the better. Before it would hurt any worse.

But Beast knew he hadn't changed one jot. He was as selfish and weak as he ever was. If he were any sort of man, he would send Brendan home.

But he wasn't any sort of man. So Beast sank down into the covers, head on Brendan's shoulder, all the while hating himself for a coward.

19

In Which Things Shatter

I f one knows the secret, magic is quite simple. Admittedly, things such as rituals and circles and sigils make it all the simpler; but in essence, all it requires is the ability to reach out, take hold, and will reality into being.

Of my kind, I am among the oldest and strongest. Not for me the fate of my lesser sisters, to be fed to the witch-fires of the New World to placate its fear of the Old Ways. I have endured the long march of time unscathed and witnessed sights no other eyes had seen, touched worlds no other hands ever had.

Magic has its own will, as any living, growing thing does, and the practitioners of its art have to be very good indeed to bend that great indomitable will to their own.

I watched the little family go about their little lives in their little cottage, hours passing like eyeblinks, and when I saw my chance, I reached out and took it.

* * *

Brendan awoke to an unfamiliar sound; soft, slow breaths, just barely loud enough to classify as snores. Beast was still there in his bed, sound asleep, a well-muscled arm outstretched across Brendan's middle. All the small careworn lines around his eyes had smoothed out in slumber, his heavy brow unfurrowed.

Brendan drew a finger, featherlight, down the bridge of his curved nose, where the fine bristles of fur met in a messy whorl. Beast shifted away with a shallow grunt, burrowing deeper into the pillows. Brendan grinned and did it again, more firmly.

This time Beast shifted, lashes catching sunlight spilling in through the curtains. Brendan admired the arch of his cheeks, the sweeping bow of his collarbones as they met at the hollow of his throat. The whole world was only this moment; a perfect, placid pool of soft sheets and slow heartbeats.

Beast hummed—or, more accurately, *purred*—into his touch.

"Hello," Brendan said.

Beast's lips curved into a sweet, sleepy smile. "Good morning." He yawned hugely, pink tongue curling. "I didn't thrash about or steal the covers, did I?"

"Not so I noticed."

"That's good." Beast wriggled onto his side and tugged Brendan close. "You kept the rose." He nodded toward the slim little vase on the far nightstand where it glowed in the daylight as lambently as a ruby statue.

"Oh. Yes. Held up pretty well, hasn't it?"

"It's magic," Beast huffed. "Why did you bring it back with you?"

"I thought you might demand proof when I arrived, that I was truly who I said I was."

"Who else could you be?"

"Ah, my one solitary flaw: overthinking," Brendan joked. He stretched his arms over his head, relishing every pleasant little ache left in the wake of their exuberance.

"I'm glad you did," Beast rasped after a long moment. "Bring it, that is." The unspoken sentiment rang across as clarion clear as a struck tuning fork.

Brendan's heart leaped into his throat. Clear morning light brought out all the gold flecks hidden in the depths of Beast's eyes, and each one caught him like a dozen tiny snares.

The kiss stretched languorously until it led to other things, and the dawn slipped past without either soul marking its passage.

* * *

236

Later, they saw the crocus.

Peeking out from the wet snow lining the cobbled path to the stables, the crocus's little yellow head nodded at the end of a slender stem. Spring had finally crept its way into the castle grounds, surreptitious as a thief slipping through an unlatched window. Beast swallowed a throng of crowded emotions, but the one that stuck was resigned acceptance. This had been inevitable. He'd hoped for more time. Just a little more.

Brendan bent down to admire the flower, fragile with newness. His sunny mood faded as he straightened, a faint line between his brows.

Beast gave his shoulder a gentle bump. "All right?"

"Oh, yes. It's just... Pretty soon the cottage garden will need plowing. I wonder how they're getting on without their great big workhorse." His smile was uncharacteristically crooked.

"Maybe they bought a new one," Beast reassured him. "I did send quite a lot of money in your father's saddlebags."

"That's assuming my imprudent father hasn't squandered every penny."

"When you looked in the magic mirror, it seemed your sister, at the very least, lives in some measure of comfort."

Brendan brightened, taking Beast's hand. "That's true."

"If it is truly bothering you, why don't you take another look? Perhaps after dinner, so you can sleep with a clear conscience."

The words were barely off Beast's lips when Brendan stretched up onto his toes and kissed him on the cheek, with all the ease of a couple who had done such a thing a thousand times before, while Beast stood as still as a startled rabbit. "Thank you, Beast. That's a sweet offer. After dinner."

Beast made himself move again, twisting his fingers through Brendan's far more elegant ones, and smiled. "You go ahead," he said when they arrived at the stables, "I have some things to attend to."

"You do?" Brendan's avid curiosity brought an interested glint to his eyes, a look Beast had gotten very familiar with and enjoyed a great deal. "What things?"

He'd gotten better at controlling his temper, but he was a creature of old, old habits, and they died hard. He quashed the snarly instinct to insist

237

Brendan mind his own business, and it trudged off to sulk in a corner.

"For the most part," he said, "the castle takes care of itself. There are, however, a plethora of small matters that require my direct attention. Every few months I must ensure all the spells on the castle are intact, doing as they ought. Lately I have been neglecting my duties, and it's unwise to postpone any longer."

Brendan's eyes widened in open fascination. "You're going to go do magic?"

Beast smirked, then leaned down to capture him in a long kiss. When they finally surfaced for air, he pitched his voice into an intangible caress. "Perhaps I'll grant you a practical demonstration, later."

Brendan flushed up to his hairline.

* * *

Brendan took Jean-Luc out for a ride, both their breaths clouding in the cold air, and during the whole ride thought of nothing but Beast. The horse could have fallen out from under him, and he still would have floated along, unconcerned, on a pink haze of happiness.

Afterward Brendan brought the gelding in, shooing the invisible hands of servants away when they attempted to remove the tack for him. It was a simple, pleasant task, as was scrubbing down Jean-Luc's hide. Good clean work, and it improved a horse's mood, being looked after and cared for.

Brendan smiled to himself. That same principle worked with other beasts, too.

Kicking snow off his boots, he returned to the castle, following the lit hallway to the western parlor. Beast was there reading, reclining on a chaise lounge with his wolfish feet kicked up on a low table. Brendan caught sight of the book's title—*Myths and Fables of Grecian History*—before Beast set it aside and smiled a welcome, inviting Brendan to join him on the chaise.

"Perimeter secure?" he teased, leaning easily against Beast's warm bulk.

"It's very important, walking the grounds and freshening up enchantments," Beast said with mock severity. "If the magic on the kitchen pantry expired, we'd be foraging for roots and grubs."

"Perish the thought."

"I've been putting it off for weeks. Everything is settled now. How was your ride?"

"Good." He began the laborious process of uncoiling the long scarf from around his neck. "Jean-Luc was momentarily startled by a falling branch, but disaster was averted and all is well." A servant whisked the scarf away as soon as he was clear of it, with Brendan's thanks. Still a bit cold, he leaned further into Beast. Beast chuckled, winding a strong arm around Brendan's shoulders, enfolding him in warmth.

The silence was as soft and comfortable as a feathered duvet, no need to speak as Beast motioned for Brendan to give him his cold hands and chafed them between his own palms, sharing his heat. Mindful of his claws, Beast stroked the pads of his fingers over Brendan's palm. Brendan swallowed a little gasp, a frisson chasing up his arm. He looked up only when those questing fingertips went very still.

Oddly, Beast was staring at Brendan's hand like it held the secrets to the universe cradled in its grasp, his expression drawn into strange lines.

"Did my hand do something to offend you?"

Beast blinked up, brow furrowed. "What? No?"

"Well, then why are you glaring at it so?" He wrapped the hand in question around Beast's own with a tender squeeze. "Is something the matter?"

Beast abruptly stood, pulling Brendan to his feet and flashing a wavering smile. "Woolgathering. Pay me no mind. Come with me, I have something for you."

* * *

"Blackberries! I'm surprised you remembered." Brendan's musical laugh rang out in the cozy warmth of the kitchens. "Thank you."

Beast ducked his head, as pleased as he was embarrassed. As if he could forget the request Brendan made, or more precisely, the intensely vivid dream preceding it. "Ah. Yes. You are, of course, quite welcome."

239

Brendan plucked the bowl off the cupboard shelf from the great array of various fruits displayed, next to a rainbow of grains and legumes in glass jars and baskets of fresh breads.

"This is only the dry goods cupboard," Beast offered. "There's a cold one over there, for meat. And a separate one for cheese and butter and things." He waved in a vaguely dairy-wards direction.

"Fascinating," Brendan murmured, taking a quick peek in another pantry, shelves stacked with dozens of red-waxed cheese wheels. "The fish told me about this. You can ask for anything?"

"Within reason. It's best to keep a ready stock of raw ingredients and let the servants put it all together. I asked for a complicated cake one time, and the results were...messy."

Laughing again, Brendan settled into a tall stool at a high kitchen table. Reaching across the table, Beast chose a single berry from the bowl and popped it in his mouth, relishing the summery-sweet taste. Brendan ate a whole handful at once, somewhat less seductively than his dream version had, though his sound of enjoyment was plenty intriguing on its own.

"This is dangerous," Brendan suddenly declared.

Beast glanced around, seeing only an innocent bowl of swiftly dwindling blackberries. "It is?"

"Definitely. I could eat all of these by myself, in an indecently short amount of time."

"Have I discovered your secret weakness, then?"

A fall of hair escaped its ribbon and curled over Brendan's ear. A wicked cast shadowed his eyes, painting them nearly as dark as the berries themselves. "I think you've already found all my weaknesses."

"Let's see, books, music, gardens,"—Beast ticked off each point on his talons—"frozen ponds, harpsichord strings, fencing..."

In a smooth, swift movement, Brendan stretched his slender body over the table until he was so close Beast could feel his eyelashes disturbing the air with every blink. "Those weren't the weaknesses I was referring to."

Beast swallowed thickly. This reminded him too much of his own weakness, his own cowardice, and he dropped his eyes to the bowl between them. Brendan slid back into his chair with a slightly smug expression on his fine-boned face that very clearly said, *we'll save this for later*, a look that sent a spark of want shooting right up Beast's spine. He ate some berries to cover the fiery flush he could feel flitting under his fur.

"So," Brendan continued as if nothing remarkable had happened, "how is it exactly you brush up these enchantments? How does one go about ensuring spells are intact?"

Beast shrugged one shoulder. "It's not easy to explain. I just do it." Much the same as his ability to control the invisible servants, it was innate, something otherworldly that didn't translate into words. Suffice to say he made his wishes clear, and then the orders were carried out. Whether this was done by magical or mundane means was inconsequential. He just did it.

"You didn't have this ability before? Before…" Gesticulating wordlessly for a few seconds, Brendan sketched the shape of Beast from head to toe in the air. "Well. Before?"

"No, not at all. I never even believed in magic until that sorceress came knocking at my door. I learned a trick or two, over the years."

Brow creasing in thought, Brendan nodded, then ate another berry. Beast resisted the urge to tweak his upturned nose. "Before I came here, I didn't think there was anything reason could not explain. But after everything I've seen here? The world holds far more wonders than I'd ever thought possible."

Beast smiled too widely, felt the tips of his canines protruding, and quickly scaled the smile down to a smirk. "Indeed. There were always stories around these parts, local legends and old wives' tales. Witches and unicorns and all that folkloric rubbish. I never paid it any credence. Now, well, let's say I'm willing to keep an open mind."

Brendan perked up in his seat. "You haven't seen a unicorn, have you?"

Beast barked out a laugh. "No!"

"Shame."

"Even if I had," Beast said sardonically, "I lacked the proper qualifications to tame one."

Brendan spluttered, choking on a berry. When he was no longer in imminent danger of fruit-borne asphyxiation, he tipped up a broad, beaming smile that left Beast equally short of breath.

He glanced down at the palm of his hand, the last blackberry dark against his golden pelt. Following an impulse, he thrust his hand flat out in front of him and concentrated until the blackberry changed size and shape, color shifting first into purple and then into bright red. What sat in his palm was now a shiny strawberry, perfect in every respect.

Brendan gasped. "How did you do that?"

"Just an illusion." Beast flashed him a quicksilver smile, there for a split second and then gone. "Go ahead, pick it up."

Reaching out eagerly, Brendan's fingers went right through the skin of the strawberry until they touched the real berry within. He exhaled with wonder. If not for the eerie sight of his fingertips disappearing beneath the surface, it was visually indistinguishable from the real thing, a perfect facsimile of shiny red flesh complete with a scattering of tiny seeds.

"That's *amazing*," he breathed, looking up at Beast in ardent admiration.

Beast stamped down a ridiculous upswelling of pride—it was just a useless parlor trick, nothing worth bragging about—and shrugged. "It's only a modification of the spell used to shield the castle from unwelcome eyes, replicated in miniature. The applications are limited. Not terribly useful."

"I think it's incredible."

"Well." Beast cleared his throat. "I thought it might amuse you. It's still just a blackberry, you know. You can eat it quite safely."

Brendan popped the counterfeit strawberry into his mouth with a grin. "So, you're a wizard."

Beast scoffed. "Hardly. Not really, no." He couldn't resist teasing back a little, "No more than you are."

"Me? How am I a wizard?"

"I do believe you have demonstrated a few...tricks of your own. Last night." Quite without his consent, his voice rumbled down a few octaves. He leaned a little closer across the table, catching the hint of his intoxicating scent; cedarwood soap with the mélange of clove and lavender the servants kept all the castle's linens in. Underneath, warm and rich, Brendan's natural scent mingled with Beast's own. The realization made the pulse thud hot in his temples, made him want to stalk on all fours and growl; a feral instinct rising to stake his claim again, and again, and again.

He had to forcibly clear his nose with a sharp exhale, wrangling himself under control.

A flush had crept above Brendan's collar. He mirrored Beast's lean and looked up becomingly through his lashes, smoke blue eyes steady though his hands traced idle nonsense patterns on the wood. "I hope you found my, er, *tricks* agreeable."

Agreeable was one way of putting it. "Positively enchanting," he whispered, flicking a lock of stray hair off Brendan's cheek. "I didn't know it could be like that."

Brendan's restless hands went still. "Neither did I," he whispered back, and pulled Beast into a fervent, breathless embrace.

His lips were soft and pliant, until he delivered a sharp nip to Beast's tongue, none too gently. Beast sucked in a shocked sip of breath, then growled deep enough for the vibrato to carry on the air. He grasped Brendan by his slim hips and lifted him up from the stool to the table.

Brendan went languid against him, body melting in eagerness as he wrapped his thighs around Beast's waist. Busy fingers searched for buttons in the ivory linen at Beast's throat.

Biting back a hungry moan, Beast grabbed a handful of hair and yanked, exposing the pale, smooth column of Brendan's throat for him to lay claim to. Brendan cursed, arching up into every touch, straining to get impossibly nearer.

Something moved in the periphery of Beast's keen vision, and he glanced up in time to see the empty bowl on the table, not a handspan away from where he was rutting up against Brendan, floating off to the washbasin as it was carried off by invisible hands.

Beast regretfully let go, and forced himself to step back. "Damn." The slight rasp of Brendan's unshaven jaw still lingered on his lips, the smell of him thick in his nostrils, which wasn't helping matters as Beast tried to compose himself.

Brendan noised a protest, hair wildly askew and pupils blown wide. "What? What's wrong?"

Beast just nodded toward the sink, where the bowl was being rinsed and dried with a swift, sure efficiency. Cupboards rattled as other servants began stacking up plates from lunch in their rightful places.

"Blast." With an unfairly adorable pout, Brendan slid off the counter and straightened his clothes. "The afternoon was going in a very promising direction, there."

All day Beast had felt uncommonly impulsive, and when another sudden desire cropped up, he didn't question it, enfolding Brendan in his arms and kissing his forehead.

When he drew back, Brendan had a dreamy smile spread across his face. "What was that for?"

"No reason in particular," Beast lied as he put some distance between them, leaning back against a cupboard. He knew why. He hadn't expected to become so fixated on this man, certainly hadn't planned for it, but he couldn't deny it had happened regardless. Foolish—utterly foolish, as he had been painfully reminded the moment he saw that cheery yellow crocus beaming up that morning. Their time together was agonizingly short, and Beast wanted as much as he could get in the limited time he was allowed, even though it would only make things harder when the inevitable happened. When he was once again alone, grieving what he had lost, pacing back and forth like a trapped animal in the same dark rooms for untold centuries still to come.

Beast knew what he had to do. He just didn't know if he had the strength for it.

Brendan had smoothed his hair back into an orderly queue. "Well, if we're not going to put on a show for the servants, do you fancy a walk through the greenhouse?"

Beast shook himself out of his dour contemplations. "If you've had your fill of blackberries. I can always summon up another bowl."

Brendan gasped in faux horror. "The temptation! Let us leave, quickly, before my willpower dissolves."

Masking a snicker with a roll of his eyes, Beast turned on his heel and left the kitchen, side by side with Brendan.

* * *

"Don't you get bored, just swimming about all the time?"

"I dunno, don't *you* get bored walkin' on those leg things all the time?"

"The fish makes a good point," Beast said over the top of his book from the bench across the pond.

"Hush, you." Brendan turned back to the lazily circling koi. "What is it you do all day?"

"Well, the swimmin' *does* keep us right busy."

"Very true," nodded the ebony fish, sucking a floating leaf into its mouth and spitting it out a moment later.

"Is that all? You two *must* do other stuff. Like, I don't know, discuss literature or something?"

"Ha! Yeah, we debate Chaucer 'ere in our little pond."

Beast interjected, "I used to let them in the library, but they'd return the books all soggy."

Bubbles of piscine laughter broke the silvery calm of the water.

Taking the ribbing in good nature, Brendan stood up and brushed petals from his trousers. "All right, I give up," he laughed, making his way over from the bank to the bench. "I was just curious."

"I've met *cats* less curious than you," Beast muttered as he set his book aside.

Brendan sat beside him, hand naturally resting atop Beast's. "It's a character flaw, I know." His thumb made slow strokes on the back of Beast's knuckles.

"There are worse ones," Beast said distractedly, holding his hand very still. "Avarice, idiocy, recklessness..."

Brendan heaved a sigh. "That reminds me, I'd better check on my family, in case Father has managed to bankrupt us yet again."

Beast snorted. "If anyone can squander that much money, it's your father."

"He might have invested it all in ocean-front property in Paris."

"Unless geography has changed radically in the last two centuries, that would be *very* stupid." Beast held out his hand, and the magic mirror was forthwith delivered via invisible servant. He offered it with a showy, exaggerated flourish. "One magic mirror, as requested."

The pleasant warmth of it immediately suffused Brendan's arm, not quite as strong as the first time he had held it, but still a palpable weight of comfort in his hands. "Thank you."

He looked at his reflection and blinked. He looked...different. Hair predictably sporting a few more months' worth of length, a slight shadow of stubble to his cheeks. But that wasn't what gave him pause. Was there a new cast to his own gaze? Did he look a little older, maybe?

No matter. He cleared his throat, glancing at Beast, who merely gave an expectant arch of his thick eyebrows. "I'd like to see my family, please." The mirror swirled blank. "Let's hope they're not in a gutter, begging for alms."

Beast chuckled. "You worry overmuch."

"It's not such a—"

A strange voice arose from the mirror in his hands, a man's whisper. "—don't want to worry the others, but I truly see little hope."

The image cleared. It took Brendan a moment to recognize the man speaking as the local doctor, the very same physician that had treated his father after he had first fallen ill. The doctor was in the corner of a room, bent close with Brendan's sister Catherine.

Catherine's hand flew up to cover her mouth. Her eyes were rimmed red. "Isn't there something you can *do*? You're a *doctor*, for God's sake!"

The doctor put his hand on Catherine's shoulder in a very familiar fashion, sounding weary. "A doctor, my dear, not a miracle worker. I can't heal him if I don't even know what's wrong."

Brendan snapped his gaze to Beast, who was watching over his shoulder with palpable alarm. "What's going on?" Brendan asked hoarsely, and the image in the mirror moved as if the viewer was passing down the hall, slipping in through a half-open door into Etienne's bedroom.

Sitting around the bed as if holding vigil, his other two sisters looked just as exhausted as Catherine had, their eyes similarly raw. Beauty wrung a wet cloth out into a bowl while Marguerite took Etienne's gray hand in her own.

Brendan gasped. His father looked half dead. The slow, unsteady rise and fall of his chest under the thick blankets was the only sign he yet lived.

Beauty shot Marguerite a worried look, and in it Brendan could read volumes of concern and sleepless nights. "Father," Marguerite called softly. "Father, you must eat. Drink something. There's some tea…"

Blinking blearily, his father was a shrunken thing, not the hale and hearty man Brendan remembered. "Where's Brendan?" came thin and reedy from his cracked lips.

Brendan froze, the mirror still warm though clutched in his cold, unresponsive hands.

"He's…away, Father," Beauty said gently, laying the cloth across Etienne's forehead. "Remember?" The man mumbled indiscernibly, subsiding into stillness.

"Mother Mary, he won't stop *asking*," Marguerite muttered.

Beauty sighed a strange, lost sound that Brendan had never heard from her before. "I know." She tenderly mopped the sweat from her father's forehead, then continued in a low whisper, "I'm going to try again tomorrow."

"*What?*" Marguerite hissed. "Beauty, no. How many fruitless trips into that damned forest will it take for you to accept he's *gone*? We need you here. Father won't listen to anyone else."

Beauty slumped in her chair with an air of defeat. "He can't just be gone, Mari."

Marguerite's hard look softened. "I know, and I'm sorry. But *think*, Beauty. Father is at death's door. We've lost our mother, our brother, and now you want to go alone to whatever doom he disappeared to? It's madness! We can't lose you, too!"

A tear rolled down Beauty's cheek, and it felt as if a great blow had struck Brendan square in the gut. "I've… I've had dreams," his sister said, hands twisting in her lap. "A voice, telling me if I had gone instead like I was supposed to, none of this would have happened. That I can still make it right."

"Well, excuse me if I don't put much stock in dreams, sister." Marguerite sniffed and briskly rearranged the pile of pillows underneath Etienne's head. "Who's to say what's supposed to be, anyway? None of us can see the future."

Etienne took a long, rattling breath, head lolling to one side. "Where is...my son...?" Faces drawn in concern, the sisters looked down as their father pleaded, pale eyes wide but unseeing.

The image began to fade. The mirror shook slightly as Brendan uncurled his cold fingers' vise-like grip around the handle. He opened his mouth, but words abandoned him.

Abruptly Beast left his side to stand in front of the pond. His shape was sharply outlined by starlight streaming in through the glass, his arms behind his back, one hand clamped tight over the opposite wrist. "You should go."

"I... I, of course, but—"

"Pack his things." Beast's order rolled through like quiet thunder. After a pause of perfect stillness, he growled, *"Do it,"* and a flurried breeze stirred the texture of the air, invisible servants hastening to obey. Over his shoulder, Beast's moon-painted profile seemed but a thin sliver of mercury. "Leave now and you'll be home by first light."

"What? If I... I can't just *leave.*"

"You will. Your horse is being prepared as we speak." Beast turned away, hands still clasped tight behind his back, and took a purposeful step along the cobbled path back toward the garden doors.

Brendan lunged forward to grab his wrist, the mirror clumsily clutched between them. "Beast, wait."

Beast spun back around, face like a shuttered window. "Don't," he warned, chin raised imperiously high.

"What is this, Beast? What are you doing?"

"I'm not doing anything," Beast hissed, yanking his wrist free. "The longer you delay, the worse your father gets."

Guilt stabbed, and Brendan's gaze dropped. Despite the truth in that, all day Brendan had been trying to find the words, trying to compose it the way he would a sonata, to tell Beast he wanted to stay with him forever, and now—

"I'll come back."

"I don't want you to."

His heart seized. "You don't mean that."

Beast's lip curled. "Don't I? You presume to know me so well? Perhaps you *want* to delay, in the hope your father's illness will worsen and rid you of him once and for all."

That stung, so fiercely that Brendan took a step back. "That's not fair."

The Beast looked away with a bitter scoff of a laugh. "Life isn't fair, any fool knows that."

Brendan reached for Beast's hand, but Beast growled and pushed him away, staggering him backwards several steps. "What is it you want from me?"

Closing the distance he grabbed Beast's wide shoulders. "Stop this. Talk to me. Can't we forget about breaking the blasted spell and just *be together*? I want you just the way you are, Beast. Haven't I proven that? Isn't it enough?" He tried to catch Beast's gaze though it slipped sideways, evasive as smoke.

Brushing off his hands as if they were a child's, Beast sneered, "'Be together.' What does that even mean? Typically foolish; some half-baked sentimentality. We've given in to our baser urges, which was a bad idea from the start. Where do you expect things to go from there? At best, you will grow bored with the novelty of bedding a freak. At worst, you stay out of guilt or pity, and make yourself a prisoner, too. You're prepared to squander your life away? To grow old and die while I remain unchanged forever?"

Brendan was, for once, shocked into silence.

Beast's canines dug into his lower lip hard enough to leave marks, and a slim whisker of gentleness intruded into his timbre. "Brendan. You're smart and capable and *young*. I'm a leftover relic, a ghost from another time. Forget me. You can have anything you want. Anyone."

Desperately, Brendan shook his head and cupped Beast's face in one trembling hand. "I only. Want. *You*."

Again Beast shoved him away, this time more roughly, eyes hard and sharp as flint. "Then you are a fool." There was nothing but the sound of breath filling the widening distance between them. "Go home," Beast snapped, unmistakably an order. "Don't come back."

Brendan looked down at the blank mirror, the faces of his anguished family still stark in his mind. It felt like a fissure had torn right through the middle of him, between the undeniable need to return home and the clawing fear that the moment he set a foot on the path to leave, he would turn around for a last look back and find nothing but brambles and wilds where the castle had once stood.

"Since when have I ever done as you've told me? I have to go, but as soon as I can, I'm coming back to you." Brendan took a steadying breath. So many times before he had tried to summon the nerve to utter these three words—small words, really, but so unimaginably heavy he had never been able to lift them from his tongue—but he had come too far to back down now.

"I...love you, Beast. I love you."

Dark, emotionless eyes locked onto his, betraying not one flicker of warmth. The Beast slowly pulled the mirror from Brendan's hands, and his shoulders seemed to lift forever with a great inward breath. When he finally spoke it was with the cold, flat finality of a glacier.

"I don't love you."

Brendan faltered a step back, swallowing against the sudden burning in his throat, heart clenching in the cage of his too-tight chest. "Beast, please. Don't do th—"

"What did you *think*?" Beast said suddenly, wildly, his great bulk menacing as he threw his arms wide. "Did you think you were anything other than a diversion? Something to while away the long winter days?" His snort was thick with derision, every syllable he spoke gathering speed like tumbling stones preceding a rockfall. "Did you think this was a fairytale, some foolish story where princes fall in love with paupers? You thought I would change for the likes of *you*?"

Brendan ceased to be, hands falling numb and useless to his sides. The words roiled in his gut, each one a butterfly with razor-tipped wings.

"You love me," the Beast jeered, brows slanted into scornful arrogance. "A few tumbles and you dare to think you have some claim on me! Did you believe I'd settle for *this*? For *you*? Did you think this could continue forever? It was only ever a matter of time before I tired of you. Were you truly *that* naïve?" He laughed, which even pierced worse than anything he'd said. "Did you actually believe you were the *first*?"

Each butterfly lurched once in Brendan's gut, then died.

"Go," Beast snarled.

Brendan stood frozen.

"*GO!*" The roar reverberated around the greenhouse, jasmine flowers quivering on their stems. Beast flung the mirror down at Brendan's feet. It shattered, splintering against the cobbles with a tinkling crash.

Brendan ran.

The Beast stood alone, swaying almost imperceptibly.

Starlight filtered down through the glass ceiling and shone up from each broken, scattered fragment of mirror. The fish wisely stayed at the bottom of their pond and said nothing.

The silence stretched, and after some time Beast left the garden.

20

In Which There is a Homecoming

The bellies of clouds were pink with dawn, and here and there the sky-clad trees wore clusters of new buds.

Plodding steadily along, Jean-Luc followed the familiar path without guidance from his rider, slumping in the saddle as if his spine were broken. A blanket of numbness had fallen over Brendan as he rode through the night. The cold had been cruel, clutching at his clothes and hair with skeleton fingers, wind-riven branches creaking under the last icicles of winter.

But it was a relief not to think. The numbness was as welcome as ice on a wound.

The further they rode from the castle, the more frost fell away, grass greening along the roadside. The dawn chorus was in full swing, and birds fluttered from tree to tree as they sang love songs to one another. A beautiful morning.

Jean-Luc caught a scent and whinnied softly, prancing with excitement. Brendan looked up from his hollow, unseeing stare. The d'Aumale cottage peeked through the receding forest, nestled between graceful beech trees, looking considerably richer and greener than he remembered it. With all his effort, Brendan gathered the little scattered pieces of himself together, drawing up tall in the saddle.

A cry rang out from the quiet cottage.

Skirts hiked up indelicately high, Beauty dashed down the path toward the road. "Marguerite! Catherine!" she called over her shoulder. "Brendan is *home!*" Behind her the house stirred, sleepy voices rising.

It wasn't too hard to paste on a smile; he'd missed his favorite sister, and the sight of her rose his spirits from bedrock to somewhere slightly higher underground. He slid off Jean-Luc's back, legs shaky and sore from the long ride. Before he had even fully turned around his arms were full of sister, ribs being squeezed so tightly he could barely breathe.

Brendan smiled—a real one this time—and swung her off her feet in a great big bear hug. "Hello, sister."

She punched him on the arm.

"Ow! What—"

"Is that all you have to say?!" As he rubbed at his bruised bicep, Beauty punched his other arm for good measure. "You disappear for *months* and all you say is *hello*?! Oh, *Bren!*" She flung herself back into another hug, sobbing. Brendan patted her shoulder, slightly at a loss.

The twins spilled out onto the stoop, overcoats hastily thrown on and hair messily pinned. As soon as they clapped eyes on Brendan, their jaws dropped. They both ran out, and Brendan was caught in a very localized hurricane of tears and womanly affection.

"You're back! You're really back!"

"Are you hurt, Bren?"

"We thought you were dead, you goose!"

"I just can't believe it! When I heard you shout, I thought you'd gone mad, Beauty!"

"Where have you *been?* We thought Father's dreadful Beast had killed you!"

The name struck him like a kick to the chest, and it took every ounce of willpower not to flinch.

"I never did," Beauty swore, "I knew you were alive! But oh! *Father!* Brendan, Father is—"

Brendan extricated himself from his sisters' grasp with some difficulty. "I know. He's ill."

All three looked at him, perplexed. "You knew?"

"How?"

"It's...complicated. I can explain everything later. Is Father still in his room? I must—" He froze. In the open doorway, leaning heavily against the frame for support, stood his father.

Etienne's halting voice was a faint wisp of what it had once been, and he was so pinched and pale that it was a shock he could stand on his own feet. "I thought I heard...Beauty say...you were home."

"Father! You shouldn't be up," scolded Catherine, wringing her hands.

Etienne stumbled a little, and Brendan darted forward to take his elbow. "Hello, Father."

Etienne beheld him with such intensity it was as if his eyes could pierce into the great empty abyss of Brendan's broken soul. He steeled himself, prepared himself for anything; for anger, for disappointment, even for wrathful fists to descend, but the only thing that fell upon him was his father's embrace.

"My son," he sobbed, pulling Brendan close. Brendan felt as if a stiff breeze could knock him over. The last time his father had actually *hugged* him was when he'd scraped his knees at the age of five. "Thank heaven you're unharmed. You are all right, my boy?"

All of a sudden Brendan was *angry*, banked coals flaring up into hot sparks; he'd been furious with his father on Beauty's behalf, for bartering her as if she were chattel, and now the man didn't even have the decency to be healthy enough to be yelled at.

"I..." His voice broke, so he cleared his throat and tried again. "I'm all right, Father."

Etienne held him out at arm's length, giving him a thorough once-over. "Look at those fine clothes! You look like a lord." He beamed weakly. "It's good to have you home, Brendan."

"Oh," Beauty sniffled, dashing away happy tears.

"Father," Marguerite said gently. "You should lie down. You are very ill."

Still smiling, Etienne shook his head. "I feel so much better already."

* * *

Once inside, Etienne was overcome with weariness and had to be led to bed. Beauty made him comfortable while Catherine unsaddled the horse, and Marguerite disappeared into the kitchen to put on the kettle.

Brendan hung up his cloak and set his pack down by the door. The house had undergone several welcome changes in the past handful of months; some modest paintings, new warm rugs, and a few extra chairs in front of the fireplace. With a basket of knitting beside the chairs and last night's embers still glowing in the hearth, the cottage looked very homely and inviting. As he built up the fire, he couldn't help but notice as pleasant as it was, the room seemed so very small.

"Father's settled in," Beauty said as she joined him. "He should sleep through the rest of the morning, I think. The doctor ought to be in to check on him this evening." She motioned for him to sit. When he lowered himself to the chair, the whole night's worth of exhaustion swept over him. Beauty sat beside him and took his hand. He shot her a tired smile.

Catherine walked in, and for the first time Brendan noticed the slight swell of her belly. "Good Lord," he cried, standing up. "Are you *pregnant?!*"

She blushed. "Sit down, silly. Yes, Gustav and I are expecting."

"Who is—wait, the doctor?"

"Yes," she said in exasperation. "We were married shortly after Christmas. I was going to wait until we'd heard some word from you, I swear we were going to, but… Well." She laid her hand over her stomach with a small smile. "It wouldn't have been proper to wait much longer, you understand."

"I'm…going to be an uncle?" Brendan turned the idea over in his mind and found it to be very agreeable, indeed.

Catherine grinned. When they had been rich and lived in the city, she had always been rail-thin, and—it must be said—a bit ferrety about the face. Now she had a pleasant plumpness to her and a rosy glow to her cheeks. Motherhood suited her.

He still couldn't resist teasing her, just a wee bit. "So, not a white wedding, then?" He had to duck as she lobbed a ball of yarn at his head.

"Tea's on," Marguerite called as she brought out a tray with cups and toast. Suddenly realizing he was ravenous, Brendan smothered butter and jam onto a piece of toast before wolfing it down.

His sisters all watched him intently, and the toast stuck in his throat. "I, er. See you bought some goats?"

"*Brendan!*" hissed Marguerite. "To hell with the goats! *Where have you been?*"

Three pairs of eyes fixed on him expectantly.

Brendan sipped at his tea, carefully lining his words up like tin soldiers. "Well. I'm sure Beauty told you where I went." He had to pause as each of them tried to ask questions at once.

"But you've been at that castle this whole time?" asked Beauty, aghast. "With that horrible man Father spoke of?"

Brendan had to forcibly will himself to answer through unsteady breath. "Yes."

Marguerite covered her mouth. "Oh, how awful. Has he held you captive this entire time?"

Catherine gasped. "No! However did you escape? Was it very terrible? Did he keep you locked in a dungeon?"

"Locked in a dungeon and given such nice clothes?" Beauty murmured, almost under her breath. Too keen by half, his little sister always was.

"Was he truly a Beast, as Father said? Did he have claws and fangs and everything?"

Brendan's knuckles went white on the arms of his chair, voice all steel and ice. "I cannot speak of it."

His sisters all fell silent.

Beauty cleared her throat and poured a cup of tea. "Of course, brother. Don't trouble yourself. I can't even imagine what you've been through." Catherine opened her mouth, and Beauty shot her a hard look until she shut it again. "You rest. Take your time. If you ever wish to, we will be here to listen whenever you feel ready."

He did his best to mirror her kind smile. They sipped tea and chewed toast in silence. Catherine levered herself from sitting to standing with

256

some difficulty, so Brendan leaped to his feet to assist. *An uncle.* With three sisters, he'd always expected to be one someday, but hadn't fully given it any thought. Maybe he would feel adequately prepared by the time the baby came, though he doubted it.

"Goodness gracious!" exclaimed Catherine, grasping his face between her hands. "You look like a highwayman."

Marguerite tilted her head to one side. "He certainly does. He looks a complete ruffian, don't you think, Beauty?"

"Well, I don't know if I'd go that far," she said diplomatically. "But he's certainly a little...scruffy."

Brendan touched his bristly chin. "Do you really think so?"

Marguerite tugged at a hank of his hair. "Your hair is nearly past your shoulders! And it looks like you're trying to grow a hedgehog on your face."

"Thanks very much, Mari," Brendan muttered. "I didn't realize it'd gotten so bad. I'll shave tomorrow, all right?"

"You didn't realize? Didn't you look in a mirror in that castle?"

Brendan's jaw twitched. "There were no mirrors, no."

The sisters again fell silent.

"Why don't you go take a nap, brother?" Beauty gave his arm a gentle push toward the attic stairs. "You look awful. Don't worry about Father, we'll take care of him. You can see him when you've had some rest."

He started to smooth his hair back into place, but the brush of his own fingers kindled the unexpected phantom sensation of someone else's threading through it, and he snatched away his hand. Weariness weighed down his limbs. "Yes. That sounds... Thank you." He ducked down to kiss Beauty's cheek, then dragged himself up the stairs, ignoring the concerned murmuring he could hear starting up behind him.

The attic room looked just the same as he remembered it, piles of secondhand books, a worn violin case lovingly set in the corner. It was as if he had never left. He fell to the narrow bed gratefully, burying his face into the pillow. At least someone had thought to change his sheets once in a while. They smelled fresh, though without the faint hint of clove and lavender he had become accustomed to.

He wrenched his wandering thoughts back into place. If he didn't think about it, then it wouldn't hurt.

He kept his mind blank by listening to birdsong until exhaustion overtook him.

* * *

He slept dreamlessly for a handful of hours. Wakefulness brought a moment of confusion; where were the bedposts with their crimson curtains? Where was the faint crackle of fire in the grate? Then reality came rushing back, and he was in his chilly attic bedroom, the fine clothes he had slept in grimy with road dust.

He shoved them down into the bottom of a drawer, where he wouldn't have to look at them, dressed in his own plain, simple country clothes, and tied his hair back in an efficient tail at the nape of his neck.

He ran into Beauty in the kitchen. She smiled brightly, lifting a small bucket of goat milk onto a table. "Oh, you look much better. Can you please take Father his medicine with his lunch?" She fished one-handed in her apron pocket for a small bottle and set it on the waiting lunch tray. "There's food here for you, too."

"How is he?"

"His color is a little better. The doctor is coming to check on him in a little bit."

He glanced at the bottle of poppy syrup, cheeks a touch warm, but Beauty seemed oblivious to his discomfort. Maybe she'd forgiven him for drugging her. An upside to being presumed dead for so long. "You need me to bring him this? Can someone else…" It was a vain attempt, and he knew it.

"Do me a favor and at least *try* to have a civil moment with him." Beauty sighed, tucking loose golden curls back under her kerchief. "He's been distraught about you, you know. He hasn't touched a drop of liquor or even played so much as a game of dice since you left."

"I shall alert the town criers," he muttered acidly, then slipped his gaze away from Beauty's disapproving frown. "All right, yes, I'll take him his tray, if that will make you happy."

"Oh, Bren." She pulled him into a tight hug. The familiar scent of her herbal hair wash was slightly undercut by the smell of goats. "I'm just happy to see you again. I missed you terribly."

"I missed you, too."

Her voice went watery. "To think you were trapped there all this time, because of *me*—"

"No, no, Beauty." But God, this was unbearable. He was making his sister miserable with his maudlin, hangdog airs, and that wouldn't do at all. He forced some buoyancy into his tone. "It wasn't like that."

A sniffle. "No?"

"No," he said, more firmly. "It wasn't all bad. Really." Only the best and happiest days of his whole life, punctuated by the worst. "I just…don't want to talk about it. Yet. Is that all right?"

She pulled back, regarding him with an incisive, searching gaze. Then she sucked in a fortifying breath and nodded once, willing to take him on faith. "Of course it's all right." A wan smile touching her lips, she pushed the tray of food into his hands. "Go on. The soup will get cold."

Fairly certain he succeeded in mimicking a suitably convincing smile, he carried the tray into his Father's bedroom. His color *did* look better. "Father?"

Slowly, Etienne stirred, eyes bleary. "You're here."

Brendan pulled a chair closer to the bed and took a seat. "I'm here."

"I thought perhaps I had dreamed it. I have had the strangest dreams." His father's voice was hoarse and feeble. Brendan helped prop him upright on the overabundance of pillows.

"Beauty says you are to eat and take your medicine." Etienne made a face but took the bowl. Brendan pretended not to see the way the spoon trembled in his hand. He measured out a dose of poppy syrup and stirred it into the tea.

Etienne grunted in thanks, handing back the half-empty bowl, and sipped at the tea. Brendan sat back in silence, arms loosely crossed over his chest.

His father heaved a sigh when his teacup was dry. "Son. You *are* all right?

Unharmed?"

It was far easier to lie to his father than it had been to Beauty. "Yes, Father, I'm fine." He flashed a tight smile, meant to reassure. Etienne looked as if he wanted to ask something else, but blinked unevenly as the poppy syrup took effect. "You should get some more rest."

Etienne murmured agreement and sank down into the nest of pillows, eyes fluttering shut. He had more silver at his temples than Brendan remembered, his cheeks more hollow. His father had been a handsome man once, though grief and drink had taken their toll there a decade before. But he'd never looked *old* before. It made Brendan feel simultaneously unsettled and helpless.

Beast made my father sick once... The ugly thought crept in and lurked in the corner of his mind, a hideous little gargoyle of a suspicion. *What better way to be rid of me than to do it again?*

Brendan watched another minute as his father's breath steadied. Then he ate his own lunch, mindful of crumbs. The sisterly wrath if he got mutton sandwich on his father's sickbed didn't bear thinking about.

As he finished the last bite, a light knock rapped at the bedroom door. Not waiting for an answer, the door swung open and in walked the doctor—or rather, his new brother-in-law, Brendan supposed.

"Ah, young Monsieur d'Aumale! The prodigal son, I understand." The doctor extended his hand heartily, and Brendan shook it. "I am most glad to see you are well. None of the girls would tell me where you had disappeared to. I had assumed, I fear, that it was in relation to some gambling debt, or some equally unsavory endeavor."

Despite himself, Brendan let loose a bark of laughter. "I do not take after my father in that arena, Doctor Thibault."

The doctor was several years his senior, but not so much older than Catherine. His fair hair was going a bit thin at the top, and he wasn't particularly good-looking, but he did possess intelligent eyes and a pleasant smile that would naturally put folks at their ease.

"I know not what manner of man your father was before you moved here to our little provincial township, but I must say he has acquitted himself well. He recently became the sole owner of the grocery in town, did you know? And doing quite a brisk business, I hear." Doctor Thibault took a few instruments from his bag and bent over the bed, taking esoteric measurements with a mien of deep concentration while Brendan watched with interest.

The doctor straightened, mouth pursed into mild astonishment. "I am pleased to say his conditions are improving. His arrhythmia has ceased, and it sounds as if the pulmonary edema has drained."

Brendan did not know much about medicine, but he did know a thing or two about words. "His...heartbeat was irregular? And he had fluid in his lungs?"

The doctor shot him a reappraising look. "Ah yes, they did tell me you were something of a scholar. I must say yesterday his situation looked very dire, indeed."

"What's wrong with him?"

"I haven't the faintest idea," the doctor freely admitted. "If his condition continues to improve, I would venture your father will be hale enough to leave his bed in a few weeks. It's still too early to make any promises, though."

"Thank you, Doctor Thibault." Brendan rose to shake hands again, but the other man held his up with a disarming smile.

"Please, call me Gustav. No need to stand on formality. We are brothers now, after all," he said with a twinkle. He pulled up the other chair and sat down with a sigh. "It's a bit of a trek to get here. We have a modest home in the town proper, but when your father fell ill, Catherine insisted upon staying here."

"Had I known you were courting her, I could have given you fair warning. My sister can be a bit overbearing at times, Doctor."

"I am *well* aware." Gustav folded his instruments back into his bag, falling silent for several beats. "I do care for your sister very much."

"I am glad to hear it. I wish..." Brendan cleared his throat. "I wish I had been present for the wedding."

The doctor rubbed at the back of his neck. "It was a...hasty affair, I am shamed to say. But I am sure you're pleased you'll be here for Marguerite's wedding, come July."

"What?!" Brendan exclaimed, then calmed himself down after a glance at his still-slumbering father. "Marguerite has gotten engaged?"

"Oh, yes. Did nobody tell you? Women can be such frustrating creatures. Monsieur Beaumont proposed three weeks ago."

"I do not know the man." Brendan blinked, feeling like a stranger in his own home, among his own family. What else had happened in his absence? It had only been a few months and suddenly everyone was getting married and having babies and buying up greengrocers.

"I take it you did not expect to find things so changed?"

"I am still coming to grips with the fact I'm going to be an *uncle*."

The man beamed with clear pride. "We were planning on naming it after you, you know."

Brendan startled. "Really?"

"My wife insisted! They were all quite overwrought, you know." A slight reproach.

Brendan carefully composed a suitable answer. "I was unable to send a letter or employ a messenger."

"I see. I will not pry, my fellow, but suffice to say, it must have been an uncommonly strange place you have been."

His tongue felt dry and heavy. "Indeed it was, Gustav. Indeed it was."

* * *

"Beauty."

She tore her attention away from her embroidery. "Yes?"

"Can you trim up my hair? You always were so good at it."

With a cluck of her tongue, Beauty set aside her work. "You'll never let me live that down, will you?" At seven years of age, Beauty had chopped her own hair off so it came right under her chin. It gave their governess *fits*.

"I doubt it," he returned with a cheeky wink. It had gotten a little easier with practice, forcing cheer back into his mannerisms. He followed her into the kitchen where she brandished her good scissors.

"It's never wise to tease a woman holding a sharp pair of scissors, you know. Sit." She wrapped a dishtowel around Brendan's shoulders. "An inch or two off, let's say?"

"No. Above the ears, please."

"Oh, *Bren*! Not all your handsome hair!" Beauty burst out, taken aback. "Are you sure?"

He pressed his lips together until they were surely paper-white. "Quite sure."

Beauty eyed him carefully for a long second, then sighed.

Long curls of chestnut hair fell to the kitchen floor with each metallic *snick*.

21

In Which There is Truth

Each day Etienne recovered a little bit more. After a few days, he could walk quite steadily to the kitchen to fetch his own tea, and had taken to joining his children in the living room for their now-customary chats every evening.

Brendan had spoken little, and his sisters treated him a bit like he was made of glass and would break apart at the slightest provocation. Sometimes he felt like that too, like he could shatter apart into a million, glittering pieces, the broken reflection of stars shining up as a roar still rang in his ears...

Stop that. He ran a hand through his short hair, still not used to having cold ears and a bare neck, or how strangely light his head felt.

Beauty had shown him around the cottage, talking excitedly of the changes she had 'suggested' to Father, all the things they had done with the money from the saddlebags. She explained about the goats, the new mare Jean-Luc seemed very enamored with, the household repairs, and the smart investments Father had made in town.

When she brought him round the back of the cottage, Brendan went very still. Twining profusely up the back of the house, beautiful red rosebushes grew in unseasonably full bloom. He'd know them by scent alone, by the merest velvet touch of their petals. They were, without question, Beast's roses.

Beauty smiled, mistaking his expression for mere surprise. "You took away that strange rose Father brought back for you, of course, but you left enough of the twig for me to plant a cutting. They really shot right up, didn't they? And already in bloom! I think it must be magic."

Brendan swallowed hard. Beauty glanced at him and paused, a narrow line creasing her brow. "I had thought Father would object to them—you know how he can be about flowers since Mother died—but he didn't." Her hand slipped into his, and he shook himself out of his melancholic trance. "He thought… Well, he thought you were dead."

And now he was to answer for his Father's unhappiness, as well? It struck Brendan as deeply unfair; time and time again, the man had left a trail of disappointment and dashed hopes in the wake of his careless actions, while each time himself remaining unscathed. Leaving others to pick up the pieces of his mistakes, especially Beauty.

He bolstered himself with a deep breath. "Sorry about that."

"Yes, well." She led him back around the house and gave him a bright, brisk smile. "Least said, soonest mended."

Then she told him how she had tried to ride to the castle herself, to find him and bring him back. "I must have circled the same outcropping of rocks a dozen times! I swear, Brendan, it was like the road itself was trying to keep me out!"

He listened and didn't say a word.

Later that week he asked if she also had gotten engaged, or if there was a suitor somewhere hidden away.

"Goodness no! There is a fellow…"

"Mm-hmm. I knew it."

"Nothing like that!" She waved a dismissive hand. "I am in correspondence with a man who owns a school in Clermont. He's going to hire me on as a teacher next year. Happily, teaching is quite unfashionable right now, so nobody cares one whit if your family is disgraced."

Yet again, Brendan was completely taken by surprise. "That's wonderful! Does Father know?"

"Yes. He wasn't sold on the idea at first, but then I told him I had already spent my dowry on travel plans. He just threw up his hands and said if

I wanted to waste my life and become an old spinster, then that was my business." Her silver-blue eyes sparkled. "But I think he's secretly proud, in his way."

"He ought to be! You'll be a brilliant teacher. And traveling all the way to Clermont? You're going to have adventures, after all, just like those stories we used to tell each other."

Beauty flushed pink with pleasure.

* * *

Most nights since he'd returned, Brendan had slept in dribs and drabs, sometimes waking bolt upright with that last roar echoing in the empty cavern of his dreams. *Did you think I would change for you? Did you think you were anything other than a diversion?* The words would play in torturous refrain like an actor trying to get his lines right through sheer repetition, and Brendan would toss and turn until the fist-like tightness of his chest finally woke him and brought some surcease.

Worse were the nights Brendan awoke aching for touch, his foolish body at odds with the rest of him, not understanding why it couldn't have what it craved as much as oxygen. Sometimes he woke up wanting Beast so badly he had to clench his hands in the sheets and count backward from one thousand before oblivion would reclaim him. But tonight had been kind, sleep coming a little more easily, his dreams not haunting him so.

A voice softly called his name. "Brendan..."

In the dreamy haze of half-sleep, he muttered into the pillow, "Beast?"

A frigid wave crashed over him, and suddenly he was ice cold, soaking wet, and wide awake. He was also on the floor, having tumbled out of the bed during his startled flailing. Struggling out from under drenched, clinging sheets, Brendan looked up at the slowly focusing shape at the foot of the bed.

Beauty stood in her nightdress, a lit candle in one hand and an empty pail in the other. "Told you I'd get you back." A single nod of satisfaction, and then without any further ado, she turned on her heel and walked out the door.

Brendan blinked as ice water dripped off his nose, wondering why fate hadn't seen fit to make him an only child.

* * *

Before long, Etienne was well enough to take short walks in the evenings, to 'build up his strength,' as he put it. While he was out, the four siblings would often gather in the living room.

One such evening, Brendan stared mindlessly into the fire until he noticed his sisters all glancing furtively about before uncovering an earthen jug from its hiding place under a basket of knitting. Marguerite poured three tiny glasses and handed him one.

"What's this?"

"Just some cider."

The first drop vaporized instantly on Brendan's tongue, and he coughed, "Mother of God! Where did you girls *get* this?"

Catherine jerked a thumb at Beauty, who blushed and explained, "It's just a little brewery, in the cellar." At Brendan's dumbfounded stare, she straightened up defensively. "What? It's medicinal."

"Tell that to Gustav," pouted Catherine, giving the jug a wistful look. "He says it's bad for the baby."

"But good for the pipes," Marguerite wheezed, taking an unladylike swig. "Don't tell Father."

"Wouldn't dream of it." It wasn't too bad, on the second sip. Likely it would strip paint off a barn, but it really tasted none the worse for that.

The girls chatted idly, their voices washing over Brendan in a comforting buzz. Last night he had been flipping through one of his old books and stumbled across a passage that had once been read aloud to him, in an enormous library while golden daylight streamed in. He had slammed the book closed and been barely able to sleep, trying to rein in memories the way a farrier did a wild horse.

Today, however, he had seen or heard nothing that reminded him of...

before. He counted it as a good day.

"So tell me," he chimed in when the conversation tilted in the right direction, "who is this Monsieur Beaumont you are engaged to, Marguerite? Why didn't you tell me you were getting married?"

It was Marguerite's turn to blush. "I thought you had enough to worry about without me adding to it. He's a tailor. He owns his own store in town."

"The tailor? I thought you and that banker fellow had an...understanding?"

Marguerite's cheeks grew even pinker. "We did! But...then I met Jérémie."

"She stared after him like a mooncalf," jeered Catherine.

"I did not!"

"Oh, you liar, you did too."

"It was quite sweet, actually," Beauty said calmly, smoothing the rankles in the building quarrel. He'd always found it admirable, her skill at that. How would she have fared against the Beast's mercurial mood swings and occasional outbursts? Better than he? Brendan wrenched his thoughts back to the present, angry with himself.

"That's half of us married off, or as good as," Marguerite said. "You're positive this Clermont fellow isn't angling for your hand, Beauty?"

"Quite sure," Beauty said firmly.

Catherine heaved an aggrieved sigh. "It would be nice to have more cousins for my child to play with. We're not getting any from Brendan, so maybe you should keep that in mind before you turn down more marriage proposals."

"I'll be sure to consider your needs very carefully when planning my future, sister." Beauty sipped her cider.

Not getting any from... Brendan replayed it in his head several times before realization hit. Good God, *they knew.* His sisters knew, and even more unbelievably, they *didn't care.*

While he had been busy reeling, they'd gotten deep into discussion about the upcoming wedding, comparing the merits of satins and tulles. He finally gathered his wits enough to speak.

"You...you all know?"

Three pairs of eyes blinked at him. "Know what?"

"You know that I—Uh." He stopped, utterly at a loss for how to continue.

Understanding dawned on Beauty's face. "Oh, *that*. Well. Yes." She gave a pointed look to the twins, and through some feminine mystery divined her meaning.

"Ohhh! Well, of course."

"We are not complete fools, Brendan. You never were interested in any of our friends we introduced you to, not even one."

"And after we moved here and you got that job at the store, if a strapping fellow ordered something you would practically leap over the counter to fetch his things."

"I certainly did not!" Brendan protested, face so hot it must have gone brilliantly scarlet.

"You did too!"

"She's not entirely wrong, brother," Beauty broke in gently.

A reluctant smile tugged at Brendan's lips. He put his hand to his chest in exaggerated shock. "Betrayal, from you of all people. *Et tu, Beauty?*"

Catherine sighed impatiently. "This is very interesting and all, but is nobody going to ask about the castle? Honestly, we've waited for *days*."

"Hush, Catherine," Marguerite said sharply. "He'll speak when he's ready."

"Can't he be ready now?" The twins launched into bickering that lasted for a full minute before Brendan and Beauty shared an exasperated look. For a split second he was transported back to his childhood, the two youngest d'Aumale siblings rolling their eyes in solidarity as the twins argued *yet again*.

Brendan dropped his face into his hands and laughed as if he'd never stop.

"Are you quite well, Brendan?" Beauty asked, setting down her cider and leaning toward him.

"I'm fine!" he choked out. "Ah, I'm fine. It's so comforting to see some things never change."

"I just wanted to know if the castle was very grand, is all," Catherine snapped waspishly.

"It was. It was very grand. A bit disheveled, in a state of some disrepair, but quite grand for all that."

Questions flooded forth, and Brendan did his best to smile and answer each of them, as they asked of gardens and stables and ornaments and never, not even once, asked about the Beast.

* * *

Brendan lay in bed, staring up at the rafters of his room. The night was so late it could be argued he was just awake very early.

Had everything been a lie? Every kiss, every touch? Had their time together meant nothing? How could have he been so wrong about everything?

It made a sick sort of sense; it had always been him who pursued Beast, who initiated physical contact. It was possible the same pattern had been repeated countless times before—lure an innocent traveler to the castle and play the brooding, tragic prince until the traveler's sympathy got the better of them. Now Brendan was back home in a routine of normalcy, surrounded by regular folk, his life at the castle felt unreal, a momentary delirium. How could he be sure of anything?

He had known, anyways, Beast hadn't loved him, or else the spell would have broken. But it was unbearable to think Beast was laughing at him. That he didn't care for Brendan at all. That he had been *used*.

Brendan pressed the heels of his hands against his burning eyes until colors burst like stars across his vision. He felt like a frayed rope, sawed away strand by strand until he was naught but one, single straining thread.

He even missed the blasted fish.

* * *

Days passed. Following breakfast, Brendan groomed the horses and helped take in the laundry from the clothesline.

It was easier to get through each day if he remembered to focus on the simple things, like the familiar smell of horses and the cool crispness in the air. It kept his mind clear, kept him from thinking himself into knots. Music would be a better cure, but he hadn't been able to touch his violin since he'd returned home.

"There you are," came his father's voice, soon followed by the man himself skirting the garden wall with the assistance of a newly carved wooden cane. "We've some time to ourselves, at last. Take a walk with me."

Nothing good had ever come from a heart-to-heart with his father. He never knew how to talk to the man. Brendan nodded down at the laundry basket, stomach twisting in apprehension. "Can it wait, Father? I...should really get the chores done." Not at all a transparently thin excuse.

The lines around Etienne's eyes crinkled as he smiled. "A little more fresh air won't do the linens any harm." The smile faded a few degrees. "Please."

Blast. "Very well."

The first two dozen steps down the path were taken in strained silence.

"You're looking better," Brendan offered, because if it was important to Beauty he and their father get along, he might as well put in an effort.

"I'm feeling much better. The doctor says he's never seen a recovery so fast and so complete."

If his father's sickness had indeed been magical, as Brendan was nearly certain it was, then that practically proved the horrible suspicion it had been fabricated solely to wrest Brendan away from the castle. The first time Beast had made Etienne unnaturally ill to draw Beauty to the castle; surely it was simple enough to manufacture a second time to force Brendan away from it.

He belatedly realized his father had asked him something. "I'm sorry, what was that?"

"I asked if you were well."

"Of course."

Etienne gave him an indecipherable look. "Unlike your sisters, I have actually seen the Beast with my own eyes, and I..."—his voice faltered—"and I know you must have experienced...terrible things, trapped in that unspeakable place."

Brendan looked away, into the dusky treetops. He felt like a charlatan, letting his silence lie for him. But how could he begin to explain? That it had become as wonderful as it had first been terrifying? The marvels he had seen? That he'd been in love, and happier there than he'd ever been before, and his heart was broken for having lost it?

Resentment burned like a hot coal in his chest, a long-lingering wound that flared up anew as if a rake had been drawn over its waiting embers. "And yet," he said with deceptive lightness, "you wagered Beauty to him anyway."

Etienne stopped, stock-still. "Ah," he said, a single note of clear regret.

Brendan ignored it. "You thought no one would ever know, perhaps?" He used an echo of that dangerously silky tone Beast had favored when furious, but his volume rose higher and higher as he went on, until his voice was raw, loud enough to drown out the ringing in his own ears. "Did you expect you could barter your favorite child away *on a game* and never have to answer for it? After all the hardship you've caused us? After you'd already ruined all our lives? After you ruined *my* life? Tore down any blasted chance I might have had to be a real musician, to go anywhere, to be *anything*, and we're all supposed to carry on and never say a disparaging word and you're never to be accountable for any of it, and—" Gasping for air, he reflexively scraped a hand through his hair to pull it back, but it was short now, offering no resistance.

Etienne waited, and when Brendan didn't add anything more, simply said, "I know. I'm sorry."

"Oh, that's all well and good then, isn't it? If you're *sorry*."

His father looked down at his hands, raw-knuckled on his cane. "Your mother would be quite ashamed of me."

The air left Brendan's lungs in a rush, sweeping much of his wrath away with it. His father had never spoken to him of his mother, not once, not since the day of her funeral.

Etienne raised his head, the line of his mouth trembling faintly. "Do you remember her much?"

Brendan swallowed. "I... Only that she had very long golden hair. Sometimes I think I can remember her voice, a bit."

A soft, wistful smile changed Etienne's face, transforming him for a moment into a much younger man. "She had the voice of an angel. My peers all told me to remarry, but how could I? I loved your mother more than I thought a mortal man could love. When I met her, my life forever changed. She made me a better man. And without her... I was alone."

A vivid memory of Beast's quicksilver smile flashed behind Brendan's eyes, and he felt a stab of longing so acute it seemed unbelievable he wasn't bleeding out on the road.

Etienne took Brendan's shoulders in his hands. "When your mother died, I felt such grief as I never thought to feel again. But I did, my son. The day you left and I realized you were gone, I grieved for you."

A lump grew at the back of Brendan's throat.

"You are my only son. I thought I'd lost you. I thought my own foolishness and cowardice led you to that castle and doomed you there. I was wrong. I was never alone; I had you, my wonderful children, and I did not do right by you. I swear to you, I am going to do better." Etienne swayed, one hand still on Brendan's shoulder while the other leaned heavily on his cane.

Brendan gnawed his lip, then guided his father to a fallen tree on the roadside. "Here. Sit, Father. You're still getting your strength back." They sat next to each other in silence for a stretch of seconds, in the dappled sunshine, among the lazy drift of spring moths.

Sighing, Etienne propped his cane at his feet. "It should have been me. I should have been willing to sacrifice myself for this family, as you were. You put your own life on the line to protect your sister. You did what I could not, my son, what I dared not. I knew you were bright; I never knew you were brave."

Brendan slid over a sidelong look, hands threaded between his knees. He'd wanted to be angry for this; anger was easy, a respite from the despairing loss he'd been wallowing in. This confusing morass of emotions wasn't as easy to parse, and left him feeling like an exposed nerve.

"You've made it quite clear over the years what you think of me, Father," he muttered, kicking at a toadstool.

"Ah." And again it was a syllable of pure regret, which tore through even more of Brendan's dwindling anger as if it were tissue paper. "Yes, I've been hard on you. You're too emotional. Ask too many questions. Always needling and poking, always challenging."

Brendan laughed dryly. "I'm aware I am as much a disappointment to you as you are to me."

Etienne winced with an inward hiss of breath. "No. You're not a disappointment at all. You are all those things, but you're also brave, talented, and tenacious. Stubborn as a mule. And far, far smarter than me, which isn't an easy thing for any parent to bear." He shook his head, the lines of his face pinched with pain. "But I was always hard on you because I feared life would be far harder." He paused for a long, long time, squinting up at the sky as if he would find what he wanted to say written in the clouds. "Harder than it is on most men."

Brendan's head jerked sharply before he could stop it, staring at his father's profile. "What do you mean?"

"Come now," Etienne said a touch reproachfully, with a sideways slant of his brow. "I'm a man of the world."

Brendan shut his open mouth with a click. Did he have it written on his blasted forehead?

"But," Etienne went on as if he hadn't completely rocked the foundation of Brendan's world in less than ten seconds, "I worried needlessly. You've grown into a fine young man, a son any father would be proud of." He clapped Brendan on the back, and mortifyingly it was that simple, rough gesture, more than anything that had been said, that made Brendan's eyes water.

But his father didn't say anything as Brendan rubbed the heel of his hand across his damp cheeks. He didn't sneer or say something cutting, but merely sat with him until he pulled himself together, hand still resting warm and solid between Brendan's shoulder blades.

22

In Which There is a Decision

Gustav pronounced Etienne well and truly cured, and the family celebrated with a cozy dinner party, both twins rosy-cheeked and beaming on the arms of their beaus, and the man of the hour himself drinking too many glasses of watered wine and loudly toasting everyone in turn.

Afterward, Catherine moved back to the village with her husband, and the next morning Etienne at last resumed his position at the grocery, much to the relief of his overworked clerk. He came home early most days with an armful of unfinished accounts, stating he would rather work in the presence of his family than alone in his stuffy office.

Sometimes Brendan would help out at the shop, while his father expounded on the details of business ownership and mercantile acumen in a rather obvious ploy to groom him to take over someday. For his part, Brendan quietly humored his father, as it was better than sitting in the attic staring at books he couldn't bring himself to read or at a violin he couldn't bear to practice. And who knew, perhaps he would take over the grocery someday.

I can't imagine you selling cabbages.

What else was he to do? His future was empty.

The evenings brought the promise of simple, home-cooked meals (something Brendan had admittedly missed in the months of dining on swan-shaped sweetmeats smothered in unpronounceable sauces) and fireside conversation. He listened far more than he spoke, asking only the occasional question.

"Any word from your Clermont fellow, Beauty?"

"The headmaster," she corrected vaguely, attention fixed on the letter in her slim hands. "He says admissions are better than he expected. And the construction on my suite is almost done."

Marguerite somehow managed to make a simple cluck of her tongue into a declaration of utter outrage. "You get your own suite?!"

One corner of Beauty's mouth ticked upwards, but she said nothing.

Parental instincts aroused, Etienne looked up from his ledger, ink stains on the bridge of his nose where he had been rubbing at a headache. "Marguerite," he began wearily.

"There are some letters for you, Brendan," added Beauty, with her uncanny ability to head off conflict. Sifting through a stack of neatly piled correspondence, she handed him a bundle. "We finally started getting our mail. Some of them had been sent to our old manor, and it took forever to get them properly redirected."

Brendan leafed through the handful of letters with mild surprise and surreptitiously flipped them over.

Marguerite noticed. "They're all sealed," she said, annoyed. "You're not interesting enough to spy on, brother."

"That's never stopped you from snooping through my things before."

"Now, now, you're all grown adults." Etienne broke in, again looking up from his bookkeeping. "Must you still snipe at each other?"

"Of course, Father. Sorry, Brendan," Marguerite immediately simpered, robbing him of the opportunity to be the first to offer apologies and appear the more mature of the pair. He shot her a narrow glare, and she stuck her tongue out at him. Beauty only sighed, returning to her reading.

Later, sprawled on his bed in the soft flicker of a small lamp, Brendan went through his letters. A few were from friends—little better than acquaintances, really—from the city, expressing their sympathies for the d'Aumale's sad state of affairs. Brendan exhaled a tiny amused snort; though it was not unheard of for letters to take months to reach their intended destinations, the messengers had certainly taken their time.

Several were from professors at the university who remembered Brendan fondly. One even tried to give him homework conjugating Latin. He chuckled, before recalling all the language translations he had done at the castle's library and quickly stamped down a pang of heartache.

His favorite music teacher wrote, *Just because your formal education cannot continue does not mean you will ever stop learning. You have a fire in you, a resoluteness some might mistake for pure obstinacy. Combined with your natural talents for both virtuosity and composition, it is in you to truly make something of yourself; I sincerely hope you do so.* Touched, Brendan reread the letter several times and set it aside to answer later.

The last envelope bore on its face, simply, *Monsieur Brendan d'Aumale* with the old manor's address below it, like all the others had, but the handwriting made Brendan's hands go very still. When he turned the letter over, the impression on the wax seal was of a crowned stag.

Slowly, he slid the blade of the letter opener under the seal and unfolded the parchment with unsteady hands. The spidery scrawl was just the same as he remembered it, swoops and whorls added in unnecessary fanciful flourishes.

Brendan,

I hope this letter reaches you. This is the only address I have, so with luck it will find its way eventually. I have heard of the unfortunate circumstances that have befallen your family, and wish to extend my condolences. It must have been a wrench for you to leave the university. I know how you loved it there.

I am well. My holdings are well, the bloody English staying off our backs for the time being, and the crops and cattle have had a fine year. I have a son now. It's strange how having a child can change the way you look at the world, but there it is. I have a wife and a child, my lands are prosperous, and while I cannot truthfully say I am happy, I can say I am doing my duty, and must be satisfied with that. I am known in these parts as a God-fearing family man. Who knows? Maybe if I pretend for long enough, it will become true.

Did you know we have a Saint Brendan? We love our saints here, a saint for every little thing. Hearing the vicar say your name in Sunday service may have been the only time I've ever actually paid attention to what the daft man said. The story goes this Welsh fellow went on a seven-year voyage to find the Garden of Eden, had mad adventures, and ate a sea monster. Saint Brendan the Bold, he's sometimes called. I thought you'd get a laugh out of that.

Anyway, I find I'm dancing around the meat of this missive, so I'll stop stalling and write it.

I'm sorry.

I know I didn't say that in my last letter, and I certainly don't blame you for never writing me back. I made a lot of promises I never kept, or even intended to keep. Things seemed different back then, and when I told you anything was possible, well, perhaps I even believed it a little. I probably cannot say it enough, but you can read this next sentence over a few dozen times until you are satisfied. I am sorry.

I want you to know I sincerely, truly, valued your friendship. Knowing you made me the person I am today, and sometimes, when I look in the mirror I think all the good things I see, you helped put there.

I must laugh, reading over what I have written. I intended only to offer my well wishes, and instead I'm rambling about myself. I suppose I'm a more selfish creature than I like to admit.

I hope you've found a bit of happiness, Brendan. If you haven't yet, well, when you do find it, you make sure to grab onto it and to blazes with what anyone else says. I ran away, but you're not the sort to do the same. You deserve to keep some joy. I could say that I regret I'm not the person to give it to you, but I think we both know it's foolish to pretend I ever could have been.

We have a saying here we use to say thanks. Go raibh míle maith agat. It means, May you have a thousand good things.

With warmest regards,

Kieran Seghainn

Brendan set the letter down and watched the moon rise over the shadowy forest through his attic window.

* * *

278

The next day, Brendan descended the stairs into an empty household.

This was odd, as there was always someone puttering around doing odd jobs, and he wondered if he had missed some previously agreed upon appointment in town. He wandered into the kitchen in the hopes of finding a day-old scone, only to find Beauty already there with a fresh pot of tea and two cups ready.

She motioned to a chair. "Come and sit." He paused warily, some element of her manner foreshadowing what this was about, but did as she asked. She poured him a cup. "We finally have the house to ourselves."

Brendan cleared his throat, turning the teacup in his restless hands. "Why do we need the house to ourselves?"

She laced her fingers together and met his eyes. "I think it's time you told me what really happened at that castle."

Brendan went as still as a hare hearing a twig snap behind it.

"You're so *distant*, Brendan. You barely eat, and every time I look at you, you're staring off into space. I haven't heard you play one single note since you've been back. What happened to you?"

He could not find the words to answer her.

Her small, knowing smile was soft with compassion. "I don't think you were kept captive, or any of the horrible things the others imagine. I think... Well, I think there's more to it than meets the eye." She took his cold hand. "I am here for you, brother. You can tell me what happened. I promise I will not judge you nor think less of you, no matter what you tell me." She waited, silent and encouraging.

Tongue dry, Brendan took a deep breath and told her everything.

At first the words staggered out, haltingly stiff-legged, but soon gathered a swift momentum that Brendan could only ride along with, hearing himself speak as if someone else was telling his tale through his lips. All the shaky walls he'd built around his hurt and heartbreak and loss came tumbling down, and the numbness that had encased him in a surreal fog since he'd left through the castle gates melted away, leaving him exhausted and aching.

Beauty sat quietly throughout the whole story. When he'd finished, hollowed-out and raw, Beauty tilted her head back and closed her eyes as if praying. Finally she said, "I'm so sorry, Brendan."

Brendan kept his head down and fiddled with the crumbs on the table. "Yeah. Thanks." She grasped his hands so earnestly he looked up, startled. Her eyes brimmed with trickling tears. He tore his gaze away; he was absolutely useless when his sister cried. He never knew what to do. "Don't cry, Beauty."

"But it's so awfu—"

"*I know it is*! You're right! It is awful. I feel like I had everything and then lost it all. I've never felt that way about anyone before, and it was so *perfect*, and I was so unbelievably *happy* and I thought he cared about me and he was a complete and utter *bastard* but damn it no matter how hard I try I just *can't stop loving him*." Brendan struggled for air. "I have enough to feel terrible about without making *you* cry, as well."

She gathered herself, wiping her eyes. "You're right. I'm sorry."

"No, it's…" Brendan blew out a heavy breath and scrubbed a palm over his face. "I'm sorry, I shouldn't have shouted. None of this is your fault. It's mine." His hands clenched into useless fists, the knuckles pale and bloodless. The lump in his throat took some effort to fight past. "I knew all along there were very few ways our relationship could end, and near none of them happy. I thought… I thought he was worth the risk."

They sat quietly. Then Beauty asked, gently, "Did you tell him before then?"

"Tell him what before when?"

"That you love him. Not in the garden, that awful night when you left, but before."

"Um," he said blankly.

"You were there all winter, Brendan, you didn't— Surely, when you…" She raised a delicate brow. "I assume you slept together?"

Brendan covered his eyes with a pained groan. "If there is one topic I don't need my baby sister to ask about, this is it, right here."

"But if you did, then surely you must have told him how you felt, yes?"

"Not…necessarily. That's not— Have you been reading those terrible romances, again?"

The rising pink of her cheeks was all the answer he needed. "I'm not claiming to be an expert," she quickly averred. "Though for all the times I've had to listen to the twins go on and on about all of their failed liaisons—"

"A not-inconsiderable amount."

A snort of laughter escaped before Beauty stifled it with her hand. "So you never told him?" He shook his head, and she clucked her tongue. "Oh, *honestly*, Brendan. You were right. You *are* an idiot."

Brendan buried his face in his hands. "I know, I know! I wanted to tell him! Dozens of times. But he had to know how I felt."

"Did he? How could he know if you never told him?"

"It... I...thought he would just *know*." He paused. "Okay, so it makes less sense when I say it out loud, but—"

She sighed. "So what was the last thing he said to you, then?"

"After I told him, he said he didn't love me, that I was just...a diversion. Something to occupy him over the winter. And..." He swallowed and had to force the words from his throat, "I wasn't the first."

"He said all that?"

Brendan nodded miserably.

"You really are an idiot."

Brendan blinked. "I admit, I'd expected a more sympathetic response."

"Oh, please. *Think*, Brendan. You remember that stray cat, when we were children? The orange one that kept coming 'round the kitchen window, and that horrible maid said she was going to poison it if she saw it again?"

"Yes?"

"How did we get it to finally go away? We yelled and threw things at it. Remember? We told it, go away! We don't want you!" She gave him a look people normally reserved for the mentally infirm, or village idiots. "I can't believe you fell for that, Brendan."

"But that—That is *not* the same!"

"I think it is."

"How would *you* know?" he snapped, hands clenching in his lap. "You weren't there! You can't know what it was like! I was a fool to think my feelings for him would be somehow enough to... I don't know. I thought it would prove it didn't matter to me if the spell broke or not. That it doesn't matter how he looks."

"There's more involved than *looks*, Brendan. I know, I wasn't there, and I can't know what it was like. But think this through. He can't leave the castle. Ever. Being with him means making yourself a prisoner, too. Would you be able to spend the rest of your life at that castle?"

Fresh, painful memories flooded in, perilous waves on a jagged shore. Honey-dark eyes burning like embers; the steady throb of a bared-throat heartbeat fluttering against Brendan's lips; the desperate, grateful gasp of his own name into his ear; the unguarded smile Beast wore only when he thought it couldn't be seen; his low laugh, his strength, his wit, his kindness. His Beast.

"Yes. Yes, with him, I would."

"Oh, Bren. You truly do love him, don't you?"

Suddenly furious—not at his sister, but with himself, with Beast, with the insurmountable distance between them he had vainly spent months trying to bridge—Brendan threw his hands out wildly to his sides. "What use is it? It obviously wasn't enough, loving him. I've never cared about *anyone* the way I care about him. I can't even *conceive* of a life without him, and it still *wasn't enough*. What use is love if it can't break some stupid spell?"

A sudden shadow passed over Beauty's face. In a soft undertone, like she was afraid of being overheard, she said, "I have been having such strange dreams since Father fell ill. Voices whispering about love, and breaking spells, and—" She leaned in earnestly. "Twirling in some mirrored ballroom, wearing a golden dress. Dancing with a man in velvet. Flowers and celebrations. Fine things, princess things..."

Wincing, Brendan turned his face away. "Perhaps it would have been for the best. Maybe you should have gone like you wanted from the start. If I hadn't stopped you that night, maybe you'd both be happier."

Beauty gave a very unladylike snort. "First of all, I'd look terrible in gold, it would wash me right out. Secondly, I don't have time to go twirling about wearing fripperies. The twins would love that, but not me."

Brendan managed a weak grin. "No, you're going to challenge conventional thinking and turn academic tradition on its head."

"What I'm going to do," she said sternly, "is teach children to think for themselves. That's what I want out of life. Maybe, someday, I'll meet someone special and have children of my own, but that will be *my* choice to make, not the choice of some silly dream." Her eyes, twin to his own, burned keenly. "Thirdly, you love him. And I think he loves you, too."

A ragged breath snared tight in Brendan's chest. He slumped over his knees and clenched his fingers into close-cropped hair. "I don't know," he whispered. "Beauty, I miss him so much it *hurts*."

"Well, then," she said briskly, "you have your own choice to make, brother. Give up, or try again." She patted his hand, rose from the table, and left him alone with his tangled thoughts.

* * *

I did the right thing.

Whenever sorrow loomed up to drown him, Beast would repeat the words in a desperate refrain. *This was the right decision.*

He wandered the empty, honeycomb hallways in a sleepwalk. He knew something wasn't right—the castle too cold, the walls too cracked, the servants trailing after him aimlessly—but none of it seemed important. He drifted, blindly seeking something he couldn't even name.

He stopped, briefly, in the doorframe of the guest bedroom. Without a guest, it was just another empty room like all the countless others, devoid save for one wilting rose on the bedside table. He touched it lightly with an outstretched talon, recoiling as half of its petals shuddered off in a dry hiss. Peering through the window panes, he stared at the great iron gate at the end of the rose-lined lane, hoping to see someone there and hating himself for it.

The servants had already changed the sheets, but Beast crawled onto the bed anyway and twisted in the covers, trying vainly to catch the smallest trace of familiar cedarwood scent.

This was the right thing.

Sometimes, it vaguely seemed something wasn't right with the woven fabric of magic that bound him and encompassed his whole world, but it didn't strike him as important, so Beast ignored the little niggle of concern until it was nothing but a faint whisper of unease at the back of his mind.

The conservatory pathways were littered with fallen leaves and petals, crunching under his clawed feet. Beast caught a faint whiff of sweetness and rot, looking up at the slender branches in puzzlement. Had the jasmine flowers always been so brown and shriveled? He couldn't remember. His vision was fuzzy at the edges, like a daydream or a fever.

The marble bench was cold, but everything felt cold lately. He sat under the dying jasmine for a long time before realizing where he was. This was where Brendan kissed him, really kissed him, for the first time. The memory broke through the fugue, for just a moment, and color bled back into the edges of the world.

He had asked Brendan about his dead mother, about living with the weakness of grief. Looking back, he couldn't believe how callously he had behaved, trivializing the loss. No, he *could* believe it. If the Beast gathered up every instance of careless cruelty he'd ever displayed, he would be unable to count them all, even if he spent another two hundred years doing nothing else. A gallery of his regrets would need a whole new wing to house them all.

"Isn't it better to let it go? To be free of that pain, rather than loving so fiercely you still feel the loss of it after so long? How can it be worth it?" he had asked, and Brendan answered almost immediately, *Of course it's worth it. Every second.*

He understood now. Too late.

"I love him," Beast whispered into the silence, "I love him and he'll never know." His head sank to his hands and he remained there for hours or minutes or days, time whiting out into stillness.

When he stood up he fought off a brief wave of dizziness. He hadn't eaten since... When had it last been? Unimportant. Beast stood over the silver pond and watched two contrasting shapes swim in overlapping circles, tracing a language he did not understand.

"He's never coming back, is he?"

The fish sounded genuinely sorry. "No."

"That is good," he said, dull and toneless, and wandered away.

23

In Which There is Love

The bell jingled cheerfully. Beauty pushed inside her father's shop and was met by a variety of d'Aumale greetings. The shop's central table had been cleared of crates and produce displays and set instead with an array of cutlery and plates. The twins bickered over who got the heel of the fresh, steaming loaf of bread Brendan had just cut.

He looked up with a quick smile. "Beauty's here."

"Finally," muttered Catherine, snatching up the heel while Marguerite was distracted and shoving half of it into her mouth.

At the counter, Etienne abandoned a stack of papers and rose to his feet. "There's my girl!" Her father wrapped her in a warm hug before guiding her to a chair. "Forgive our impatience, my dear, our hunger has gotten the better of us. We've worked up quite an appetite during the morning rush." He flipped the sign in the window to 'closed' and helped her set up a very respectable luncheon.

"We must have had half the town in here today, seems like," said Brendan as he poured them all some wine. "It's been a busy morning." He looked good with his hair short, Beauty finally decided. It made him look older, more mature, while at the same time bringing out the line of his jaw and the color and clarity of his eyes, soft blue like the feathers of a heron. Though she supposed it was somewhat vain to think that, as the two of them shared that particular feature; one of the gifts their departed mother had left them, along with her sense of adventure.

"That it has," their father said as he unwrapped a fine haunch of cold ham. "I would have been lost in the weeds without your assistance, my boy."

"Happy to help." There was a strange, nervous timbre in Brendan's tone, like an instrument with one note off-key. Beauty looked at him askance.

Luncheon served, the conversation meandered over simple things, like the dreariness of the weather, and the new fabrics Beaumont's had gotten in that morning. Catherine declined the wine to sip at water instead, explaining sourly that Gustav had insisted spirits were bad for the baby.

"All the other pregnant women drink wine," she grumbled. "It's all this silly nonsense about medicine he natters on about. He's even making me eat awful things like iron filings, for the *vitamins*." Her mouth twisted on the word like it tasted, indeed, of metal.

Marguerite snorted. "If Jérémie tries shaving off bits of horseshoes into *my* food, I can tell you it will not go well for him. However do you manage it?"

"Well, it's only a little bit. And not every day," Catherine conceded.

"Isn't this nice!" exclaimed Beauty over her sisters' grousing. "Such a good idea, Brendan." She gave him a smile before nibbling delicately at a biscuit.

Etienne's face crinkled into lines of fondness. "A very fine idea indeed. It does my heart good, having the whole family together again."

Brendan's hand snuck up to pinch the bridge of his nose, as if he were attempting to stave off a nasty headache. Beauty wondered at it, but let things lie. She could always wrangle an explanation out of him later.

"Yes, well, on that subject," Brendan said, smoothing his napkin several times, despite having nary a wrinkle in it, and realization struck. Beauty's heart swelled with pride, tempered with worry and, she was dismayed to find, a smidgen of grief. When he left this time, it was a very real possibility she would never see her beloved brother again.

"I actually had an ulterior motive for asking you all here." Brendan lifted his chin and said, "I'm going back to the castle."

There was an immediate outcry. "Certainly not!" cried their father.

"What? That's ridiculous!"

287

"Whatever for? You must be mad, Brendan!"

"I know you all probably have questions—"

"Damn right we do!" Marguerite slammed down her glass so hard wine sloshed over the table. "After everything that happened to you there, what on earth could possess you to go back to that horrid place?"

Face florid, Etienne shot to his feet. "I absolutely forbid it!"

With a rueful smile, Brendan shook his head. "Father, I'm nearly twenty. My decisions are my own."

The twins stood up as well, and out of ingrained courtesy Brendan followed. Beauty remained sitting; she may as well finish the last biscuit, since nobody was paying any attention to her. She picked off a raisin and took a bite as above her head Catherine railed.

"You're going back? To that…that *monster*?"

"He's no monster, Catherine. Just a man."

Their father stared at him, aghast. "I don't understand. I have seen the Beast with my own two eyes! I know the danger you are proposing to walk back into! I have experienced firsthand his barbarism, his cruelty."

"He is my friend, Father. He's been alone a long time, and I…I want to be with him."

Etienne fell quiet, confusion written in the careworn lines of his face. Marguerite sucked in a shocked breath, trading a glance with Beauty, who did nothing aside from very slightly raise her brows and finish her biscuit.

"Beauty!" Catherine flapped her hands at her erstwhile silent sister. "Have you nothing to say? Tell him what you think of all this!"

"Safe travels, brother," Beauty said softly.

He smiled down at her. "Thank you, Beauty."

Catherine gawped at Beauty. "How can you be so *calm*? After all we went through? You yourself must have made a dozen trips into the forest trying to find him! Now, he's just going to go skipping back, and you're all right with that?"

Unruffled, Beauty sipped her wine. "I hardly think he'll be skipping, Catherine." The others may rant and rail all they wished, but the adamant set of her brother's stance meant he would not be swayed.

288

Hands on her hips, Catherine huffed with exasperation. Marguerite lowered her hand from her mouth to her heart, her shock fading into something else. "Are you really sure about this, Brendan? I mean, really, truly, *completely* sure?"

Without a shadow of hesitation, Brendan said, "I've never been more sure of anything in my life."

Catherine pursed her lips and stared at her brother for several long heartbeats. Finally, she sighed, hands up in resignation. "If you insist upon this foolish endeavor, you must at least make me a promise. Promise you will come back to us someday." She framed the swell of her stomach between her palms. "I don't want him growing up without an uncle." She glanced away and cleared her throat to mask the roughness of her voice. "When are you leaving?"

"Right away. Tonight."

"But you can't!" Marguerite burst out, near tears. "What if you miss my wedding? We need you!"

"No, you don't, Mari. None of you do." With a half-hitched smile, he leaned forward and brushed a kiss to her forehead. "You'll all do fine without me."

Etienne's posture was slumped in defeat. "But...what about the shop?"

"Father, you and I both know I'd be a useless shopkeeper. I'm glad to have helped out, but you'll do fine. Better than fine. You've done so well here already."

It was perhaps the first time Beauty had ever heard her brother give their father a heartfelt compliment, and she had to resist the urge to let slip a few happy tears.

"But... I still don't understand." Etienne sounded truly lost, the slope of his shoulders painting him older than his years.

"I know, Father," Brendan said, laying a hand to Etienne's arm in a clasp that became heartier and less hesitant the longer it remained. "I don't know if I'll be able to explain it to you. I do not mean to cause any of you distress. But you all have found your callings. You've made your choices and are living your lives. It's time I do the same."

Beauty got to her feet and reached for her cloak.

"Beauty," Etienne asked, "where are you going?"

"Home," she said briskly. "Somebody ought to pack my dear brother something to eat for his trip, don't you think?"

The smile Brendan gave her could have illuminated a darkened room.

* * *

Night softened as it gave ground to the ineludible approach of morning, the forest still slumbering around him. The first time Brendan had made this trip, it had been all freezing rain and cloudy skies, sharp winds and muddy roads. The second time he had been so numb he barely remembered it, riding through a thick and clinging fog of heartbreak.

But this time every step of his journey was made in crisp clarity. He followed the thin road through the ancient forest until it was naught but a slim ribbon of dust cutting through the grass, all the while strikingly aware of every fleeting detail. The susurration of branches swaying overhead, the weaselly tang of some distant skunk, the steady jolts of Jean-Luc's hooves against the ground. He was alive; as present and aware as if he had just awakened from a long and stifling sleep.

Brendan had no idea what to expect when he returned, none whatsoever, and in some measure, that very uncertainty was welcome. Perhaps Beast would be glad to see him. Perhaps he wouldn't. Perhaps he would be furious, or penitent, or grateful, or perhaps a hundred unpredictable, shadowy outcomes—but all Brendan could do was follow each step with another. The future would have to sort itself out. The feeling was extraordinarily freeing, each step forward a decision remade.

Trepidation was still there, perched in the back of his mind, but caution was a tiny and unimportant thing compared to the absolute certainty this was the right decision; perhaps even the *only* decision. Since he'd left the castle, running home clutching the pieces of his broken heart, Brendan had been lost and adrift, a bit of flotsam atop a white-cresting sea. It was only now, going back, he could feel the waves pushing him to land, the solid shore under his feet.

Even if every bladed word Beast had said that night in the garden had been true, and even if it had been by his magical arts that Etienne had fallen ill and Brendan driven away, it didn't change the truth. His place was with Beast. There was nowhere else.

He let his hands rest loosely on the reins, trusting in the horse to remember the way and praying fervently the magic wouldn't turn the road back on itself and deny him entry.

Through the evening Brendan rode, into the night, through those small still hours of gray that prefaced the dawn, and remembered the color of Beast's eyes as they opened to the morning, endless amber lit up with gold like tiny sparks of sunlight.

At last, the towering shape of the great iron gates appeared at the end of the uneven path, and Brendan urged Jean-Luc into a hasty trot. Any relief he felt was immediately occluded by surprise; the gates were now tangled in thick vines, climbing up the bars with leaves as wide as his outstretched hand.

Perplexed, Brendan slid out of the saddle. He touched an iron bar through a wild spray of ivy, his fingers coming away flecked with rust.

There hadn't been one speck of rust on this gate when he'd left. He tried to swing the doors open, and the hinges creaked like an old woman's complaints, but did not budge an inch. Brendan planted his boots firmly and pulled at the gate with all his might, but he may as well have been trying to yank down the moon.

Foreboding traced goosebumps up his spine. Something was very, very wrong. Was there some trick to this, some hidden latch? Suddenly he remembered being in the kitchen with Beast murmuring against his ear, and shivering with the words, *I do believe you have demonstrated a few tricks of your own.* He tried to shove the memory away, to fix his attention on the present.

After another appraising look at the gate, Brendan returned to his horse. "I think I can squeeze through, but there's no way I'm getting you in there. Think you'll be all right out here, Jean-Luc?" The gelding whickered softly

291

and put his velvety nose into Brendan's palm. "Brave boy." He hitched the reins on a bit of iron and left his bulky cloak draped over the saddle.

It took some careful maneuvering to slip between the iron bars, but with a few minor scrapes he was through, brushing rust from his clothes. When he looked up at the castle, a choked gasp died on his lips.

* * *

Beast stood with his head bowed at the castle's tallest tower, a jutting spire still standing from the original stronghold. Long ago, each brother had been given a piece of territory to rule as their own. This land had once belonged to an even older great-great-great uncle as a country hunting lodge. Each generation added as their holdings grew, their wealth increased, the noble lineage thinning as royal blood grew scarcer. So many had gone before him in this very castle, trod upon the very stones Beast now stood, and he had treated it as his personal pleasure house, wherein everything and everyone had existed merely to keep him occupied and amused.

How empty he had been.

How empty he remained.

A mere husk, a shell, a twisted body given to shape the ugliness he had always truly been.

He had sent the servants away, no longer able to bear the brunt of their silent accusations, hoping beyond hope that when the inevitable finally descended upon him, *they* at least, might be free.

This tower, this castle, this land, was irrevocably his. He was its lord absolute, with power unmatched. And it was nothing. He held nothing in his hands but his own regrets.

* * *

Brendan stared. The castle was a ruin, weathered and crumbling as if it had been doing so for years beyond counting. The beautiful stained glass windows that had once looked out like gemstone eyes from the castle's face were all smashed and yellowed. The grounds lay in a careless mess as if neglected for decades. Weeds and saplings grew up through the cracked cobblestones leading to the main stairs, and all flanking it the red roses on their bushes were as dry and withered as drops of old blood. The air felt dead, as quiet as a graveyard.

It looked as if time had forgotten this place for hundreds of years. A sudden fear gripped his heart, fear that everything had been some kind of dream, a hallucination, that his memories of fine marble and grand gardens had been some sort of mad delusion, and all that had ever stood here was the broken bones of some long forgotten keep.

"Beast." The whisper slipped from his lips unbidden, and the sound jolted him from his frozen horror, and he ran toward the doors. He had to find Beast. He would never have allowed his castle to fall into such disrepair, never, not unless he...

Brendan violently shook the thought from his head, falling against the doors in his haste. They had both slid off their hinges and keeled against each other. He reached for a knocker, but it fell off at his feet with a hollow thud, more rust than metal.

"Beast!" he called out, near frantic. "Let me in! Please! Beast? Anybody!" Not a sound, not a whisper. Not even the whisk of movement from one of the servants. He tried tugging at the fallen doors, but as with the iron gates, they would not move. They only groaned ominously, as if they would topple over on him.

"Beast!" Brendan beat upon the door with his fists, the sound swallowed up by the plants choking their way up the castle stones. How had they grown so much in only a few weeks? Why was nobody answering the door?!

With a frustrated growl, Brendan tore himself away and dashed alongside the wall. There was a side door, past the hedge maze and the sculpture garden, near the stables. If he could just get there, then surely he could find his way inside the castle, and Beast would be all right and everything would be fine and... He drew in a shuddering breath.

Damn it, why had he been gone so long? *Mother Mary, is this my fault? This castle stood for centuries until I interfered! Somehow, I am to blame for this.*

He circled the stepped reflection pool, barely recognizable as the same one he'd almost drowned in without its concealing blanket of snow. He could see now it was surrounded by fountains, dry as bones and falling apart. *If Beast is hurt, and I am responsible... Or if he's...*

The thought went unfinished. Instead he remembered a crooked grin cast across the fencing *salle*, Beast twisting his rapier with careless grace.

Roots and brambles seemed to spring up under his feet, and he nearly tripped several times rounding the corner. As he got closer he had to slow down, weaving through thornbushes to get into the sculpture garden. Corinthian pillars flanked the path, once proud, tall columns the color of new parchment, but now as dirtied and worn as Roman ruins. He once walked this garden with Beast, and he remembered the way Beast had held his hand, unsure and bold in equal measures.

The air felt eerily too cold, the fine hairs on the back of his neck all prickling up, and he caught the slight scent of a lightning storm.

A woman stepped out from around a crumbling column. She was not entirely human, this was instantly apparent. Though she had the usual assemblage of arms and legs and so forth, and arranged in a very beautiful manner, her eyes had the high unnatural shine of polished onyx and her black hair moved like weeds underwater.

"Honestly," she said, clarion voice ringing strangely, echoing where no echo should sound. "What do I have to do to get you people to act as you are supposed to?"

* * *

This was as good as any place to lie down. Beast let his mind drift. It had been such a short time, really—just one winter out of two hundred—but that one winter had held the only days of his entire life he had been truly happy.

He descended into memory, into images he'd imprinted in the gallery of his mind's eye. Brendan's easy smile, his eyes alight during an impassioned discussion, his clever fingers coaxing music from ivory keys. His head thrown back in ecstasy, the flush of his skin, the soft chestnut fall of his hair.

Grateful even to be left memories, Beast closed his eyes with weary acceptance.

* * *

"Why didn't the girl come, instead of you? Have you no sense of narrative imperative?"

Brendan eyed the sorceress warily, for he knew without a shadow of a doubt this must be her; she was exactly as the book had described her, silver-black and gossamer-clad. He managed to find his voice. "I am very stubborn."

"That is readily apparent." She looked like a woodcut, all ink and blank paper.

"What have you done to him?" If she had hurt him, if Beast was harmed in any way...

"The prince? Not a thing. I have done nothing more than endeavor to weave a tale, child. It is what I do." She watched him the way cats watched garden voles; circling around with amused indifference right up until the time came to pounce. "Though I find myself curious, stubborn boy. What exactly would you do, if I *was* intending to do something with the prince?"

"I'd stop you."

"Would you really?" The woman smiled, perfectly even teeth glinting like ivory. "Are you a sorcerer, by chance? Know you the hidden, eldritch ways of magic?"

"I can wiggle my ears, a bit."

She stared at him, this cold apparition of a woman. Then she threw her head back and laughed in a way he had never heard a lady do before, loud and unselfconscious. Her black stone eyes warmed, and the ground at her feet started to sprout little seedlings. "The prince must have had his work cut out for him with *you* around."

Brendan didn't like the way she spoke in past tense. He narrowed his gaze, jaw tightening. "If you've hurt him, witch, I will end you." Silence stretched taut in the air, his hands closed into fists.

"This little scholar suddenly turned warrior before me, hm?" The sorceress studied him with the same intensity people gave horses they were considering for purchase. "Not a bad story, come to think of it," she mused, almost to herself.

Realization suddenly coursed through him. "You…you did all this." He felt like a fool for not thinking of it sooner. Of course Beast hadn't made his father sick; *she* had. The one responsible for everything. The sorceress who had set the entire thing in motion. The one playing games with Beast's life. "You made my father sick. Sent Beauty the dreams. I suppose you are to blame for the state of the castle, as well."

"You mean this?" She indicated the decaying grounds around them with a dove-white hand. "No. The spell itself despairs and falls under its own weight. This happens, sometimes, when spells get very old and they adopt some measure of autonomy. I had no part in it. I have no wish to see all my hard work wasted. As for your other suppositions, yes. I arranged matters with your family."

Something ugly roiled in Brendan's gut. "My father almost *died.*"

Her hand made a gentle, brushing motion like a falling feather. "No. My spell would not have claimed his life. It was only necessary for a few chapters."

"Why?"

She shrugged one elegant shoulder. "My reasons are my own."

"How, then?" Despite the dire circumstances, he couldn't stave off his curiosity. "How did you do *any* of this?"

"There are powers far more ancient than your sacrificed god and your virgin goddess."

Taken aback by this ecclesiastic turn, Brendan blinked. " I… What? The Virgin Mary isn't a goddess."

"Is she not? As you say." The sorceress looked amused. "The most ancient of powers is that of stories. What is it you think the very first people did, huddled around their fires while the dark of night shrouded the world in mystery? They told stories."

"And you… What? Twist people's lives into stories?"

"I weave them," the sorceress corrected, watching Brendan carefully for a long moment, the full weight of her inhuman eyes boring into him. "Done right, stories can live on forever. Nothing else is truly eternal, not even the strongest magic. The proof is all around you." She turned her gaze to a nearby statue, marble in cloven chunks at its base.

"Your point?"

"Magic fades, like memories. Neither one so quickly or so easily as we tend to believe, but they do. In time it will fade for you, Brendan." He barely masked his reaction, jerking back as she spoke his name. "This place will crumble into earth—no magic now can keep it standing—and you will forget."

Anger momentarily stole his voice. As he struggled to regain some measure of control, blood pounding in his temples, the sorceress took a gentle, fawn-like step forward.

"I have upset you. You misunderstand me. I am offering you a gift."

An incredulous scoff made its way past Brendan's teeth. "A gift?"

"You came here to save the prince. A noble tale, but doomed to failure. You could not have known what you chose was an impossible task. When a ship sinks, no mere man may deprive the ocean of its prize. There is no reason for it to drag you down as well." The sorceress leaned toward him, her words a conspiratorial whisper. "I can make you forget. You can return to your life; to your fine, loving family, to a new life, to an open world of endless possibilities." Her placid face expressed only sincere, earnest kindness. "It is what *he* would want."

"You act like you know everything. Like you know me. You don't. I didn't come here to *save* Beast. I came here to be with him. And nothing you say can dissuade me. Keep your gift and let. Me. Pass."

The sorceress looked at him as if she could see right through him, saw his heart beating beneath clear, glass skin. She sighed, expression changing sphinx-like and inscrutable, to reflect some unspoken decision. She inclined her head toward him, as one did when meeting an equal. "Sometimes, one has to trust in the story. Old wisdom, the very first lesson taught to my

297

BRENDAN & THE BEAST

kind. One I may have neglected to consider."

"What you have neglected to consider," he returned heatedly, shoulders squared, "is that time is wasting. I know Beast is here somewhere, and he may be *dying*, and yet you still stand in my way."

Her eyes raked over him. "You know," she put her head to one side, and with a crescent-moon smile said, "you'd make a decent protagonist."

Brendan shook his head, wanting only to get past this strange colorless woman and find his Beast. "I don't know what you're talking about."

"I would not expect you to." She watched him for another moment with her head half-turned, like a bird. "It is rare for anyone to pen their own story." She tapped finely carved fingers against her wrist. "I believe there is a common saying about curiosity. It would seem I am as susceptible to it as any feline. I will not hinder your passage."

"Is this a trick?"

"No."

Brendan let out a breath he hadn't even realized he'd been holding. "Then let me pass."

Without any further conversation, she stepped aside, the hem of her filmy gown flowing around her bare feet like water. Still leery of chicanery and trickery both, Brendan edged along the path, not daring to take his eyes off her.

Just as he was ready to turn, she spoke. "May I impart some wisdom to you?"

Warily, Brendan nodded.

"Remember this; sometimes once a thing is done, it can never be undone. That is the second lesson taught to my kind."

Puzzled but suspicious, Brendan stepped out of the sculpture garden onto the grass. He turned back for a moment, but of course, she had disappeared.

* * *

Moving was laborious, so he stopped. He was so, so tired. Each breath brought with it new sorrow, harp strings cutting sharp and discordant through Beast's heart.

Brendan.

Every endless second, Beast ached for the slightest touch of his hand, the merest whisper of his voice. If fate was kind, far kinder than it had been to himself, Brendan would live out his days happily, making music and visiting libraries and laughing low and sultry over candlelit dinners with someone far better suited for him than some broken antiquity.

With the last vestiges of his strength, Beast wished only for another's happiness.

* * *

Finally Brendan's feet found the riding path leading back to the castle. After what felt like ages, he found the door, completely hidden behind briars. He tore at them, grunting at the pierce of thorns. The door had warped in its frame, but he managed to wrench it open, hinges wailing in protest.

He burst through the doorway, yelling Beast's name at the top of his lungs. The shadowed hallway devoured Brendan's voice, and he faltered. Deep cracks crept up the walls, bits of plaster fallen and rotting on damp, threadbare carpets. Everything was in ruins. Lamps did not light as he passed them, no gentle nudges directed him, and every little absence only amplified the sensation this castle had been long abandoned.

It was dark, only the faintest of pre-dawn light sneaking its way in through filth-encrusted windows. He moved as if walking in a nightmare, legs too slow to respond, like slogging through thick mud. He passed the doors to the library, paused, and pushed them open. There was a good chance Beast might be in there.

A portion of the shelving had collapsed, and books were scattered over the wooden floors, leather covers curled back with some long-ago dampness, now so dry they were disintegrating as he watched. At any other time, had circumstances been less dire, Brendan would have mourned their loss; so much knowledge now only appreciated by dust mites and booklice. He remembered sitting in this library, how Beast would laugh while sounding surprised at his own amusement, as Brendan joked about long-dead authors over the dregs of a wine bottle.

He backed out of the room. Where should he search first? The greenhouse? The solarium, his bedroom, the music room? The castle possessed more rooms than Brendan could begin to count, and probably dozens more he'd never even known existed. Without question, he would search each room, each hall, every parlor and foyer, and in every last cobwebbed corner if he had to… But what if he was already too late?

Brendan put his face in his hands, forcibly holding back a shaky sob. Why had he waited so long? Why had he spent so many foolish days agonizing over the decision to come back? Too indecisive to leave his old life behind. Too proud to go back to someone that had hurt him so deeply. Too much of a coward to hear the man he loved turn him away again.

There was a light touch on his arm like the brush of a spider, and he spun around with a startled gasp to nothing but a dark and dusty hall. As his heart moved from his throat back down to its proper place, the familiar brush of air heralded the presence of one of the servants, a welcoming ambiance Brendan had unknowingly become attuned to. He grinned with relief, nearly giddy at the company.

"I am *so* glad to see you. Well, not *see*, you know." Actually, he *could* see something, when the light shifted, like an outline, a thin, oily haze where the edges of a body might be. He tilted his head to the side. "What… What has happened to you?" The servant grabbed the cuff of his sleeve and pulled him away from the library doors. "Right. You know where Beast is? Take me there. Is he all right?"

Without warning, the servant staggered, the grip on his sleeve weakening. Brendan automatically tried to reach for them but grasped only shadows. "Are you hurt?" He couldn't catch the servant's smoky outline; it was only visible when the light was just barely there, still half-shadow. The grip became firmer, and the servant regained their footing, yanking insistently at his sleeve. All Brendan could do was follow.

The hall opened to a narrow chamber cluttered with an armory's debris. Brendan picked his way carefully over rusting suits of armor, prone on the tiles, like soldiers who had simply given up their vigils and laid down at their posts. He stepped over a red-plumed helm, a hand on the wall for balance. Fingers skimming across the exposed plaster, he remembered being pushed up against the wall of the portrait gallery, Beast's kisses stealing the breath from his lungs.

"Is it much farther?" he rasped. The servant paused at a doorway, twisting from side to side as if unsure which direction to take. With a pang of worry, Brendan tried to lean in toward his unseen guide. As frantic as he was to get to Beast, this servant did not seem well. "Stop a moment. You seem confused. Are you unwell? Is there anything I can do for you? To help you?" The fingers on his sleeve yanked him a step further, and then another. "Okay, okay. Let's go."

The servant led him through a moldering parlor, down another darkened hall, to a small and unremarkable door. Oddly, it was flanked by twin sconces bearing unlit torches. Most of the castle Brendan had seen had been outfitted with newer lamps and chandeliers. Perhaps this bit was older than the rest, or had just never been important enough to change it from its medieval fittings.

The thick plank door opened to a long set of narrow stairs, winding upwards to a tower Brendan had never seen before. His boots scraped against the steep slab steps curving up and around the central pillar, thin arrow slits letting in slivers of the rising dawn. In between the spaces of shadow Brendan could sometimes catch sight of the servant's shape, undefined but certainly there.

The hand guiding him trembled, sliding off his arm. He could barely make them out, a mere suggestion of shape bracing itself against the outer wall.

"Take it easy," he said anxiously. "The spell is failing, and you're a part of that, right? You shouldn't waste your strength—"

A hand set itself on his shoulder and pushed him hard, urging him up the stairs on his own. "Is Beast up there?" More firmly he was pushed again. "But...will you be alright?"

Two hands shoved him this time, as if to say *just go, you idiot*!

He lingered a moment more only to utter a fervent, "Thank you," then dashed up the stairs as fast as he could, taking two or three at a time. It was a tall tower, and by the time he reached the top his lungs burned. He propped himself against the arched doorway, struggling for breath.

The stairs opened into a circular room, all stone and open windows carved into the facsimile of delicate lace, perhaps at one time a watchtower or observatory. A breeze ruffled his shorn hair through the arched windows, the rafters of the pointed tower creaking above him. The room stood empty except for a solitary heap of cloth and furs in its center.

The heap moved. A shallow breath in. Out. And in again.

A singular instant stretched for an hour, every muscle in Brendan's body locked fast. When he was finally able to move, he ran and collapsed to the floor. "Beast," he whispered, throat too tight for anything louder, and braided his fingers through much larger ones.

A sharp indrawn breath as dark amber eyes blinked open.

"Beast!" Brendan rolled him onto his back. His heart was a tangled tumult of relief and fear and happiness and dread.

Beast's head lolled toward him. "Another one," he croaked, his hand limp and uncommonly cool in Brendan's.

Eyes roving, desperately searching for injuries, Brendan could barely hear him. "What?"

"Another one. Dream. This is a…strange one, though." Beast's eyes fell shut, as if speaking had exhausted him. Brendan leaned over him and kissed him, lightly, to prove to himself this wasn't a trick, some kind of leftover illusion the sorceress had left as a cruel joke. But the mouth beneath his own was familiar, the same lips that had been haunting his dreams every night he had lain awake in his cramped little attic room. He cupped that proud face between his hands, shaking with relief.

"Hey, hey, don't fall asleep. I'm here, I'm here. I'm not a dream, Beast. I'm really here." He smiled, though it felt watery. "I came back."

Beast grunted, sitting up a little.

"Are you injured? Where are you hurt? We have to get you down from this tower, get you somewhere warm—"

"Not hurt." He lifted a hand, laboriously, and gently caressed Brendan's

302

cheek. It felt like all the wind knocked from his chest, and Brendan closed his eyes and leaned into the touch, sliding his own hand atop Beast's. And for a moment, everything was perfect.

"You're here," Beast grated. He blinked, lucidity returning to his honeyed stare. "You're really here."

"I'm here, Beast."

Leonine features hardened. "You shouldn't be. I told you to go. Why? Why didn't you listen to…" Shutting his eyes and swaying, Beast swallowed thickly.

Brendan tried to shape a feeble smile. "I never do what you tell me to, remember?"

Beast's laugh twisted into a cough. "Your one flaw." Brendan laughed too, though it had a low, hysterical edge. "Shouldn't have come back. Seen me like this."

Brendan shook his head. "I had to."

"Didn't think…after what I said…" Shame shadowed Beast's face, and he turned away. With a soft touch Brendan turned him back, close enough to share breath.

"I had to come back," Brendan whispered. "My life is empty without you, Beast. I love you."

Beast's eyes squeezed shut, as if hearing it caused him physical pain. "Brendan…"

"Shh. You shouldn't talk. Just…just take it easy, I can go get help—"

"Please." The word, so plaintive and so rarely heard from that tongue, gave Brendan pause. "You said you saw… That you saw a good man, in me. I wish… I want to be that. Be that good man you see. If someone like you can see worth in someone like me, maybe…maybe it's really there." Something almost like a smile flickered on Beast's face, though each of his breaths grew more and more labored. "I have done so many bad things in my life, Brendan, so, so many. Made so many mistakes. But right now. My only regret." Again his furred hand came up, skating over Brendan's cheekbone, tracing the line of his jaw. The red dawn painted his eyes into golden fire. "My only regret. I never told you… Never told you I—"

"Shh," Brendan insisted desperately, covering Beast's lips with his finger-tips, shaking his head in refusal. This was killing him, ripping him apart piece by painful piece, when Beast's every labored breath was saying *goodbye*. He couldn't bear it, the finality in that splintered voice. "You don't have to say it. You shouldn't speak, you need to rest, you need—"

Beast weakly moved Brendan's hand from his lips, holding it fast to his heart as he whispered, "My only regret is I never told you I love you."

And his eyes fluttered shut, his head sinking to the stones. In that great chest a breath rattled, then went still. His hand fell limply from Brendan's grasp.

Too stunned to move, to think, to even breathe, Brendan remained still, the cold seeping up from the stones into his knees while a clamor of silence rang in his ears.

This wasn't how things were supposed to go.

This couldn't be the way it ended.

"Wake up, blast you." He wasn't even conscious of speaking, bare skeletons of words scratching their way from his throat unbidden. He clutched at Beast's collar, crouched over his prone form, the only sound rising to the creaking rafters his own strangled breaths. "Wake up," he whispered hoarsely, his forehead on Beast's unmoving chest, where he'd lain only a handful of times before, lost in the steady drum of a heartbeat while counting the minutes and wishing they would last forever.

The book, the fish, his sister, the witch; all of them had lied. This wasn't how the story was meant to end, an abbreviated ink splotch drying on a blank and uncaring page.

No blood stirred that heartbeat. No sound. No breath.

Brendan stayed there, no intention of ever being moved from this spot. Let the castle crumble, the tower fall, the earth swallow them up, let night descend forever, it didn't matter. Nothing mattered. Not anymore.

He took no note of the handful of dried leaves drifting in through the open windows, or of the sudden gust that sent them skittering in circles on the stone floor.

The dawn spilled in brightly as if the wind carried it aloft, its strength building like a flame on a fresh lamp wick, spreading until it touched every stone and crevice of the circular room, until the light glared so brightly it shone red through Brendan's closed eyelids.

Reluctantly, he raised his head from Beast's unmoving body. The breeze abandoned the dancing leaves and tugged instead at their clothes, so strongly it could not simply be a trick of the wind, and with none of the telltale gentleness of the servants.

Brendan sat up, alarmed. An unseen force pulled Beast's body away from him, drawing it up off the ground. Beast's head hung back limp as he rose up, russet hair trailing across the stones.

"No!" Brendan lunged forward. "You can't take him!" He clawed desperately for Beast, a lax arm slipping out from his grasp as Beast was lifted higher and higher. Light separated into tendrils of brilliance that oozed around Beast, wrapping him tightly within, every limb enveloped, the glow swelling tenfold, so burningly bright that Brendan had to shield his eyes or go blind.

There was a sound like the world breaking, a soft, soughing shatter.

As suddenly as it had arrived the gale died down and the glare faded, once again only the gentle illumination of dawn.

Blinking spots from his vision, Brendan turned back. Words couldn't describe his relief that Beast's body was still there, no longer ethereally floating. Then the body moved, and Brendan's heart stopped, hope welling up within him.

"Beast!" he cried, quickly scrambling to his side.

"Brendan?" Beast muttered, weakly, but alive. *Alive*, praise every saint he'd ever heard of, and even those he hadn't. Light-headed with elation, Brendan threw himself onto Beast and scattered kisses over his face, his neck, his hands, anywhere he could reach.

Beast seemed to regain his strength quickly, returning the kisses with enthusiasm, his tongue scraping over Brendan's lower lip, a hand stealing up to entangle in his hair. Abruptly he pulled back, scrutinizing Brendan as if seeing him for the first time. He frowned.

"You cut your hair."

Brendan gaped, then laughed in pure and undiluted joy. "Is that all you have to say?"

"But...it's *short*."

"Do you like it?"

"No."

Again Brendan laughed. "You were dead and now you're not, and all you can say is—"

Beast dragged him back down and captured his mouth, pressing up into him hot and ardent. "Was I really?" Beast murmured into the kiss. "Was I really dead?"

Brendan's hands spasmed hard enough to bruise, and he was able only to answer with a tremulous, "Yes."

"I'm all right. Never felt better." Beast pressed his lips to Brendan's temple. "You're here." Brendan melted against him and they surged into another deep, jubilant kiss, Beast softly drawing claw-tips over the nape of Brendan's bared neck.

"Wait." Beast's heavy brows crashed together, and he pulled back his hand in alarm. In one smooth motion he got to his feet, and Brendan clambered up after him with slightly less grace.

Beast stared down at himself in disbelief. He let out a low, anguished growl and brought up both hands, flipping them from back to palm repeatedly. "But... No, this isn't right." Beast frowned at his taloned feet and lashing tail. "The spell broke. I can *feel* it. I am no longer bound by it, but... This is wrong. The spell said I would have my true shape restored to me. What trickery is this?"

"No, it didn't," Brendan breathed.

"What?"

"It never said that at all."

"Brendan, what in God's name are you talking about?"

"I saw the book. It said, 'like a beast you shall remain, until you learn to love and are loved in return.' That tricky witch." He shook his head in a sort of wry, twisted admiration.

"I don't... I don't understand." Beast's shoulders were hunched, his voice lost and forlorn.

Brendan took Beast's hands and reveled in their warmth, the silk of their golden pelt. *"'Once a thing is done, it can never be undone.'"* Still seeing no glimmer of understanding, Brendan smiled gently. "This is *you* now, my love."

Beast took a step back, shaking his head. "But I'm still a monster!"

"No, you aren't. I think monsters, and beasts, only exist in here." Brendan placed his hand over Beast's heart, where it fluttered like a frightened bird. He held Beast's cheek in his cupped hand. "This is your true shape now. This is who I fell in love with. And you're still that same man. I must admit, I'm actually relieved."

A disbelieving snort through that curved, aristocratic nose. "Why the hell would you be relieved?!"

"I'm relieved because anything else would be like…like kissing a stranger." Brendan nuzzled into Beast's neck, breathing deep his comforting scent of wildness and warm velvet.

Beast's arms tightened. "No kissing strangers."

"I faced an enchanted forest, crumbling ruins, and a very intimidating sorceress to reach you, and already you're questioning my fidelity?" He had meant it lightly, but his grin faltered as Beast's eyes locked on his own, bright with unshed tears beneath the curve of his golden brows.

"I lost you once, Brendan. It nearly killed me."

Brendan's breath caught at the faint tremble in the words, the naked honesty of them, and before he could answer he was tugged into a hard, searching kiss. When their lips parted, both gasping slightly, Brendan's voice had gone rough at the edges. "You won't lose me. No matter what shape you're in, Beast, I won't be parted from you again."

The glad rumble from Beast's broad chest was very nearly a purr. "Well," he husked before claiming another kiss, "I suppose I can live with that."

Brendan laughed between kisses, gladness painting everything beautiful.

"I love you," Beast whispered against his lips, sending a spark of electricity through Brendan's every waking nerve. "And…you still love me?"

"Of course I do."

The last bit of tension went out of Beast's shoulders, and he grinned brightly, fangs and all. "Good." He nodded toward the windows and beyond, at all the castle in wreckage, his home for over two centuries now only rubble and ashes. "What now?"

On the horizon, the sun rose warm and golden over the roses and brambles. Down on the lawn distant shapes of people gamboled merrily, ghosts made flesh and enslaved no more. Some embraced or danced or strode purposefully toward the gates, leaving the castle behind them. Brendan wished them every happiness.

"How do you feel about Prague?"

"Prague?"

"Always wanted to see Prague," Brendan continued lightly. "Third on my list."

Beast rolled his eyes. He flexed his claws out in exaggeration and touched them to the tips of his pronounced horns. "Splendid idea. You know, if I wear a collar like a pet, we might merely be hanged instead of burned at the stake."

Brendan cast him a grin that felt sly enough to have been stolen from a fox. "You remember when you showed me the blackberry trick?"

"The...blackberry trick?"

"You made it into a strawberry." His expectant look was met with blankness. "To be more precise, you made it *look* like a strawberry. Do I need to draw you a picture?"

An amazed smile slowly dawned. "You're *brilliant*."

Brendan grinned. "You think you can manage an illusion on something a bit bigger than a piece of fruit?"

"Well, I'm certainly no wizard, but with practice, I believe so." Beast shook his head in admiration. "As I said, you're brilliant."

Brendan shrugged. "It doesn't *have* to be Prague, of course. We could start somewhere closer. Or stay in the country. Or—"

Beast gathered his hands, his smile bright and honest and *happy*. "I don't care where we go. As long as we are together." This kiss sang, a chorus playing back and forth between them, giving and taking in perfect harmony.

Brendan gasped, burying eager fingers into Beast's thick mane of hair. His lips traveled to a pointed ear, and let his voice hit the throaty depth that never failed to make Beast shiver. "Always."

Beast murmured agreement, and they stood simply wrapped up in each other for a long while, perhaps hours. Reluctantly Brendan turned, light footsteps taking him to a lacework window. He looked out at the vista of broken marble and overgrown hedges. "It's such a shame about your castle, though."

Beast's careless shrug was one of unfettered freedom, his joyful smile a mirror to Brendan's own, and nearly as intoxicating as the fullness in his heart. "Let it be forgotten. Its time is done. Ours is just beginning." Beast extended his hand, waiting.

Grinning, Brendan took it.

"Shall we, then?"

And they left the castle together.

Epilogue

Some Time Later, Greece

In the privacy of their rented room, with no need to wear his manufactured illusion like a familiar, well-fitting jacket, Beast stood by the dresser and folded his shirts.

No matter how long he had been attempting to master the skill, no matter how often he practiced, he remained persistently terrible at it, resulting in shirts creased in places it shouldn't be possible to crease. Nevertheless, he was determined to learn how to do things properly, without the benefit of servants. Once Brendan had offered to do it for him, to which he had gruffly replied, "You aren't my *wife*." Brendan had laughed in that open, honest way that had always driven Beast a little bit crazy, and suggested they hire a valet instead. A single, scoffing snort expressed what he thought of *that* idea, and so Beast continued to obstinately mangle his clothing by himself.

A mirror hung over the dresser. In its reflection, just over Beast's shoulder, he could watch Brendan lounging bonelessly in a plush chair, absorbed in a sheaf of written music. Every few seconds he would hum softly to himself, unconsciously swaying his quill in the air before making notes in the margins. Beast couldn't help but smile at the sight. Brendan set down the papers with a sigh and rubbed his eyes.

"Nervous?" It wasn't Brendan's first concerto by any degree, though it just might be the largest. Word on the street had it a visiting daughter-in-law of some Ottoman sultan was planning to attend. There was no shame in being a little jittery at the prospect; Beast himself felt the occasional quaver of nerves on his lover's behalf.

"Oddly, no." Brendan stood, banishing stiffness in a long, lean stretch. He tucked his hair behind his ears and pressed himself to Beast's back, arms wrapped around his chest and chin nestled as high as he could reach, his warm breath tickling the back of Beast's neck. "After all, one of us has to make some money," he teased, nibbling at Beast's ear. Beast twitched it forward out of reach, but Brendan chased it down with another tenacious nip. Abandoning his hopeless task and leaving his shirt crumpled, Beast snorted.

"We have plenty of money, love."

"Always good to have more to send to the nieces and nephews."

"Hmm. Perhaps this time, we will have reached the magic amount that will finally endear me to your sister."

"She'll come around eventually. Father did."

"Only after we had that fight. Do you suggest I try the same strategy with Catherine?" Beast smiled, leaning his head back against Brendan's.

Brendan shook against him with mirth. "I most certainly do not. Father backed down; *she* definitely wouldn't. I like you with all your pieces intact."

Beast huffed in amusement, basking in the closeness of Brendan's body, letting the tips of his talons sneak under lapis silk sleeves to trace slow caresses against slender wrists.

Brendan broke the companionable silence with a hesitant cough. "There is, er, something I wanted to talk to you about, my heart."

Meeting the reflection of Brendan's eyes in the mirror, Beast said, "That sounds ominous."

"Now, I don't want you to panic."

"That *definitely* doesn't sound good."

Reaching up, Brendan unlaced the neck of Beast's loose linen shirt. Beast growled, the electric touch instantly tantalizing. "Is this just a cunning attempt to seduce me?"

"No! Well. Maybe. We'll see." With an impish grin, Brendan pulled down the collar and dug his fingers into the thick fur trailing down Beast's chest. He was unable to bite back a low, rumbling purr. Brendan chuckled, propping his chin on Beast's shoulder. "Pay attention, you. I'm trying to break some bad news, and you are making it very difficult."

"What is more likely, Brendan, that there is bad news buried in my chest hair, or that you are just looking for a new excuse to get your hands on it?"

"I need an excuse now? As much as I do enjoy fondling you, my heart, look here."

Obligingly, Beast followed the path of his fingers in the mirror and nearly jumped back in shock. He looked down, just in case the mirror had made a mistake, but no, there it was. A single silvered hair, curling brazenly from the golden thatch of his chest.

Beast stared in open amazement as his heart eventually started beating again.

A gray hair.

He had a gray hair.

Elation coursed through him, heady and rich as fortified wine. He wasn't stuck forever in some prison of static stagnation. He would not watch the world pass by while he remained changeless forever. This was utter, irrevocable proof the spell was finally, truly, broken. They could grow old together; he *could grow old*.

Practically drunk on happiness, he scooped his lover into his arms and swung him around the room in a big hug, Brendan putting up only a token protest before melting into Beast's glad embrace.

"I hope you don't expect me to be this thrilled when I get *my* first gray hair," Brendan said with a joyful laugh, and kissed him.

And they lived, not 'ever after,' as eternity is an unkindness to wish on anyone, but very happily indeed.

The End

About the Author

Fox Beckman lives in the Twin Cities and is utterly incapable of working without a curated playlist in the background. She writes queer fiction, especially stories about diverse nuanced characters creating found families, and monsters becoming lovers—or even lovers becoming monsters. Fox occasionally wrangles kangaroos and forages for (probably) edible mushrooms, and enjoys fencing and archery—any hobby where she gets to stab things, basically.

If you enjoyed this book, please consider leaving a review on the site you purchased it or on Goodreads. Recommend it to a friend, share on social media, and thank you so much for supporting an independent artist!

You can connect with me on:
- https://www.foxbeckman.com
- https://twitter.com/foxbeckman

Also by Fox Beckman

The Trust Trilogy (Coming Soon)
  Stolen from Tomorrow
  Shards of Trust
  Built from Ashes

 **Stolen from Tomorrow**
Ravi Abhiramnew's job is simple: hunt down and neutralize supernatural threats. Until he meets Cayenne, a charismatic time traveler who claims to know everything about him—even his most closely guarded secrets. Going to dinner with Cayenne is probably a bad idea. Going on a romantic island getaway *definitely* is.

Really, it serves him right when a monster picks their resort as its hunting ground.

With Ravi's combat skills and Cayenne's time magic, it should be a breeze killing the monster and getting their vacation back on track. But it turns out the real danger lurks much, much closer...

Coming April 2023 from Ninestar Press!
  https://NineStarPress.com

Printed in the USA
CPSIA information can be obtained
at www.ICGtesting.com
LVHW050531151223
766409LV00001B/111

9 798218 180140